PRAISE FOR JAMES A M...

"*Seven Forges* is an excellent, enjoya... ...hly entertaining fantasy debut into a new ... ...nd sorcery, complete with romance, intrig..., ...u danger."
Attack of the Books

"Wow, that twist. In some ways I think I should have seen it coming, and I kind of did, but *Seven Forges* just lulled me into security and BAM! Craziness!"
Starships and Dragonwings

"*Seven Forges* is a well written fantasy adventure with a very interesting premise and a big world to explore."
Celtic Frog Reviews

"*Seven Forges* is a perfect story of political intrigue, brutal fighting, beguiling magic and assassinations. [It] has the WOW factor."
The Book Plank

"James A Moore entertained the hell out of me with *Seven Forges* and also made me think. If he writes more books in this world, I'll definitely read them."
Shelf Inflicted

"I highly recommend this and all of his books."
The Crows Caw on Smile No More

"*Deeper* is pulp fiction at its most exciting, but it's Moore's talented writing style that raises the novel above just another forgettable monster-romp."
Dark Scribe Magazine

JAMES A MOORE

The Blasted Lands

SEVEN FORGES, BOOK II

**ANGRY
ROBOT**

ANGRY ROBOT
A member of the Osprey Group

Lace Market House
54-56 High Pavement
Nottingham
NG1 1HW
UK

Angry Robot/Osprey Publishing
PO Box 3985
New York
NY 10185-3985
USA

www.angryrobotbooks.com
War is inevitable

An Angry Robot paperback original 2014

Copyright © James A Moore 2014

Cover art by Alejandro Colucci
Set in Meridien by Argh! Oxford

Distributed in the United States by Random House, Inc., New York

ISBN 978 0 85766 392 4
Ebook ISBN 978 0 85766 393 1

Printed in the United States of America

9 8 7 6 5 4 3 2

This one is dedicated to Christopher Golden, Tim Lebbon, Martel Sardinia, Anya Martin, Lee Harris, Caroline Lambe, Marc Gascoigne, John McIlveen, Cliff Biggers, Mike Underwood, Ro Moore, Steve Moore, Nela Bell, Eric Bell, Brian Bell, Dimi Kosmakos, Andrea Cummings and the memory of friends and loved ones past. Thank you all for making this journey an interesting one.

And to Pete and Nikki Crowther for the bow tie emergency repairs and for being wonderful souls.

ONE

The wind howled furiously, but it did not howl alone.

The Pra-Moresh joined into the fury, their voices breaking into warped laughter, sobs of sorrow and snarls of rage.

Andover Lashk listened to the noises and gritted his teeth to stop himself from screaming. His heart stuttered in his chest and his stomach clenched into a fiery fist. He had heard of the beasts, but never seen one before.

That was about to change and he knew it.

His iron hands wrapped around the long haft of the hammer and the blade he'd forged into a proper weapon. He felt the familiar weight and concentrated on unwinding the tension in his arms.

Jost, the girl who'd taught him the most about unarmed combat, said the secret of fighting was to be relaxed: tension slowed the body down and he would need all of his speed.

The cackling and weeping of the things came closer and danced around him in a slow circle. The Pra-Moresh fought in packs. He knew that much. He could see shapes but they were barely visible through the dust and snow whipped around by the storming air of the Blasted Lands.

Something charged from his right. It was a shambling mountain of fur and claws and he saw the mouth of the thing open in a feral grin. Andover pushed back across the frozen ground with his left leg and slid his weight onto the right. The paws of the thing swept the air where he'd been a moment before and he used his left leg to kick back a second time, sliding across the icy surface a few more inches.

The shape came closer and he swept the weighted end of his hammer back, letting the balancing point swing up toward the beast.

A sound like a weeping man came from the thing and it swatted the air a second time to see if the point of the weapon was a serious threat. The paw slapped the sharp tip knocking it aside easily.

This was exactly what Andover hoped for. He used the momentum of the attack to help him bring the heavy hammer's bladed head around in a hard arc and added his own meager body mass to the swing.

The impact ran up his arms and the shriek of pain from the beast set his teeth rattling in their sockets. The thing staggered back, shaking its brutal head. Something vital had been broken. A stream of blood ran from the nightmare's face. While it was moving around in pain, he brought the blade up a second time and shattered the monster's jaw.

More of the things were coming. He couldn't tell how many, only that they were there. It was their damned voices; they sounded like they were everywhere at once. A wall of fur came from the dusty air and he stepped toward it, sweeping the heavy hammerhead up and around in a savage arc. The hammer bounced off the back of the Pra-

Moresh and an instant later Andover was knocked to the ground as the monster loomed over him. His head hit the hard, frozen earth and his vision faded to gray.

The monster swept a paw at him and he blocked, the reaction more instinct and luck than anything else. And his hammer was knocked into the distance.

A wailing sob of victory came from above and the vast mouth of the thing dropped toward his face. Andover reacted instinctively and shoved his hands forward to protect himself.

The iron fingers of his hands caught the teeth and lips of the Pra-Moresh and he grunted as the thing tried to bite down. Hot, stinking saliva bled across his metallic fingertips as he strained. He was not strong enough to stop the mouth from closing, but his hands proved too much for the monster's teeth, which broke off against the living iron.

The beast pulled back, no doubt surprised by the unexpected pain. While it was shaking its face and working its jaw, Andover reached up and grabbed the thick fur of its throat in his hands and squeezed with all of his might.

Had his hands been flesh it might have made no difference, but metal fingers clenched and punched through meat and fur and cartilage and shattered the monster's windpipe.

It reared back again, lumbering to the side and gagging, trying to breathe, while Andover pushed himself backward and looked for any method of escape. It was impossible to say if he could get away. As for weapons he could use, there was nothing. The first of the demons was alive and recovering and enraged. The second was coughing and gagging–

The thing fell down and shuddered, but did not rise. The torso of the monster vibrated and it thrashed in a frenzy, but did not get back up.

Madness. Andover felt a grin peeling his lips apart.

He rose to his knees and looked around. There were two of the nightmares near him and neither was making noises now. He tried to see his hammer but it was lost in the storm.

The bow was still slung across his back. The quiver of arrows still contained a few though some had been lost when he was thrown down.

He drew an arrow and slid the bow from his back, struggling past the heavy fur cloak that stopped him from freezing to death.

The dust slapped across his eyes, making him blink furiously. The first of the Pra-Moresh was eyeing him angrily, its ruined muzzle bleeding a constant stream of steaming hot blood. The second convulsed violently and then stopped moving.

He took careful aim at the first of the creatures and drew back the bowstring, breathing as he'd been taught. The shaggy head continued to face him, but the monster did not charge. Not yet at least.

The arrow cut through the air and punched deep into the flaring nose of the thing. He had been aiming for the eye. The Pra-Moresh reared up, bellowing-crying-giggling, and then came down on all fours, charging him, a mountainous heaving bulk that would surely crush him.

He drew and fired and missed. And then it was there. The body of the thing plowed into him and carried him easily from the frozen ground. Andover let out a groan that was lost under the noises from the brute.

The great arms wrapped around him and began squeezing. Pain ripped into his sides and forced the air from his lungs and his hands reached – sought what he had previously missed with his arrow. The fingers caught one of the dark eyes and he dug as hard as he could. The other hand found the fletching from the arrow buried in the nose and he pushed down with all he could muster.

To call his hands miracles was not an exaggeration. The hands were a gift from the Sa'ba Taalor's god, Truska-Pren, their god of iron. In his short lifetime Andover Lashk had never had much need of gods but one had granted him new hands when his had been ruined by the city-guard. The hands were metal. No doubting that, but he could feel with them, and they moved under his command. So he felt the raw juices that vomited from the ruptured eye of his enemy and he felt the arrow drive deeper before it bent and broke under the pressure from his grip.

Those sensations were miracles. The way the Pra-Moresh threw him like a horse might throw a kitten was simple physics. The beast screamed. Andover screamed and sailed and tried to find the way to land without hurting himself.

He failed.

Some rules are simply universal: When kings call to arms, the soldiers fall in. That is one such rule.

When the fighting was done and the soldiers from Fellein had fallen, King Tuskandru looked down upon his enemies and allowed a grim smile. He was physically exhausted, battered, bruised and cut in many places. Three of his people were badly wounded and many more were injured to the point where they would need to mend before they could easily fight again. They had been outnumbered four to one. Injuries were unavoidable.

Still, the enemy lay dead and dying. He called to Brodem, his mount, and the great beast padded over to him, panting and well fed on the horses of the enemy. He patted the bloodied muzzle of his ally and then reached into his saddlebags, fishing until he found the great horn he'd wrapped carefully before the trip began.

Tusk blew four hard, sharp notes into the air and felt the winds change as the sounds rang out. He did not wait for a response. He knew that if the gods willed it, the soldiers would come to him.

The battle was over. They had won. In time there would be a victory feast. For now however there were other considerations. Tusk called to Blane and Ehnole to pass the word around. The bodies would be taken home. All of them.

The ride home to the Taalor Valley was uneventful. Saa'thaa moved across the broken landscape without complaint and they only stopped when nature demanded or to give Swech a chance to slide into her furs and armor. The air was cold, the winds were violent and while her mount might easily endure the elements, she preferred to wear protection.

They rode past the remains of several horses and the broken weapons of different fighters. Swech called Saa'thaa to a halt and examined the find carefully, reading the signs of the battle. Her people and the soldiers from Fellein. There were no bodies from either side to be found, but she would have been surprised if there had been.

The fight had been brutal and short. She had no doubt of that.

She would have been there for it, but the Daxar Taalor had given her other orders and one does not question the will of the gods. Whatever she missed was secondary to the demand to kill not only an Emperor, but also his military minds. Only one had been spared and she was grateful to the gods for that.

She had aimed the blade for Merros Dulver's heart, fully intending to kill him much as the notion hurt her. And instead the voice of great Wrommish filled her being and told her to spare him. The blade that should have ended his life instead merely cut across his jaw and while he recovered from that she fled the room.

Being captured was not within the plans of the gods. She made sure she was not taken.

It was exactly that simple for her.

So now she rode home, to the valley of the Seven Forges and she looked at their guiding light as she made her way and felt her heart swell with joy. The dark clouds meant nothing in comparison to the warm glow of the volcanic mountains that lit their underbellies.

Soon enough the vast mountains dwarfed the raging storms and sheltered them from the harsh winds. The light from above reflected down onto them and warmed their flesh. The great black shape of Durhallem welcomed them home. They rode through the obsidian tunnel beneath the vast mountain and into the valley proper. The others she had traveled with were there, and they had gathered a large force to help them. A few people nodded as she passed, but there were no greetings and the work continued for those gathered. They did not have time to rest and neither did she. Wrommish demanded more of her and she obeyed.

Wrommish was one of her favored gods. The Daxar Taalor demanded that they be served and the Sa'ba Taalor served without hesitation. All that was right in their world was a gift of the gods. To do other than serve them was foolish and wasteful. And while each of her people served the gods, they were not served equally. Inevitably one god or another was favored by individuals. The philosophies of Wrommish and Paedle were the ones that she liked best. Wrommish believed above all else that the body was a weapon. Paedle's philosophies often agreed. Paedle stated that war did not need to be a business of sword against sword when a properly placed dagger or bared hand could determine a victory or win a battle before it was fought.

Swech believed that the greatest weapons were the body and the mind. Together they could accomplish amazing feats. Wrommish and Paedle best exemplified her beliefs and so she followed them above all others.

And now she would either be rewarded for her beliefs or she would be punished. She had no reason to believe she would be punished – except that Merros Dulver was alive and she couldn't say with complete faith that the gods wanted him that way. The heart can lie to the mind – time would tell.

The Taalor Valley was as lush and green as she remembered and the air was sweet after the acrid stench of the Blasted Lands. She eagerly peeled away her excess layers of fur and armor when they stopped to eat. The sky was clear for the first time since they'd entered the Blasted Lands and she looked at the sun and reveled in the warmth it caressed her flesh with.

Merros Dulver's face haunted her. The look he bore when he realized she was the assassin. The sound of his voice when he called her name and begged her to stop. She sighed once and then pushed him from her mind. She served the gods. She obeyed. There was nothing else.

Two days of continuous travel had her at the foot of Wrommish. The mountain was jagged gray rock, littered with occasional greenery and draped in several waterfalls that descended from the snowcapped top of the vast, sheltering shape. It was home and she loved it as she loved each and every one of the Forges.

To her west was the vast fortress wall that hid the city of Predayne. One of her homes was there. She would not be visiting this day. Instead she patted Saa'thaa on his muzzle and looked him in his great eyes. "Go. I head for the Heart of Wrommish. I do not know when I will return."

The bond between rider and mount was unique. From what she had heard of man and horse from the people of the Empire, they did not share the connections that she and Saa'thaa experienced. How very tragic and hollow their lives seemed on so many levels.

Saa'thaa stared back and then sighed. A moment later he was bounding away from her, toward the west.

Swech climbed the mountain. There were no pathways, but like most of her people she was used to physical challenges. Many people had made the trek over the years but that did not matter. Wrommish did not want easy ways to reach the heart of the forge, where the god rested and waited. The Daxar Taalor did not offer a life of ease; they offered life. Struggles were to be conquered.

She stopped only to eat, and then it was a quick meal. Though the voice of Wrommish had made no demands for haste, there was a deep-seated need to hurry.

There were stories told that Wrommish hid the entrance to the cavern from anyone He did not wish to see. She had never had a problem entering the cave and could not testify to the truth of the matter. Whatever the facts, she reached the entrance to the natural cave she had passed into on four separate occasions. Each time she had come alone and each time she had not left the area without being changed. One cannot meet with gods and remain unaltered. That simple wisdom was one of the first lessons she had ever learned.

Though there were no torches, there was no worry about illumination. Metal seams ran through the rock of the cavern that gave off a warm golden light. The luminescence was not natural; it was another gift of Wrommish. As she walked into the heart of the mountain, Swech stopped long enough to remove her clothes, setting them into a small pile near several other collections of leather and cloth alike. The veil covering the lower half of her face was removed last, and she sighed in simple pleasure at the air that ran across her nose and her lips. The gods had decreed that the people of Fellein were not worthy to see the true faces of the Sa'ba Taalor. One look at them made clear why. So, since they had met the strangers, the group that traveled with them had hidden their faces away. Two days back in her homeland and the veil had become so much a part of her that she never thought to remove it. Now she was free from that order and it was a good and lovely thing. She breathed deep the warm air of Wrommish's breath. She was not alone today. There were other pilgrims, either called forth or here on their own journeys. Like her, they had set their clothes into neat piles, knowing none would consider touching their possessions or taking from them in this holy place.

There was nothing to fear here. Fighting could occur anywhere, but none among the Sa'ba Taalor would ever fight in the hearts of the Forges, simply because it would be disrespectful. Should Wrommish demand that she strike and kill a hundred of her brethren she would do so, regardless of place or time. But, to her knowledge, none of the Daxar Taalor had ever demanded bloodshed within their mountain homes.

The cave around her was different than the last time she'd entered. The walls were still stone, and the ground still soft sand and pebbles, but the patterns of the stone cavern had changed and the sand had a lighter color. It was different each and every time, as the mountain was alive. She could feel the beat of the mountain's slow, steady pulse with each step she took. The ground beneath her feet was almost the exact same temperature as her body, and she stretched and sighed and reveled in the comfort that the sand offered her. The walls glowed brighter the closer she came to the core of Wrommish and, though the heat from the fires below should have roasted her flesh and crisped her hair, she felt no discomfort. The aches of her long journey faded and her exhaustion was washed aside by the love of Wrommish.

The sand faded, solidified and became Boratha-Lo'ar, the fabled crystalline bridge, the thick translucent stone floor that ran the width of the vast chamber of Wrommish. The heart of Wrommish glowed beneath her

feet and lit the cavern in shades of gold and autumn. The
fires of the mountain ran below her, and Swech held
her arms wide and basked in that warm, wondrous glow.
By all rights she should have been dead. She knew that.
She was not foolish. The heat below her was more than
enough to cook her flesh away and the gasses that rose
from the molten core were poisonous. It was the will of
Wrommish that all who entered the mountain were safe
from the heat, just as the will of the gods kept the raging
storms of the Blasted Lands at bay. Merros Dulver's gods
had never offered him any evidence of their existence.
He was raised to believe that faith alone would protect
him from certain fates, but none of the gods ever offered
proof of their power. The Daxar Taalor offered miracles
every day. The wise understood that.

She was aware of the others who stood near her, but
they were not significant. For the moment she felt the
delicious heat of the god's heart and savored it. Merros
Dulver had spoken to her of his people's gods and how
some of them were feared, angry forces of retaliation.
The concept was preposterous. One should not fear the
gods. One should only feel their love as the love of a
parent for a child: unchanging and ever-present.

She closed her eyes and said a silent thanks to
Wrommish for the love she felt and when she opened
her eyes she finally acknowledged the people around
her. They were her kin and her people. In some places
she might have killed them on sight, but here, in the
Heart of Wrommish, they were family.

N'heelis, Chosen of the Forge of Wrommish and King
in Gold looked upon her and spread his arms in welcome.
He wore no crown, but his long hair was wrapped in

heavy golden thread and draped down to the small of his back in a coil as thick as her leg. She returned the gesture, enchanted by his beauty as she always was. His flesh bore the scars of a thousand battles and almost as many victories. He stood naked before the god and the deep slash marks on his chest formed a serpentine pattern that ran from his left nipple down to the middle of his right thigh. The heavy scars were the mark that Wrommish himself had placed upon N'Heelis when he was chosen as king. She had borne witness to that event herself.

When N'Heelis spoke it was not with his voice, but with the voice of Wrommish. His lips moved but the sound was too low, too deep and resonated across the entire chamber.

"You have served the Daxar Taalor with honor, Swech Tothis Durwrae."

Words could not express her joy. Instead she merely held her arms wide apart and bared herself to her god.

N'Heelis walked closer. "I ask more of you still. I ask that you leave this land again and become the instrument of my will." There was no question of refusing the command. For Swech, for any of her people, it would be easier to forget how to breathe and see than to deny the gods.

N'heelis'shands reached out and held her face. His eyes locked on hers and the will of Wrommish spoke into her soul, telling her all she needed to know.

She smiled and almost wept. Great Wrommish was generous. There would be great glory in her works to come.

N'Heelis let go of her and smiled. Swech leaned forward impulsively and kissed the palms of his hands. Then she turned from her king and kindred and walked to the edge of the crystalline bridge. The fires of Wrommish blazed below her and the rising heat, here exposed and unforgiving, dried her eyes and made her hair wave and flutter. Here, as nowhere else, Wrommish was present and his power was undeniable.

Swech stepped from the edge of the hard floor and allowed her body to fall, plummeting into the glowing core of Wrommish's molten heart. Behind her three others followed suit, each called by the god for their own tasks.

For only one heartbeat she wondered about the life growing inside her, the child of her union with Merros Dulver. As with all things, the child would be born to her if the Daxar Taalor wished it.

The heat blistered her flesh and Swech's hair burned away long before she was swallowed by the molten gold of Wrommish's heart. Fires scorched her lungs and eyes even as she whispered the god's name one last time.

There was no darkness.

There was light: brilliant and soothing and all-encompassing.

And then there was rebirth.

Her body was fire. As she rose into the night the flames congealed, solidified and became flesh.

Swech climbed from the blaze in two quick motions, ignoring the fluttering sensation in her stomach. Wrommish had told her she would be placed in a different location, carried by the flames. For the moment she had no fear of the fire, as she was shielded from the heat, but that would not last. The flames crackled and popped, and even as she climbed from them she had to duck under the meat roasting above her. The ground was cold not ten feet away, but where she rose the air was as hot as the pit fire.

Swech looked around for only a moment before spotting her chosen prey.

A careful examination of the area let her know that most everyone was occupied. Eyes looked elsewhere and people ignored her presence, as Wrommish willed it. Most were gathered together into tight knots of flesh, huddled in the cold and talking, relaxing, or just sharing each other's company.

The one she sought was alone, her back to the fires and her body almost hidden in shadow. The woman stared out into the darkness and held council with the night. No one else was near her, and that was for the best. Unlike so many of the females she'd met in Tyrne, this female was not soft and pampered, but wore comfortable attire. Her hands were callused, and a long thin blade rested near her. This one could fight, her posture even when resting spoke of her abilities.

Swech did not carry a sword. At the moment she was naked.

She used that to her advantage and stepped in front of the woman.

There was a moment of shock at her unclothed body, and then a heartbeat of curiosity. When recognition flared in the woman's eyes, Swech struck quickly; a hard blow that knocked her opponent into a daze. Before she could recover Swech killed her. A deft strike to the throat and the woman coughed softly and then choked on her own blood.

Another quick look around told her that no one had noticed anything. Wrommish was good to her.

The chill of the night air made itself known and so Swech took the woman's clothes. She could not leave the body to be found. There were too many witnesses who would surely ask questions. Instead she crouched over the cooling corpse and lifted it onto her shoulders.

Her skin felt wrong. Her mouth felt wrong. Every part of her felt off from the way it should have, but that was not an issue. She would adjust. Beyond the fire's edge there was forest. The caravan the woman traveled with was on a wide road, well paved and tended, but there were no signs of towns or cities, and not more than twenty or so people looked to be taking this journey together.

She did not bury the body, merely hid it beneath a layer of loam that had not been disturbed in many months. Scavengers might find it and eat it, but they would not cause a problem. The people around her would be moving on with the dawn's light. Wrommish had told her that much and shown her a great deal more.

Swech moved back to the campsite and gathered the belongings of the woman she'd killed. They were hers now, along with the woman's body and face, name and memories.

Even as she settled for the night she felt the thoughts and beliefs of the woman in the back of her mind, like a constant echo from a hundred different people. She would adjust and endure if the Daxar Taalor willed it.

She wondered what went through her victim's mind when she saw herself approaching, naked and unarmed. Ultimately it did not matter, but curiosity was one of the many aspects of life that she enjoyed. The world was full of new wonders. She would see as many of them as she could on her way to Fellein's capital.

They gathered the bodies and carried them, sometimes hefted on shoulders and other times dragged by their heels, but all of them were accounted for. By the time Tusk and his retinue had reached the apex of the mountain they had been joined by two hundred additional members of the kingdom.

Tuskandru, Chosen of the Forge of Durhallem and Obsidian King looked down into the heart of the great mountain and saw the fires below and knew that they were good.

Without hesitation he raised the body of the man he knew only as Colonel Wallford above his head and heaved the corpse of his first victim into the punishing heat rising from below. As the body flopped bonelessly downward and smashed into the liquid fire he bellowed out his god's name and then watched the body burn. One after another his people followed his lead, raising the bodies high and then tossing them down, calling out to Durhallem with each offering. Nothing of the enemy was kept as a trophy. All that they had carried with them was offered to the god.

And when they were done, Tusk led his people from the top of Durhallem's highest peak and down to the Great Hall where they would feast and celebrate the start of the great battles coming their way. And feast they would, for Tusk was hungry and soon enough the Council of Kings would be gathering across the valley in the Palace of the King in Iron to discuss the destruction of their enemies.

Sometimes the gods are kind.

TWO

The Guntha told stories of massive black ships crewed by demons. The demons were allegedly horrible to see and impossible to kill. They were, according to the Guntha, the main reason that the island people had attacked Roathes again and again.

Each time island-dwelling Guntha had been repelled until, finally, there had been a sort of peace for the last three years. No one expected them to try again after their last defeat.

Then the Guntha started amassing their troops as they had in the past along the finger of land called the Blade of Trellia once again. They always gathered there first, for Trellia was one of their earliest queens and she had declared that strip of land sacred long ago.

This time when Marsfel had asked for assistance from the Emperor the result was different from times past. Instead of weeks of correspondence and requests, the long-time enemies of Roathes were killed in one simple attack by a handful of strangers sent by the Emperor as a favor to King Marsfel.

Marsfel had expected a few soldiers to come along, look at the gathering forces and send word back to the Emperor that, yes, troops were needed to reinforce the meager army of the Roathians. That was what had always happened in the past. The troops had to be paid, the Empire sent money, Marsfel skimmed a bit of currency and everything went on as it had before.

Only not this time. This time the Guntha were massacred. This time Marsfel had sent a small group of mercenaries to detain the eleven people who had allegedly slaughtered over a thousand of the islanders, and his mercenaries had never returned.

Their remains were found on the King's highway. The eleven got away. According to Lanaie, Marsfel's emissary and daughter, the man who had led the eleven was now in charge of the entire Imperial Army.

Could it get worse? Marsfel had asked himself that question after reading the latest news from his daughter. The answer was yes. Of course it could get worse. It already had. The Guntha were no longer a problem. That would have possibly been good news, but the reason they were no longer a problem was because at least one of their islands had exploded.

Fire had erupted from the sea and the islands had been buried in flaming rock and the Guntha had been burned to ashes as their islands merged into one massive, growing land mass. The islands had once been tiny specks on the horizon, but now they were one large pillar of flame and ash that covered most of the skies above. The waters of the Corinta Ocean were cloaked in black clouds that rained gray ashes down upon all of Roathes, as far as he could tell.

The ashes covered the land, the people, the buildings and the water alike. Hideous clouds of black ash came in from the waters, stinking of death and worse. The plague-winds had come to his kingdom and the people he ruled were succumbing to them. Some grew sick and recovered. Some simply grew weak. Others died, and there was nothing to be done about it. Even kings cannot force the winds to blow the opposite direction.

The tides that rolled in were greasy and stank of dead fish and rotting meat. The waters were too hot, and the air was hotter still. Roathes was cooking away, stewing in its own juices, and he was powerless to make it stop. The raging storms over the growing land mass out there had not abated, and roaring hot winds were washing in regularly, tearing apart the shoreline and washing away anything that was too close to the waters. The Blade of Trellia was already gone, submerged or washed away. Who could say? The waters were too hot, and the fish that had long been a staple for the area were either dead or had fled. Fishermen aren't much use without fish.

And reports kept coming in of vast, black ships on the horizon. Ships large enough that they could be seen even against the backdrop of the fiery island and the falling ash and lightning storms. If they were really out there and not merely nightmares, they were supposedly filled with demons.

The ships had not come in from their distant location yet. That was the good news for Roathes. The only good news.

Most of the boats in Roathes were for fishing. There were a few naval ships and they were being readied, but, really, there weren't nearly as many warships as Marsfel had claimed for a very long time. There hadn't been much need, after years of peace. Corinta had the closest naval fleet and they really never came this far north.

The absolute worst news? Well, he had asked for help from the Emperor after being caught in a lie, and the man who would ultimately decide whether or not he needed assistance was a man he had attempted to capture or kill.

Marsfel considered all of these things while he waited for word from Lanaie. She was still in the Summer Palace, because the Emperor was dead, assassinated by gray-skinned strangers from the Blasted Lands.

He had never been to the Blasted Lands. He never wanted to go to the Blasted Lands. He could not understand why anyone would willingly go to the hellish place to begin with. All he had ever heard of the desolate ruins was that they made the raging storms coming in from the sea seem relatively calm. That was a horrible notion.

And yet the Emperor had sent emissaries for some insane purpose and so now he was dead. Was there a connection? The people from the Blasted Lands were gray-skinned. They came from the same direction as the black ships.

He might well have continued on that thought process, but instead he stopped when Turrae showed up, shaking his head and running. He was not normally a nervous man, one of the reasons that Marsfel had chosen him as a steward.

"The ships are coming closer, Majesty." Turrae's voice was weary.

The ships? "The black ships? From near Guntha?"

"Yes." His voice shook. "Majesty, they are so much larger than we thought."

Marsfel shook his head. "Show me."

Turrae led quickly and climbed the stairs to the highest level of the stone keep Marsfel had lived in his entire life. There a dozen soldiers were standing together and arguing over who got to look through the spyglass that was a permanent fixture on the side of the tower pointing toward Guntha, or rather, where Guntha used to be.

"Leave us!" Marsfel roared the words, and the soldiers vacated as quickly as they could while maintaining their dignity.

Without the glass, there were a few distant specks that might be ships in the distance between the flaming island and the shoreline. He used the cylindrical contraption that had been one of the treasures of his people for as long as anyone could remember and looked around at the waters carefully. The specks were indeed still there and, as his steward had warned, they were ships. They were indeed much larger than he'd expected.

The ships were as black as iron, and bloated. They sat low in the waters and their sails were drawn tight as the winds from behind them pushed them toward the shores. It was hard to count how marsf of them might be on the waters, but with an effort he made out fifteen of the vessels. Fifteen ships cutting closer to the land. Very large ships, if he was guessing correctly without the benefit of any reference points.

Marsfel sighed and shook his head. "Call to arms. Prepare for battle."

"What if the ships are merely investigating?"

"Then they will see our forces preparing for them. There is no way around that."

"Yes, Majesty." He heard the regret in the man's voice and felt it in his own heart. They were not ready for a war.

"And Turrae?"

"Yes, Majesty?"

"Send word to the capital. We need help. We need it as soon as possible." He did not expect an answer, and certainly not a positive one, but it was all he had left.

How long does it take to bury a man? How long to give his spirit rest?

In the case of Wollis March it had not taken long. His spirit had gone on and, in the traditions of his people, his body had been burned and the ashes collected. When his wife and son finally showed themselves they would be presented with the ashes, which would then likely be scattered to the winds with the appropriate ceremony.

In the case of an Emperor, however, there was a great deal more involved. There were kingdoms to notify, you see, and they in turn had to send emissaries to present themselves before the Imperial Family, and then, likely, there would be declarations of regret and more promises of fealty and, of course, there was the matter of replacing the deceased with the next in line to rule the Empire.

It was a statistical nightmare, and for well over a month the Summer Palace had been as tempestuous as the skies above the Corinta Ocean.

Merros Dulver left most of that to the people who took care of such affairs. He was busy enough without having to consider seating arrangements and who had to make offerings to whom.

There was a war getting ready to happen and it seemed he was in charge of preparing the city for any possible attacks.

For over a month he made himself known to the soldiers in Tyrne, and they in turn made themselves as ready as they could for the rage of their new commander.

His anger was not as great as they believed. He was merely loud and more than ready to be louder. He bellowed out of necessity. He leveled orders and he watched with hard eyes to make certain that the men under his command met his demands. From the highest-ranking officers to the greenest recruits, he made himself seen and known.

There were walls around the Summer City that needed reinforcement and there were watchtowers that had fallen into disrepair that needed to be mended. The structures were solid enough, but the long years of peace had led to a lack of readiness. Buildings that should have housed guards were instead storing supplies and in one case – he would eventually track down the culprits responsible by all the gods – housing a brothel.

Soldiers who had grown relaxed and soft were soon put to work at fixing those problems, and more, and woe to the foolish that suggested that workmen might be better equipped to handle the matter.

The City Guard were drafted to handle more work than they were used to, and while there were a few protests, they did not last long.

At first a few men tried to desert. Merros Dulver put an end to that quickly enough. Had they run in combat they'd have been killed. Instead of death they were given options after meeting with the General. Most chose one of the less extreme punishments he offered, especially after the first would-be deserter attempted to call his bluff of being hanged. It seemed that the new commander of the Imperial Army did not believe in bluffing.

While the people of the Taalor Valley made their ways home and prepared for what was coming, Merros Dulver did the same. A few claimed he did all that he did out of fear of the Sa'ba Taalor. A small number of soldiers, who'd known him from before his meteoric rise to power, believed he did what he did out of grief for the loss of a man who was very nearly a brother to him.

Most just did the best they could to follow orders and stay well out of his way. In the long run, they were the wisest of the lot.

The body of Emperor Pathra Krous was presented before the royal family of Fellein and from there he was carried to the wagon waiting to take his mortal remains to the waiting barge on the Freeholdt River. The royal family had a very large crypt and he would be buried with the rest of his family in Canhoon despite his love of Tyrne and the Summer Palace. Some laws cannot be changed on a whim.

The First Advisor to the Emperor and the legendary sorcerer Desh Krohan walked beside the casket carrying the body the entire way to the river, keeping pace. He had been there for the birth of Pathra Krous and he said his farewells to a man he'd called his friend on more than one occasion. From the river, the Sisters would stay with the Emperor's body until he was placed within the tomb and they would seal the great building to ensure no one foolhardy or greedy enough to try for the alleged riches within the tomb would succeed. Pella, Goriah and Tataya were his most trusted allies and he was going to be far too busy seeing to the ascension of the next ruler of the Fellein Empire to consider making the trip himself.

The women stood before him, their heads lowered and their cloaks in place. The air was passably warm, but along the river and heading toward the proper seat of the Empire, it would get colder. Spring was fully upon the land but the cold winds from the north and from the Blasted Lands weren't quite done with the area yet. Desh knew that better than most.

"Be safe and be alert." He made a point to look at each of them. They nodded their heads. "This is not a good time for any of us but now in particular there are plenty who would see me dead and gladly eliminate the three of you in the process of trying help me reach that state of being."

Krohan looked at the elaborate coffin one last time and touched the wood, muttering unheard words in the process. The body would remain unmolested. Of that he was absolutely certain.

Without waiting, he turned and started the long walk back to the palace. The hood covering his face kept anyone from seeing the worried expression he wore. Most would have backed away in fear if they could have caught a glimpse of his anger.

After a dozen paces, Tega met with him. Tega was young and blonde and had caught a few eyes, despite the fact that she dressed in simple enough clothes. The blossom of youth was still with her and that made a difference, he supposed, though he had not been young in a very long time.

"Are you well, Desh?"

He looked at the girl and managed a smile. "I'm horrid. My back hurts, my head hurts and in an hour's time I'll be having a meal with over half of the royal families in Fellein. It would be all of them if the rest were done traveling here."

"Oh." She looked down at the ground.

"Calm down, Tega. I'm not the least bit angry. I'm just being truthful. And even if I were angry, it wouldn't be you who had to face my wrath. You've done nothing you shouldn't have."

That made the poor girl breathe a little easier. He wished her relaxed state would last longer.

"You called for me, Desh?"

For the first two years they'd known each other she had called him *Master Krohan*, not because it was the title he preferred, but because he wanted her to know her place as his apprentice. Reflecting on the practices he had seen some of the sorcerers use on their apprentices, he considered himself positively mild in comparison. These days she was allowed to call him by his first name because she had learned her place very well and because she was an excellent student. She had earned the right to call him by his first name and she had long since proven herself worthy of being his apprentice.

Desh Krohan had only three rules for his apprentices. First, they had to study and practice every day. Second, they were never to perform any of the more complex rituals before getting his approval – he'd lost two apprentices in the past to foolhardy attempts – and lastly, they were to obey him in all of his orders.

In return for that last there was an additional rule for himself: he was never to consider his apprentices as either servants or slaves. They were sorcerers in training and as such needed to be respected. The average wizard tended to have an amazingly long memory.

With those simple rules in place Desh Krohan looked to his apprentice and did something he did not at all want to do. "Tega, I need you to set aside your regular training for the present time. I need you to gather information for me."

"Of course, Desh." Her response was automatic. Part of him was glad of that. Part most decidedly was not.

"No. This is not a standard request from me. On this you can deny me without consequence."

That got her attention. She stopped walking and looked at him with hard eyes. He stopped in return and met her gaze. "What are you thinking, Desh Krohan?"

He looked around them and sighed. There were people aplenty moving in their vicinity. The City Guard was in force, currently, moving people along and preventing too many from blocking the roads away from the funeral procession. There were plenty of hawkers and cutpurses alike in the area, looking to make a few extra coins. Most of them were wise enough to stay well away from the two of them. Desh Krohan's name was well known and the majority of people wisely avoided getting his attention.

"We will speak more in my chambers. Meet me there if you will. First I need to have a quick discussion with General Dulver."

His apprentice nodded her head and stepped into the crowd. She was gone from his sight in a matter of seconds, lost in the flow of people.

Desh moved toward the Summer Palace and the people parted for him as if he were a very large rock in a fast moving river. He met the newest commander of the army in the throne room. Currently the room was covered in papers and maps and Dulver was standing next to the largest table in the place and staring at the very maps he had brought back from the Seven Forges himself. Like everyone else, he was worried about the attack that might well be coming their way.

Merros Dulver was a good soldier and a better man. He was also currently brooding. Desh liked that about him. Had he been as calm as some of the other generals he would likely have not been the right man for the task before him. Planning a war is not an easy thing to do, after all.

"How are you today, Merros?"

Dark eyes regarded him from under dark brows. Merros Dulver was tanned from his time in the field. His hair had recently been cropped to a length that could easily fit under a snug helmet and he'd started shaving his face clean again. When Desh had first met the man he'd been clean shaven, and when he'd seen him the next time he'd been on the road and traveling for over three months, most of that time in the harsh environment of the Blasted Lands. He'd grown a full beard and his hair had fallen almost to his shoulders. The first time, he also hadn't looked quite as haunted. The wizard blamed himself for that last part. It was he who had hired the retired military man for an expedition into the Blasted Lands that had ended with absolutely surprising results.

The Sa'ba Taalor were not what he'd expected anyone to encounter in the endless, raging storms that hid away most of the areas to the north of Fellein. An occasional nightmare made flesh, one of the Pra-Moresh or the even more vile creatures that populated the wasteland, were all he'd honestly thought the men might run across on their journey. All he'd truly hoped for was that sending the Sisters along would give the soldiers and cartographers a chance to map out the pathways to the Seven Forges.

Thinking about that made his stomach twist and his heart ache. His damned expeditions had cost a few lives over the years, but he'd never expected the constant quest for knowledge to result in the death of the Emperor or an encounter with an unknown race.

The Sa'ba Taalor. The people of the Forges. They spoke a variation of the Old Tongue as one of their languages and they had skin the wrong color. Desh Krohan had met people from every part of the known world. He had seen people with a dozen different hues of flesh but never before had he run across a species of people who had gray skin. Had they not been so very vital he might have thought them animated corpses.

Merros responded and brought him out of his reverie. "I'm not having a very good day." His face made clear that he was being kind.

"You are currently hating your existence and wondering if you can back out of being a general in the Empire's army. The answer is 'no'. You cannot back out. I need you and Fellein needs you. More importantly, you are one of the very few men I trust at the present time to ensure the safety of Nachia Krous."

Nachia Krous, another issue to deal with, and soon. She was next in line to ascend to the throne of the Empire. Several different members of her family felt someone else should be taking that honor.

Merros looked him up and down. A lot of people refused to look him in the eyes and Desh was fine with that. He preferred it, actually, as it meant they were justifiably concerned about the rumors surrounding him. Very few men felt they could look him in the eye without fearing for their lives, their souls and their freedom.

Merros Dulver might have been worried about all of those things, but he still looked the sorcerer in the eye. Desh admired that about him.

"What is it you need from me?" Merros spoke softly. Both of them were grieving, and he knew that. While Desh was walking the Emperor's body to the river Merros Dulver had been working through the rebuilding of the city's defenses and adjusting to the death of a good friend. The death of a soldier did not warrant the sort of vast ceremony required in the passing of an Emperor. That didn't make the impact any less.

Merros Dulver had lost his best friend. Desh Krohan had lost a man he'd helped raise from childhood to become the ruler of the Fellein Empire. He didn't consider his loss any greater than that of the soldier before him. He knew better.

"I know you are grieving. I'll do my best to give you time to do so, Merros. I just wanted to remind you that there will be a feast in the Emperor's honor tonight, and your presence will be required." The General shook his head and his lips pressed into a thin line. "I know. I can think of a thousand or more things I could do with that time, not the least of which is mourning. But you are the ranking military officer and you have to show your support for the Empress-to-be."

"Of course. I'll be there." The General looked at him for a moment longer and then his eyes crept toward the maps.

"Thank you for that." He paused a moment longer. "I have to speak with Tega for a bit and then I'm coming back in here to look over those maps with you."

Merros nodded his head. "Good. I'd like your opinion on a couple of these symbols." His hand waved at the map halfheartedly. "They are unfamiliar to me."

That was hardly surprising. The maps had been provided by the Sa'ba Taalor, after all. They were a gift before everything went insanely wrong. Now they, along with every item offered by the people from the Taalor Valley, were suspect. "I'll be back as soon as I can to discuss the matter."

Without another word the wizard left the room, using one of the hidden passages to allow him easier access to his chambers. The tunnels were narrow and they were well hidden, but they were not completely a secret. Most of the Krous family knew about them, at least the ones he wanted to let know about them. There were advantages to being as long-lived as he was, especially if one had a good memory for things that were not written down anywhere.

By the time he reached his quarters Tega was already there and pouring herself a mug of the tea Desh brewed almost every day. Three additional cups were already waiting. Two of the Sisters were standing in the room, looking his way with smiles. Flame-haired Tataya stepped up and grabbed the exact mug he'd been eyeing. It seemed she had a gift for taking what he wanted. Not that it mattered. The cups were identical. Pella shook her head, sending dark curls waving, and rolled her eyes and waited until Desh had chosen before grabbing the last of the cups for herself.

"Goriah is well on her way. She'll make sure Pathra reaches his destination without incident." Pella took a sip after she was done speaking and closed her eyes, savoring the sweet flavor.

"Just the same, best if everyone thinks all three of you are riding with him. It stops people from getting foolish when they think they might be outnumbered."

Tega sighed. "Why would anyone want to harm the Emperor's body?"

Desh answered that one himself. "Because no matter how kind a soul he might have been, Pathra Krous made enemies merely by being the Emperor. For some the act of harming his remains would be revenge and for others it would be a step toward humiliating the Krous family. The next ruler might act foolishly if properly provoked."

Tega nodded and took a long swallow of her tea.

"Time to get on with this." Desh sighed and drank from his own cup. The tea was soothing but his nerves still felt tightly wound. "Tega, I would not ask this, but the Sisters are already being sent off to handle tasks of their own. They must be away and even if I could go myself I would need someone here to take my place." He looked into her eyes and made sure she understood the gravity of his words. "We are in volatile times and I must make sure that I have the very best knowledge available. I've already employed the Sooth and done all I can to interpret the signs they have given me, and now I have to ask a very great favor of you."

"Desh, anything, you know that. I was willing to go to the Seven Forges for you, and I would be there now if things hadn't gone so wrong."

When Pathra Krous was killed, General Hradi, the head of the Empire's Army, had foolishly decided to send troops after the visitors from the Seven Forges. His soldiers were not up to the task. Their fumbling demands had been enough to make a bad situation far worse. While it seemed that the Sa'ba Taalor had actually planned out and assassinated the Emperor, the matter should have been handled with greater tact, and now war was inevitable. If the gray-skinned people came back any time in the near future, Desh had no doubt they'd do so while leading their armies into combat against the Empire.

"None of that was your fault or mine, Tega. There was nothing to be done for it. But now, we must do all we can to either prevent a war or end it quickly, and that means I need information from the one place I can think of that the Sa'ba Taalor do not go."

She frowned up at him. "I don't understand."

Desh nodded and looked toward the Blasted Lands as if the palace wall were a window and he might see what was out there. "I know. Some secrets I keep closely and others I simply never share. In this case the knowledge has been kept close to heart because there is no need to give away our possible weapons and, as I have said to you many times, knowledge is as powerful as any sword."

He put an arm across her shoulders and led her to the window looking out over the city. The Sisters moved with them, silent and careful not to be seen from the window. "There is a place in the Blasted Lands that the Sa'ba Taalor will not visit. Their gods have forbidden them to go there, and for that reason we must go there ourselves. We must know what is there and what their deities want to keep from them."

"Why?" Tega was a brilliant disciple, but sometimes the most obvious things avoided her, while she sought the answers to the complicated mysteries of the universe.

"Whatever is there is something that is hidden. More importantly, it is something being hidden from our enemies. We must know what it is because it might be a useful weapon against them."

"What is this place?"

Desh looked away from her for a moment and then looked to the Sisters. "It's called 'The Mounds', by the Sa'ba Taalor. That is honestly all that is known. Anything else I say would be conjecture. The Sisters have been far closer than I have. The Sooth told me that the Mounds are important, but they would not say why."

Tega closed her eyes and shuddered. She had dealt with the Sooth only once, and that was enough for her. The spirits of the Sooth were often greedy, and they took as much as they could and offered as little as possible in exchange. They could offer glimpses of the future, promises of things that would come to pass, but they always hid those promises under layers and layers of deception and obfuscation.

"And you would like me to explore these Mounds?"

"Absolutely not. I would much rather you stay right here and remain safe, where I can find you at any time. But that is no longer an option. I need you to explore the Mounds, to see for me everything that I cannot afford the time to see for myself."

Tega walked away from him and even without seeing her face he knew she was worrying her lower lip and that her eyebrows had knitted into a knotted frown. He said nothing. The Sisters were likewise quiet, understanding all too well what he was asking and that he would never demand anything of that magnitude from one of his apprentices. They had walked where Tega walked now in their own times.

They understood the dangers.

Finally she nodded. "I will go." She did not turn to look at him.

"I'll do everything I can to protect you, Tega. You know this."

"Of course." She cast her eyes in his direction but did not meet his gaze. "When should I leave?"

"Immediately. I'll have a horse and an escort for you. And supplies, of course."

"I'll want to see my parents." She hesitated to say the words.

"Of course, Tega. See them. But not a word of where you are going. Tell them you're going to Trecharch. Tell them I've sent you to study the Walking Trees and to ask questions of the Mother-Vine. That should keep them from worrying too much."

A moment later the girl was leaving the room and heading to her chambers. Directly after that the Sisters looked to him with questioning eyes. "You are both needed elsewhere." He hated that his voice carried a defensive tone. "There are missions that require instinct and there are missions that require a properly devious mind. Tega is many things, but devious is not yet among them. We'll start working on that when she gets back."

If she gets back, he thought, but did not say.

"For now, my ladies, it is time for you to leave here as well." He sighed and shook his head. "And time for goodbye speeches about good men."

• • •

Merros Dulver ate without tasting, chewed and swallowed. He was not alone. There were a great number of people in the room and many of them sat within ten feet of him, but he might as well have been by himself for as little as he cared about them at the moment.

The sort of people who, only a month earlier, would have had him sweating through his clothes, surrounded him. Some of the most powerful people he had ever met were present and most of them were wearing enough finery to pay the salary of his entire military career with ease. Diamonds, gold, silks, fine leathers and dress-swords of every possible make.

Bite. Chew. Swallow. Even the wine, which he knew, intellectually, was a very fine vintage, tasted like ash. Also, every bite reminded him of the new scar along his jaw.

Wollis March should have been at his side, making snide comments under his breath and reminding Merros to at least try to enjoy the moments when the finer things in life were offered up. Instead Wollis was gone. Dead. His body was ashes, and those ashes were waiting for his family to arrive; the family that was expecting to be reunited with the man, not with his memories and a jar of gray dust.

How was he going to face them? He'd never met Dretta March, but he'd heard many stories of the woman and seen her and her son Nolan alike when last he rode to the far north, the very edge of the Wellish Steppes, and gathered Wollis for their expedition into the hellish Blasted Lands.

He could not quite be surprised that Swech killed Wollis. He'd been witness to her abilities, had seen her kill or break a few men before they made their way to the palace in Tyrne. Thinking her incapable of violence was rather like thinking a bonfire incapable of causing a few burns. It made exactly no sense. Still, he hadn't expected her deception.

He couldn't say he'd fallen in love with her, but he had very much enjoyed her company. And having her gone, having her be the one that had killed poor Wollis, well, that merely added to his sorrows.

His sorrows. He bit back a snort of derision at that. He was mourning the loss of a good friend and feeling wounded because his most recent lover was the cause of his grief. The people around him were mourning the loss of their Emperor and their family member. If nothing else, he'd have to respect their loss because they outnumbered him.

His eyes flickered to Nachia Krous, who sat straight-backed and held her grief tightly locked away. Her eyes shone with unshed tears and her mouth pulled down with a desire to cry out, but she held her own. Surely her loss was as great as his. She had lost a cousin after all, and according to the rumors they had been very close.

Of course she stood to become the Empress in a few days at the most, so he supposed that was a reason to celebrate. Or at least it would have been if not for the current insanity running through the Empire.

War. There hadn't been a war in Fellein for hundreds of years. There had been skirmishes, to be sure and he'd been on the front line of a few of them, but the simple fact was that the Fellein Empire was the most powerful nation in the known world and no one in their right minds would consider getting into a long fight with the sort of forces now at Merros's command.

At least that was what everyone believed. Having seen
the state of the Imperial Guard, the very finest soldiers
that Fellein had to offer, Merros had his doubts. Their
armor was lovely, quite shiny and remarkably well-kept
– now that he'd demanded repairs – but the men wearing
that armor were more show than substance and that was
a very sincere problem, because the Sa'ba Taalor were
easily the most dangerous fighters he had ever seen.

No. He was being unfair because he was worried to
the point of nausea about the idea of a war. The Imperial
Guard were good fighters and well trained. But next to
the coming enemy he was unsure of their skills.

His hands trembled just the slightest bit at the
knowledge that ten of the people from the Seven Forges
had killed over a thousand people in one evening. He
had borne witness to their actions.

Well, to part of the fight. He'd been sneaking in for a
closer look when he got caught by one of their enemies.
The ten had crept past and never been seen. He'd been
spotted. Luck or not, he had failed where the ten had
succeeded. He'd managed to defend himself and end the
life of his attacker.

Wollis would have told him he was being far too hard
on himself. Wollis had been good that way.

And if he had been bragging, Wollis would have
been the very first to slap him back down into his usual
reserved state of mind.

Cut. Chew. Swallow.

A very large man with too many rings on his fingers
was picking at his roast and staring silent hatred in the
direction of Desh Krohan. He was a hard man, by the
look of him, and likely a skilled fighter by the way he

carried himself, but he was softening and growing fat. The look on his face meant he was likely a Krous who was not going to ascend to the throne, and just as likely a very foolish man. No. He knew the man's name. Laister. He was one of the people who thought he should be the next Emperor.

He did not need or want to know more about the man just yet, but he marked him in his memory, because at some point he knew he'd need the knowledge.

Wollis was dead. Over a fortnight had passed and he was still having trouble getting past that simple fact.

Desh Krohan was talking with passion about Pathra Krous and he envied the man his oratory skills. He had never been a speaker. He was a soldier, pure and simple.

Well, except that now he was a general in the Empire's Army. The thought made his head hurt.

Applause exploded from around the room and Merros looked left and right before focusing on the sorcerer. Apparently he had finished his speech. He moved solemnly back to his seat near the future Empress and took a long sip of his wine.

Anger bounced through Merros. It was irrational, but it was real. The problem was that he was sitting down and eating a very fine meal – tasteless to him currently, but that was not the fault of the chefs – and the people around him were applauding moving speeches and the entire Empire was sitting on its laurels and waiting for an invasion.

To the north and west the Sa'ba Taalor would be gathering their forces soon, if they had not already started. They had to cross the Blasted Lands, yes, but he had no doubt that they would find their way home faster than any of the Empire's people ever had. Why? Because they were traveling on those damned mounts of theirs and the great beasts were much faster than horses. And when he had been with them, the very air seemed to bend to their needs when they traveled. Maybe that was his imagination, it was hard to say, but they seemed to traverse the desolate wasteland far faster than he had managed before meeting them.

To the south, Roathes was seeking his help. The kingdom that had chased him and several of the gray-skinned warriors from their palace after the Sa'ba Taalor had decimated – Gods, could it really have been over a thousand people? – the Guntha invading their lands. The Guntha were apparently gone now, destroyed when their islands erupted into a great volcanic mass and from the remains of those islands? Well, several people had seen large black warships circling the newly formed land mass. Those ships were either piloted by the Sa'ba Taalor, held by an unknown enemy or mirages created by the smoke and fear the eruptions caused.

Roathes was in chaos and the King there, Marsfel, was desperate for help from the Imperial Army.

Somebody should do something about that.

The part that made him angriest?

That somebody was him.

The Princess Lanaie moved to his table and sat in the seat next to him. The seat had been empty the entire time, not because there were seats to spare, but because, as was tradition, a place had been set to his left in honor of Wollis. The setting was present, a platter, a knife, a goblet and a fork. But in this case the cutlery faced in the wrong direction. He was a soldier. He knew the tradition too well.

The woman apparently did not. He knew her immediately. He had seen her sisters at her father's side not all that long ago and thought that they were truly some of the loveliest women he had seen. He had met her later, when she clarified the half-truths that her father had been telling the Emperor in order to gain assistance against the Guntha.

She had dark hair, dark eyes and skin several shades darker than his. Her features marked her as a Roathian as surely as they marked her as a daughter of King Marsfel.

Merros stared at her for a few seconds. He wasn't trying to be rude – she was already doing that by sitting in the place reserved for his dead friend – but he was damned if he could think of any reason why she would want to speak to him.

"I am Lanaie, Princess of Roathes. My father is King Marsfel and I would speak with you, General Dulver." Her lower lip trembled and her eyes were moist. She was nervous and he sincerely doubted it was his presence that caused her so much distress.

Then again, her father had tried to have him killed recently, so that might just be a cause for dismay in her opinion.

"I know who you are. We've met." That wasn't what he meant to say. He meant to ask how he could help her, but currently the wine and his grief were working against his better judgment. "You are sitting in the seat of my dead friend." He spoke calmly and made it a point to look her in the eyes. He might have overlooked the offense, but at the moment he was remembering the fight he'd had had with the men her father had sent after him.

"I don't understand." She looked worried for a moment her face pinched in concentration and then her eyes grew wide with horror. "I am so sorry." Her voice broke and he could tell by the tone that she was restraining herself from making a scene.

A flash of guilt crept through him. It was one thing to scold a soldier being foolish and another entirely to chastise a distraught woman, forget the fact that she was also royalty. It seemed a day for catastrophic social mistakes.

"Never mind," he said as gently as he could. "What can I do for you, Princess Lanaie of Roathes?"

"My father has sent news. The ships. The ones they heard of. The black ships that the Guntha spoke of. They have been spotted. My father. The King. He saw them with his own eyes."

Ah. She wanted his help.

"I am not the person you need to speak with. You should be speaking to the Regent. Desh Krohan is currently the official head of the Empire until such time as the new Empress is crowned."

"He has not taken the time to see me." Her voice broke.

"He is a very busy man." Merros wanted to be gentle. He did. He also wanted to be left alone. "He is also far likelier to help you than I am at the moment."

"But you are the head of the army…"

"I am a soldier. I fight wars. I do not choose which wars I will fight." *And if I did, I would most assuredly not run to the aid of your father*. He did not add the last, but he certainly considered it. He was human after all and currently not enthusiastic about assisting the man who'd tried to have him murdered.

She won the argument not with words but with actions. Instead of throwing accusations at him or pleading for his interference, she looked down and her lower lip trembled. Merros started to look away because he knew what would happen next.

Wollis always said women were his weakness and the man was not wrong.

Princess Lanaie looked back up at him and tears fell from her large, dark eyes. She looked so damnably lost and afraid and he had always been raised to believe that a woman in distress needed to be a gentleman's first priority.

"Damn me. Fine. I'll arrange for you to see the Regent. Just, please, stop that crying."

That didn't work as well as he'd hoped. She just cried more.

Not ten feet away Laister Krous was looking on with a scowl on his wide face. Either he had not been raised as a gentleman or he felt left out. Either way, Merros didn't much like him. He kept that opinion to himself. A wise man knows when to keep his mouth shut.

THREE

The winds were still roaring around him, but Andover Lashk did not feel them. The bitter scent of ash was still present, but the air that should have been cold was instead warm and there was a scent of roasting meat that made his stomach roar.

Andover opened his eyes and saw that someone had managed to build a shelter over his head. It was a nice surprise, as the last thing he remembered clearly was being hurled through the air by the monster he'd just maimed.

He tried to take a deep breath and immediately regretted it. Pain washed through his ribs and he winced.

"You're awake." The voice was deep and friendly enough. He looked to his left and saw Drask Silver Hand's massive form not three feet distant. "We were beginning to wonder about that." The man was sitting on a bedroll and looking directly toward him, his eyes alight in the gloom of the shelter.

Andover sat up very slowly, wincing the entire time. He was having trouble breathing.

"You have broken ribs. Bromt bound them for you." Andover looked around and saw both Bromt and Delil, the other two people he was traveling with. Well, he had been traveling with them before they disappeared. Only they were back now, weren't they?

"How did you find me?"

"We were never far away. We were watching."

Anger flared in his chest and, despite the pain, he turned to look hard at Drask. "Then why didn't you help me?"

"Are you alive?" Drask's eyes gave off that odd glow his people's eyes all seemed to hold inside.

"Of course I'm alive."

"Yes." Drask leaned back and shrugged. "Then you did not need our help."

Andover opened his mouth to say more and then closed it. Being angry with Drask was foolish and would get him nothing but dead.

Delil moved through the small shelter in a crouch and squatted next to him, looking at his chest and moving her hands over the tight bandages there. He'd have noticed them before but he was too busy recovering from being alive. "These are tight but you can breathe. Do not move too much. It will only hurt."

She turned away from him for a moment and her arms got busy over the fire in front of Drask. When she turned back there were several slices of roasted meat on a small wooden plate. "Eat. You need to gain your strength. Tomorrow morning we travel again."

Her tone was not kind, nor was it harsh. It was simply perfunctory. Still, her eyes managed what he thought was a small smile, as he took the offered food. As always, the damned veils hid their faces away too well for him to see much beyond their eyes.

The entire shelter rattled as ice and dirt lashed against it. Delil cut more slices from the slab of roasting meat and folded them over on themselves before sliding them under her veil. For a moment he saw her chin through the fabric. It looked like a perfectly normal chin, well-rounded and shapely enough. At least as shapely as a chin could manage to be without anything around it but cloth. He couldn't understand the secrecy any more than he could understand the strange quality of the Sa'ba Taalor's voices.

"How far away from the Seven Forges are we?" He took the time to ask the question only after he'd rammed the first cut of juicy meat into his mouth and chewed it into nothingness. His hunger did not abate in the least and he intended to eat as much as he could manage in a single sitting. He couldn't remember the last time he'd eaten. The meat was gamey, and heavy with enough fat to make it tender. His stomach fairly roared for more.

Drask shrugged his broad shoulders. "We could be there in a week or less. We will probably take much longer. The storms will not abate for at least another day or so, if I am right." He shrugged again. "I am normally right." Bromt nodded his agreement.

"Why will we take longer?"

"You are not healed yet, Andover. You must be mended before we head through Durhallem's Pass. There will be challenges for you there and you must be ready to face them."

A great, low note sounded. The noise was loud enough that the tent wall vibrated with it. Andover flinched and immediately regretted it as his ribs flared. All three of the Sa'ba Taalor looked toward the sound, their bodies tense.

"What *is* that?" Andover had to shout to be heard as the roaring noise slowly faded away.

"The Mounds." Delil's voice was harsh. "We are closer than we should be."

Drask said something to her in a different language, one that was unsettling to his ears. Whatever he said, the tone was argumentative. If he'd expected Delil to be cowed by the large man, he was mistaken. She argued back vehemently until Bromt interrupted them both.

For a few minutes the only sounds were the winds outside and then Andover decided he was done watching the three of them locked in a staring contest and spoke up. "So tell me what the Mounds are."

"We do not know. We are forbidden by the Daxar Taalor to approach them." Delil's voice was low and seething with tension.

"Then tell me about Durhallem's Pass and why I need to be healthy before I get there."

Drask was the one who answered. "You will be challenged there. You are unknown and you come to our land as an outsider. This challenge is the first of several for you."

"I'll be with you, won't I?" He frowned. This wasn't what he'd been expecting when he agreed to the journey to the Seven Forges. He wasn't really sure exactly what he'd expected, except that he was to work as an ambassador of sorts between Fellein and the Sa'ba Taalor. He was supposed to come with them, in part as payment for the miraculous hands he now had, replacements for the ruined lumps Menoch and Purb, of the City Guard in Tyrne, had left him with.

"Possibly," Drask answered. "That is for the gods to decide. Durhallem's Pass is the entrance to the valley we live in. I cannot say that the guards there will challenge you, but they might."

"But I don't have–" He bit his tongue.

Drask looked at him in silence for several seconds, his face unreadable. "You have no weapons?"

Andover nodded.

All three of the Sa'ba Taalor sighed.

"I know. I have my hands." Andover mumbled the words and looked down.

It was Delil who hit him with her fist and knocked him back into a prone position. She barely seemed to move, but he was on his back and his face was first numb and then burning where her hand struck him.

She leaned over him and her eyes flared with anger. "Did I teach you nothing? Do you wish to have another lesson, boy?" The word "boy" had never seemed so insulting.

A month ago he would have whimpered. A year ago he would have run.

Andover reached up and struck her in the chest with his closed fist. Delil slipped back before the blow landed and the damage was minimal, but had it connected properly he knew he'd likely have left her in agony.

Delil continued the motion he had started, falling backward. As her arms caught her weight, her left foot came around and the heel of her boot cracked him in the stomach hard enough to leave him gasping.

Bromt and Drask watched on, offering no help on either side of the argument.

Andover rolled over, ignoring the pain in his chest. There was pain, yes, but in comparison to what he had already endured in his life it was minor. He reached for her leg with every intention of doing his level best to break it. She was gone by the time his hands should have been closing on flesh.

And then her hands were on his wrists. Before he'd been injured Andover had been working in a smithy; he'd worked the bellows and hammered at metal for hours on end, learning from one of the best blacksmiths in Tyrne. Despite his size, he was muscular enough.

Delil was not only faster, she was stronger. She pinned his arms in short order and he bucked and fought and did his best to get away while she held him in check.

Drask leaned in closer and looked at Andover, studied him.

"She has leverage on you. She has you at a disadvantage. You are not without moves you can make to break free."

Andover looked to Delil and saw that she was looking back, her eyes watching his face. She did not look angry. And he understood. Wounded or not, this was his training. There was no reprieve for bad weather or his injuries, just as there would be none if he fought for his life.

Her weight was forward and pinning his arms. She crouched in front of him and he could not possibly reach her with his body. If he tried she would move to one side or the other and either attack or once again pin him. His arms could not move, but if she intended to keep him where he was, hers could not move either.

Andover lunged forward and slammed his forehead against hers. Delil fell back and he had his moment. He had his momentum. He was off balance, but there wasn't far they could go, and if he was going to fall, he intended to fall on his enemy.

Delil saw him coming and moved, sliding away from where she had been and moving like water around a falling tree. He hit the ground and turned as quickly as he could, but it wasn't fast enough. By the time he'd recovered from his attempt, the woman was cuffing him across the side of his head.

She could have killed him. He knew that. It didn't make him any less angry.

Andover let out a small growl and lunged and she slithered away again, not letting him hit her.

Bromt, who seldom seemed to take the effort to talk, spoke up, "Anger is a tool, Andover Lashk. Never let it be the master. Think before you attack. Delil is not going to let anger make her foolish. You can ill afford to make that mistake."

The entire time Bromt was speaking Delil was moving, half crawling over their supplies in the small area of the tent, watching him as a cat watches a wounded bird. She was not the least bit intimidated by him.

Delil spoke to him as she moved. "You are an unscarred baby, Andover Lashk. You are afraid of hurting me." There was no venom in her words. "Let me worry about my injuries. When next I come for you, I will attack you in earnest. Do you understand? I will hurt you. Badly."

He nodded. He believed her. He knew better than to think she was bluffing.

When she came he was prepared. He calmed himself, watched her and did his best to anticipate.

She dropped lower still, slid across the ground on the balls of her feet and brought her hands toward his face. He grabbed at her wrists and, while he was trying to pin her, she brought a knee into his side hard enough to send him stumbling. Before he could right himself she had a handful of his hair and slammed his face into the ground. She turned his head with her pressure and avoided breaking his nose, but he understood that this was her being nice. She had him. She could have ended the fight with one brutal move.

Andover got to his hands and knees and shook his head to clear the ringing from his skull. By the time the noises had stopped, Delil was sitting cross-legged on the ground and eating again. She looked at him and shook her head, though he could see the smile in her eyes. "Do not tell me you do not have a weapon. Your body is a weapon." She reached down and pulled her tunic open enough to show the ugly blemish on her light gray flesh. The bruise caused by the knuckles of his hand when he'd struck her, apparently harder than he had realized. "We watched you fight the Cacklers. You broke the teeth out of one of their mouths." She leaned toward him and let her tunic fall back in place. Her hand touched his wrist and slid up to the back of his hand, her fingers lightly moving over the smooth black metal. "You have hands of iron, Andover. Before we reach Durhallem's Pass we will show you how they can be used best to fight."

Bromt nodded and pointed to their supplies. "Besides, your hammer is over there. We found it when we found you."

Drask chuckled. "That's your lesson for tonight. Get rest. When the storm abates we move on. Before then, each of us will show you how to fight in close combat." His eyes looked Andover from head to toe. "You need the lessons."

Andover nodded his head.

Drask leaned in again and touched his hand. Silver fingers prodded iron. "Truska-Pren had gifted you, Andover. Gods do not make such gifts lightly. Before you told me you would meet with our gods and offer your thanks. I will keep you to that. But before that happens you have to prove yourself worthy to meet with the gods, or their representatives. You met Tusk, the Sa'ba Taalor. You have not met him in his role as King Tuskandru. Not really. He has not spoken to you and he has not accepted you. Tuskandru's people are the guardians of Durhallem's Pass. If you do not prove yourself to them, you cannot prove yourself to Tuskandru. He is the first of the kings you must meet."

Andover thought hard on that. He had made promises. He had new hands. They were his gift and they were his to keep, that he had already been promised. He had fought the men who'd taken from him, who'd crippled him, and he had returned the favor to both of them. That had been the price demanded by Drask, and he had paid it. But there were other duties that came with his hands, and those included meeting the Sa'ba Taalor's kings and offering thanks to their gods. He knew there was more to it. There had to be, didn't there? But he did not fully understand the details.

He moved and winced at the pain in his side. Delil had reminded him about pain without even trying. He looked toward the girl again. She was curled up and her eyes were closed. She had called him "unscarred". She was not quite right. His wrists were all scars, weren't they? But, next to any of the people in the tent, she spoke a bit of truth. He could see the scars on her skin highlighted by the small fire. Her arms, her legs, her hands... there were scars everywhere. The same was true of Drask and Bromt alike. Bromt seemed more scar tissue than regular flesh.

He wondered how long before his skin was similarly decorated. Part of him was terrified by the thought. A look at his wrists, at the graying skin where his iron hands met his flesh – a stain that was growing, however slowly – and he knew that he was changing, becoming something other than he had been before his flesh and blood hands were taken from him. Another part found the notion oddly appealing. And that thought was just as unsettling to him as anything he had ever encountered.

There are some who say that kings rule by divine right. If that is the case then surely the kings must answer to their gods. That was most assuredly the way of the Sa'ba Taalor. The Daxar Taalor called their representatives together and, as they demanded, so it came to pass.

From each of the mountains the kings came, some with retinues and others with either no one for company or only a small number. There had been times when the seven kingdoms were at war, but those times were past and any grudges carried were cast aside as ordered by the gods themselves.

They met as equals, surely the gods were equals and therefore their representatives were as well, but they met in Prydiria, called the Iron Fortress, the vast keep of Tarag Paedori, the Chosen of the Forge of Truska-Pren and King in Iron. The great hall of the keep was opened and the kings met at one of the huge gray marble tables and settled themselves there to eat and discuss the only subject that currently mattered: the coming war.

Tarag Paedori was the host of the affair, not that it much mattered to any of the attendees. Tuskandru walked into the hall and nodded his greeting to the man. They had been allies more often than they had been enemies. That was true of all the kings when it came to Tusk. He was an easygoing sort, so long as you didn't offend him, and as Durhallem did not believe in mercy, most of the kings had the common sense not to give the Obsidian King a reason to hold a grudge. Both of the men were of exceptional stature. They had to be. Though all of the kings celebrated different aspects of war in their daily lives, few would have argued with the fact that both kings required physical strength above nearly all other attributes.

In comparison N'Heelis, the Chosen of the Forge of Wrommish and King in Gold, was leaner and smaller. His muscles were cords and bands that ran under his flesh and his scars were so plentiful that it was far harder to find a portion of his body that was unblemished than it was to find a wound that had healed. Though he was slight in comparison, he was highly respected. The representative of Wrommish had met each of the kings in combat previously and taught all of them a good number of tactical maneuvers for unarmed combat.

Wheklam's chosen was Donaie Swarl, the King in Lead. She was lean and tall and dark. Her skin was several shades darker than most of the others and she wore a dark blue sash wrapped around her head and draped down to her waist. The fabric was said to have cost several people their lives over the years. More than one had tried to take it from her and died for their efforts.

Of all of them, Donaie had met the most outsiders. For years she and her ships had cruised through the waters well beyond the Seven Forges and made raids on multiple lands. Wheklam demanded the sailors be prepared for when the Great Tide was upon them and the King in Lead had obeyed.

Several asked her questions about the destruction of Guntha and she answered their questions. She rolled out the maps she had made of the world and on those maps the newly growing island was carefully marked in.

Ganem, the Chosen of the Forge of Ydramil and King in Silver, entered the hall with Lored, Chosen of the Forge of Ordna and King in Bronze. If there was ever a sign that times were changing it was that the two came in together. For over a decade the only thing they had shared was their hatred of each other. Lored's right eye and the area surrounding it had been replaced by a partial mask of bronze and everyone in the room knew that Ganem was the cause of that particular wound. Ganem was not a woman to be angered lightly and Lored had offended her many times. Still, the Daxar Taalor demanded peace and so both sides offered peace.

Either the last to enter the room, or possibly the first, was Glo'Hosht, the Chosen of the Forge of Paedle and the King in Mercury. It was incredibly rare for any of the kings to see Glo'Hosht, who warred with everyone and no one. Glo'Hosht was often called the King in Shadow and the Bone King, because Paedle, as everyone knew, was the god of silent deaths. Glo'Hosht was also androgynous. No one could decide which gender was the King's and he or she volunteered nothing.

Seven Kings and Seven Gods met in the great hall. They were not the only ones to meet there.

The business of kingdoms and empires does not stop. In seven days the new head of the Empire would be crowned. It was, not shockingly, the topic of much conversation.

Merros found he did not care. There were other things on his mind. First, there were the men under him, many of whom he was only just meeting and assessing for the first time.

He was dressed in new leather pants and a simple shirt with a leather tunic. He was supposed to be dressed in a uniform that had been tailored to his body, but he hated the damned thing already. He would wear it when he had to, but not now. For now he preferred to meet the men around him in relative comfort.

Getting used to being one of the commanders of the army was a bit confusing for him. Not because he hadn't been in command before – he had been a captain before he retired and he had led the expedition into the Blasted Lands, after all – but because of the sheer scope of his command.

He was used to a company, a battalion, possibly a squad of men. This was an army, and as he stood on the parade grounds and looked at the hardened men in front of him, he was almost comfortable. Then he remembered that each of the soldiers he was facing was in charge of a battalion, or a squad or a full legion.

"Durst, how many more are supposed to be here?" He'd almost called the man Wollis, but he caught himself this time. Taurn Durst had been along with both men on the last expedition and he was a competent soldier. He was from Trecharch and, like many of the people there, he tended to be direct and honest in his opinions.

Durst walked closer and pursed his lips. His thick hair was receding from his forehead like a slow moving wave drawing away from his eyebrows. He looked to have deep trouble with the idea of handling any task harder than remembering his name, but Merros knew the appearance was false. Durst was excellent with numbers and a very capable fighter.

"Might be one or two missing, General, but if they are, I suspect we can have a talk with 'em and handle the matter." He spoke slowly and, when he contemplated the notion of punishing the , Durst's broad mouth pulled into a dark grin. That smile alone made Merros recall why Wollis had respected the man. Durst was fond of discipline and precision. Anything that fell short of those lofty ideals was something the man felt should be crushed under one of his thick heels.

"Fair enough." Merros eyed the crowd again. Most of them were standing at attention. He noted the ones who weren't and made sure to have Durst copy their names onto a sheet of paper.

"We are here today because we stand close to war." He didn't waste time on pleasantries. He'd take care of those later. Merros scanned the men and watched their expressions. "Make no mistake about that. I doubt another season will pass before Fellein is drawn into bloody combat with warriors you do not want to take lightly."

The soldiers started muttering among themselves. Not all of them, but a sizable percentage. Merros frowned at that.

Durst frowned too, then he stepped forward and bellowed, "Shut it! Keep your tongues still until the General is finished with you!"

Several of the soldiers looked shocked by the outburst, and one or two of them had expressions that said they were contemplating arguing. Durst's head lowered a bit, his neck thrusting forward. His posture practically begged for someone else to interrupt.

Merros said nothing for a moment, but instead waited for calm to come back.

"Some of you know me. Most do not. Get used to my face and my voice. If you have questions, I'll be available to answer them and we'll discuss matters, but for now, it's time to listen."

A few of them got smart and responded with, "Aye. Ho, sir."

"Let's hear that again, lads!" Durst roared the words and the men caught on.

"Aye! Ho, sir!"

Merros nodded. "We are all aware of how long it's been since Fellein has been in a real war. Believe me. This is likely to be a very real war. Not a skirmish, not an argument between neighbors. Ten of the Sa'ba Taalor killed a thousand Guntha."

That caught the rest of them up and several started to speak. This time it was Merros who shut them down, bellowing at the top of his lungs to get their attention. "I said it's time to listen!" The silence was complete and immediate.

"Ten of them killed a thousand. I saw it with my own eyes. They did not engage in formal combat. They used stealth and they crept in among numbers that should have never allowed them to gain access." Again he looked over the soldiers. "Most of you have fought the Guntha. You know they were hard fighters and brutal enemies. They are gone now. Dead. We've all heard the stories about the burning seas and the new island growing where the Guntha lived. The stories are true."

He walked a few paces and let them consider those words. "The latest messages from Roathes say that black ships with black sails are cutting along the coast. They stay out in the waters for now, but those ships are supposed to be the very forces that caused the Guntha to attack again and again. They were trying to escape what they claimed were demons."

One of the men in the crowd snorted and muttered something just loud enough to catch his attention. Merros turned to eye the man sharply. "What's your name again?"

Not being completely foolish, the man stood a little straighter and answered directly: "Lockner Horast, General. Captain of the First Lancers Division."

"Lockner Horast." He kept his eyes locked on the man until the other soldier looked ready to get nervous. That was exactly what Merros wanted. "Captain Horast, you sound doubtful. Tell me what's on your mind."

"All respect, General, but everyone knows the Roathians like to talk a good war. Most of us have been down there a time or two fighting the Guntha."

"Absolutely right. What's your point?"

"The Roathians tell me a hundred ships are along their shoreline and I'm probably going to expect a dozen men fishing in paddle boats."

Merros smiled. "Aye. And you'd probably be right. Except that this time there's information coming from other sources too. This time one of Desh Krohan's Sisters is studying the situation. If you'd like to talk with the wizard and ask how often his associates lie about the facts, I can arrange that."

Horast shook his head. "No, no. That's just fine, General."

"There are ships. Just how many we don't know, but it's over a dozen." He paused a moment and then pointed to the south. "The great clouds you see from that direction are coming from where the Guntha Islands used to be. They're gone. They've been burned away and a new island is growing out in the Corinta. And between that island and the Roathians there are ships.

"That's one problem. Next problem is that Emperor Pathra Krous is dead. He was murdered right there, in his own palace. With a hundred members of the Imperial Guard within hailing distance." He looked hard into the audience of soldiers. "How is that acceptable? How is that ever acceptable?"

The men in front of him looked around, but no one came up with a good answer. He gave one himself. "It's not! That happened because as an army we have grown soft and lazy."

That got them. Several of the men made noises now and almost all of them were staring with angered expressions.

Merros held up a hand. "Don't take my word. Instead let's talk to Morton Darnaven." He gestured to his left and the man came forward. "Darnaven can tell each and every one of you what he witnessed when he met the Sa'ba Taalor. He did not travel with them. He saw them when they were watching our finest soldiers being trained." Darnaven was a heavyset man, but none of him was flabby. He was a long-timer, not quite as long for the service as Merros himself, but he'd been in combat against the Guntha and had been farther to the south than most of the men in the room had ever traveled. He had worked the skirmish lines across most of the Empire at one time or another and he was a hard bastard with a particularly mean scowl. That was why he was now a colonel.

"Colonel Darnaven is going to talk to you about the Sa'ba Taalor. He is going to explain to you why they are dangerous and why we need to prepare." Merros looked at the crowd and then he smiled. It was not a pleasant expression. He normally reserved it for when he was about to deliver punishments. "He's going to explain why we are now going to have new soldiers coming in and how hard we are going to work to train them for combat."

He walked a few paces, eyeing the men and making sure he had their attention. "First, however, we are going to make sure that the coronation of our new Empress goes smoothly. There will be no disturbances. There will be no unruly crowds. We will have a peaceful coronation. Or I will have heads to mount on the walls of the Summer Palace. Do I make myself clear?"

"Aye! Ho, Sir!"

"War is coming. We will be prepared for it." Merros walked away from the soldiers and left them with Darnaven.

As he walked, Durst kept pace. "I want that list of names. Durst. Every one who wasn't paying attention when we started, and the ones who didn't show. When Darnaven is done with them, send them to my office to wait for me."

"Aye, ho sir."

He thought for a long moment and then added, "I want a post and a whip in the western yard, Durst. I won't use it, yet, but I want it there. I want them to know we're serious."

"Aye, ho sir." Durst didn't hesitate and didn't argue. Merros did not like using punishment to make a point and the man knew it. But like Merros, Durst had seen the Sa'ba Taalor in action. He knew how serious the situation was.

"Also, it's time for a few competitions. Work it out. I want the best ten archers. The best ten swordsmen we have. Everyone competes. Best ten lancers, best ten horsemen. There will be cash rewards for the winners and very likely a few promotions."

From there it was back to the palace for another round of meetings. The coronation of Nachia Krous was only a few days away. There were a thousand details to see to and more.

And, of course, there was always reason to expect a few unpleasant surprises.

FOUR

In the distant past, the Wellish Steppes were a place of horror and tyranny. The Overlords in charge of the area had been bested long ago, but a number of people still claim that the land was cursed. To be fair, the fact that most of the region ran alongside the edge of the Blasted Lands didn't help the area's reputation. The land was fertile, but not much grew there beyond fungus and scrub grass. The one distinct advantage to the place was that it's mostly flat. Large caravans and small groups alike could travel it without too much worry about unseen threats.

It was so calm there, in fact, that even without paving the pathways through the area had long since been well established. "The roads along the steppes practically pave themselves," was a fairly common remark among the soldiers in the Imperial Army. For that reason alone it was not unusual to find those very same soldiers looking forward to marching across the area.

There are exceptions to every rule.

The damp was constant and heavy. The moisture clung to everything and slowly, methodically seeped its way through clothes, shoes and supplies. Had it been any warmer, there would likely have been worries about the supplies mildewing. Instead they just marched on, keeping a brisk pace in the hopes of staying warm in the chill, misty air.

The caravan came from the east. They traveled the Imperial Highway, and those who had horses were glad of them. Those who did not, carried their packs and their supplies and walked the distance from Old Canhoon at a steady march. The road here was old but well tended, and cut into the low-lying hills. In some places the paths were deeply enough worn that the soldiers almost disappeared from sight, and in others they were level to the ground. Nolan March was charged with watching the flanks of the entire column, and it was occasionally amusing to watch the men seemingly sink into the ground fog, like the specters he'd heard tell of as a child.

March preferred walking the edges of the column and keeping an eye out. It broke the monotony of staring at the backs of the men in front of him when he was forced to march the column.

Nolan carried himself easily enough. He'd grown up in the north, joined the army when he was of age and had now been trained as a soldier. Canhoon was where he was assigned and where he'd expected to stay, but now he was on his way to Tyrne, where he was supposed to join the Imperial Guard and where he would see his family again.

That had been the plan before he found out about the death of his father, Wollis. He hadn't seen the old man in a long time and now it looked like he would never see him again. The thought was a hard one to accept. He'd grown up believing his father was nearly indestructible. The man had been on the road and traveling for most of Nolan's life, but he'd always seemed almost like a giant when he was home, and he'd always been the first to tell stories of the military life and the people he'd fought with and against.

Thinking about Wollis made his chest swell with pride and his heart ache with loss at the same time. He would be missed.

The man who'd been his father's commander had sent for him. The plan had been to reunite the entire family and Nolan was grateful for the effort, even if it hadn't worked out.

"First thing I do when we get to Tyrne, is I take the money I've saved up and buy myself a new pair of boots. These bastards are falling off my feet." The voice came from Darus Leeds, who could rightly enough be called Nolan's friend. Which is to say he was one of the people in the battalion that Nolan liked and additionally was one of the few he trusted. Nolan was not big on trust. His first few weeks in the army had taught him that many people are thieves. Those same weeks had taught a few of the thieves that stealing from Nolan was a very bad idea.

Stonehaven was a long ways off, but the lessons he'd learned in his hometown stuck with him. Most of the people in the area, not surprisingly, worked in the quarries and worked hard for what they owned. That tended to make them a bit reluctant to let go when something was taken from them.

Darus was fairly tall and lean, but Nolan had already learned that didn't mean much. While he was nowhere near as solidly built as Nolan he was as strong as an ox and had a fearsome way with a sword. They often faced off against each other in practice matches and from time to time teamed up against other members of the battalion. Darus came from a good distance to the east, somewhere near Elda. From what he'd told Nolan, the people in his area still trained hard with sword and shield alike. Nolan saw no reason to doubt those claims.

Darus was looking his way and expecting a response. "What?"

"I said what are your big plans when you get to Tyrne?"

Nolan looked away. "I'm supposed to meet with a family friend." He muttered the words and a little twist of guilt nibbled at his insides. It was unjustified but the guilt was still there.

"Your family has friends in Tyrne? Didn't you say as you're from up north near Trecharch?"

"Stonehaven. A bit east of Trecharch."

"Yeah I heard of that one." The way he said it let Nolan know his friend was lying. He didn't take offense. Darus had a need to sound knowledgeable about everything he encountered. Several people had called him on his claims in the past and Nolan ignored them as easily as he ignored the false claims. Darus was a friend. It was precisely that simple for him.

"My father." He paused a moment to swallow the lump trying to form in his throat. "The man he was riding with is in Tyrne. He's asked to see me. He wants to present my father's ashes."

Darus made a noise and nodded his head. That was all there was to say on the matter. Darus had left home when he'd joined the army and had no intention of looking back. What his parents might have done to inspire the cold distance within the otherwise friendly man, Nolan did not know. He merely understood that Darus had no desire to speak of it.

Nolan thought back to his one meeting with Merros Dulver. He'd seen the man ride up on horseback and thought him a striking figure. He was tall and rugged and solid. He carried himself with confidence and he'd shaken Nolan's hand and spoken highly of his father's prowess in combat. He'd liked the man just fine right up until the time his father decided to go off with him.

There was nothing fair about that, of course. He knew Dulver was a good man. His father had said so on several occasions.

Still, his father was dead. And the man who'd taken him away was one of the men in charge of the entire army.

"What you should do is find out what this fella says about how your father died."

Nolan nodded his head and looked around. They were following the same road they'd been on for longer than he cared to think about. Up ahead the sound of horns came back their way and the foot soldiers dutifully stepped to the sides of the road and waited, most of them grateful for the chance to rest their legs for a moment. The last time they'd been called off the road had been to let the escorts past with the body of Emperor Pathra Krous. That had been a somber moment. An escort of mounted Imperial Guards had dominated the road, and a great black wagon moved between them, the windows covered and the Imperial crest gleaming on the sides. Nolan, along with every other soldier, had held his sword out above his head as the wagon rumbled slowly past, and several of the soldiers had done their best to hide tears.

Tears for a man none of them had met. What a mad world they lived in.

Somewhere up ahead a loud noise came their way, as if to prove the point. It was a warbling cry, a trumpet call that he was not familiar with.

The response was immediate, by a good number of the foot soldiers. They grabbed their shields and their weapons and prepared. The men sported swords or axes. Those that did not, brandished spears. The road almost immediately bristled with pointed, sharpened steel.

"What the hell is happening up there?" Darus was squinting against the glare of the sun's attempt to burn away the mists, trying to see what was causing the disturbance, but with no luck.

Someone called out, "Spears to the front!" and immediately the foot soldiers with spears came forward, sliding past the swordsmen and preparing themselves. A lanky man with graying hair moved into position in front of Nolan and dropped into a crouch, holding his spear with the point aimed high, but easily lowered should it be necessary.

No one questioned whether or not this was a drill. The sounds of conflict came from further up the road. The view was obstructed by spearmen and by the curve of the road itself.

"What the hell?" That was Darus again as a deep roar cut the air and was immediately followed by the sound of several men screaming.

"Spears, ready! Here they come!"

"They" were impossible to see at first, but hearing them was easy. The sounds of metal and men joined together in a loud tidal roar, but that was nothing to the other sounds clashing for attention. The noises were unsettling, alien, and made Nolan's skin crawl. There were low growls and higher sounds, a keening noise that barely made sense to his ears.

The lines of men that bordered the road began to falter and spear tips that had been raised high wavered and then dropped as something came closer. Whatever that something was, the spears were attacking, doing their best to pin it in place.

A vast shape took to the air for just a moment. A blur of dark fur, darker leathers and metal and, unless he was mistaken, there was a person atop that lunging, flailing insanity. Yes, he saw an axe coming down even as the massive thing yielded to gravity. Several spears went sailing in the wrong direction, their points falling like saplings in a sudden flood. But more weapons went in the right direction and a moment later the roars and screams of the furred nightmare were faltering and then dying completely.

Ahead of them, along the line, soldiers screamed and broke ranks. The squad leaders called out for order and a small handful began listening, drawing back into the proper ranks, but some did not pay heed, too enthralled by what they were seeing, apparently.

Darus shook his head. "Can't see a damned thing."

Nolan was about to agree when the shape came through the ranks. It was low-slung and charged across the ground, roaring and swinging clawed front limbs that slapped people aside with too much ease. There was indeed a man riding on the beast's back, but he was dead near as far as Nolan could tell. The man's skin was gray and his body sagged to one side, flopping and flailing with each move of the creature. Soldiers screamed as they were hurled through the air, broken and bleeding. Some only staggered a few feet, but a few truly unfortunate souls were thrown twenty feet or more with a single sweep of the monster's limbs.

Nolan backed up and looked for a better access point. Darus moved with him, looking for a moment as if he planned to run away. But that wouldn't happen. The punishment for running from combat was death, and they all knew it.

There were few people from the north who couldn't climb a tree. Trecharch and the surrounding areas had trees that practically begged to be climbed, and so Nolan resorted to older skills, found the best looking tree for the job and scampered up as quickly as he could. Flinching a couple of times when his equipment snagged itself on a branch or rough bark.

Not far away, the soldiers he'd trained with were scattering away from whatever the hell they were fighting and he saw them for the first time. The great furred nightmare he'd seen was down, killed by the footmen. Easily a dozen of them had gone down in the process, but they had taken man and mount alike.

Moving over those remains, demons from the worst kind of nightmares charged, slashing at the soldiers too close to them. The attackers moved quickly, but they were not faster than the eye.

What he'd thought was one enormous attacker was actually several. From above he could see the breaks in the forms, close together and pushing along the same path to give the impression of one body. The large shapes could easily have broken away from each other and moved through the entire area, but they stayed stubbornly on the road and they continued to follow the path even when the foot soldiers and cavalry were in their way. Horses and riders were knocked aside and torn apart if they got too close. Any men standing nearby when the odd shapes got closer were slapped away or violently attacked. As he observed, one of the shambling things reached out and yanked a man into its embrace. Within a heartbeat's span the captured soldier was screaming and dying. As he died, four of the spearmen attacked, driving the points of their weapons deep into the loathsome thing that shuddered and wailed and died.

Before he could see much of the dying creature, the next in line rolled forward, crawling over the dying man and monstrosity alike.

He clamped his teeth tightly together and looked down at Darus. "Get to the supplies! Get to the wagons!"

"What? Why?"

"I want to try something."

As they spoke the column of nightmares tramped closer, pushing past or through the men fighting them. Spears and swords rose and fell and a few more of the things fell to the weapons. But the next in the line kept coming in a slow moving tide of unnatural flesh.

And as the people fighting them looked at the creatures, occasionally a trained fighter would back away, disgusted or horrified or simply unbelieving of what they were seeing. Nolan wasn't sure which was stronger: his desire to know what was so unsettling or the part of him that never wanted to be that repulsed.

Nolan dropped quickly from his perch and ran toward the wagons, hoping that Darus was with him. The things were coming closer and he had a momentary fear that someone would see them running and think they were trying to flee. He remembered his father telling him about two occasions where he'd had to discipline a soldier trying to flee from a fight. Neither of the men had lived through the experience. The idea of a spear in the back or a noose around his neck did not appeal at all.

Death did not come, but the things behind him were definitely getting closer.

The wagons were in motion. Not because they were supposed to be, but because the horses apparently did not like what was coming their way and they were trying to get up the sides of the well-worn road and drag their wagons with them. The men trying to calm the beasts were not having any luck. One wagon had fallen to its side already and the draft horses were straining and trying to haul their burden along despite the added resistance. The men riding the wagon had fallen. One lay broken on the ground and the other was pinned under the weight of the capsized vehicle.

Nolan didn't take time to think it through. Instead he pulled his axe and climbed atop the wagon, hacking at the couplings until they broke. It didn't take much effort as the wooden connections had already fractured. Darus followed his lead and took a long knife from his belt sheath and cut the leather straps at the same time. A moment later the horses were free and the wagon was no longer moving.

The man under the wagon was not moving. He was alive, but his eyes had rolled back and his skin was pale and sweating. It would take more than the two of them to free him. The wagon was too damned heavy.

Nolan shook off his worries for the downed driver and climbed over the wagon. The canvas cover had broken and the supplies inside were spilled halfway across the road, only adding to the chaos as other wagons and horses tramped over the supplies within.

He'd been hoping for one of the armory wagons, but was not that lucky. The spilled contents were from the larders.

Behind him, a wagon succeeded in climbing the rise and lurched off the road. The driver did not make it along for the ride and let out a yelp as he fell backward and flopped down the hillside back to where Nolan and Darus were waiting. He was battered and looked a bit surprised to find himself in the mud, but he got back up on his own. His round face was familiar, but there was no name associated with him in Nolan's mind.

Nolan looked the man over. "Get a weapon ready!"

The man nodded and pulled at his sheathed axe. It was more a tool than a weapon, unlike like the one Nolan himself carried, but it would cut a monster as sure as it would chop wood.

Nolan looked at the debris, searching for any possible tools to help them, and then looked up at the road ahead where the monsters were still coming.

No time.

The closest of the things was almost on them and he saw the head of the beast again and wished that he did not. It should not exist and yet it did. Had someone taken a dozen men sculpted of soft clay and decided to make something different from the originals, what was coming at him might have been the result. Faces were distorted and pressed into new shapes, crushed against shoulders and torsos and bent by angry fingers into a new, rough form. He could see mouths and broken teeth, he could spy a nose mashed into a semi-flattened shape and smeared into an eye socket. The eye was still there, rolling madly and possibly seeing the world around it or merely staring blindly. Arms and fingers were broken and bent and pressed into that rough-hewn face. And it wasn't only the heads of the people used to make the shape. There were legs and torsos and there were broken swords and shields and armor twisted into that moving, impossible mess.

There was an Imperial Guard insignia crushed into the side of the monster's face. Part of the thing. The crest of a shield was warped into that nightmare, a piece of the unholy whole.

The bloated nightmare pushed forward and ran into the wagon, not stopping, not slowing but continuing along the same pathway. The wagon did not budge; it was a very heavy obstacle to be sure, but the thing kept shoving forward, the heavy forearms of the monster slamming into the overturned affair and smashing into it again and again, pummeling wood and iron that began to break and bend under the assault.

Darus had to drag Nolan back as the brute continued forward. A moment later and he'd have been crushed when the wagon fell toward him as the monster kept coming.

The beast was the last of them, apparently. It kept moving, trying to push along the same road, but behind it the soldiers had finished their bloody work and had hacked and stabbed the rest of the monstrosities into immobile carcasses.

Revulsion got the better of common sense. That was really the only way to put it. As the bloated, loathsome thing kept pushing up the road, not the least worried about Nolan as it moved along, his mind went dark and red.

Nolan let out a battle cry and swung his axe in a great arc, bringing it down on the mottled, vile back of the thing. The blade cut deep and the creature let out a sharp bleating noise and started turning back to examine Nolan with its repulsive piecemeal, rudimentary face. He hacked again and again and felt himself climbing onto the thing's great back as he pulled the axe free and snarled at the impossible head.

There was nothing rational to his actions. Deep inside his skull, buried under the insane rage that consumed him, Nolan wondered at what he was doing and whether to not he would survive his foolish attack, but it didn't matter just then. He wanted this abomination gone, and more than anything else that was what drove him.

His axe rose and fell and rose and fell, and he felt his throat go raw as he screamed again and again and kept hacking, dark blood splattering its way up his arms across his face and down his chest, painting his uniform in the color of the thing's vile juices.

He was dimly aware of Darus next to him and others coming closer, but they did not matter just then.

It only mattered that the thing be dead; the better for him to pretend it had never existed.

And then the fight was done and he stood on the bloodied remains and panted, looking at his trembling hands and then slowly around him to see Darus and the man from the wagon and a half dozen others staring his way with wide eyes and unsettled expressions.

"Well then." Nolan's voice was coarse and raspy. He stepped back from his grisly work and shook his head, trying to clear away the last of the red rage that had consumed him.

Nolan's legs gave out, and so he fell back until he landed on his rump in the dirt.

"Well then," he repeated. "That's that."

It was close to an hour before he recovered enough to move. He heard the people speaking around him but was too exhausted to care. Considering what he'd just done, it seemed the rest of the troop was fine with letting him alone.

News of the Emperor's death had spread faster than tales of other events. Though the great eruption in the Corinta Ocean was certainly a topic worthy of discussion, and the destruction of the Guntha was a situation most would be speaking of for months to come, it was the death of Pathra Krous at the hands of an assassin that overtook conversations. The reason was simple enough: the changes wrought by his death would surely be more far reaching.

Still, even that news took time to cross the continent. First there were rumors, and those are often ignored. Then there were confirmations and from there the true wave of guesswork flowed wildly.

The Pilgrim did not care for speculation or hearsay. Both were the work of weaker minds.

When he heard of the Emperor's death he sighed once and then rose from where he'd been resting for a very long time.

Pathra Krous had been a good man. He had been an important man. His death was what mattered, however. The Sooth had spoken to the Pilgrim of Pathra Krous's dying and what it meant to the world around him.

It was the sign he had waited for.

It was worth rising for.

The Daxar Taalor were not the only gods that made demands.

The Pilgrim struggled from the murky waters where he had rested for so long and shook off the sediment that covered his flesh. The air was hot and sticky with humidity. His clothes clung to him like a second skin. He was aware of the fabric as he was aware of the heat: as a secondary consideration. The most important thing was the news that Pathra Krous was gone.

Everything else was secondary to that one portent, that one sign that his time had come at last.

The Pilgrim had slept for so many years and now he would fulfill his destiny.

Muscles that should have atrophied and withered long ago moved stiffly at first, but as circulation returned to his muscles, so too did the ease of movement he had known before.

How long had he slept? He did not know. He did not care. It was enough to know that he was needed again.

He called out with his mind to the gods, and frowned as he waited for their response.

Silence.

Only silence. Still, he walked. He had a great distance to cover and there were people he needed to gather to his side if he were to succeed in his holy mission.

The bodies were heavy, and they felt greasy to the touch. Nolan did not like handling them and he liked being in charge of guarding the remains even less. Still, someone had to do it, and Sergeant Niles insisted that it was the sort of honor that would eventually lead to promotions.

Of course, Niles was also known to say the same thing of digging the holes they pissed in whenever they made a camp for the night, so his word was hardly trustworthy.

The bodies were covered in salt and then wrapped in cloths in the hopes that they might make the trip to Tyrne intact. There was a firm belief that whatever the things were, the leaders of the army would want to examine them.

Nolan would have dealt better with that thought if the damned things would stop moving around. Everyone said it was the motion of the wagons they were piled into, but Nolan didn't believe it for a second. They moved just as much when the column was at rest. They'd finally turned south and moved alongside the Freeholdt River. According to the maps, that meant they were almost to their destination. He'd had doubts, too, until they finally saw the city in the distance.

Tyrne was immense. That was the only way to put it. Even from half a day away, they'd seen the tallest buildings. Now they headed into the city proper, and he did his best not to gape as they walked. He was not alone. Most of the soldiers he was with had never been to Tyrne and a goodly number had never been to any city of size except for Old Canhoon. Canhoon was large to be sure, and with a sizeable population, but it wasn't so very tall. The outer buildings were not so enormous, but the ones further in rose higher than he would have thought any buildings could be built.

It took most of a day to get to Tyrne and that was long enough for some of the awe to wear off. And as they got closer they were joined by other groups coming to the capital in a stream of humanity. Many of the people coming seemed to be taking care of regular business – carts, loaded with goods to sell, or leaving the city and heading toward other destinations with supplies, were common sights – but there were more who bore a desperate air with them, who seemed to be heading to the city in the hopes of escaping from the inevitable war that people they encountered were certain was coming to eradicate them all.

War. That was an unpleasant notion. Darus shook his head and spat as they walked together. "You think there's anything to the notion of war?"

Nolan looked at the man and cocked his head to the side. "I expect yes. We just fought some sort of monsters and we're heading for the capital. Not just us, either. There's more soldiers behind us and more ahead. I saw a full regiment of cavalry making for the city up ahead."

Darus spat again, squinting up the road as if he might see the horses and their riders. Nolan knew better. His friend had eyes meant only for seeing things close by. The further out he looked, the worse his sight.

"You sure?"

"I saw them." Nolan was about to say something else, but whatever it was fell away from his lips unspoken. Up ahead the road was clear enough to let him see what waited in that direction. The great wall of the city and the open gateway, and through the gate he could see the long road leading upward into the heart of Tyrne. He could see the path leading all the way to the palace.

"Can you see them now?"

"No." His heart hammered in his chest. "No. I don't know where they went."

"Well I guess we'll see for ourselves soon enough."

Sergeant Niles came toward them from further up in the column with his usual swagger. His eyes were dark splotches in the sunlight. "Nolan!"

"Aye, ho, Sergeant?" He didn't much like Niles, but he could respect him well enough. There was a difference.

"Got a note from the Office of the Commander General, says you're to go to the palace immediately and bring your prizes with you." He pointed to the wagons loaded with rotting flesh. "Get to it and take Darus, Tolpen and Vonders with you."

Nolan nodded and started to head for the carts. It was Darus that asked the question that had already started ringing in Nolan's head. "Why us?"

"March because he was asked for. The rest of you because the Captain says you deserve recognition for killing those things." The sergeant didn't wait around any longer. Before Darus could ask another question the man was heading back the way he'd come.

"What do you make of that?" Darus's voice was soft.

"I make nothing of it. We'll learn what we need to know when we get there." Nolan wasn't sure he believed that himself. He just knew he needed to get to the palace. He wondered if Merros Dulver would be there. He knew the answer, of course, but he wasn't sure how he felt about that knowledge.

Desh Krohan swept into the throne room with a smile on his face. Merros looked at the man as if he might have lost his mind. What in the name of all the gods was there to smile about?

Nachia Krous looked up from the throne with a similar look of puzzlement on her face.

"Oh, look at the two of you." Desh shook his head. "It's like watching two children trying to study their letters with their eyes closed. The sun is out, the clouds are fading to the south and the day is young. Nachia, you're to be Empress of this land within a week and Merros you've been promoted to the head of Nachia's armies. Try to actually enjoy that fact for a moment, will you?"

Merros cleared his throat, trying to find the right way to respond without having himself reduced to cinders by the man.

Nachia was more direct. "I don't want to be the Empress. I want my cousin back."

The wizard shook his head. "I know. Still, you can't have Pathra back. He's gone from us and wanders now wherever the spirit goes when the flesh is sundered." He leaned closer in to the woman who was supposedly his ruler. Supposedly because Merros was almost certain that no one ever actually ruled over the man. "I know that look. Calm yourself. Tantrums won't help you now. You're ascending to the throne. There's no choice in this."

Merros sighed. That was the problem with the wizard. One of them at least. He tended to be very sure of his declarations. He also tended to be right. The General did not like that combination very much. Not that he could do much about it.

"So let's have a chat, shall we?" Desh walked to the table where paperwork sat for the Empress's consideration and pushed the papers away from one edge, the better to rest his hip and buttock against the marble. "I think it's time to get past the losses we've suffered and move on to running the Empire properly."

Nachia opened her mouth, her lips peeling back in an angry grimace, but before she could respond Desh shook his head. "I don't mean we forget the death of Pathra. He was one of my dearest friends. I mean we don't let his death stop us from keeping his Empire safe. He wouldn't appreciate his hard work being allowed to fall into ruin because our souls are heavy with his loss."

That stopped her. She closed her mouth and slowly nodded. "What do you suggest, Desh?"

Merros felt himself release a breath he had been unaware he was holding. The simple fact was that angering the future head of the nation was a bad idea, even if you were working on her behalf. Desh Krohan was not his friend, exactly, but he was definitely a benefactor. He needed a few of those.

"Merros, here, has been bolstering the city's defenses and that's a wonderful notion, but we need to do more. There are soldiers coming here, forces gathering, because we need them, but they need to be supplied, they need to have places to sleep."

"There are ample barracks, Desh. I've made sure of that." Merros couldn't keep a defensive edge from his voice.

"Oh, to be sure, Merros. I know that about you. If I didn't think you were up to the job I would have never recommended you to Pathra as strongly as I did."

Merros resisted the urge to snort at the comment. Nachia Krous did not. "Recommend, he says."

"The papers were signed by your cousin, Nachia."

"I know that. You know that. But I have no doubt as to who was holding the pen in place for him." She was not angry as she spoke. If anything, she seemed to be teasing the man. Merros had no idea what sort of relationship they had, really. He had seen both of them repeatedly, but most of their interactions had been in front of an audience of people and now they were positively casual with each other.

"I merely make suggestions, Nachia. Same as I always have."

The gesture she made was universally accepted as a rude one. Merros managed not to laugh out loud. It was possible that both of them were trying too hard to get along, but he rather liked it. The camaraderie, forced or not, was closer to feeling natural than the stony silence that had held sway over the palace since the murders.

"What do you want to do about the black ships in Roathes, General Dulver?" The sorcerer, advisor to the Empire, looked his way, as if he might be asking about the weather.

"Well, I suppose we could send a few of the Sa'ba Taalor to handle the matter." His response was automatic, offered in a dry voice and completely inappropriate. It was the sort of thing he should have saved for when he was speaking to Wollis March.

Both the future Empress and the sorcerer who technically ruled the land until her ascendency looked at him for a long moment in complete silence, and then the wizard started laughing out loud, his face reddening as he let loose with a raucous cackle. Nachia joined in only a moment later.

And when they were done he sighed and shook his head. "I suppose I should send troops that way.

Just to ensure that if there really is a problem it gets handled quickly."

"You doubt the existence of the black ships?" Nachia's voice was low and curious. He sensed no hostility. She merely wanted an honest answer from him.

"I do. Mostly because King Marsfel has already proven himself to be untrustworthy." The man had lied, and repeatedly, in an effort to gain financial assistance from the Empire. He had apparently made a practice of it as his father had before him.

"True enough, but the claims aren't only coming from him. They are coming from a dozen different sources."

"And yet these black ships that are supposed to be running around in the Corinta near Marsfel's shores have made no move to attack. They are simply out there sunning themselves like lizards." Merros shrugged. "I have made no secret of my dislike for the king. That has not changed my decision a smattering. I don't think we can afford to send too many forces to chase after phantoms when we are very likely at war with the Sa'ba Taalor."

"No 'very likely' to it. They aren't welcome here and, if they show themselves, I'll expect you and your soldiers to cut them down." Nachia's voice held a sharp edge.

"We have a company of two hundred men missing in pursuit of them. I expect we'll hear from them all too soon, Majesty."

Desh raised one eyebrow and said nothing.

Nachia sighed. "So, we wait on the ships then?"

Merros lowered his head rather than stare at her. "I'll do exactly as you tell me, Majesty, but I would suggest waiting. We have seen no sign that the ships mean harm and even with a dozen reports we've little proof that they even exist."

"I'll defer to you, Merros. I'll trust in your judgment. Now, tell me what happens with the city's defenses."

"They've been finished, Majesty. The gates are back in working order, the areas where the walls needed repairs have been mended and the structures that had taken root along the outside of the wall have been taken down."

"Taken down?"

"Yes, milady. Several buildings had gone, up using the outer wall as a support. They weren't supposed to do that to begin with, and they might be used by the Sa'ba Taalor to allow their mounts to climb over the wall."

Nachia contemplated the great beasts that the enemy rode and then nodded her head. "Are we safe from attacks without those structures?"

"Safer, I suppose. I honestly don't know how well those things can scale a wall, but I know they made it out of the Blasted Lands without having to resort to the Temmis Pass, and we have never managed that on horses."

She nodded her head again. For a moment there was silence and then Desh spoke up again. "Onto the next matter at hand. Regarding the defense of the Imperial Roads…"

It was going to be another long day, Merros supposed, but at least it seemed they were able to move on a bit. There was much to do and it seemed they would have very little time to get anything accomplished.

He had no idea.

FIVE

It seemed help would be a long time coming.

Marsfel looked out at the dark waters of the bay and sighed softly to himself. No one to blame, really, but himself. He had angered the Empire's military commander. What could he possibly expect after that?

There were no stars to see. The clouds had blacked them out again. He knew that the Great Star was in the sky, as bright as ever, but he could not see even that light through the ash and the heavy foulness that tainted the air.

The rains had come down throughout the day and painted the sands with gray and black patterns of soot. Every building within sight of his palace was black now, and even the trees were darker in color than they should have been.

The only light, outside of a few torches, came from the fire raging in the distant ocean and in the lightning that sometimes stabbed the waters where the new island covered over the remains of the Guntha.

The Guntha had never been friends. They had been enemies for most of his life and occasionally they had been allies when all parties felt there was some use in alliance.

No matter what they had been, however, they had always been a part of his world and now they were gone.

Much, he suspected, as his kingdom was soon to be gone.

Even if the black ships never came in to attack, the fish were gone and the stores of supplies were wearing thin. A lot of his people had left their homes and fled to the north, seeking aid from the Emperor or at least a place to stay where the air did not stink of death. The erupting mountain in the ocean was not going away, and the cloud of filth that belched from it was not leaving either.

It seemed likely to him that they had the right idea. It might well be time to move on soon. His needs were few, but keeping his family and his people safe definitely qualified as something the King wanted to accomplish in his lifetime. And for the first time since he had taken residence on the throne, he had doubts that he could accomplish that task to his satisfaction.

A barrage of lightning danced through the clouds in the distance. The flares were bright enough to let him see the ships in the water.

"Turrae!" he bellowed his assistant's name and as always the man responded in moments, slipping through the door as if he had been standing just outside and waiting for hours for the first call of his king.

"How may I help you, my Lord?"

"The ships, Turrae! They are at the shore. They are so much closer than they were before. Sound the horns and light the signal fires. It is time!"

The man stared at him with wide eyes in the near darkness of the room. For just one moment the fear was clear on his assistant's face. Then it vanished, replaced

by his usual calm. "Of course, King Marsfel." Turrae
vanished from sight and Marsfel stalked across his
room, his hands fluttering nervously as he reached for
his weapons. He had armor, but despite having worn in
several times for the fittings, he really didn't much know
how to put it on, not without help. And there wasn't
time. The ships were too close and his daughters had to
be protected. His kingdom needed defending. He would
not stand by and wait for the enemy to come to him. Not
here, not now when so much was at stake.

The Ghurnae blade was long and curved, heavy with
one sharp edge and a jagged point that could gut a man
with ease. He had trained with such blades since he was a
child and while he was heavier than he had been before
taking the throne, Marsfel remembered well the lessons
he'd had. He slid the sword and hilt over his shoulder
and took two long daggers as well. The set was matched
and had been presented to him many years ago by his
father when he came of age. They had been well cared
for and well used over the years.

Marsfel was many things and, while a few would
disagree with his personal assessment, he was capable as
a leader and as a fighter alike.

Still, his hands shook and his heart raced.

By the time he left his personal chambers the call
had gone out. Several of the watch still called out on
the great bone horns and as he strode toward the front
entrance of the keep the way was lit by two of the great
signal fires. His soldiers would come.

He would lead them into battle and they would
live or die together. Turrae stepped next to him,
carrying his own Ghurnae blade and daggers. A small

shield was strapped across his back, but otherwise he had no armor.

The guards were a different matter. They always wore their armor; it was a part of their duty. They stepped with him, falling into loose formation. At another time he might have demanded a closer step, a better pacing, but that was not a consideration. They would fight.

Fires lit the paved road leading toward the shoreline and, as he progressed, the mercenaries he had hired to bolster his soldiers came forward, most of them riding horses. He hadn't thought about that, hadn't considered having the horses readied.

Marsfel shook his head and swallowed harshly, his throat a tight, dry lump. He hadn't thought of so many things. He'd known this was coming and yet he was ill-prepared.

The leader of the mercenaries stared at him. He couldn't think of the man's name. Turrae mumbled "Jepphers" under his breath, and Marsfel could have kissed him.

"Captain Jepphers. It is time."

"Do you lead this fight yourself, Majesty? Or do I lead with my soldiers?"

A damned good question. The mercenaries were there to fight for him.

"Lead the way, Captain, and we shall follow." He shook his head. "I have no horses."

Jepphers nodded his head. He could see the man was well aware of the situation and that he was also keeping his tongue. The Captain had brought a good number of mercenaries with him. Turrae could have said exactly how many, but Marsfel couldn't hope to guess.

Jepphers blew a loud, whistling note between two fingers and his hired men turned their attention to him and followed as he led them in a charge toward the beach and the ships that had settled near the shore.

The winds were harsh and hot and the clouds over the waters were as dark as a sinner's thoughts. The ships that had seemed large before were enormous as he and his troops marched up the road toward the beach. The waves crashed against the vessels, which rocked in the waters and occasionally groaned a soft protest.

He saw the mercenaries riding hard and felt a grim satisfaction in his choice to hire them. He'd hoped for help from the Empire, but prepared for whatever might come his way. The sword felt good in his hand and, despite his fears, he believed he was prepared to defend his people and his kingdom.

How many people could the ships hold? Marsfel had no notion. The boats his people used were much smaller, and even the largest would be dwarfed by the black shapes. They seemed nearly impossible and he couldn't see them well enough in the rough weather to determine much beyond their size.

Turrae coughed into his hand and shivered as the winds picked up. The air was warm and his condition had nothing to do with the breeze. "They are so damned large…" It was the only time Marsfel had ever heard the man curse.

He was trying to find the right encouraging words when the flurry of arrows rose from the ships and plummeted toward the approaching riders. Had he wondered how many people could hide on the vast structures? It was hard to say with any certainty, but most definitely enough to kill fifty men with one first volley. The arrows rose silently and dropped in graceful arcs. They stopped in the bodies of mercenaries and horses alike, some peppering the shoreline, but most landing in flesh and crippling or killing.

The soldiers were far enough ahead that it took a moment to hear their screams. But he could see them as they fell, some dropping to the ground and others clinging to their horses even as their mounts collapsed or bucked and tried to escape the unexpected pain.

A second volley of arrows rose and fell, missing more targets as the animals bolted and took a number of fighters with them. But the respite was brief. When Marsfel looked to the ships he saw silhouettes in the shape of archers moving to the edges of the vessels, bracing themselves and taking careful aim. Several riders tried to break away, but the assault seemed nearly endless, and most died with arrows in their backs.

He had meant to lead his men into glorious battle. He'd told himself that this would be an easy thing, a certainty, really, because so much was at stake, but as the men he'd hired to fight for him were cut down by archers, he felt his courage blowing away with the ashes in the wind.

How could this be? How could this happen?

Turrae said something, but Marsfel did not hear him. The sound of the dying and wounded was too close and too loud.

Turrae screamed this time and struck him on the shoulder, roughly, to get his attention. Part of him wanted to turn and lash out at the man, but he resisted.

His assistant's voice rang clearly enough. "They're coming! They are leaving the ships!"

The shadows were dropping from the side of the ships into the rough, shallow waters. He knew they must surely be on ropes but he couldn't see the lines and as a result they looked more like man-sized spiders scaling down the sides of the great vessels than anything else. The notion sent shivers through his body.

The forms flowed down the sides of the boats and into the turbulent waters. They did not hesitate to move toward the shore, swimming, walking or carried by the waves, he could not say. He could only see them coming, see the odd gray glow of light where their eyes should have been, and wonder if the Guntha who claimed demons pursued them had been telling the truth.

He had seen the Sa'ba Taalor, had seen their odd eyes in the daylight and in a well-lit room, but this was different. The light seemed stronger and it unsettled him.

He wanted to run. Oh, how he wanted to leave as quickly as he could, because the shapes coming toward him were fast, and even moving through the water they were intimidating.

Kings are not allowed to be afraid.

"Come then! Let's kill a few enemies!" Marsfel roared the words and moved, sweeping the heavy Ghurnae sword in a few wide arcs to test the feel of the weapon. His men followed. He could feel them moving with him and that knowledge gave him strength. A king leads. That is what a king must do.

The ashes in the wind whipped through the air and stung at his eyes, but Marsfel did not care. It was time to teach these fools a lesson. Time to show the Empire that he was a king to be respected.

Before he knew it, he was running, charging on thick legs and driving toward the surf, a feral grin pulling at his lips. He was a king! He was a warrior!

The woman who met with him wore leather and carried two thin swords. Her hair was wrapped and pulled away from her brow by a thick blue length of cloth.

Marsfel swept his blade toward her head. It would make a fine prize to show his enemies when this was over.

His hand fell away from his body. The sword he carried flipped through the air with his hand and landed in the sand and surf.

The woman crouched and whipped one of the swords at his knees and fire ripped through his legs where metal met flesh.

Marsfel could not keep to his feet. He fell forward and landed on his good left arm and his bleeding right stump.

The pain was immediate and ripped away all hints of confidence he had sported.

She stood over him and for the first time he saw the face of the demon that had crippled him with ease. The Sa'ba Taalor had worn veils. This creature did not. The eyes were fine, the nose long and elegant, despite a heavy scar that ran from below the left eye and down to the right cheekbone.

But below the nose? Oh, truly, there must be demons in this universe!

"What are you?"

Rather than answer his question, the demon spoke, her words carrying the odd echoing sibilance he'd heard from the Sa'ba Taalor before. "You are King Marsfel of Roathes?" Her eyes regarded him coldly and her twin blades glimmered.

Turrae tried to come to his aid. The man ran silently, but his words broke that silence. "I am Marsfel," Turrae hissed.

Marsfel looked to his second. The man came in proper stance, his sword held before him to guard against possible strokes, the heavy tip at the right level to easily gut a foolish opponent.

The woman was not a fool. Her arms moved; the left sword struck against Turrae's blade and sent that deadly tip to the side. She stepped closer, close enough to let Marsfel count the heavy laces on her boot, and then her right sword drove through Turrae's mouth and opened the side of his face all the way back to his left ear. The left sword whickered through the air a second time and cleaved into his neck from the other side. When she stepped back, only a strand of gristle kept Turrae's head from falling completely away from his body.

She looked back to the King. "You are Marsfel?"

His mind wanted to lie. His heart would not allow it.

"Aye. I am Marsfel, I am the King."

Her voice remained calm through the exchange. Around her, beside her and to her flanks, more of the demons came out of the waters and attacked the people who ran with Marsfel. They did not leave survivors. His men were brave at first, and then they were afraid. It seemed they did not fight humans. Nothing should have been as savage as the things that came ashore and killed.

"I am Donaie Swarl, Chosen of the Forge of Wheklam and King in Lead. This is my fleet. Do you surrender your lands to me?"

"Will you show my people mercy if I surrender?"

"I will offer the same mercy I gave the Guntha if you do not." Her hand gestured to the waters behind her, where the column of flame and ash and smoke continued to roar into the skies.

"Spare the people in my palace then, and I will surrender."

"I do not negotiate." Her swords barely seemed to move, but the points found themselves in either side of his neck just the same, and the movement cut through to bone with ease.

His death was fast, but Marsfel died just the same.

The cold was an old friend now. It wrapped itself around Andover Lashk and wove its spell through his skin and muscles alike. He did not shiver. Shivering took energy. Instead he walked, one foot forward and then the other.

The perpetual twilight was no better than it had been, but now the sky above was bloody and clearly showed the silhouettes of the great mountains he had heard so much about.

The Seven Forges were before him and Andover found the cold hardly mattered at all. His exhaustion was still there, but that too seemed a trifling thing in comparison. The mountains were enormous. So much larger than he'd have thought possible before.

Delil walked next to him and he saw her eyes looking at the vast black surface facing them. The only highlights he could see were the places where the reddish light from the clouds accented the more prominent edges of stone.

"You face Durhallem," Drask spoke from directly behind him. When last he'd looked, the man had been almost a hundred feet to his left and now he was only a foot away. How a man that large could move so quickly, so quietly, still unsettled him.

"That is the mountain? Where is the tunnel you spoke of?" Andover looked but could see no sign of the gate he was supposed to pass through in order to enter the valley of the Taalor.

Drask chuckled. "We are not close enough for you to see it yet."

He looked away from the mountain and stared hard at Drask. "We're not?"

"Not nearly. We have two more days of traveling before we reach the passage."

"Two more days?" He looked back at the mountain, which already consumed most of the horizon. "We're still two days away?"

"Durhallem is a very large mountain, Andover Lashk. We have at least two more days of walking before we are there."

Andover shook his head.

Bromt walked closer and without preamble he swung one massive fist at the side of Andover's head. Andover worked on reflex alone and ducked under the blow, skittering back and staring hard at the man.

Drask spoke as if nothing had happened. "That is two more days to make sure you are ready for whatever you face in the Pass."

Bromt came for him again, his eyes the only sign of his features in the darkness.

Look to any map of Fellein and at the very southern edge is the Corinta Ocean and on some of the more sophisticated and detailed maps there is an indication of the Brellar below that.

There were people who had come from Brellar and a few of them had made it as far as Roathes in their time, but most of them were stopped long before they planned on ending their journeys. Roathians were not known for their tolerance of anyone with knowledge of the seas.

Still, it happened. There were tales written of the Brellar, and a few of the older books at the Imperial Academy had illustrations of the Brellar and careful depictions of the scars they placed on the their bodies.

In total there were seventeen recorded situations, determined to be historically accurate, of the Brellar making it to Fellein and living to tell their tales.

So this time around Desh Krohan sent a representative to find them and talk to them first hand. Because she was particularly good at dealing with sensitive issues, he sent Tataya across the ocean. She went with his blessings, a rather large supply of gold and gems, and a ship full of men who knew how to behave themselves around sorcerers.

There are maps that are more detailed than those most commonly found. Most of them belonged to Desh Krohan. The man, who had paid several fortunes over the years to find and map the Seven Forges, was not new to the notion of learning all he could about the world around him.

Tataya and Captain Callan were standing together on the prow of his ship, a sleek, fast affair that bore no name, when the lookout called "Land ahead, Captain!"

Captain Callan was a lean man with wind-tanned skin and an abundance of freckles. His hair was a dark auburn and he sported a thick mustache and a grin that was always eager and just a little bit ravenous. Tataya liked him immediately. He claimed to have encountered the Brellar before, thought there was little to prove it. Still, as he was exactly the sort of man who tended to ignore the rules he did not agree with, she could easily believe that he might have had a run in or two in his time.

He managed to take his eyes off of her for a moment and looked to where the young man crawling along the top of the sails was pointing.

"Well now, looks like we might just be in luck this day, milady." His voice was cheerful and his grin stayed in place.

"That would be a lovely thing, Captain." Far to the north the ocean was a foul mess of ash and dead fish. Here the skies were calmer and the waters were a clear and lovely shade of blue. The air was pleasant and the wind whipped a few stray strands of her hair around. Most of her locks were bound with a leather tie, but some escaped, almost inevitably. The Captain kept staring at her hair as if it might be the most amazing thing he'd ever seen. At least he was good enough not to speak directly to her breasts, which was more than could be said for several of his crew.

"Do you want to set into a port, if there is one?"

"'If there is one?' I thought you said you'd met the Brellar before."

His grin grew larger. "I have. Our ship met theirs. We waved and I managed to purchase a few trinkets and several crates of fruit from them."

To be fair, that did actually qualify as an encounter. "And that is the only time you have run across them?"

"I have never had a reason to go this far south before, milady."

"Why did you go now?"

Callan's smile actually grew brighter. "A beautiful woman offered me a great deal of money."

She allowed a small smile and a nod as acknowledgement of his words. "Perhaps we should see if there is a port where we can land."

He called out to his first mate and they exchanged a quick flurry of words in the slang-heavy dialect employed by the Guntha, until that people had been slain. Likely he thought she had no knowledge of what he was saying, and she chose not to disillusion him of that belief.

"What can you tell me about the Brellar, Captain Callan?" Her voice was calm and the question was casual enough. She had asked him before and he had carefully avoided giving her answers that offered any details. That alone was reason enough for her to doubt his claims, but not enough to make her call off the expedition.

"They're friendly enough, I suppose, if they've a mind to be. I've only met them the once and we exchanged trinkets and food. The captain of their ship spoke the common tongue,, but it wasn't his first language. If he hadn't, I'd have been hard pressed to deal with him properly."

That was a lie and she knew it. He'd already displayed knowledge of several languages. He simply didn't understand that she shared his knowledge. The Brellar might well speak the common tongue, and so much the better if they did, but the good captain was hardly without resource when it came to communication.

Still, it was a small enough lie.

"And if they have other notions?"

"The Brellar don't have a home. What I hear was they had a place to call their own, once, but the good people of Fellein took it from them and cast them out. That'd be a few hundred years ago. No country, so they took to the water. Found new places to call theirs." His eyes looked into hers as he spoke. He made sure he was looking at her properly when he continued on. "You need to know they're not supposed to like Fellein much."

"What do they like then?"

"What they can take as theirs, mostly. They like easy prey and if they find a ship that isn't properly defended, they've been known to take it and everything on it."

"And the crews of those ships?"

"Some of them survive. Others float in the water till the sharks come along."

"Do you suppose your ship is defended well enough?"

His smile flashed out brightly. "I bought fruit and trinkets. A wise man has a crew large enough to handle troubles."

"Well, I wonder what they'll think of my offer."

"You brought an abundance of gold and a promise of more?" Callan's smile was wider still and she half expected him to purr. "I expect they'll meet you with open arms. But I do not expect you should trust whatever they agree to."

"Are they liars?"

Callan shook his head. "No. They are opportunists."

He would give nothing more on the subject and she knew it. "And what do you know of the Guntha?"

The Captain looked at Tataya and sighed. "That they are mostly dead now."

"Mostly?" She looked back at him and raised one eyebrow in question.

"They are a seafaring race, milady. Not all of them were on their islands when the great fire took them."

"What has happened to the rest of them?"

The Captain shrugged his shoulders and looked away. "I expect they'll do what everyone does in such situations. They'll survive as best they can and fade away."

"And do you know others who have been in such situations, Captain Callan?" She found herself looking carefully at his face, wondering what he was thinking. There were ways to find out, of course, but none she chose to employ at the time.

Callan's smile faltered. It did not completely fade, but it seemed to her that he held it in place by force of will.

Neither of them spoke of the rumors just starting when they left port. A few spoke of the black ships finally closing in on Roathes. If there were truth to the stories, it remained hidden from them.

Much like Desh Krohan, Tataya hated not knowing with a certainty what was occurring.

"Well now," he said. "I've met a lot of people in my time, milady. Travelers always do."

"I've been known to travel myself." She looked away from him. Not because she was done studying his reactions, but because he wanted her to not look at him for the moment. There were few who could tell what a person wanted as well as she could. She had been trained to understand the finer aspects of desires.

Callan pointed to one of the crew with his chin. "Vondum tells me you've actually been to the Seven Forges. Is that true?"

It was Tataya's turn to be cryptic. "I have been to the Blasted Lands."

Callan was ready to ask another question when the youth climbing across the top of the sails called out again, "Ship coming, Captain! Ship coming fast!"

The Captain looked up and followed the lad's pointing finger with his eyes. And there it was, a longship heading for them. The sails were clean and well tended. There was neither flag flying nor any colors to indicate alliances, but there were none on the ship she rode on, either. Flags tended to fly when there was a reason, and currently there were no countries fighting against each other that she knew of.

Callan squinted and looked closely at the approaching vessel. "This could well be the day I earn my money from you, milady. That would be a Brellar ship."

"How can you tell?"

Callan smiled again. "Might not be Brellar running that ship, but it's definitely built by them. You can tell by the metal along the sides."

Looking closely at the approaching vessel she could see what he meant. There was a rail along the entire length of the ship, and it had the dull gleam of steel.

"Why do they have a rail?"

"They use it to tie lines to the ships they're planning to board."

"Why would they need that?"

"Most times the Brellar run across another ship, they either make a sale or two, or they take what they want in tithings."

Tataya looked to the Captain and shook her head. "You couldn't mention that before?"

Callan shrugged. "Hardly seems good business to have you too scared to go looking for them before you've paid me." He smiled and waved an arm around to indicate his crew. "Besides which, we're armed and you have money. One way or another, we'll work these things out."

There were many ways to work out the potential issues facing them, and not all of them involved spending the gold she'd set aside for negotiations.

"The money I brought with me is to deal with the Brellar in an official capacity."

"Oh, to be sure, they'll act very official when they get here." Callan's voice was as cheerful as ever. She found she liked it less under the current circumstances.

As she contemplated the best possible answer to his latest words, the ship ahead of them doubled and then tripled. Three ships. Three.

One quick look let her know that the Captain was no longer quite as confident as he had been moments before.

The skies were just as blue as they had been a moment before and yet the feel of the air was a bit chillier.

"Do the Brellar normally run in fleets, Captain Callan?"

"To my knowledge, which is limited, no, milady."

Tataya nodded to herself and then looked on as the three ships came closer. "And what do we do about that situation?"

"I would expect we wait and see how they receive us." Callan shrugged his shoulders. "There isn't much else we can do, to be fair."

Tataya nodded her head. There was a great deal more she could do, but she preferred to see how the situation progressed.

There was no love lost between Danieca Krous and her much younger cousin, Nachia. That was a fact that few people outside of the immediate family knew. Desh Krohan knew, of course, because he made it a point to know. Amazingly little got past him along those lines. The careful study of the Krous bloodline was an extremely important part of his duties as the Royal Advisor. Currently he was also the man in charge of the nation and deciding who would ascend to the throne. He had actually already made his decision, but that didn't stop the majority of the Krous family from continuing to demand he change his mind.

Currently it was Laister Krous who wanted that change to happen the most. Laister felt he should be the Emperor. He'd felt exactly the same way when Pathra ascended to the throne and he would likely feel that way regarding who should rule the Empire for as long as he was alive and possibly into any number of afterlives as well.

To make his point clear, Laister had run to his second cousin, Danieca, who controlled a substantial fortune in her own right. Danieca was a large woman and, while few would have believed it, in her time she had been a true beauty. A life of excess had been unkind to her, but had not, unfortunately, calmed her attitudes in the very least.

Her voice was like the sound of a crying baby, shrill and impossible to ignore. Far worse was the fact that Desh could not make himself stop staring at the rash at her hairline. It was a fairly ugly rash, to be sure, but the angry red marks seemed to flare with every breath she took.

"I am hearing ugly rumors, about you and Nachia, Desh." Her lips snapped shut for a moment and she glowered. "Ugly. Rumors."

"The same sort of rumors once floated around regarding you as now float around regarding your cousin. Neither has any validity." He forced himself to focus on her eyes. Hard to believe that she had ever been capable of seducing a man with the baleful things, but in her time she had managed repeatedly.

Danieca didn't so much as blink. She sucked in a great breath and prepared to continue the debate at a new volume.

Desh held up his index finger before her and made sure it got her attention before he spoke. "Think very carefully about what you're about to say. The wrong words will go a great way toward determining your lifespan."

She paled. "Are you threatening me?"

"Not at all." His eyes remained locked on hers. "I'm reminding you who you speak to; no more, no less. I have about had it with your accusations regarding my relationship with Nachia, who will be the new Empress in a matter of hours."

"I could protest this."

"You already have. You've been protesting since Pathra was slaughtered." She flinched at his words. "You and yours seem to have forgotten that part. He was murdered."

"And his murderer remains unpunished!" Danieca slapped her meaty hand onto the table and leaned toward him. "Where is the assassin who killed our Emperor, Desh Krohan?"

"I'm still investigating that very question, Danieca." He spoke softly, but his eyes kept their grip on her gaze, not letting her look away. "Very little else has been on my mind of late."

The woman no longer looked comfortable with the current discussion and, if he had to guess, it was the tone of his voice that was responsible for the change in her demeanor. When the latest wave of demands had started he'd been as patient as he could, but his tolerance for screaming was wearing thin.

Desh Krohan rose from the seat where he'd been leaning a moment before and rose to his full height, looking down on the woman who had, as a young girl, done her very best to seduce him – sometimes he thought it was a game all of the women tried to play as surely as the males of the Krous family tried to bed the Sisters – and spoke softly. "This conversation is over now, Danieca. The decision is made. I have listened to the endless prattling of Laister and yourself, and even done my best to ignore the veiled accusations you've thrown my way, but this ends now."

"I have merely done what I must to ensure the safety of the throne in these troubling times, wizard." Danieca's voice was harsh, but of a lower volume. She was not cowed, but it was just possible she was remembering whom she was talking to.

"The throne is not the issue here. Your concern is Laister. Your concern has always been Laister. Let me make this clear to you one last time. Pathra Krous, the last Emperor of Fellein, stated who would ascend the throne when he passed. He named his cousin Nachia, as was witnessed not only by me but by the Lords in residence at the time. I have shown you the signed writ. I even allowed you to examine the royal seal before it was opened. Nothing has changed. Nothing will change. Laister is not fit to run the Empire. Nachia ascends to the throne before the end of the day."

"You overstep yourself, Desh Krohan." Her voice now was softer still, the faint whisper of a serpent preparing to strike. She was afraid of him, but she was not backing down.

Sometimes a person picks the wrong battles to champion. "No, Danieca."

He was still trying to find exactly the right words to end the discussion when she continued. "You forget yourself. I am not the Empress, that's true enough, but you would do well to remember who you speak to. I have a great deal of influence with the right people and you know that to be true."

"I do." Desh nodded his head. "I know exactly how much influence you have. I know how much you are worth. I know your fortune is vast. I also know that Laister has done several scandalous things that have been brushed away by your influence."

She started at that. Likely she would have tried to speak, but he continued on. "I am aware of everything that happens, Danieca. I knew about your delving into sorcery when you were younger, and I know exactly how well that went for you. I could, if asked, point to precisely where the bodies are buried." He leaned closer. "Really, Danieca, not everything you read about sorcery is true. I speak from experience here. I wrote most of the books that are studied.

"I know where Towdra keeps his money. I know who you trust to watch your wealth when you are away. I know exactly what you own and where you hide it." His voice rose, though he was doing his best to avoid actually yelling. The good fortune of the day was that Danieca had come to his private offices before preparing to make her latest threats and the rooms were excellent at keeping their secrets. "I know more than you understand, Danieca. As clever as you think you are, there is *nothing* you have done that remains a secret from me for long."

"You're an advisor, Desh Krohan. Nothing more than that. You'd do well to remember your place."

"My place?" It was Desh's voice that became a whisper then. "I am not an advisor. I am the First Advisor to the Throne of Fellein. I am the Regent to the Empire. Until I surrender the throne to the proper heir, I am in charge of the Fellein Empire, the greatest single power in the known world."

Desh managed to stand even taller. "And you? You are an old woman with delusions of importance. Would you like to test me, Danieca?" He leaned down until their faces were only inches apart, knowing full well that what she saw most clearly were the shadows of his hood. There had been a time when he'd allowed himself to go casually around her, but those days were long past. They had not been friends or allies for many a year. Instead she was a thorn he tolerated. Sometimes he found her charming in her own caustic fashion, but not at the moment. He had had enough of her veiled accusations of impropriety and the barely concealed warnings of how powerful she was.

"You won't be the first member of your family to threaten me. You likely won't be the last. But I will tell you exactly what I have told previous members of the Krous bloodline that have tried to force my hand. You do not want to push me any further. If I decide that you are a real threat to me, I will defend myself."

That got her attention. The woman who had pushed into his office with a dozen demands now looked at him and nodded her head fearfully. She opened her mouth to speak and he stopped her again.

"Just to make this very clear, Danieca, I will defend myself in any way I feel best suited to protecting myself, the Empire and the interests of the Empire. Consider very carefully the stories you heard about me when you were growing up and contemplate whether or not you wish to test their validity."

She did not run out of his office, but she left with as much dignity as she could muster while walking at three times her usual pace.

Desh sighed and settled back into his seat. Usually one or more of the Sisters was there to stop that sort of confrontation, but they were away and he missed having the buffer.

His fingers found their way to his temples and once there started worrying at the knots of tension just under the skin.

The sound of Nachia entering his chamber was a small one, but he heard it.

Desh looked up and smiled at the woman. Nachia Krous was a beauty, much like most of her family. The entire group had married for money and success for generations and somewhere along the way they'd found a way to breed attractive children. He wasn't quite sure where things went wrong as they aged, but in most cases that seemed the case.

"My family has been here to see you again?"

"Of course they have." He grinned and winced both. "Haven't I told you it would be best to avoid sneaking into my chambers by way of the hidden passages?"

"Of course you have. But I'm about to be the ruler of the Empire, so I figured I could just ignore that rule."

"There is that, I suppose." Her logic was much like Pathra's. That alone made him believe he was making the right choice by following the dead man's wishes. Pathra Krous had been his friend as well as the Emperor of Fellein. He had been groomed and chosen by Desh himself. While Pathra had definitely been the one to suggest Nachia, it was also true that Desh had been planting that suggesting for a long time before the decision was made and that he'd spent a fair amount of his time grooming her just as he had her cousin.

"Have they convinced you that Laister is the better choice?"

"The world is many things, Nachia, but it has not gone completely mad. Laister will not be the Emperor. It's you walking to the throne when the coronation takes place."

"Have they all shown up?"

"Do you mean your family or the royal families?"

"Both I suppose."

Desh sighed. "Well, it seems King Marsfel will not be with us."

"Being dead tends to cause difficulties." Nachia spoke under her breath but Desh heard her just the same. He almost scolded her, but in the end he merely smiled indulgently. She was behaving herself. She seemed to understand as well as Pathra had that she could say things to him that were decidedly not for the general populace.

"As his heir apparent, Lanaie has asked for aid in securing her kingdom." Desh looked at her carefully as he poured himself a small goblet of sweet wine to ease the pressure in his skull. He poured a second for her as an afterthought.

Nachia took the small treat gratefully and sipped. "And have you made a decision on that, Desh?"

"Of course not. I'm setting that particular challenge aside for the new ruler of the Empire."

She made an obscene gesture and Desh almost choked on the wine he'd just raised to his lips. "Really, is that the sort of thing Empresses should do on their coronation day?"

"So long as I am wise enough not to advertise the fact. Isn't that what you always told Pathra?"

"He always did talk to you too much."

"More than you know, 'old man'."

Desh rolled his eyes but could not keep a smirk from his face. "I'll not live that name down for a while then, I suspect."

"You are old and you are a man. It's a fitting title."

Amazing how the right words from the right person eased his tension far better than wine had ever managed.

"Sit down, Nachia. Relax for a few minutes before you have to start getting dressed."

"I'm contemplating a drastic change in fashions." She shook her head and sneered just a bit as she took a seat.

"I'm sure you are. Just the same, that dress you wear tonight will be the height of any fashion."

"I'm not wearing it so much as having it built around me."

"I have no doubt you will look amazing."

She paused and looked away from him. "I'm scared. You know that don't you?"

"If you weren't I'd be horrified for the fate of the Empire. You should be scared. It's a very large responsibility you will be taking on."

"That's not actually comforting, Desh."

"It's not meant to be. But I will be by your side, Nachia. You understand that much at least. I will be by your side at all times."

She nodded and blinked several times. Her face was already showing the stress of her future upon the throne.

"So there's that. Today you ascend to the throne." Desh sipped at his wine and savored the sweet warmth it offered. "Tomorrow we begin dealing with the affairs of the nation properly." A slow grin spread across his face. "And next week we start looking to find you a suitable husband."

"Excuse me?" Her voice did not quite shatter, but it most definitely cracked.

Desh smiled. "One of the duties of the Empress is to have an heir. It avoids problems like the one we're facing with your family right now."

"So would killing them all." She was joking. He knew she was joking.

Still, "That could be arranged."

"Shame on you, Desh."

"I'm just acting in my official capacity as your advisor, Majesty."

"Not for a few more hours." She shook her head. "Not just yet." She said the words like they were a plea to the gods.

The gods did not answer.

SIX

The Coronation of Empress Nachia Krous went off without difficulties. That was the part that mattered. The rest of the world falling into pieces was merely an unfortunate side effect of the times.

Merros Dulver shook his head and looked at the courtyard before him. The Summer Palace was a vast place, to be sure, and it would be easy to get lost within the many halls of the place. The courtyard, however, was not a location where getting lost normally seemed remotely possible. The lawns were carefully cultivated; the hedges trimmed down and tended with regularity. It seemed a horrid waste of labor to tend to the place in Merros's eyes, but the fact remained the entire area was a beautiful, wide open spread that ran in the front of the Summer Palace and looking at it now he couldn't imagine the hedges would survive.

The long stretch of cobblestone road leading to the palace was clear, but on both sides were vast crowds of people, all of them looking on with awe. And, closer in, wooden platforms had been raised to seat more people and to give a clear view of the coronation. He had understood Tyrne was a very large city, but never had Merros seen so many people in one place, not even in the numerous border clashes he'd been part of.

There were musicians aplenty, and they made sure to spread joyous music for all to hear. He wondered who paid them for their efforts, but he had enough to worry about without adding that particular consideration.

Nachia Krous was crowned with all the appropriate celebration and decorum. Merros himself stood on the platform with her – he had even escorted her with a full battalion behind him – and he had watched while Desh Krohan introduced her, and the heads of each of the different churches in Tyrne had offered their blessings on her Majesty. She made her vows and she was given a spectacular crown to place on her brow above a dress that surely had enough fabric to make a dozen uniforms.

And while all of that went on he looked around for any sign of cutthroats, assassins, or even anyone with a good arm and a rock, because sometimes people wanted to get attention in the worst possible ways and didn't consider their actions until after the fact. Nothing. Sometimes silence was lovely and other times it was nearly perfect; of course there were exceptions. He should have been delighted but instead the lack of anything untoward made Merros tense.

He shook his head. Perhaps that was the recent past rearing up to bite at him. There had been a time when he'd been a bit more optimistic. At least he thought there had.

A roar went up from the crowds as Empress Nachia was revealed to them in her full regalia, wearing her crown and holding the sword that had last been used to crown her cousin. He observed her with as detached a mind as he could. She was a lovely young woman. She was also capable of having him executed with little more than a thought, not that he believed she would. Still, it helped to have a little perspective.

Instead of looking at his new Empress, he scanned the crowds, looking for anyone who stood out, who did not follow the general mood of the crowds. It was easy enough to see them. The entire Krous family seemed to stand out along those lines. Brolley Krous was standing close by his sister and seemed delighted. Laister Krous looked less pleased. His expression was exactly the same as if he'd realized he'd just inhaled a bug in his sleep.

They were amusing on both sides, but there seemed no threats from either side of the Krous spectrum.

Taurn Durst moved closer to him and spoke just loudly enough to be heard over the din of people applauding. "We have to move now, sir. You said you wanted her back in the palace fast as could be."

Merros nodded. The man was right, of course. "Let's get her in the carriage and get back to where we need to be." The notion of moving a woman a hundred yards in a carriage seemed almost comical, but not really, not when one considered the massive crowds.

He looked around and saw the armed soldiers along the wall, each with a crossbow and all of them alert. Had they looked at all bored he'd have made examples of them and they knew it. This was a moment to be careful. It had been only a short time before that a careless moment had caused the death of the last Emperor.

He gave a nod to Taurn and the man moved, calling out sharp orders to the Imperial Guard around them. The soldiers were in formal armor, wearing the dark blue coat of arms for the Empire and gleaming in the twilight. When they moved it was with nearly perfect precision, and Merros allowed himself a brief flash of satisfaction. Nothing less for this event. They had to look perfect in order to make the people understand that the Empire was strong.

Even if he doubted that strength was enough.

New recruits kept coming in, moving into the barracks and then quickly discovering that all of their previous training was only the start of their learning. The new soldiers, the old, all of them were fast discovering that they were not up to standards. Merros was serious about preparing the troops.

One hundred of the best the Empire had to offer held the way for Nachia Krous and Desh Krohan. Merros Dulver walked four paces behind them and, as they passed, the troops lined up behind him.

How the new ruler of the Empire managed to fit herself and her gown within the confines of the carriage would remain a mystery for all time in Merros's eyes, and yet she accomplished that feat and left enough room for her advisor.

And a moment later the eight black chargers were moving on, pulling the head and heart of the Empire into the Summer Palace and leading the way for Merros and his troops.

And when they were inside and the main gates had been closed, the General allowed himself a little breathing space.

Only a little, however, as the celebration would surely go on for a good number of hours, regardless of whether or not the new Empress wanted to celebrate.

• • •

Nachia Krous sighed and fidgeted. "I hate this damned dress."

"The coronation is done with. You can now head to your chambers and find something more comfortable if that's your desire." Desh Krohan's voice was low and calm and he stared at her with that damn half-smile of his in place.

"You don't approve though, do you?"

"It doesn't matter, Nachia. You are now in charge of this nation. I merely offer advice."

"By all the gods," she shook her head. "You're actually glad to be done with ruling, aren't you?"

"I've never cared to rule, Nachia. I prefer to observe and offer assistance."

Before she could respond the wizard's face pulled into an expression of pain.

"Desh? Are you well?"

He shook his head and held up a hand for silence.

"You should take the time to get dressed in something more casual, Nachia. I have… a task to attend to."

"A task? What do you mean?"

"The Sooth are making demands."

He had spoken of the Sooth before, but she shook her head. Sometimes he spoke of the Sooth as a mystical art and sometimes as the spirits that art dealt with. Perhaps it was both. Whatever the case, she knew from experience that he did not like dealing with the Sooth.

"You said you don't like handling the Sooth alone, Desh."

"Not a matter of choice in this case, Majesty." His teeth were gritted and his brow stippled with beads of sweat.

"What is happening, Desh?"

He looked up at her; those eyes she knew so well were dark and desperate.

"The Sooth almost never make demands, Nachia and when they do, I do not dare ignore them."

The carriage came to a halt and, as it did, Desh rose from his seat and opened the door, sliding quietly into the crowded area. When Merros Dulver offered her a hand down there was no sign of the sorcerer.

"Your Majesty…" He held an arm out for her and she took it, mostly because the insane dress she was wearing made walking without help feel nearly impossible.

"I need to get to my chambers."

"Your chambers?"

Nachia stared hard at him. "I'm not wearing this thing a damned moment longer than I must. I want comfortable clothes and I want them now."

"As you wish." He stifled a smile and walked with her, a dozen armed men following behind them.

"Are they necessary?" Nachia didn't like the idea of being followed wherever she went.

"At least for tonight, Majesty. I'd beg your tolerance. We can't take chances. Not on this night and not when you have enemies who are already attacking your Empire."

She nodded her head and pressed her lips together and once again wished desperately that her cousin were still here and the ruler of Fellein.

"What news from Roathes?"

"There is no news, Majesty." Merros shook his head. "We can only believe that the worst has happened."

"What are you doing about it?" She didn't mean to sound harsh, but the thought that the entire country of Roathes might be under attack or conquered already did not sit well.

"I have sent several scouting teams to tell me exactly what is going on." Merros looked at her closely. "They'll be reporting back soon. Now that your coronation has been taken care of and I have enough troops here, I intend to see about sending help, if we can."

"If we can?" She didn't like the sound of that.

"If we can, Majesty. My first priority is taking care of Tyrne and you. This is a very large Empire and we do not know exactly what has happened yet."

They moved through the hallways at a solid pace and Merros kept his eyes moving, seeking any sign of troubles despite the security he'd left within the confines of the palace earlier.

Merros continued, "Until I know exactly what has happened, and what is left, sending any help would be a waste, despite the wishes of Lanaie."

She bit back a sudden question as to whether or not his delays in assisting were of a personal nature. In the time they'd known each other she'd already decided that Merros was an honorable man. He'd done nothing to change her mind and she wouldn't allow herself the luxury of alienating the man over a trifling suspicion.

As if he'd read her mind he answered, "This is not a personal thing. We have a very large army, Majesty, but they are spread out across the Empire and I need to assess the needs of the Empire before I offer help to what might already be a lost cause."

"Of course, Merros. I know that." She hoped her voice sounded as assured as she wanted it to.

When they reached her chambers – she had not yet moved herself to the suite her cousin had occupied and was not completely sure if she would – Merros entered the room before her to make certain that no one waited within. There were three women there, the very ones who'd helped her into the preposterous affair she was currently wearing. If they were unsettled by him entering the rooms unannounced, they were wise enough to keep their opinions to themselves. Only when he was comfortable with the security of the room did he step outside.

As he passed her he shook his head. "Do I need to make any comments for Desh Krohan as to appropriate attire and timeliness, Majesty?"

She chuckled. "No. I have heard them all. I'll be ready in a few moments, Merros."

She barely tolerated the maids helping her remove the full regalia and ostentatious gown that went with it. When they had finished she smiled her thanks and immediately went over to her closets, sorting quickly through the clothes and throwing down a heavy blouse of white and dark brown riding pants. When the maids started to make noises of shock she shushed them and went about her work, getting dressed.

Within five minutes she was back in the hallway and looking at the moderately surprised expression on Merros Dulver's face.

He managed not to say anything, but she could see him thinking it.

"What?" she demanded.

"It's not for me to speak on how the Empress of the Fellein Empire dresses herself."

"You're right, it's not."

"But if I were going to speak on the subject and having seen what your cousin's choices in hair stylings did to the men in the courts, I would point out that remarkably few women in the courts can carry off riding breeches with quite the same level of flair."

She shook her head. "What do you mean?"

"No disrespect meant, of course, Majesty, but have you seen the backside on your cousin Danieca? I dread the notion of her trying to squeeze into a similar set of breeches in the name of fashion." His voice was direct and dry and he made it a point to be looking elsewhere when he spoke.

"Oh, by the gods, Merros! You're as bad as Desh!" Her laughter carried down the expansive corridor, momentarily dwarfing the sounds of the score of men walking behind her in perfect unison.

"Speaking of gods, Majesty, I was thinking we might want to have a discussion with a few of the church elders who helped at your coronation."

"Whatever about?"

"Well, mostly I feel if we are dealing with people who look to their gods for answers, we should at least consult with the representatives of our own deities."

Nachia considered that and nodded. "What if they don't give the sorts of answers we like?"

Merros let a lazy half-smile flicker across his mouth. "We might want to investigate finding new gods…"

Desh made it into his chambers as quickly as he could, blinking back the bloody tears that burned at his eyes. There had only been seven occasions in his very long life where the spirits of the Sooth had come seeking him, and each time it was agony. The last time had only been a month or so earlier, and that had ended with a massive eruption and the murder of one of his closest friends.

He was not looking forward to what the spirits might have to say. He wiped the blood from his eyes and staggered over to the dark wooden cabinet where he kept the offerings he made to the Sooth. The stones took weeks to carve just the right way and required energies he could rarely afford to sacrifice. To those who understood their value, the simple stone spheres with their elaborate markings were worth a hundred times their weight in precious gems. To the Sooth they were the only guarantee of getting information without being tortured in the process.

Desh grabbed four of the stones, blinking away crimson tears and heading for the small room off the main chambers he called his home.

The floors of silver, pounded thin and meticulously polished, the walls of oiled iron, the ceiling of deep red liquids best not contemplated too carefully. The chambers never gave him comfort, but they gave him something else he needed: a chance to understand what was coming his way. A hint of the future that he needed from time to time.

The meeting place of sorcerer and spirit.

Desh fell across the floor and grunted in pain as he rolled onto his back and looked up at the ceiling above.

He did not need to speak and so he chose to remain silent. Instead he opened his eyes and looked toward the seething red waves above his head and they flowed toward him and covered him in their unkind embrace.

Sometimes the cost of knowledge is minor, but no sorcerer would ever expect truth to come without pain.

Desh Krohan was not disappointed.

SEVEN

The mountain dwarfed everything Andover had ever seen before. He'd known that for a while now, certainly over the last two days the vast slopes of the black shape had grown to hide the grit and storms of the Blasted Lands and replace them with its brooding presence. He could no longer guess how high the mountain rose, because the top of it was lost in the clouds.

All his life the largest thing he had ever seen was the city of Tyrne, where he'd been born and raised. The city was immense to be sure, but it was a structure built by man, and for the first time in his life he understood that nature could build on a much grander scale.

The cave before them was another example of that scale. The gates of Tyrne were possibly higher at the main entrances to the city, but the Durhallem Pass was a fiery tunnel cut through the entire mountain and looking into it was unsettling. Dark stone lit by streaks of red light that seemed almost to pulse as he looked at it.

Andover's voice sounded small even to his own ears. "Are you sure it's safe?"

Drask stood next to him, his face lit by the reddish hues, his eyes ablaze with that same light. "If you mean, 'will the mountain fall down?' it is safe. If you mean 'will you survive entering the pass?' that is up to the followers of Durhallem and the King Tuskandru."

The answer was not at all comforting.

"So, what now?"

"We walk." Drask started forward and the other members of their troupe did the same. With no other choice, Andover followed. His hand slid along his side until he felt the haft of his weapon and took comfort from the grip. The Sa'ba Taalor walked with no real change in their demeanor, meaning they remained alert and their bodies moved with the same predatory grace as always. He gave no thought to the way he walked, but might have been surprised to know how much of that same relaxed gait he'd adopted over the last few weeks.

Delil walked next to him and Bromt stepped to the side, his eyes narrowed into slits. He could never tell if the man was angry or merely trying to see something far away when he looked that way, but the appearance was one of great rage, barely suppressed, so he kept his distance just to be safe. As he had been struck no less than a thousand times by the man in the last few weeks of travel it seemed the safest course of action.

Delil spoke, and for that briefest instant he was taken aback by the soft voice. The weather in the Blasted Lands, never gentle to begin with, had been stormy, and all of them were virtually buried under layers of armor and cloaks. Well, except for Andover. He didn't have any armor. Just a lot of clothes and the gamey hide of a Pra-Moresh. "They will be with us soon, Andover."

"Who?"

"The guards of the pass."

"What will happen?"

Delil turned to look at him and her eyes wandered over his form, assessing his appearance and taking his measure. "They will challenge you."

"Why?"

"You are tiny."

"I'm taller than you!"

"No. At best you are my height, but you are tiny. They will challenge you just because it is fun to see you squirm."

Andover nodded his head. So really they were bullies. He had met his fair share of them over the course of the years, hadn't he? Memories of Purb and Menock flashed through his mind: recollections of a dozen times they had shoved him around and brought him to the edge of tears because he'd let them. And then of course, there were his hands...

He remembered the hammer coming down, the pain of flesh and bone exploding under the impact.

He remembered how it'd felt to return the favor after he had been granted his new hands.

They stepped out of the shadows. He'd been looking but had not seen them. The four men were dressed in black armor and sported black weapons. Two carried axes and two more had swords. All of them had bows. The two furthest back, the swordsmen, had their bows readied. The men with the axes stepped forward and rested hands on the handles of their weapons.

Drask called out sharply and the men looked to him. Once again they spoke in whatever language the Sa'ba

Taalor shared with themselves and with no others, as far as Andover could tell.

The closest guardsmen looked at Andover and came closer, their eyes glowing with the odd and unsettling light that all their kind seemed lit up with inside. One of them came closer and Andover let himself relax as he looked the man over from top to bottom.

None of the Sa'ba Taalor seemed to have uniforms, not as far as Andover could tell. They'd explained their beliefs of weapons and armor alike: that it was best a person make their own, the better to be certain the tools of war were as close to a perfect fit as they could be.

This man was no exception. His armor appeared rough, but Andover immediately understood why. It was designed to imitate the walls of the great cavern they were traveling through. At a distance the stone seemed almost smooth, and in the areas where volcanic glass was lit with the rage of Durhallem it was often closer to smooth, but the stone had been carved by the Sa'ba Taalor after their god Durhallem demanded it. They'd expanded the tunnel the god had created until it had satisfied him. In the process they had left the marks of their tools and that is what the armor mimicked. It was an impressive level of craftsmanship.

The axe he carried sported an equally rough looking blade of obsidian. A really very large blade, to be sure, cut from the black volcanic glass. From what Bromt had explained to him, the followers of Durhallem were occasionally gifted with an offering of obsidian by their god. According to what the man had told him, the obsidian was harder than steel and considered a great honor.

The man was enormous – which seemed to Andover one of the two sizes of most Sa'ba Taalor men: enormous and gigantic – and carried himself with as much strut and posture as the most offensive of the City Guard back home. Purb would have been proud.

"Why do you come before Durhallem today?" The man's voice was rough, his use of the common tongue was adequate but with a thick accent. Had Andover not grown accustomed to the accents of the Sa'ba Taalor, he'd have been at a loss for what the man said.

He answered in the language that the Sa'ba Taalor shared with others, an archaic form of the common tongue according to Desh Krohan, but different enough that Andover had spent as much time learning it as he had how to fight. "I am here to pay my respects to your gods and to thank them for the gift of my hands."

His voice was much calmer than he'd expected. His eyes looked the man over continuously, reading the man's motions, his stance, and what little he could see of the stranger's face behind the black veil hidden under his black helmet.

The man stared back and was likely doing the exact same thing. And then the guard stepped forward and looked down at him, physically, as he was easily a head taller. He switched to the same language that Andover was using. "Why would the gods care about you or your hands?"

Andover sighed and pulled away his gloves, revealing the cold iron of his miraculous limbs. The eyes of the guard looked from the hands to his face and back again, studying carefully.

And when the man's hand reached for his axe, Andover stepped in close and drove his right fist into the guard's throat as hard as he could. It was purely reflex. He did not stop to think if the guard was reaching for a weapon or scratching at an uncomfortable part of his armor, he just stepped in and struck as soon as the man moved.

And as the man gagged and stepped back, he hit him again. There was a part of Andover that was perfectly fine with his actions, but it was a small part, really, barely large enough to notice. The rest of him was horrified. The guard had merely asked him a rough question. That was hardly reason to attack.

And yet his left hand dropped down and caught his enemy's wrist in iron fingers. His hand clamped down on that wrist with all the power he could muster and broke skin, tortured muscles, and crushed bone before the hand reaching for the axe could pull the weapon from his belt and drive that lethal blade through his face.

Andover Lashk used his other hand to strike the guard's jaw savagely and felt bones breaking against both of his iron hands.

And that little part of him roared in triumph as the guard staggered back from the pain.

The other guard was moving now, heading for him, and his weapon was already drawn as he came closer.

Andover shoved against the guard he was fighting and staggered him backward toward his companion. The first guard was bleeding and broken, the second stepped to the side, moving around his wounded friend.

Andover shrugged a shoulder and his hammer dropped to his waiting hand with practiced ease. As the second guard pushed past his injured companion, Andover was already bringing his hammer around from a lowered position, his muscles straining and accepting the demands he made. The grip felt as natural in his hand as if it were part of the same metal. In truth, it was, as he'd forged it from the remains of the very iron used to create his amazing hands.

The second of his enemies blocked the punishing blow from his bladed hammer and snarled something in a language Andover did not speak. Still he could understand an insult by the tone used and he stepped in closer, crouching down and pushing toward the man with his weight.

The guard was larger than him and had a longer reach. From any sort of distance the man had an instant advantage. Delil had explained that and Bromt had reinforced it. Drask had listened to their words and watched their actions with barely a change in is expressions, but he nodded his head now as Andover swept the heavy head of his hammer at his enemy's knee, instead of using it conventionally. The guard hissed as the heavy weapon slammed into his knee and sent him staggering, trying to keep his balance.

Andover let out a hiss of his own as the axe came up in a hard arc aimed at his face. His free hand caught the edge and he felt the metal surfaces scream across each other. Say what you will and call it a blessing that his hands were metal, but he still felt that edge trying to cut and it still hurt enough to make him scream.

His adversary had reach and he had weight advantages, too. Andover saw his arm coming and could do nothing but try to get out of the way as a fist the size of his face smashed into the side of his head. He was not fast enough to get away clean, but he avoided part of the damage. His ear burned and his head rang but he was conscious.

As Andover reared back, trying to shake off the blow, his enemy pushed into him, limping from the blow to his knee but not nearly stopped by it. Andover hissed into the man's face as he pushed back and felt himself sliding across the ground, unable to resist the sheer bulk of his enemy.

He pushed himself in close again and used his left hand to scrape and claw at the man's face, pulling at the veil covering the lower half. Metallic fingers caught cloth and flesh alike and ripped.

The guard howled in pain and pulled back as much as he could. His face was bloodied and Andover felt wet heat spilling across his iron fingers. There was a certain dark, visceral satisfaction in the man's agony.

Andover hauled his hammer up in a tight grip, letting his hand slide up the long haft before he brought it around. The hammer's uneven head brushed his fingers. Close to his thumb, the rounded head pushed down with comfortable familiarity. The heavy blade on the other side of the hammer covered his fingers like a shield and he heard himself screaming as he drove the entire affair up into his enemy's face.

The guard fell back soundlessly, bleeding from the great gash Andover's hammer had opened across his nose and his mouth alike. Whatever the veil had hidden was ruined beyond his ability to identify any features. Teeth and blood alike slopped over his hand.

He was horrified by his actions, but that little voice that was so pleased to be in a fight was crowing with joy now.

No time for that.

The first guard came at him again, and this time he was better prepared. The axe blade skidded down the length of Andover's hammer and then took a slice out of his outer thigh, just above his knee.

The pain was impossible to ignore, but, despite that fact, Andover had no choice. If he took the time to think about the pain he would be a dead man. The same rules applied as had before: the man was larger and had a better reach. Up close and personal was the only chance he had of surviving this.

The hammer was tight in his hand and he stepped in closely and used the blade of his weapon, ramming the wetted edge into his enemy's armored stomach with all the force he could muster. It was a small wound , but it was a starting point, and as the man grunted and tried to get away, Andover bent his knees and dropped a bit lower, then lifted with both legs, forcing the hammer's head into the wound with all of his body's weight.

The axe caught in the heavy hide of the Pra-Moresh and was lifted and brought down one time, twice and a third time, each blow smashing into Andover's bound ribs with crushing force.

Andover used his free hand and sought to catch his enemy's wrist, but failed. His close-quarters tactic was working, but not completely. The axe wasn't getting through his thick cloak but each impact was agony. He either finished this quickly or he was going to die.

The hammer's blade was still pushed into the man's torso and warmth slicked his fingers. He pulled the hammer free and let it drop down. He felt the heavy weight sink into his enemy's thigh, the blade cutting through muscle and sinew and catching on bone.

The guard only grunted and stepped back, pulling his axe free from the hide that had impeded it. The obsidian blade whipped back and the guard went with it, dropping into a defensive posture.

Andover stepped back and felt a grin pull at his lips. "You've lost. Yield." The wound in the man's stomach was moderately worrisome. He would heal from it in time, barring infection. But the hammer had cut deep into his leg and a heavy flow of blood poured down his trembling, weakened calf. He would bleed out very soon.

The man shook his head and spat.

Andover could not believe that any sane person would continue to fight until the words Delil and Drask had both used a hundred times rang in his mind: *Durhallem does not believe in mercy and neither do those who follow him.* The guard brought his axe around and let loose a bellow that shook the walls of the pass. Despite his readiness, Andover flinched and then did his best to block the blow.

The axe's blade screeched along the iron rings wrapped around the hammer's haft and carved into the wood of the handle. It stopped against his iron fingers and caused a bark of pain. Andover let the hammer drop and rammed the palm of his hand into the guard's face, felt bones crack and bleed under the veil and watched the man's head snap back at the impact.

The other hand he used to block the axe again. And then he stepped back as the guard tried to come for him and fell to one knee, his leg giving out. Andover did not let himself think. His foot caught the handle of the hammer and he hooked it upward, catching with his right hand.

Then he brought the hammer up over his head and brought it down with all of his might. His enemy looked on, trying to bring his weapon up to defend himself, but failing as the axe fell from blood-starved fingers.

The helmet on the guard's head let out one loud clang as the hammer crushed it into a new shape and the man fell forward, dead.

Andover looked over the dead men and reached for his hammer. Two more. Two more and he might have a chance of surviving the fight long enough to meet up with Tusk.

King Tuskandru. The man whose guards he had just killed. No. Only one. The second guard's face was a bloody pulp, but he was still alive. He still breathed.

Andover looked at Drask and saw the two other guards behind him. They had arrows aimed at him. He was not foolish enough to think that he would survive if they fired the arrows. He was also not foolish enough to think they would accept his surrender. There was a compromise, he knew that, but he could not wrap his mind around what it might be.

And then the words came to him again: *Durhallem does not believe in mercy and neither do those who follow him.*

He took three steps toward the fallen guard and brought his hammer down upon that ruined head. The man died a moment later, his body shuddering.

Drask Silver Hand looked at him for a moment and then nodded. He did not speak. He did not have to. Since they had left Fellein, Drask and his associates had spent their time schooling Andover on the ways of the Sa'ba Taalor. This test, at least, he had passed.

Both of the remaining guards kept their eyes on him and one of them spoke in harsh tones. "You will wait here. You will not move. King Tuskandru will be here soon."

Andover nodded his head and rested his weight on the handle of his hammer. The other guard blew several harsh notes into a horn, the sound echoing madly down the length of the pass.

Drask walked closer to him and pointed at the bodies. "Whatever of theirs you like you may take if you wish."

"What?" The idea of taking from the dead did not sit well with him.

"They are your kills. According to Durhallem if you wish to take what they have, you have earned it. That is not the way with all of the gods, but Durhallem accepts it."

Andover looked at the two corpses for a long moment and then reached down and took the obsidian axe. The blade was impressive. If nothing else, he intended to study it.

Delil walked closer to him. She looked at the blade and shook her head.

"What?" He couldn't keep the defensive edge out of his voice.

"You should worry less about trophies and more about the fact that you are bleeding badly." Her eyes looked pointedly at his leg and he followed to where she was looking, surprised to see a thick runner of blood streaming down to the ground. The cut he'd taken was far worse than he'd guessed originally.

Until that moment he'd been only vaguely aware of his wound, but upon looking at the damage he felt the pain he'd made himself ignore before. The axe fell from his hands and he let out a groan.

Drask looked at the wound from where he stood and sighed.

Bromt dug into his various bags, not speaking at all, but searching. "I've not got any."

Delil spoke, "Of course you don't. You never have any. You just hope to scab up and survive."

"Am I alive today?" Bromt's voice was low and filled with irritation.

"That is up for debate." Delil's voice, in contrast, was amused. She pulled a satchel from her back and dropped it before her, pouring the contents out on the ground. Half a dozen different objects fell out and she sorted through them with care, as most had sharp edges. He had never seen that large a collection of knives and arrowheads left in a pile on the ground before. What she reached for was a stick made of silver, which she then tossed toward Drask without looking up.

Drask caught it effortlessly and looked from the four-inch long rod to her, and then to Andover's leg.

"How do you have this?" There was no accusation in Drask's voice. He was merely curious.

"You gave it to me."

His brow knitted with concentration. "When?"

"A long time ago. Before my first Great Scar."

"You have a better memory than me." Drask shrugged and walked over to Andover. "You are bleeding. I can stop the bleeding, but it will hurt."

Andover looked up at the man and gritted his teeth. The last time Drask Silver Hand had told him something would hurt he'd had the new hands bonded to his flesh in a moment of the greatest agony of his life. The pain had been so overwhelming that he'd been buried alive by it and had woken several hours later.

On the other side of that coin, Tuskandru was the king here and he'd just killed two of the man's guards. There was a very real chance that the man would want to rip him in half with his bare hands and if he wanted to defend himself from that particular pain, he'd need to be as intact as he could be.

"Do what you have to."

Drask nodded his head and pulled at the gaping wound in his pant leg. The larger man yanked at the cloth until it tore, allowing him better access to the torn flesh beneath. Then he held out the silver. "This will touch your wound. If Ydramil decides you are worthy, he will mend you. If not, nothing will happen."

Andover shook his head. "How can he decide if I'm worthy? We have never met."

Drask stared at him for a long second, shaking his head slowly side to side. "Ydramil is a god. He knows what he wants to know." He slid the metal between his metallic fingers. "Besides, I'll be asking on your behalf."

"Oh." It was all he got out before Drask's thick fingers were pinching the wounded edges of his flesh together roughly. A yelp slipped out before he could stop it and Drask shoved the silver rod against his skin and spoke softly in words that made no sense to Andover.

And then the world went momentarily too bright for him to see as the silver between Drask's miraculous fingers melted and poured directly into the wound on Andover's leg.

"If you move, I will stop and you will bleed." Drask's words were loud enough to get past the pain. "Do not move."

The hands on his hammer's haft gripped harder and he winced, but made himself stand still. The pain was great, but he had endured greater in the past.

A moment later the pain was gone and Drask was leaning away, looking at the wound and the long line of reddish metal that was rapidly cooling. His skin should have blistered and blackened from the heat. Andover knew that for a fact. He had burned himself more than once as a blacksmith's apprentice. Still, the pain was fading and his flesh was undamaged. In fact, the line of metal was cooling quickly and as it dropped in temperature the pain vanished.

A thick line of silver was clear across the sealed cut, a metallic scar on pink flesh. But the pain was gone.

He had just enough time to marvel at that thought before the riders came, the great beasts of the Sa'ba Taalor and the riders who commanded them. They seemed larger than he remembered. That was always the case with the mounts and their riders alike, as if his mind refused to accept the fact of their scale.

They came at a leisurely pace, Tuskandru at the head of the column. It was impossible to forget the helmet of the man and he couldn't imagine anyone else in similar garb.

The group came forward at slow pace, not hurried and not concerned about the people they were facing. When Tuskandru dropped from his mount, his hand rested on the hilt of a weapon. Andover could see nothing but the hilt and the sheath and that was enough to leave him worried.

Drask Silver Hand lowered his head and held his hands away from his weapons. When Andover saw both Delil and Bromt doing the same, he mimicked the gesture. Tusk looked at the bodies of his guards and then looked at each member of their party, waiting until the last to look at Andover.

"Who killed my people?" Tusk's voice was lower and deeper than Andover remembered, but that could have just been the terror that was eating at him. He had held his own against the Pra-Moresh and successfully survived not one but two separate battles against multiple opponents, and not a one of those situations worried him as deeply as the King of Durhallem's Forge.

"I did." He could barely believe it when his mouth opened and started making noises.

Tusk looked at him for a moment and then looked at Drask. "And did he have help?"

Drask stood up and shook his head. "He had training, that is all the help he needed."

"They were good guards." Tusk looked at the bodies again.

Delil shook her head. "Not that good. They underestimated him."

"He's tiny." Tusk gestured toward Andover with one hand. "He is smaller than you, and you are a runt."

Drask laughed. Bromt laughed. The Sa'ba Taalor with King Tuskandru laughed. Delil made what Andover assumed was a rude gesture.

Andover did not laugh.

He looked at the bodies and reached down, once again taking the axe he had chosen as his prize.

Tuskandru watched him as he lifted the weapon. It was a very heavy blade and lifting it was not as easy as he might have hoped.

The King walked up to him and held out a hand, gesturing for the axe. "May I?" Andover was surprised to hear the man ask.

Just the same, he handed the weapon over.

Tusk looked at it for several moments, moving the blade so that he could look at it better in the red light of the great tunnel. And then he handed it back.

"That is a fine piece of obsidian. When you use it, you should place it within a weapon that you make yourself. Do you understand?"

Andover licked his lips and nodded. When they had met before Tuskandru had not spoken directly to him. And now the King had addressed him.

"I will, your Majesty."

Tuskandru looked to Drask and spoke several words that meant nothing, followed by the phrase "Majesty". Whatever he said, Andover suspected it was a question.

Drask made a few gestures and spoke a few words of gibberish back. When he was finished Tusk nodded his head and looked to Andover again. "I am King Tuskandru. When you speak to me as a leader that is what you call me. When you address me as a person you may call me Tusk. You understand?"

"Yes."

"I am not 'Majesty'. I am Tusk." There was no room for discussion on the matter. "Now, come. You are welcome in Durhallem and you need to clean yourself and make yourself presentable."

"I do?"

"You are going to meet a god. It is best to be prepared for that."

"A god?" he shook his head. "I'm going to meet a *god*?"

Drask spoke softly, "Durhallem wishes to meet you. You will meet a god."

Andover nodded. He could think of no words to say to that.

"What did you call this? An 'adventure'?" Nolan's voice was a harsh crack as he looked to his left at Darus. His friend was crouching lower over his horse and holding the reins for dear life. The horse below him slid and stumbled on the icy, rough ground, but managed to keep running. He did his part by not falling from the saddle. His hood was up around his face and his eyes were squinted half shut. Beneath him the horse was squinting, too. That was almost inevitable. The winds of the Blasted Lands were utterly miserable to contend with and the cold had long since numbed Nolan's exposed skin.

Darus waved one arm to the blackness coming their way from behind. "That will undoubtedly be an adventure."

Vonders Orly was riding up on Darus'sother side and he bellowed to be heard. "We're making camp!" Nolan started to say something but Vonders shook his head. "No choice! These are cutting winds! We stop now, or we will likely die out here!"

Vonders was from the Wellish Steppes and, if he was to be believed, he and his family had made several raids into the Blasted Lands in the past. They'd gone looking for anything they could sell and they'd found things on a few occasions. He wore a ring made from a very odd piece of metal: misshapen and hammered by wind and worse, the circle around his middle finger was heavy and the myriad fragments of what looked like melted gems that ran around the edges and fused together into a multicolored lump at the center were unusual enough that Nolan did not doubt the origin.

There were two ways to get that sort of piece: be very rich or go find it yourself. Vonders came from a family that had gotten wealthy selling the pieces they found.

"How long?" Nolan's voice sounded like a distant mumble to his own ears.

Vonders pointed back the way they'd come and Nolan saw that the wall of blackness coming toward them was eating the distances at a terrifying pace.

Seen from the top of the Temmis Pass the Blasted Lands had looked almost calm. There were whorls of mist and cloud, but they were hardly violent in appearance. The pass went far deeper than most people realized, several hundred feet down into the lower levels that held the raging storms of the Blasted Lands at bay. From the inside, the clouds of mist revealed themselves for the tips of the endless winds and the nightmarish dust and frigid air. Nolan preferred the view from above, really.

The four men rode only a hundred feet further before they scrambled to pull blankets for themselves and their animals. While Nolan and Vonders drove spikes into the merciless ground to anchor their tent, Darus and Tolpen quickly set about sliding the heavy cloth of the blankets around the horses and securing the straps that would keep them from blowing away.

Calling their shelter a tent was a bold exaggeration. It was shelter, yes, but hardly as noble a structure as a tent. The horses gathered together at one of the three posts that held the structure up. The supplies stayed at the second post and the men gathered at the third. Darus had pissed and moaned about hauling the posts along for the ride. Each horse had trailed one of the heavy beams, and Vonders's horse had hauled the heavy leather sheets on a small wagon. As the beast had been bred for hard work, it also carried several heavy stones that they were using to anchor the sides of the shelter, now that it was built.

Darus looked to Vonders and shook his head. "I was wrong."

Vonders did not gloat. Instead he merely nodded. "Brace yourselves. It's coming."

A few seconds, later the harsh hiss of wind and grit and small stones slapping the leather and canvas sides of the structure drowned out nearly all other sounds.

Nolan shook his head, shocked by the violence being unleashed against their protection. The walls seethed and buckled and whipped in a frenzy as the winds tried to tear them down, but Vonders's instructions had been very detailed and Nolan had listened. He was almost certain the tent would hold.

The horses stayed surprisingly calm and Nolan thought that a good sign. Not that he could be certain. He'd seen horses many times, and he'd been trained to ride one without falling off, but they were still a fairly new experience to him. His thighs and hips and backside were likely never to forgive him the sin of taking up riding.

When they'd been summoned to the palace in Tyrne, he'd thought they were going to be questioned about the beasts that they'd hauled with them from the battle. Nolan could not have been more mistaken. He'd expected to see Merros Dulver, and on that front too, he was disappointed.

Instead of meeting with a general he met with the Empress and her advisor, a sorcerous thing called Desh Krohan. He'd heard of the wizard, of course. Nearly everyone had heard stories, but the truth was so much worse. The wizard towered above them in a great cloak that seemed alive, and no matter how hard Nolan had stared he'd never been able to see a face within the cowl of that hood.

He'd almost ignored the wizard, he'd been so busy looking at the Empress. That she was a beauty was a given.

She had reddish hair and a lean body, and she'd been wearing a crown on her head, but she didn't seem like she was capable of ruling the whole of the known world.

Tolpen was the one who figured out how to bow properly and the others followed suit very quickly. There were two guards at the doors of the immense room where they met the Empress and the sorcerer. The throne she sat on was surely elaborate enough, and he supposed that the fact that she sat there should have been his warning, but the notion of bowing to a girl barely any older than him had not sat at all well until Tolpen did it and made him realize what was supposed to be done.

Empress Nachia did not show the least bit of concern over whether or not bowing got done. The wizard seemed less interested in that notion and more concerned with talking to the four of them.

After that it all sort of blurred. One moment he was focused on the Empress and the next he was trying to figure out what sort of nightmare was hiding under that sorcerer's cloak and then Tolpen was nodding and promising that they would not disappoint the Empress or the wizard.

It was only when they were choosing horses from the royal stables that Nolan realized they were going somewhere.

Turned out they were going to the Blasted Lands. Something about being heroes of the Crown and needing to go to protect a young girl who was on a mission to find out more about the enemies of the Empire.

Nolan cursed himself for not paying better attention.

Vonders had opened his bedroll and was sorting himself. His ring kept catching the light from the lantern. They didn't quite dare a full fire, but two lanterns burned in the tent with them and kept the entire assortment of soldiers and animals in semidarkness.

"How much did you say a ring like that costs?" Darus kept eying that ring like it was the crown on the Empress's brow.

Vonders shook his head. "Didn't cost me a thing. Found it out here in the Blasted Lands. Keep your eyes aware and maybe we'll find you a treasure of your own."

"You think so?" Darus managed to sound both hopeful and dubious at the same time. Like he couldn't quite believe the pretty girl he'd been looking at might like him in return, only more so.

Vonders yawned and curled his furs around his shoulders to keep the cold at bay. "Trust me. It ain't so hard to find stuff. You just have to know how to look."

That was the last word spoken during the night. The winds were shrieking and being heard was impossible.

The next morning was more of the same and the men sat in their shelter and ate dry rations and drank water and then tended to their horses. Fresh water and oats, and the animals seemed perfectly content to stay put. Vonders said that was a sign it was time to stay where they were, and not a man among them much argued with his logic. The winds and the screaming hail were enough to stop anyone from being foolish.

The tent was holding well enough, but Vonders instructed them on several occasions to beat at the sides when the storm seemed to grow quieter. His reasoning was sound. The silence was brought on by a thick sheet of ice building on the outside of the structure. Had it been left there was no doubt the entire thing would have collapsed under the weight. By the time the worst of the storm finally abated there were splits along a couple of seams and the taste of ash and dirt coated the inside of every mouth.

So far, the beauty of the Blasted Lands did not impress Nolan.

Darus spoke up as he carefully rolled his gear back into a bundle that could be carried on his shoulders. "So, where are we going again?"

Vonders pointed in a direction that meant nothing at all to Nolan. "That way. The Mounds."

"What are the Mounds, exactly?" Darus did like his questions. No two ways.

"No notion as to what they might be, except they're big and the Sa'ba Taylers ain't much for 'em."

"Sa'ba Taalor," Nolan corrected.

Vonders nodded, taking the correction in stride. "The bastards that killed the Emperor don't like 'em and that wizard sent his sister to go look 'em over. We're supposed to make sure she gets back in one piece."

"What? He sent his sister into this?" Darus's voice squeaked at the very notion.

"Maybe they aren't close."

Nolan shook his head. "Long as we get there soon and get back. I don't care much beyond that."

Vonders shrugged and then secured the supplies in his wagon. The tent itself went over the top of the supplies and Nolan helped him tie the furs and canvas in place. Whatever else he might think, he'd never doubt the man from the steppes when it came to the weather again.

They were on their way within another fifteen minutes. An hour after that the horse that Tolpen rode slipped the wrong way on the ice and broke its hind leg. Tolpen managed to roll free before the animal could crush him.

If Nolan needed proof that the man was a hunter he got it right then. Tolpen put an arrow through the screaming animal's head, killing it instantly. Within ten minutes after that, he was hiding the carcass and cutting thick slabs of meat from the animal's body. Much as the notion horrified him, Nolan's stomach rumbled at the thought of fresh meat. Their dried rations kept them alive but tasted like the air in the Blasted Lands.

They packed away as much flesh as they could on the supplies and Tolpen took turns riding behind the others to avoid exhausting the other horses. That night they ate fresh meat.

Not much more than a day later they met the woman, Tega, and the two guards who'd been watching over her.

When she was a young girl, Tega's parents had worried about her. They felt that she was too serious to be a child. Really, that was something that never changed. Even when she was lying to them and telling them that she was going to Trecharch and planned to visit with the amazing flora of that area, her parents felt she was too serious.

They'd have been far more worried along those lines if they'd known she was heading for the Blasted Lands.

There were six men traveling with her. All of them had eyed her with appreciative looks. They did so when they thought she wasn't looking, just as they saved their uncivilized comments regarding how well they could warm her nights for when she was in her private wagon and they thought she could not hear them.

She did not let the way they looked at her or spoke of her affect her ego. As Desh had said more than once, the least attractive can be a beauty when compared to solitude.

In the public times, they were very proper, but ultimately they were men and they were soldiers. In other circumstances, the two often led to a problem with crude humor and occasionally with inappropriate behavior. The latter was not a worry. Fear of Desh Krohan and of sorcery in general was enough to make sure they behaved, even if they hadn't each been watching the others for foolish behavior.

They were soldiers, true enough, but they were also men who were promised extra monies if they returned their charge undamaged to her mentor.

Their expedition was much smaller than most that attempted to enter the Blasted Lands. Not small enough to be foolish, but very close to that in most eyes. The Pra-Moresh were a danger and a very real one. Several people had allegedly seen the great beasts in the northern areas of late, and Pella had heard them up in the Wellish Steppes. While it was not unheard of for the nightmares to wander those areas, it was a rarity.

The guards did not complain about their small numbers, not even when they thought Tega was too far away to hear them. They were grateful for the money and the opportunity to prove themselves to Merros Dulver. The new head of the Imperial Army was a harsh man to please, but gaining his favor and his trust could surely not hurt a soldier's career chances.

The men with her were all chosen by Desh himself as examples of brave soldiers with a powerful sense of duty and a proven talent for defending their charges.

They had fought some sort of abominations on the road to Tyrne. They had done so well, in fact, that Desh had sent them to meet up with her by way of the Temmis Pass. She had ridden down the narrow cut away in the vast pit that held the Blasted Lands, and sweated the entire time. Twice she'd traveled that stretch now and both times she'd wondered if the wagon she was in would survive the trek. So far, her luck was holding.

The group had stopped for the night, such as it was. The wind and ash blew just as hard and the cold tried to sink through the wood of her wagon even more vigorously at night than in the daytime, the only other difference was that the darkness was more solid than before. The faint light of the sun was gone; the great orb set for the evening and the light of the Great Star that often shone down at night was lost behind clouds and grit.

Outside her shelter, the tents had been set up and the animals had been protected as best possible against the howling storms.

The storms did not seem to care. The winds were harsh enough to batter and shake her wagon.

A hard knock at the door of her wagon had Tega nearly ready to let out a yelp before she caught herself. The sound was simply so unexpected that she had no idea how to respond to it.

When she could breathe again she answered the door, one hand held behind the wooden barrier and holding a dagger. Just because the men had behaved themselves so far did not mean they would continue to follow that trend. In any event she did not want to take any foolish chances.

The winds tried to rip the door from her grip and the dust from outside entered the cabin in a rush. Tega squinted her eyes against the worst of it and looked at her unexpected guest.

The man on the other side of the threshold nodded his greeting. "According to the best guesses we can make in this weather, we should be at the Mounds tomorrow, if this storm lets up." That was very likely the most words Maun had spoken to her since Desh had introduced them. He was a lean man, and hard, with several scars on his arms and his neck alike. He was unsettlingly quiet at the best of times. When they'd left Tyrne he'd said nothing, leaving most of the comments to the other man guarding her, a burly fellow named Stradly Limms. Stradly liked to talk and had filled her with a dozen stories about the City of Wonders. She enjoyed each of the tales, having never once been to the area often called the Old Capitol these days. The actual palace remained there and the majority of the Krous family lived there, but she'd never been herself. The stories Limms told honed her curiosity.

"Do you think the storm will abate?"

Maun stared at her for a moment without responding and finally gave a very small nod of his head. "Likely. At least according to Vonders." Vonders was as close as they came to an expert in the area. He was, aside from her, the only person who'd ever entered the Blasted Lands before.

Tega thanked the man, but he did not leave. Eventually she decided to ask him why.

"We can't tell for certain, the storm is too bad, but it's possible there are others out here. Might even be some of the enemies are following us at a distance."

Tega nodded her head. "Thank you for the warning. We'll talk again after the storm lets up."

Maun nodded and slid backward and into the winds, his hair flipping madly around his face. A moment later he was gone.

She did not like the man. There was something about him that was unpleasant, though she could not quite decide what it was. She would trust him only because Desh said she could, but she could not bring herself to be comfortable around him.

The winds continued their screaming fit and the wagon shuddered and groaned along with it, a victim of the raging abuse the wind delivered.

Outside the winds calmed for a moment and then a low noise thrummed through the air, through the ground itself, and set her entire body to vibrating along with everything in her shelter. Tega closed her eyes and felt her lips drawn down in a scowl of discomfort. The sensation was unpleasant at best and bordered on painful.

She knew what it was, of course. The sound – low vibration that rattled her bones in her flesh – was nothing other than the target of her investigation. The Mounds.

There were stories about what had happened in the Blasted Lands. Those different tales were one of the reasons she'd chosen to apprentice with Desh Krohan in the first place. He was supposed to be wise and ancient and if anyone would know the mysteries behind the ruined area it would surely be the man nearly old enough to have been there.

His tales were as broken and sporadic as the rest. There had been a great war, that much was a given. There had been sorceries on a scale not seen since and those powerful spells had caused the devastation. But what, exactly had happened? No one knew for sure.

According to Desh there was a very real possibility
that the Mounds rested over the remains of Korwa,
the greatest city that had ever existed. Korwa, where
magic was first studied and taught, where the seat of the
known world had been before the Cataclysm. Vonders
and his family scavenged the Blasted Lands for the
tiniest relics, but what might still be waiting if there was
anything left of Korwa? Certain sorcerers, like Desh,
had long since prepared their most important items to
withstand amazing damage. It took time and power, of
course, but according to Desh there were a few items of
his that could not be destroyed by lightning, by fire, or
sword. They could be hurt, yes, but it would require an
army's worth of effort.

What might still wait where sorcery got its start?

Despite herself, Tega felt her heartbeat faster at the
thought of the Mounds. Not with apprehension, though
surely there were plenty of reasons to be worried. Not
with dread of what might be waiting in the place that
could make noises low and strong enough to rattle her
teeth in their sockets.

No. Her pulse quickened at the thought of what she
might find if she could, indeed, discover a way to enter
the area that the Sa'ba Taalor were forbidden to seek by
their gods.

Ultimately, she knew that Desh had sent her for
his own reasons, but in this case, she had decidedly a
secondary purpose of her own.

She had questions, and now, by the gods, she just
might have a way to get answers.

EIGHT

Four days passed before Desh Krohan came out of his chambers. No one, not even the new Empress, was quite foolish enough to knock on the doors to find him. Nachia Krous did indeed *visit* his chambers – twice, actually – but she did not find him. Instead she saw only the sealed door to a room within his personal area, and left without a sound. She knew that the door there lead to an area where he locked himself away to do whatever it was that sorcerers did when they dared not be disturbed.

There were stories aplenty of what sorcerers did, of course, but Nachia had never much cared about that. She was a very bright student when she was growing up, and she had always been inquisitive enough, but when it came to magic and the casting of spells, she had no interest.

It was not a lack of imagination so much as a simple understanding. She would never be allowed to practice any sort of sorcery, and so she did not waste her time with it. In this she was completely different from Pathra Krous. He had always desperately wanted to know more of everything that was forbidden him. She had never decided if that was a strength or a weakness in her cousin. Either way she missed him.

When Desh came out of his locked room he staggered to his personal chambers and immediately poured cold water from a pitcher into a goblet and a ceramic bowl. He drained the goblet, filled it two more times and finished it thrice. Then he washed his entire body, carefully splashing away the worst of the blood. There was a great deal of blood, more than he had expected.

When he was mostly presentable he draped his great robe over his body and moved into the main work area, lamenting, again, the lack of the Sisters to aid him.

Nachia was not in the room when he got there, but in less than twenty minutes she made her presence known. By then he had called for a servant to fill his bath properly and was busily eating pabba fruit, cheese and bread with desperate appetite. Four days without food or water had left him feeling wasted away, though he looked much as he always did.

"Where have you been?" Nachia's voice was just a little demanding.

Desh didn't even bother looking up from his food. He chewed, swallowed and washed the latest bite down with a splash of wine and answered, "Dealing with the Sooth. I'm glad you're here. You've saved me the trouble of coming to you."

Nachia was surprised not to hear his usual admonitions about privacy and the possibility of rumors but brushed that aside. "What's wrong?"

Desh finally looked up and took another sip of his wine. "A great deal, actually. But the thing we should focus on for now is the need to move everyone out of this city immediately."

"What?" Her voice cracked like a whip, and Desh imagined he could hear the echo from the other side of the palace's courtyard walls.

"A little quieter, Majesty. We would rather not share state secrets with the enemies of the Empire."

"Desh, what are you talking about? Have you lost your mind?"

The man's skin was still pale and his eyes a touch feverish in appearance. He had cleaned himself fairly well but had not yet bathed, and as a result there were spots around his hairline where dried, crusted blood could still be seen.

"Possibly," he said. "But I don't think so."

"We cannot move everyone out of the city, Desh. It's impossible."

"It's hardly impossible, Nachia. Difficult, to be sure, but well within the realm of possibilities I imagine."

"Where would we take them?" Nachia stared at him and shook her head. Her brow knitted into a tight "V" above her eyes, a sure sign that she was vexed. He rather enjoyed that aspect of the conversation, as she was normally the one putting him into that state of mind.

"There is a very large Empire beyond the walls of Tyrne, Majesty. You know this. You've lived beyond them for most of your life."

"Desh Krohan, you are my First Advisor and I have always respected your opinions, but I need more than that to convince me to move an entire city's worth of people."

Desh sighed and stood up. His great robe fluttered and moved and shimmered and looked as impressive as ever, but with the cowl down the effect was lost. He was simply not as terrifying when he had a face.

"We need to move the people from the city, Nachia, because the Sooth have warned me that it has to be done."

"What are these Sooth, anyway? And why do you listen to them?"

Desh frowned. Describing the Sooth was rather like trying to explain the distance between the Great Star and the sun. There was no proper measurement that he knew of.

"They are spirits. They don't exist in the same way that we do, and they can often see events that haven't happened yet."

"How?"

"I have no idea. All I can tell you is that they can often tell what will happen and it strikes their fancy they can share that information." The "V" between her eyebrows grew more pronounced. "Honestly, Nachia, you look like you're about to have a fit."

"I'm not going to do anything of the sort." A wave of her hand, brushing away a pest. "Explain why these spirits say we should abandon one of the largest cities in the Empire."

"Because they say the city will be destroyed."

Nachia's eyes sought something and when she spotted a chair she nodded and moved over to it.

"How? How will the city be destroyed?"

Desh felt his face grow a bit hot. "Yes, well, that would seem to be the problem I've encountered."

"Excuse me?"

"They can't tell me how, only that it will happen and soon."

"How soon?"

"Well, that would be the other problem I've run into. The Sooth don't understand time as we do, you see and so they can't exactly point to a precise moment."

Nachia's mouth dropped open in surprise and then slowly pulled into a tight line of disapproval. Desh found himself puzzling over how mobile her features were.

"Desh. I need more than that before I can do anything."

"Why?"

The Empress shook her head. "Because I can't very well demand that every person in the entire city abandon their homes over what amounts to the faintest possibility of a problem."

Desh shook his head in counterargument. "Of course you can. You're the Empress. You can tell them whatever you want and they have to listen."

"Are you mad?" Nachia's voice broke for the second time.

"We've already discussed the possibility, I believe. Listen, Nachia, I would love to argue this out with you, I would, but I rather got the impression that time is of the essence and we have a lot to accomplish if we're going to evacuate an entire city the size of this one." He scratched at the dried blood along his scalp line and looked at the chamber where even now a very large tub of refreshingly warm and clean water was waiting for him.

With the usual disregard for his needs, Nachia crossed her arms and shook her head. "This can't happen, Desh!"

"It has to happen, Nachia. I mean that. I know it's inconvenient, but it's absolutely necessary."

Nachia stared hard at him, a child, really, the difference between them amplified by decades, by centuries, not merely by years. "Then I fear we may all die here, Desh Krohan. I need more than the thought that the city might someday come to an end to move us."

"Nachia! You have to listen to me." He strode toward her, and stopped himself from grabbing her shoulders. "We have to leave here. Go back to old Canhoon. Go to the proper palace and easily half the population will follow you soon enough."

"Give me a proper reason, Desh. Find out what is going to happen here and explain it to me. Give me more than the spirits giving vague warnings." Her voice was steady and so was her gaze. Desh cursed himself a bit for picking as well as he had who would rule when Pathra died.

"Then how's this for a reason? The Sa'ba Taalor have only been in one city. This one. They know where it is and they will surely strike here when they attack."

"If they attack."

"Ask Merros Dulver if he thinks they'll forgive the slight against their king." Desh kept his voice calm. Anger would only fall on deaf ears and she would not listen to anything else from him at the moment. She was as stubborn as ever, just smarter about listening.

Nachia nodded. "I will. And while I'm doing that, you find some proof of these troubles. Anything I can use to justify moving tens of thousands from their homes."

Desh nodded his head.

Nachia waved a hand in his direction as she headed for her secret passage. His secret passage, which she had gleefully usurped. "And clean yourself, wizard." Her voice took on the faintest note of teasing. "You still smell like a slaughterhouse."

For once Desh had no additional words. He moved toward his bath and disrobed, desperate to be clean.

Every morning Merros Dulver rode past the red brick wall surrounding the palatial home of Wollis March and stared at the closed gates in front of it. It had become a part of his routine, a path he rode to let himself think in relative privacy.

This time, for the first time since he'd started his ritual, the gate was open. The sight was enough to stop him in his tracks. He did not stare with his mouth hanging open. He had more control than that, but he was decidedly surprised.

And when the woman stepped past the threshold of the gate and looked at him he still kept his calm, but inside he felt a river of frost spilling into his insides.

He had seen Dretta March only once before. She looked much the same, but the angles of her face seemed harder. Her eyes, dark as her husband's had been, assessed him for a long moment and she nodded her head.

"You are Merros Dulver."

Merros nodded his head and slipped carefully from his saddle. His knees wanted to shake but he did not allow them that luxury. Instead he walked stiffly toward the woman and laid one hand on the hilt of his sword. He had no intention of striking her, and certainly no desire to attack, but old comforts are often the ones we seek when confronted with uncomfortable situations. The pommel was familiar in his grip and he needed that, if only for the moment.

Merros Dulver dropped to one knee before the woman who looked back with mild surprise. His eyes wanted to look down, but just as he could not let a soldier flee in fear without penalty he did not allow that. He stared into her eyes and forced his voice to remain calm.

"I can never take back Wollis's death. I would if I could. He was the finest man I know and he was my friend. I miss him."

Dretta March looked at him for a long moment and then shook her head. "Stand up, you damned fool and come in here with your oversized horse." She turned away from him and called over one shoulder, "We have much to discuss."

Merros listened, though the ice in his guts tried to fill his very soul at the notion.

Despite the intimidating wall, the house beyond it was not overly large. The land was cleared and the grass in desperate need of a proper grooming, but that was to be expected. No one had been there to care for the place since Wollis's death.

Merros made a note to send a few soldiers to handle the matter. There were plenty on his list who needed a reminder that he was still watching them and expected improvements.

Dretta led him and his horse to the front of the villa, where a table had been set with chairs and freshly baked bread and meats. Two servants looked at the General and nearly quaked to see him. Still, they recovered quickly enough and began pouring wine and water into goblets.

Dretta gestured to the closest seat. "Sit and eat with me. Tell me how my husband died."

Merros sat and stared at the freshly prepared food. He should have been ravenous, but looking at the widow before him he found his appetite faded completely.

She brushed away the hands of the closest servant, a man trying to cut into the roast, still steaming in the early morning air.

Merros had no idea what to say and simply stared as she carved into the meat, skillfully slicing thick pieces away.

"You've come past my home every day since I got here," she said. "Likely since before then. In all that time you've found nothing you wanted to say to me?"

"I don't know where to start."

"I've already told you. Tell me how Wollis died."

He nodded and swallowed. "He died, bravely, trying to stop the woman who murdered two generals and very possibly the Emperor."

She merely nodded and stared, and then she waited as he slowly told the tale of how Wollis had saved his life when one of the Sa'ba Taalor had a knife aimed at him.

"So, you see, he saved me," Merros finished.

"Well, then, that would be a fine end to my husband's life." Dretta's voice was low and soft and looked at her expecting hatred or contempt but found none of that.

"How do you mean?" His own voice was soft and broken with grief.

"Wollis considered you a good man and a good friend. He died saving you." She eyed him carefully. "What can be more noble than saving the life of a good person? He died a good death."

"I would rather he still be alive, myself." Merros looked at her and felt his insides finally begin to thaw.

"Oh, and I'd prefer the same, Merros Dulver." Her eyes looked at his calmly enough, but he could sense what Wollis had spoken of so many times when it came to his wife: a deep and abiding strength. "I'd very much prefer my husband alive, even if it meant your death. He was away from me for too many years and several of those were spent with you. That is not something I have forgotten. But if he had to die, there are worse deaths he could have suffered."

"I am so very sorry, Dretta." The man who commanded the largest army in the world heard his voice break and tremble and could not stop it. His vision shattered into hot tears. "I could not save him."

There was silence from Wollis's widow as he cried. A distant part of him burned with shame. Soldiers do not cry and men do not cry before women, but still it happened ,and he could not stop it. He lowered his head and made fists of his useless hands and let out great, braying gasps of grief.

And when he was done with the worst of his unexpected grief, he looked up to see Dretta March looking at him with a calm face. Of the servants there was no sign.

"You could not save him." Dretta nodded. "But he saved you. And you, Merros Dulver, you are supposed to save us from these Sa'ba Taalor when they attack. That's what I keep hearing. That you are a hero and will keep us safe from the people that killed my husband." Her voice was calm as she looked away from him to layer slices of roast meat and bread on his plate.

When she looked up at him again her eyes were dry. "Keep us safe. Keep me safe. And while you are doing that, I want you to find the bitch that murdered my man and I want you to carve her head from her body." Her voice was still calm; as if she were discussing the crops she might plant on the last lands of her villa. "Bring me her head and prove to me that my husband made the right choice in dying for you."

The northerners were known for being a harsh people. That was true in the past and, if her words were an indication, it was true now.

Merros did not respond, save to pick up his knife and to cut into the food his hostess had set before him.

He was hungry. He had not felt hungry in quite a while.

The next morning when he headed for his offices, Dretta March was waiting outside the gate and they had breakfast again. It was not long before he realized a new ritual had become a part of his routine.

Goriah tended to her duties as she always had, with a meticulous attention to detail. That was necessary at the present time, as she was handling the work of three. Pathra Krous was buried in his ancestral tomb, placed next to the remains of his father and his father's father. When he had been settled and sealed in his location, she carefully set the wards that would keep the bodies of the Krous bloodline safe from prying eyes and greedy hands.

And then she got to the business that had brought her to the City of Wonders.

Old Canhoon spread out before her, a sweeping series of structures that seemed to have grown from the very ground. The appearance was deceiving, of course. The city had been built, but over such a vast span of time that many of the buildings had acquired a layer of dust the same color as the ground they were built on.

Of course, in some places the appearance was exactly what it seemed.

The palace looked nearly identical to the Summer Palace, but seemed larger still and was surrounded by concentric rings of walls, ancient barriers designed to keep out invaders that never showed themselves. Unlike in Tyrne, however, the walls were well kept and still guarded. The military forces in Canhoon made sure of it, as the city was where the largest number of soldiers were trained and lived. As she set the wards, several hundred soldiers stood at formation around the tomb, silent and somber and armed and waiting.

As the vault was sealed again, the orders were given, and in slow procession the battalions of armored men passed before the great doors to the tomb and saluted before returning to their duties.

And while the military leaders in the area said their goodbyes, Goriah looked to the dignitaries waiting with her. They were leaders of the vast city, the Commander of the City Guard, the men in charge of the vast universities and colleges that gathered within the oldest city in the Empire, and the men who were charged with making sure that the Gem of Fellein remained well polished in the absence of the Empress.

In the absence of an Empress to impress they were doing their very best to catch the attention of one of her personal advisors.

In the absence of the First Advisor, they were perfectly glad to suck up to Goriah, who was one of his personal assistants, and to the illusions she'd created of her sisters. Tataya and Pella seemed distant, but that was rather common, really. None of the Sisters had a reputation for being easy to know.

Goriah remained suitably unimpressed, but listened to the dignitaries just the same.

There were endless questions, of course. Who were the Sa'ba Taalor and what had started the conflict? What was being done about the murder of the Emperor? Why had the Imperial Highway not been better tended north of the Lishter Gap? Would the Empress be approving a request for more soldiers along the Imperial Highway? Was there news of what had really happened in Roathes? The list went on for nearly as long as the funeral march that brought the Emperor's corpse to the city.

Goriah did her best to answer a few questions and promised to bring many more questions to the attention of Desh Krohan and thus to the attention of the Empress.

Three faces she had hoped to see where woefully absent from the final farewell. She would have been surprised if any of the wizards had shown themselves, but still she had hoped.

As soon as she could, she sent her illusory Sisters on their way. Pella bid farewell first, offering her formal smile and courteous bows to the men who were doing their best to get to know her better. Not long after Tataya left as well, and when they were both gone and Goriah could finally allow herself to relax a little, she took stock of her situation and decided it was time for her to leave for real.

When she had made the proper goodbyes and promises to convey messages, Goriah slipped away from the large crowd of dignitaries, leaving more than a few wondering exactly how she had vanished so easily.

Desh Krohan had taught the Sisters the secrets of sorcery. She never quite understood why so many people forgot that fact.

The universities and colleges around Canhoon were vast things, more often than not: old and well respected and in some cases among the largest structures within the city.

The sorcerers did not advertise their school. There were no signs pointing the way and if one asked around the requests for directions were likely to be met with blank stares and puzzled expressions.

Goriah did not need directions. She found her way back with ease and entered through the front doors without bothering to knock. The structure was built of stone and better kept than many places. Despite the warmer weather outside, the interior would have been chill if not for the fires burning in several hearths.

No alarms were raised by her presence and no one came to see if she needed assistance. She walked the long corridors and drank in the atmosphere of a place that would always be home in many ways. She found the offices of the headmaster, well hidden though they were.

The chambers where Jeron studied were as large as the throne room at the palace but nowhere near as neat. The walls of the room were paneled in dark wood and decorated with shelves that held more books and scrolls than most people would ever see in their lives. A total of ten sets of heavy doors were placed along those walls, none of them seeming to fit where they were, rather as if they'd just wandered into the room and then decided to skulk along the walls in the hopes that no one would notice them. In the center of the room was a table of immense scale. That table was covered with more books and more scrolls, often stacked in precarious heaps and occasionally set alone into cleared areas as if that space were destined to hold that one volume and nothing more.

Roughly at the center of the chaos was a large and very comfortable chair. The arms and seat were covered in soft leather and stuffed well. The man who sat in that chair leaned heavily to his left and studied a manuscript written before the Fellein Empire had been even a distant thought in the first Emperor's mind.

Jeron looked up from his studies as soon as she entered the room. He was a solid man with arms nearly as thick as her thighs, and though when last she had seen him he'd been sporting a beard and a mane of hair, he was currently bald and clean-shaven. His jaw looked better with a beard, but she said nothing of that. Instead Goriah smiled and gave an informal bow.

"You look well, Jeron."

"You always look well, Goriah." He rose from his desk and pushed past the vast stacks of papers that covered it. Jeron was always happiest when he was reading. Desh had once said that he felt Jeron would be perfectly content to spend the rest of his days studying words that had been written in the past and Goriah had no reason to doubt that comment's validity. Neither did Jeron, who merely chuckled and nodded when Desh had made the comment.

He ambled over and hugged her to him. He was easily a head and a half taller than she was, and he hugged like a bear, with great strength, barely restrained. Still, nothing was broken by the contact, and she sighed contentedly. He had always given wonderful hugs, even when they had been children.

"How are you, little sister?"

"I am tired, and I feel like a hundred years have passed since I had a proper bath. I miss my bed and I suspect it will be a long while before I am properly comfortable again." She smiled as she spoke and Jeron chuckled.

"Do you ever not complain?"

"Do you ever tire of asking me foolish questions to which you already know the answer?"

One thick thumb from the paw of his right hand stroked the side of her face and she smiled. "I never tired of hearing you speak. How could I then grow weary of asking questions that will make you answer me?"

"Are the others here, Jeron?"

"Of course." His broad face moved into an easy smile. "Where else would they be?"

"Out and handling the affairs of the school? Perhaps seeking knowledge and wisdom?"

"Well, yes, that could possibly be a good goal for them, but there are many dire warnings of a war coming our way and so I sent for the rest." He put a familiar arm around her waist and led her gently toward the doors. He was not urging her to leave, but rather guiding her toward the very goal she sought.

"You were expecting me then?"

"I was expecting you or one of the others. Desh does not change."

"Desh sent me, of course. He wants to know what might be known of the Sa'ba Taalor and what you have learned from the old writings."

"He could have just asked," Jeron's voice was only half in jest. "Or he could come to visit."

"That's why he has us, you know. So that he doesn't have to travel as far."

When they reached the massive doors he'd been leading her towards they opened of their own accord. Neither of them was the least surprised by that miraculous event. They crossed the threshold without hesitation and continued along their way.

A careful observer would have noticed that the corridor down which they walked was far too long for the house that Goriah had entered. That observer might also have noticed that the air was substantially warmer than in Jeron's offices or in the main entrance. Both of them noticed, of course, but were unimpressed by the change.

They walked only a dozen paces before entering the next room. There, sitting around a comfortable table and picking at the foods laid out for them, a gathering of several very powerful sorcerers looked up and smiled warmly when they saw who Jeron had brought to visit them.

Goriah smiled back and one by one she hugged and was hugged by some of the only people in the world who knew her before she wore the face she had chosen to call her own.

There were smiles aplenty in that room, but that couldn't hide the fact that the people she was facing were scared and had a very good reason to be afraid. Whenever the Sisters came to visit it was because Desh Krohan had sent them. And when Desh took note of the sorcerers he had trained, it was because he had need of them.

It could be said, and fairly, that few people wanted to be noticed by the wizard and less of them wanted to be needed by him. That sort of attention inevitably led to changes of an extreme nature. One needed look no further than the transformations in the life of Merros Dulver to understand that.

When the greetings were done and they had all settled themselves down to eat and drink and Goriah herself had made them mugs of sweet hot tea, she looked at the people gathered with her and spoke not with her voice but with the voice of Desh Krohan.

"These are dangerous times, my friends. And they are about to get much darker."

Desh Krohan and Merros Dulver stood together and looked toward the south, where the dark plume over what had been the Guntha Islands remained like a distant storm cloud.

"What news from your Sisters?"

Desh leaned along the parapet and let the wind play with his hair. He'd scrubbed himself several times in scalding hot waters before he'd felt properly clean again and now that he was, he wanted to savor the sensation.

"Pella travels to the east. She's gathering knowledge and will contact me soon, I hope. Tataya is far to the south. She's been speaking on our behalf to the Brellar."

"The Brellar?" Merros frowned at him.

"Well, we need to have a proper navy, don't we?"

"We have a navy." Merros frowned. "At least I think we have a navy." His frown became a proper scowl. "Why don't we have a navy?"

"We did. Actually we had a fleet of ships and boats, many of which were supplied by Roathes and the descending kingdoms to the south." Desh gestured toward the distant cloud of darkness. "The Guntha blew up. And then Roathes was taken by black ships. And now we don't have a navy so much as we have plenty of promises that when the time comes, if it comes, a few ships will be spared for the use of the Empire."

"Would you care to explain how that works, please? Are there ships or no?"

Desh looked at the General and raised an eyebrow. "Mostly there are ships. They are held by the different kingdoms and assigned to the Empire, should there be a war. At least, that's the way it's supposed to work."

"So why are you now looking to hire a naval fleet?"

"You misunderstand, Merros. I'm preparing for the events that could happen."

"No. You're deliberately not telling me something. You have placed me in charge of defending the Empire and now you're hiding things. Tell me what you're hiding or find someone else to run this affair."

"You can't possibly be serious."

"I did not come out of retirement to be lied to. I came out of retirement because you promised me a preposterous amount of money and told me I would be in charge of the military forces." Actually that was a lie. He'd been told that he would be a general and in charge of defending against the possible threat of the Sa'ba Taalor. The murder of the Emperor and most of his military staff had facilitated the rise to general and head of the army. "I can't run anything if you hide secrets that can impact my ability to command our forces."

Desh sighed and shook his head. "You know I really do prefer a certain level of blind obedience."

"Which is fine when I'm not running an entire Empire's military forces. Besides which, as we've already discussed, you're paying me far too well for me to give less than my all." He looked sideways at Desh. "Really, it's embarrassing how much you're paying me."

"I could always arrange a cut in your salary."

"Don't be hasty. I'm perfectly willing to be embarrassed from time to time. I just don't want to be left ignorant of important facts."

"The facts are simple enough. There's been no need of an Imperial Navy for a long time. We have access to ships and we've made the most of it. But there might not be enough ships ready and waiting any longer and the best method of handling the situation is to bolster what we have with support from outside of the Empire."

Merros shook his head and chewed at one edge of his mustache.

"No. We need to build more ships."

"We're currently under attack."

"All the more reason to build more ships."

"We can't possibly justify building more ships if we don't have the support of the Empress, and Nachia's not likely to want to bother if you can't prove your worth."

"What do you mean by that?" Merros'svoice took on an edge.

Desh smiled. He liked knowing the man was paying attention. "What have you done about Roathes?"

"I've sent scouts." His voice took on a defensive edge.

"And what have the scouts come back with?"

"Remarkably little."

"Why is that?"

"You know why, Desh. They haven't gone far before they returned."

"Because?"

"Because there's nothing there. The land is a ruin. It's burned and blackened and the people are gone."

"Gone where?"

"Mostly up this way, it seems."

"How many?" Desh looked at Merros carefully as he asked the question.

Merros sighed. "Not enough."

"Then you need to find out where the rest of them are, Merros Dulver. You need to find out where they are and you need to gather them together. The Roathians know how to build ships and boats and you want to build a navy's worth of both. So find them and have them get to work."

"And how do you propose I manage that?"

"What were you telling me only minutes ago? You've been put in charge of the greatest army on the planet. Find a way." Desh waved a hand and stared out at the distant plume.

"Damn it."

The wizard smiled. "Indeed."

"You knew it would come to this." Merros jabbed a finger at the wizard and stopped himself just before it would have touched the man. He was brave and he was angry, but he was not foolish. It was one thing to speak his mind with the sorcerer and another to touch without permission.

"Lanaie is now the queen of her people. Find her and ask her assistance."

It was Merros who looked out at the horizon then, staring at the dark smudge that pointed toward the ruins of the Guntha.

Far to the south of the Fellein Empire, Captain Callan steered his ship, carefully following the orders that the Brellar had given. Next to him Tataya stood firm and swayed with the movement of the waves. Next to her was a complete stranger who was possibly the most important person in the world just then. Because he was the reason none of them were dead.

He hardly seemed especially significant. He was average height and a little on the slim side, with dark hair pulled back in a ponytail and a long, thin mustache that was well suited to his long, thin face. He also sported a sword on his hip and no less than three daggers, but that was hardly unusual with the Brellar. As a rule, they remained heavily armed. Like all the Brellar he had scarred most of his arms and parts of his face with symbols that meant nothing to Callan. He knew only that the markings told stories or noted achievements. The scars were small, but numerous. He supposed that was to make room for more claims of greatness.

Ahead of them were four ships. Behind them were three more.

The man the Brellar had sent along to keep them company walked closer and took the wheel from Callan. He was not demanding, but he did not have to be. As the man currently in charge of their fates, he chose to be gracious. Callan was grateful.

The redheaded beauty that'd hired him watched the newcomer as he steered the vessel into the docks where the Brellar were waiting. They had caught a good wind and rode it all the way to the land where they came to a rest. Captain Callan had never been this far south and east. He did not know if they were at an island or if they were touching a larger land mass.

They had left the areas he knew seventeen days earlier. Now he was doing his best not to get killed. He had doubts about his success rate.

Still, they were all still alive when the men on the docks started securing the ship.

Callan felt a bit intimidated, really. He called his boat a ship, but, in comparison to the Brellar vessels on all sides, it was rather like calling a stunted pony a warhorse. The Brellar's vessels were monstrous in comparison, and all of them were in fine shape.

Their Brellar escort gestured quickly and headed for the gangplank, chattering away in the common tongue about the beautiful weather and promising a meal for everyone.

Callan did not know that he trusted the cheerful mood, but he went along with it.

The redhead, Tataya, walked with calm assurance and glided her way down the to the docks. Several of the men gladly followed behind her. He doubted that their luck would be any better than his, and he'd been trying to woo her without the first hint of success since the day they'd met. The wind shifted and he caught a hint of his own scent. Perhaps if he'd bathed a bit more regularly.

Up ahead, a large group of large men with large swords was standing at the foot of a long staircase and looking toward the redhead with an odd expression on their faces.

No one was more surprised than Callan when the gathered strangers dropped to their knees in supplication before her.

Except, just possibly, Tataya herself.

Nachia Krous paced the throne room in long strides, her hair flapping in her wake. She seemed incapable of sitting still, and Merros was obliged to at least follow her with his eyes. He'd actually given up trying to walk next to her when she was in a mood like this very early on, even before she was properly crowned.

'There's no one left? No one at all?" Nachia asked the question for the third time and for the third time he answered.

"No one. My scouts didn't even find very many corpses, Majesty."

"Well, what did they do with them?" She looked toward him with wide eyes and a slightly dangerous expression.

"I have no notion. I've spoken with Desh about it and he said he'll try to investigate. Didn't look at all pleased by the idea, actually."

"Gods!" She pointed at one of the guards in the room, a man picked by Merros himself for his loyalty. "You!"

The man flinched.

"Darfel. His name is Darfel, Majesty."

"Darfel! Go immediately to Desh Krohan's chambers and tell him I demand his presence!"

Darfel responded with a sharp salute and immediately left at a brisk walk. Merros suspected the man thought he was being sent to his own death, but he listened.

"You know he's likely ready to wet himself at the notion of bothering Desh, don't you?"

Nachia looked at him for a moment with a puzzled expression and then managed to relax a bit and chuckled. She shook her hair back into something resembling a proper position. "I guess if one doesn't really know him, the old man is rather intimidating."

"Actually he's just basically rather intimidating all the time."

"Are you intimidated by him, General Dulver?"

"Majesty, I deal with people who can order me executed on a whim. Why should one who can turn me into a spider and squash me under his foot be any more intimidating?"

"Do you really think he could turn you into a spider?"

"According to the rumors I've heard over the years, he could just as easily turn me into a butterfly or kill me with a glance. After a certain point you just accept that the man can kill you any number of ways."

He kept his tone light, because the Empress needed a bit more levity in her life, near as he could tell.

"Well, you may rest assured I'll only have you executed with good reason and if I do I'll allow you a fair chance to argue your case."

"You know, I really don't know you well enough to get if you're joking when you say that sort of thing, Majesty."

"Of course I'm joking." She shook her head. "I'm just getting used to you. I would rather not go through finding a replacement."

"Still not sure if you're joking."

"Good. I rather like keeping my staff guessing as to my motives."

"You have been around that damned wizard far too much."

"I should rather not be described as 'that damned wizard', thank you." Desh's voice had an edge of annoyance. He hadn't been there a moment before, but he stepped out of the shadows and looked at Merros with a scowl.

Nachia shook her head. "You're not to consult your damned spirits about the Roathians."

Desh looked at her for a long second with narrowed eyes. "I wasn't planning on it."

"Good. That's good. I'd prefer you not disappear for several days again."

"Pity that. I was planning on going to Roathes myself to see what happened there."

"What?" It took Merros a moment to realize that he and the Empress had spoken simultaneously.

"I'm going to Roathes. I need to find out what happened there and I have no one else here I can trust with the examinations."

"Send more soldiers." Nachia was shaking her head, her lips pressed into a thin line.

"Soldiers won't answer the questions. I need to go myself."

"Send one of the Sisters." Nachia's expression brooked no argument.

"Can't. They aren't here. They're otherwise engaged." Desh crossed his arms and shook his head.

"I know you can talk to them over long distances. I've seen you do it."

"I can be there and back before any of the Sisters could manage and I need to see this myself, Nachia. It has to happen."

"What if I need your counsel?"

"I am the First Advisor, not the only advisor."

"Fine. Take soldiers with you."

"They'll only slow me down."

"Desh…"

"Nachia. I'll be back within five days." He shook his head. "Ten if you make me drag along soldiers."

Merros watched the two of them as if they were engaged in a proper duel, with throwing knives.

"What do you need from the area to know what happened, Desh?" He asked the question with a sigh.

"I need to see what I need to see. I need to touch the sand and examine different homes. I need to investigate for evidence of what transpired. It's not as simple as merely asking an inquisitor to get answers from witnesses, Merros. There are no witnesses. There's no one there at all from what you've said."

"Couldn't you get the answers from the soldiers who made the trip?"

"No. I need more than they can offer."

Nachia cleared her throat and both men looked at her. Merros felt a quick flash of guilt. For just one moment he'd forgotten he was in the presence of the Empress.

"Five days?" She looked so damned young staring uncertainly at her advisor.

"No more than that. Possibly less."

"Then do it if you have to, but be back soon."

Without pausing for so much as a breath, she turned to Merros. "You need to send men to watch him."

"But, milady, he said–"

"I don't care. Send soldiers. They'll follow behind him and stay out of his way."

"Yes, Milady." There were logistics to consider. That, and Desh Krohan was looking at him as if he might be more useful as a spider. He apologized to the mage with his eyes, but ultimately they both served the Empress.

"Does this mean we're at war, General Dulver?"

"Well, I suppose it must, Majesty."

"Then I do not wish for this to be a case of waiting and wondering, General. I wish the armies mobilized. Look at your maps and find the best way to invade the Taalor Valley."

Merros bit his tongue. The very idea of trying to move an army through the Blasted Lands was one of the problems that had kept him up and sleepless more nights than he'd managed to rest.

"I've been preparing, Majesty. It's been a matter of waiting for everything to be readied."

"Waiting for what, exactly?" She wasn't being terse. He knew that, but it certainly felt like she was. His chest felt constricted his uniform. He hated the formal attire, but had to wear it in the palace, even when the Empress was running around in her riding clothes, which was most of the time.

"Majesty, you've seen the Sa'ba Taalor. We have them in numbers, but our army is spread across the entire Empire and theirs is in a single valley. It has taken me time to prepare our soldiers, to make sure they are properly armed and trained."

"Well, you are in your position because you have the trust of your Empire. But now it's time to move forward, General. Prepare for war. By the time Desh Krohan gets back here, I want our troops ready to strike into the Blasted Lands and attack the animals that murdered my cousin."

"Aye, your Majesty. As you command." He bowed formally. They had a fairly casual relationship and he was grateful for that, but when the Empress gave an order he would obey, even if he feared the consequences.

Desh stared at Nachia Krous for a long moment in silence and then looked toward Merros. The General could not read any expression at all from the sorcerer. He may as well have been looking at a statue of the man.

When Desh spoke it was with a soft sigh. "I suppose I should ready myself. We're all going to be very busy when I get back."

NINE

Andover spent one week in the company of Tusk and his people. He was treated as an equal, which is to say he was treated well enough, but expected to handle his own troubles.

When they left the Durhallem Pass they moved down a short passage to an area that had been set aside for the sole purpose of allowing travelers to rest. The sun shone down on the space and for easily ten minutes, all Andover did was close his eyes and feel the warmth and light of the sun on his skin. It seemed forever since he had felt that simple pleasure and he reveled in it. According to Drask the gods had decreed that the location be tended and left for any Sa'ba Taalor who hunted in the Blasted Lands. As the spot was on the side of Durhallem's mountain, it was his followers who tended to it.

There was a bathhouse, there were stables old and new, and there were rooms with simple but functional beds. For some it might have seemed rather simple, but for Andover Lashk, who had lived more than once on the streets of Tyrne while he was growing up, the bed was a luxury and after the long walk through the Blasted

Lands to get there, the baths were as fine a treat as he could recall.

What he found unsettling was the moment when he was joined in the baths by several members of the Sa'ba Taalor, male and female alike.

The room had a few wooden benches built into the walls where people could sit and take off their clothes. In the center was a rather elaborate collection of stone troughs that could be filled with water by working a series of chains and levers. Andover tried to watch while one of his hosts worked the devices but, really, they weren't the sort of thing he was used to. Mostly, if one wanted a bath, one went to a place that offered them or one carried the waters from the Freeholdt River and took matters into one's own hands. As he'd been apprenticed to a blacksmith, he'd simply washed in the waters there and called it done, over the years, and before that when he was a child his mother had prepared his weekly baths. On a few occasions he'd snuck down to the river in a private area and after making certain no one was around to observe his naked state, he'd managed a few quick baths in the extremely cold but fresh waters.

In all that time he had bathed alone, as the gods had surely intended. He listened to the echoes of the water splashing as he settled himself. It sounded like he was in a cavern, not a structure built by people.

According to Drask, again, the waters were warmed by the fire within the mountain, and then released into the long troughs and allowed to cool down from a hard boil to something that wouldn't actually cook flesh. The method meant nothing to him, but the end result was a delight. He had just settled his body into the heated waters when Drask and Delil both entered the room and stripped down, discussing their reunion with their mounts, who had been waiting in the area when they arrived.

Andover felt himself blush across his entire body, lowered himself in the waters and tried to think himself somehow smaller and less noticeable. Neither of them seemed to have noticed him at first and he was feeling rather pleased with that notion when Bromt and Tusk and seven more of Tusk's people entered the chambers.

To be fair, seeing Delil and the other women take their clothes off certainly solved a few mysteries of the female body that he had been wondering about for a long time, but watching the men with them peel off their clothing was rather unsettling. Seeing Delil naked also awoke his arousal, and Andover prayed fervently to the gods that no one would notice. Andover had never been in the military and he had most assuredly never bathed with anyone else, male or female. Seeing that much unclothed flesh was unsettling in the extreme and he was fairly certain that sooner or later they would truly see him and make fun of his naked state of being.

The groups continued their talks while they disrobed and then climbed into the waters around him.

King Tuskandru sat immediately to his right. Sheer fear that the gigantic man might accidentally crush him against the side of the trough had Andover sitting up again in an instant.

Tusk was as naked as the rest, and Andover saw more of the man's body than he wanted to by a long stretch. Nearly every inch of him was scarred. His muscular chest was hairy, which did nothing to hide the signs of old wounds. He had to resist the urge to check if the king's penis was as scarred as the rest of him.

The only thing any of them were wearing was their veils. Tusk's was covered with fine metal rings.

Andover contemplated the best ways to make himself seem either so small as to be beneath notice or large enough to feel less like a child around the Sa'ba Taalor. He was of average size, and he knew that, but by the gods even the women of the gray-skinned people seemed more muscular than he.

Tusk looked at him. "You are so pink..."

Andover looked at his hands, at the flesh that had tinged with gray where the iron limbs were fused to the rest of him, and lifted them to where they could be seen by the king. "Not everywhere." Really, it was all he could think to say.

Tusk roared laughter and cuffed him in the shoulder. He had to assume it was a playful gesture as he was still alive.

"Why are my wrists changing?"

Tusk looked at him for a long moment. "The metal, I suppose."

Andover looked at him, trying to understand.

Drask leaned over and spoke in their native tongue.

Tusk spoke back and nodded.

When he spoke again it was in the common tongue. "You have not seen our children. You will. When you do, you will understand better. We do not start off gray."

"You don't?"

Tusk's eyes shone in the room. "No, Andover. We are not so different, your people and ours. You will see." The King called to one of his people who listened and nodded.

A moment later, the man was rising from the waters and baring his body to everyone there. Not a one of them seemed to care. Andover had to make himself look away. He had never seen so much bare flesh in his entire life. People should be clothed, that was all there was to it.

The man walked to the doorway of the bathroom and cupped his hands, calling out. A moment later he nodded, responding perhaps to words Andover could not hear, and then climbed back into his bath.

When he spoke to Tusk, he spoke in the common tongue. "Trumdt will bring them."

"Who is Trumdt?"

Tusk waved a hand. "Trumdt is here to tend this place. He will be here in a moment with his children."

A moment later the man approached. Like the rest of the Sa'ba Taalor he carried weapons strapped to his body. He also wore a veil. The two young children with him did not. They were dark haired and their eyes bore the same sort of gray color as the rest of the Sa'ba Taalor, complete with the odd light that seemed nearly to come from inside their skulls. But both of the children, no older than five or six years, if Andover had to guess, had dark hair, and their pink skin was tanned from many hours of being outside.

He stared at them as if they simply did not belong where they were.

Tusk spoke his native tongue and the man and his children nodded alike and promptly stripped their clothes away. The children were both girls. They did not hide their nudity. Neither did their father.

Trumdt's body was a map of scars, a book written in healed flesh and callused palms. He was as much a warrior as any of the others around them. Both of the children bore scars as well, though nowhere near as many.

"Do you understand now?" Tusk's voice caught him off guard.

"Why are they pink?"

"Why are you pink? They have not yet met with the Daxar Taalor. They have not yet worked the metals and shaped their weapons. They are only just learning the ways of the Sa'ba Taalor."

The older of the two children eyed Andover suspiciously. The younger stared as well, but without any seeming hostility.

Drask spoke up. "You are wondering why they are pink. They are wondering why you are pink."

Tusk spoke at the same time and the man nodded. He and his children climbed into the baths as well.

"I've worked metal for a few years. My skin has not changed color because of that. It's changing because of the hands, I think."

"There are differences in working metal for your people and ours, Andover." Drask spoke casually enough. "I watched you when you forged your weapon. Your metal is taken from the ground, yes? And heated by fires until it is molten."

"Yes, of course."

"Our metal is a gift from the Daxar Taalor, heated just as these waters are heated." His silver hand splashed slowly through the water, making a small wave but nothing more. "Our metal is the lifeblood of the mountains, the lifeblood of the gods themselves. They give to us, and when they give to us, and we accept, we are changed."

Drask reached down under the waters and Andover nearly jumped when he felt the warm silver fingers touch his leg. "Look at your scar, Andover."

Andover looked down at the place where silver metal had healed him before. There was indeed a thick scar there, but looking at it under the water something seemed wrong. He raised his leg for a better view and let out a small gasp when he saw the flesh properly. The skin was tinted there, much as scars can be, but the tint was gray and looked almost dead in comparison to the pink flesh elsewhere.

There was a harsh ringing noise in his ears for several moments. Andover'd had enough surprises in his life to know that noise was not real, merely in his head. "Am I becoming one of you?" The words were spoken softly enough that he wasn't sure anyone heard him.

Tusk looked at him and answered just as softly: "Would that be a bad thing for you, Andover Lashk of the Iron Hands?"

An hour after he'd settled for sleep Andover sat up and took in a deep breath. He'd been having a pleasant dream about Tega and the thought of her in his dream was enough to startle him awake.

He rose from his simple bed and looked around. A few beds were occupied, but many were not. After listening in the darkness for a few moments he heard the sounds of people talking and followed them.

Just beyond the doorway, outside in the night, Drask Silver Hand was speaking in low tones with another man Andover had never seen before. The man was smaller than Drask, but not by much. His elbows rested on his knees and he squatted next to a small fire. The air had grown much colder since the sun went down and the fire was a necessity. One half of the man's face was a ruin of scar tissue. His left ear was nothing but a hole amid the pitted mess of ruined flesh. If he had an eye on that side of his face, Andover could not see it in the light from the fire.

Andover coughed into his hand and both men looked in his direction. He did not need to cough, but suspected that startling any of the Sa'ba Taalor would be foolish in the extreme.

Neither of the men looked at all surprised by his presence and he wondered if they'd already known he was there.

Drask tilted his head a bit. His hair was down and fell around his shoulders, across his back. "You are awake? I thought you had gone to sleep, Andover."

"I was wondering if you'd heard about Tega or the rest of my people? We've been so busy I forgot about the travelers who passed us on the way here."

"The soldiers." Drask stared at him for a long time. "They are dead. Tega, the girl, I think went home."

"The soldiers are dead?" There was no moisture left in his throat.

Drask answered calmly enough. "Your Emperor died. He was killed, to be precise. The soldiers tried to accuse Tusk of killing him." Dry mouth, yes. But now there was the problem with his knees feeling weak, too. Drask continued, "Tusk and the rest of the people with him killed the soldiers. The girl, Tega, was with Tusk at the time and under his protection, but she lifted into the air like a bird and soared away."

"Oh. I. Oh. Um." There were words he wanted to say, but they were hiding themselves very well.

"Nothing more has happened yet, Andover. The kings have met to discuss matters, but that does not change your position here. You were invited by the Daxar Taalor themselves. No one here will blame you for the actions of the soldiers."

He nodded his head, swallowed the dryness and desperately wished he had a drink.

"You have questions?"

"Oh, yes." Andover nodded vigorously. "Many questions."

"You may ask them of Tusk in the morning. He is sleeping and I would not awaken him without good cause." Both of the men offered smiles at that comment. He suspected there was a story behind those smiles, but just then could not make himself ask after what that tale might be.

He was alone among the most violent fighters he had ever met, and apparently his nation had attacked them.

Andover had no possible idea how to respond.

"Would you drink with us, Andover?" Drask held a skin that sloshed with fluids.

He nodded and the man tossed the skin to him. A moment later he took a deep drink of the cool, sweet wine within it. He had not consumed many wines but rather liked the taste.

A moment later a pleasant warmth ran down his throat and into his stomach. Within a dozen heartbeats that warmth was moving through his entire body.

He nodded his thanks and tossed the wine skin back. The man with Drask caught it and offered a ruined smile from the ruined face.

Andover smiled back, though he felt like screaming in fear, and then waved his good nights.

He moved back to his bed and settled in, but he did not sleep. Instead he found himself lost in thoughts of Tega flying like a bird and armies clashing over the body of a dead Emperor.

The following morning the entire group, excepting only Trumdt, his two children and the others that tended to the place, rode and walked up the steep slope of Durhallem, scaling the mountain at a steady pace. After the time spent in the Blasted Lands, the trek was easy enough for Andover. He did not complain and felt no reason to, instead he enjoyed the view as he climbed.

Tuskandru was well ahead of him in the procession and he contemplated how to approach the man about the attacks and the deaths he'd heard of. How to find out what the King knew of Tega.

There was an odd sense of guilt lingering in his mind. When he'd left the city she had been on his mind constantly. Now? The girl he'd adored from afar for so long was almost gone from his mind.

That was for the best, perhaps, but still he felt as if he might somehow be betraying her.

The valley below was lush with greens and other hues. He had not expected that. He wasn't sure what he would expect after walking through the desolation outside of the mountain range, but truly the notion of farmlands had never seemed a possibility.

"Who tends the farms, Delil?" He couldn't imagine a farmer among the Sa'ba Taalor.

"Mostly the children."

He looked at her to see if she was having a jest at his expense, but the girl seemed completely sincere.

Andover stopped to look long and hard at the distant fields, and Delil stopped with him. "How?"

"How does anyone tend a farm, Andover? They plant the seeds, they grow the crops, and they cut them down and harvest them. It is different for each kingdom, of course, but Tusk's people teach the children to farm so that they will always be prepared to grow whatever foods they need."

"I have never seen a farm before." The words were out before he knew what he was saying.

She looked at him for a moment and her eyes smiled behind the veil. "Then we shall have to take you to see one."

By the time the sun was on its way down, they had stopped at a wall of buildings. That was the only way he could think of it.

According to the stories he heard, the people in the area had once lived in stone huts they built themselves, but after the Mound Crawler came, that great and terrible beast that Tusk had killed when he became king, Tusk ordered his people to change their ways and change they did. The people lived in the mountainside, in homes that they carved from the rock themselves, though it had taken years to accomplish the task.

Stairwells cut into the rock of the mountain itself led to openings at different heights, some of them only a few feet from the ground and others that required climbing nearly a hundred feet from the flat plateau where the odd town was settled.

There were rooms and they were solid, as they should have been, seeing as they were hacked from the side of

198 THE BLASTED LANDS

the mountain. The work was not primitive, as he'd first imagined it might be. Instead the rooms were smooth walled and even floored and as squared and balanced as any he had ever been in. Some were simple in design and others far more complex. It seemed to depend entirely on who lived there and what they did to complete their dwellings.

He was given a room in the same structure as Drask and Delil and Bromt. None of them lived in the area and so all of them were hosted in places set aside for visitors. The rooms were comfortable and functional, with little or no decoration.

What little Andover carried was left in his room without fear of it being taken. The idea seemed insane for a moment. Back in Tyrne you kept your possessions close by and hid them away if you were going to leave them behind. Here the idea was as foreign as he was. The Sa'ba Taalor did not have much of a problem with theft, according to Drask. Thieves had to fight to keep what they might take, and especially where Durhallem ruled and mercy was not an option, it seemed one would only risk theft if one was willing to die for what was taken.

It was a very different place from what he was used to. Then again, he was a very different person. All he had to do was close his eyes and think back on the fights he had survived to know that.

After the sun had set, there was a feast before the wall of structures. A broad area had been cleared of all brush and artificially leveled. He could see the cut marks where stone had been meticulously chiseled away until the area was as flat as a well-planed board.

In that area, there were four deep pits and in each of those was a fire. They proved necessary as the sun set and the chill of the night came across the mountain. From their height the people could see the entrance to Durhallem's Pass and also see into the valley far below. Andover saw rivers and lakes that he had spotted when the sun was still up. They were a different shade of black in the darkness of the valley and from time to time he could spot fires along the edges of the water.

Drask Silver Hand joined him in observing the valley, as more and more of the people from the area came down from their homes and started gathering around the four fire pits.

Drask gestured with his hand. "The valley is larger than it looks from here."

"It does not look small. How many days would it take to travel the length?"

Drask assessed him for a moment, his eyes once again catching whatever light was around and reflecting back a silvery glow. The more he stared, the more he suspected the light was internal somehow.

"To walk the Taalor valley would take you at least two weeks from end to end."

"Impossible." The word was out before he could stop himself and he dreaded the man would take offense.

Drask's eyes smiled behind his veil. "As I said, it is larger than it seems. There are seven vast mountains, Andover. They are not neatly lined up. They are staggered. You cannot see the other end of the valley from here."

"Which mountain do you call home, Drask?"

Drask shrugged his shoulders, a gesture he had picked up from the soldiers he'd traveled with a while back. Very few of the Sa'ba Taalor ever seemed to shrug, now that he thought about it.

"I follow Ydramil and his King in Silver, Ganem. I have a home near the top of Ydramil, but I have not been there in over a year now. I have been busy."

"A year?" Andover frowned at that. "Why so long?"

"Ydramil makes demands of his followers. We are told to study much of the world. I have been visiting each of the mountains, each of the kings and each of the gods."

"Like I'm supposed to?"

"Just so." Drask sighed, the thin veil fluttering with his breath.

"Why the veils, Drask? I have seen every one of you naked, but still you wear veils."

"We do not question the Daxar Taalor. They have not yet said you are ready to see our faces and so we cover them."

"What is so special about your faces?"

Drask chuckled. "What is so special about yours? To us, they are just faces. We are who we are."

"Does your face look like mine?"

"No more than my skin looks like yours or my hand looks like yours."

He held out his silver hand and placed it close to Andover's right hand. Both were metal. Both moved through sorceries Andover did not even try to understand, but beyond that they looked like hands and had five fingers, there was little that they had in common.

"Your children do not wear veils?"

"The children have not yet met with gods."

"Like I'm supposed to meet with them?" That thought was still too large to completely take in. It was easier to try to study the whole of the sky and count the stars than it was to comprehend meeting actual gods.

Drask looked away. "You ask many questions. I can only answer a few. You will meet the Daxar Taalor. They have reasons for wanting to meet you that they have not shared with me." There was no anger in his comment, not even disappointment. Drask merely stated a fact. "I can tell you only this: no one stands before gods and remains unchanged by the encounter."

They were silent for a while, lost in their own thoughts as the sounds of people gathering and preparing food came to them. At each of the fires, carcasses were spitted and set above the flames. There was a time when the notion of eating a Pra-Moresh would have been repellent, but having endured the Blasted Lands and eaten even stranger things – for strange things indeed lived in the wastelands – Andover found the idea had a certain appeal. His stomach rumbled agreement.

"I'll be leaving after the feast."

"Feast? Leaving?" Andover frowned at the other, larger man.

"Ydramil tells me I must go back into the Blasted Lands. He has plans for me and I will obey."

Andover shook his head at the notion of speaking directly to a god. The notion refused to sit comfortably. "Where will you go?"

"The feast is in your honor. You should remember to thank Tusk properly." Drask stood up, not answering the question. "Should we meet again, after you have spoken with the gods, you may ask me more questions. Until then, Andover Lashk, the Daxar Taalor watch over the both of us."

The man who had taught him harsh lessons tapped him lightly on one shoulder and walked away, his thick dark hair swaying with his steps.

Andover was uncertain how he felt about that. In part he felt he was losing a friend, though in truth Drask had done little that could be called a kindness.

Aside from teaching him not to die. That had been a very large kindness indeed.

Andover contemplated all that Bromt and Delil and Drask had done for him, even as he ran one hand gently along his bound ribs and felt the area where the pain still flashed if he pushed. The ribs were mending. They'd felt fine when he was fighting – too busy staying alive to care about the pain, and he'd been fueled by the thrill of combat – but now his side ached with a dull throb again.

He heard Bromt laughing and saw the man walking with a few other men of similar stature. They wore no armor at the present time, though all of them still sported weapons. He imagined this was as close to relaxed as they managed.

Delil talked with several others, men and women alike, and though Andover wanted to speak with her, he did not wish to interrupt her homecoming.

Tuskandru walked toward him. He was again taken by how large the King was, how striking a figure. One of the soldiers, who had traveled with the Sa'ba Taalor to Tyrne, a man named Wollis, had told Andover that Tusk cut a Pra-Moresh nearly in half with one swing of a sword. Despite having seen the monsters, having fought them, he did not have trouble believing the outrageous claim.

The King wore a tunic and leather breeches, the same as he had when Andover had first seen him. His necklace of teeth was wrapped twice around his thick neck, and his hair was pulled back into a heavy braid, wrapped with leather and decorated with a few small pieces of onyx. He did not carry any weapons. That fact alone was unsettling to Andover.

Tusk stopped before him and nodded. "Drask said you want to know what happened with your people."

"Yes. Yes, I do." His voice only cracked a little as he spoke.

"They came for us. One of them claimed that your Emperor is dead. He said that someone killed the Emperor and said we must go back and speak with your generals."

Andover nodded his head. He'd been on the receiving end of demands from the City Guard and, in comparison to the soldiers, those men had almost no authority. Certainly not as much as generals in the Imperial Army.

"They did not ask. They tried to command me. I am a king. I do not answer to your Emperor or his generals. When they would not accept that, one of them drew his weapon. I killed him."

Andover nodded again. He could think of nothing at all to say to that.

And so instead he asked, "Tega. She flew away?"

"She spoke with the voice of her master, the sorcerer. He asked that your soldiers not attack and they did not listen."

"So is she safe?"

Tusk crossed his massive arms. "None of my people hurt Tega. She was under my protection and helped me speak with your soldiers."

"Good. That's good."

"You wish to go home? To your people?"

Andover shook his head. "No. I made a promise to you and your gods, Tusk. I keep my promises."

Tusk nodded his head. "This is good. In the morning, I will show you how to reach Durhallem."

"You'll show me?" His voice broke a second time. "Are you not coming with me?"

Tusks eyes looked at him hard, their light burning. "No one goes before Durhallem who does not walk alone. That is Durhallem's demand."

Tusk gave him an amiable thump on the arm. Andover managed to keep his balance, but it was a close call.

A moment later the King was moving away, heading for one of the fires and calling out cheerfully in his own language. Andover understood a few words of the greeting, but only enough to feel embarrassed that he had not yet learned more.

Of course he had been learning other things.

"Tusk!" He called out before he could let himself think too much.

The King turned to look at him. He did not walk back and it was clear that if Andover wished to speak discretely it would be he who did the walking.

Instead he ca'led out, "Are our people at war?"

Tusk looked at him for several heartbeats and nodded. "We are at war. Fellein has attacked us. You will be asked to defend that attack before the kings of the Sa'ba Taalor."

Oh yes. His heart hammered away in his chest and he nodded. "When?"

"First you meet the Gods of the Forges. Then you answer to their kings." Tusk spread his arms wide in a gesture that almost looked like he wanted to embrace. Only the fact that he'd seen the gesture before let Andover know the move was the equivalent of a shrug. "You will be given the chance to prepare."

"Can I speak to my people?"

"You have agreed to be here. Unless they send you a message, no."

Andover nodded again and Tusk started walking. This time he didn't try to get the King's attention again.

Andover shook his head. He'd rather hoped to know the love of a woman before he died. That seemed less likely all the time.

TEN

The Krous family was powerful, to be modest. There was remarkably little that even the lowliest members of the family wanted for. Even the bastard children of Towdra Krous had more money than most could conceive of, and it is fair to say that Towdra cared little for any of his offspring, legitimate or otherwise.

Most of the family was quite content to stay where they were, fully aware that anything they desired was theirs so long as they behaved themselves.

There are always exceptions. Towdra himself was fine with the current situation. He and his great-niece got along well enough; though there were many members of the family who believed he felt otherwise, Nachia sitting on the throne suited his purposes.

Laister Krous was not as content. He believed that he was better suited for the throne, that his long years of making connections and preparing the way for his eventual accession should have paid off already. For him, Nachia was a nuisance and a problem. The only purpose the girl could have served in his eyes would have been as a good bartering tool to the appropriate parties. Want a country to behave? Offer them a fine looking woman to serve as obedient wife and mother of royal children and call it done. But Nachia on the throne was offensive to his sensibilities.

She was now on the throne and that was a problem, but not one that couldn't be surmounted with the appropriate actions.

It was for that reason that the men were sitting together in a small tavern called the Adze and Axe just outside of Freeholdt. A night's hard ride would have him back in Tyrne and no one the wiser and he had chosen his timing flawlessly. The sorcerer was gone on one of his very rare excursions from the castle. Nachia herself was too busy looking into the possibilities of war – or perhaps pleasuring herself with her new general, who could say? – to notice his absence. Brolley was, of all places, with Desh Krohan on his little search for answers to what had happened to the Roathians. The boy was hardly an issue in any event, especially after his public humiliation at the hands of the barbarians Pathra had invited to visit from the Blasted Lands. Since then, Brolley seldom let himself be seen in public. Most likely it was Nachia keeping him out of harm's way. She was an overprotective sibling and Brolley needed all the protection he could find. Danieca was staying well away from everything ever since she'd tried confronting Desh Krohan. Whatever the man had said to her was enough to convince her to keep herself to herself for the present time, but Laister already knew where she stood on matters. She was with him.

The rest of the Krous family was a herd of simpletons as far as Laister was concerned. They would follow whoever was leading and for the moment that meant they obeyed the whims and desires of Nachia.

The men in the room with him were not as loyal or as easily swayed. They required hard coin for their devotion and a great deal of it. Laister himself was not at the table where the negotiations were taking place. He left the particulars to Losla Foster, his personal assistant. Losla was a quiet man with a quiet way about him. Most everyone who met him forgot he was even there, which was exactly why he was so very successful in his endeavors. Losla sat in the shadows of the tavern's western corner and spoke softly to men who were far easier to remember and much more likely to cut a throat. They were exactly as hungry for money as they appeared, and they looked to be starving for the stuff.

There were four of them, all from the east. It seemed all the best mercenaries came from the east, normally from Elda or even farther away. Laister did not listen to the negotiations. Instead he concentrated on his surroundings and seeing everyone in the room. There were the five men concentrating on their shadowy business. There was the fat sow of a tavern keeper's wife, a woman who had long since moved from buxom to unpleasant, though at the right angles a ghost of her old beauty lingered. There was the tavern keeper himself who was even larger but had an infectious smile and a pleasant attitude. The two of them made sure customers were happy and otherwise stayed out of the way. There were three others in the place: two road-weary men who looked like they would be finishing their meals and then taking rooms upstairs, and a woman who might or might not have been an aging whore. She was attractive despite her peasant's clothes and her common features, but old enough that Laister wouldn't bother even if he were so inclined. Whatever the case, she paid him no attention and, aside from noting her presence, he returned the favor.

The biggest danger, in other words, was that Laister would grow bored enough to find the whore an interesting notion.

Losla saved him from that fate by nodding and rising from the table. The men with him did nothing to indicate that they much cared one way or the other and Losla left the tavern after gathering his cloak and saying a few words to the tavern keeper.

Laister would wait a few minutes before meeting him outside. He had no desire to be connected with anyone in the place. The inquisitors tended to investigate when dignitaries died and Laister had already endured enough polite questions regarding Pathra's death. They were always polite when dealing with the Krouses. It was in the best interests of everyone to avoid offending the Imperial Family.

When the tavern's owner started talking with the men Losla had spoken with – nothing untoward, merely pleasant chatting as he cleared away a few emptied mugs – Laister slipped outside.

It was time.

He met up with Losla on the road back to Tyrne, riding in the darkness with relative ease. If he could say nothing else for Pathra, he could agree that his dead cousin had managed to keep the roads well tended.

Laister asked, "The situation has been handled?"

Losla nodded his head, looking away from the road ahead long enough to eye the surrounding area for possible bandits. They rode at night and that meant a certain element of danger.

"They are good at what they do. Your cousin will be dead soon enough."

Laister shook his head. "Pity. I always rather liked Nachia. I just don't see her as the sort who should run an Empire."

"She's a lovely girl. I made them promise she'll feel no pain."

"Poison?"

"Likely. Their leader is a man I've dealt with before. He does excellent work."

"Have you had a lot of people poisoned before, Losla?" He already knew the answer, of course. The man had worked for him for over fifteen years.

"Me? Hardly. I'm just a facilitator. All I do is answer correspondences and occasionally make certain appointments are kept."

"Must be hard work."

Losla smiled. "My employer can be demanding from time to time, but he pays well enough."

Laister snorted. Losla was paid handsomely indeed. He kept his mouth closed and he handled everything Laister did not want to handle. For that reason he was worth every coin he earned.

"When will it happen?"

"Your cousin has been very good about letting herself be seen. Probably the next time she goes out in public." The light from the tavern grew brighter, highlighting the side of Losla's face and the back of his head.

Laister looked, wondering for a moment if the hired cutthroats had decided the offer of coin would be better handled as a reward for turning in the men who planned to kill the Empress. Stranger things had happened, true enough, but neither Laister nor Losla were foolish about these things. They were wise enough not to pay much in advance, only enough to whet appetites.

There were no lanterns following them, nor men on horses charging to find the traitors. Instead, the tavern was burning, the roof of the place fully aflame and lighting the night sky.

"Gods, man, what happened?" Laister's words were out before he even thought about it.

Losla looked over his shoulder and frowned. "Perhaps they decided it best not to leave witnesses. Dead tongues cannot tell secrets."

Laister nodded his head. Sometimes innocent people had to die in order to accomplish goals. He did not have to like it, merely to accept the fact of it. He'd always liked Nachia well enough. She was one of his favorite relatives, but she stood in the way and had to be removed as an obstacle. The burning tavern merely proved a proper reminder of that fact.

As he looked back toward the road, the roof of the Adze and Axe collapsed in on itself with a faint groan, and a gout of fire danced toward the Great Star.

Without another word, the men moved toward home. The ride would be a long one and the night would hide their secrets.

Swech shook her head and took the closest horse. She did not like the animals, but she could ride them well enough. Her body knew how, just as it understood the secrets of the face she hid behind.

She had listened to the fools whispering their plans of murder and waited until the men paying them left the tavern and then she had done as Paedle told her she must. The mercenaries died as they lived, choking on the poisons she slipped onto their drinks and food.

The tavern keeper looked at the dying men and opened his mouth to scream. Swech ran her blade across his throat before he could make a noise and then buried the same knife in his wife's heart. The other woman was heavy and dropped with a thump. The last two men had been sleeping, but at the sound of the tavern keepers' bodies hitting the floorboards of the place they awoke.

Swech broke their necks as quickly as she could and then started away from the tavern.

When she heard the sounds of someone above her whispering, she merely shook her head and carefully climbed the stairs. There were four rooms. Two of them were empty. One of the occupied rooms held a sleeping man who kept one hand on his sword. His death was fast enough to prevent him drawing the blade from its scabbard. The last room held the whisperers: two lovers who knew nothing of the murders below and merely spoke softly to each other.

They died as one, the borrowed sword cutting through both hearts in one stroke.

After that, setting the fire took only a moment.

Sometimes the best way to win a war required the deaths of thousands of soldiers. Other occasions required the deaths of innocents who knew nothing of the war. Whatever the case, Swech was ready to do what was required of her to show her gods that she was loyal and worthy of their trust.

For the present time the Daxar Taalor wanted Nachia Krous kept safe.

Swech would see to it as surely as she had seen to the death of the previous Emperor.

"That's just the problem. *Nothing* was supposed to be out there." Jeron gestured at the old maps, which had likely been hanging in his walls for longer than he could remember, and then at the new maps, copies carefully drawn out and given to him only a few days earlier by Goriah herself. The main difference was simply that a large portion of the area left blank previously had been expanded as a result of meeting the Sa'ba Taalor.

Goriah shrugged. "Well, we now know differently. Now we need to know what is out there and you're one of the very best at scrying. Desh needs you to do this."

"First Desh needs my knowledge of history and now he needs me to scry."

Goriah let out a low chuckle. "You're the one constantly telling me and the Sisters that you are a man of many talents. Though to be fair you normally tell us separately."

The man had the decency to blush a bit as he smiled. "You win. I'll make an effort."

"We need to know what's north of the range as well. We need to know whatever you can find."

"If it were easy we'd have mapped the entire thing out centuries ago."

"If it were easy, Jeron, Desh would have asked a lesser sorcerer to handle the task." A little flattery often went a very long way; a lesson Goriah had learned a lifetime earlier.

"Several of us, those adept at the Sooth, believe there are dangers in Tyrne."

Goriah nodded. Desh believes so, too. Right now he's actually gone out to investigate the possible causes."

"He actually left the Summer Palace?" Jeron leaned back in his chair and crossed his arms. "I thought the walls there too jealous to ever let him escape."

Several of the others, who had been remarkably quiet during the exchange, added their laughter to Goriah's. Most of them knew Desh Krohan well enough to understand how seldom he left the side of the ruler.

"Given the gravity of the situation, Desh is making an exception." Her smile quickly hardened into a sterner expression. "Still, we must do what we can here to prepare for the challenges coming our way. If they do listen and do leave Tyrne, a great number of people will come this way." She shook her head. "Most of them, really. We need to start preparations for taking in, well, thousands and thousands of people."

"This is called the City of Wonders for a reason, Goriah, as well you know."

"Of course."

She had not been alive then, though both Jeron and Desh Krohan had. Still, she'd heard the stories. Disasters happen. They are inevitable. Great storms batter shorelines, the earth itself shrugs and the land changes shape. Old Canhoon, the original and still formal capital of the Empire, ran across a disaster once upon a time. The earthquake caused a rip in the ground and a portion of the city had fallen away into that unexpected chasm before the land closed shut around it. No one was certain exactly how many were lost, but the number was well above a thousand. Foolish people made their share of mistakes along the way and fires blossomed in the rest of the city.

Canhoon trembled and burned, many of the structures collapsed, burying still more people. Back in those days the people of the Empire had tried raising a city that towered all the way to the clouds. After the Great Cataclysm, Canhoon was the largest city in the known world, second only to the memory of Korwa.

The city was old, but the Empire was new. The wounds on the face of the world were still fresh and sometimes bleeding and the nations around the Fellein Empire still fought against the notion that one ruler could make the world a better place. Kings had sent armies to break the crown and sunder the Empire. They'd have succeeded, too, if not for the wizards.

The Empress, she could not remember which one of the Krouses it was, had demanded the help of the sorcerers. In exchange for that assistance, Desh Krohan had demanded the title of First Advisor, a role he had already been handling but without any formal compensation or recognition. The Empress agreed.

Desh Krohan, Jeron and their peers had been the ones who'd stopped the fires and reclaimed the land. The City of Wonders had risen from the flames and ashes, from the desolation of most of the city. The buildings had grown forth from the ground. The streets paved themselves. The great walls that still stood today had been raised in a moment, and the Silent Army had stood against any who dared attempt an attack.

The Silent Army was long gone to dust, but their sacrifices held a nation together, as surely as the sight of the City of Wonders rising from the flames and ruination had cowed many an attacker and brought out the fiercest determination from the people of Canhoon.

That had been a very long time ago, however, and there were not so many of the sorcerers left these days. The cost of raising Canhoon had been high indeed and few were willing to endure that sort of sacrifice twice in their lifetimes.

Jeron looked down at the table before him, his eyes lost in the memories of what had gone before. Goriah knew the look well enough. She saw the same expression on Desh's face when he thought no one was paying attention.

"Still, Jeron, perhaps it would be best if we did all we could before having to summon that sort of power again, yes?"

He chewed at his lip for a moment and nodded. "Indeed. Most decidedly. Let's see what can be done. I'll have Seshu and Corin look into it." He turned his head to the two he'd named. Seshu nodded her head and rose from her seat with a tight smile. Corin nodded but did not rise. He would go at his own speed and remarkably little would ever change that.

"So, while we're all together, have any of you ever heard of the Mounds?" Goriah pointed at the new map and the odd symbols marking the place the Sa'ba Taalor claimed was forbidden by their gods.

Seshu looked over her shoulder and stopped at the doorway. She'd just been ready to cross through. Like the rest, she stared at the point on the map of the Blasted Lands.

When Seshu spoke her voice was hesitant. "It's impossible to say for certain, of course, but by the map's size, I could guess that it is close to the center of the Blasted Lands. If that is the case, if that is true and the lands settled as quickly as Desh believes, these Mounds you speak of could be over the site of Korwa."

Goriah nodded. "Desh said something similar."

Jeron sighed. "Korwa was destroyed. We know that. The land itself was shattered. Nothing could have survived that sort of devastation."

Goriah looked to the man and then lowered her head. "You are the expert, Jeron. That's one of the reasons I was sent here, to check with you. If not Korwa, then what?"

"Who's to say? These Sa'ba Taalor have their own gods. Perhaps they have their own demons as well."

Corin spoke up, which was a rare enough event that Jeron actually flinched at the unexpected noise. "These gods of theirs. Has anyone spoken with the temples and churches here to see if there is any connection?"

Goriah shook her head.

"I've certainly not the time, but might I suggest that someone do that very thing? Gods have power." Jeron gestured with one hand in a sign that maybe they did and maybe they didn't. Contrary to his words. "That is the claim I've heard all my life at least. Perhaps it's time someone found out if there is truth to the claim."

"I'll mention it to Desh. He might have a few notions." Goriah smiled. "And I must be on my way. I have to find him and that's going to take a bit of time. Thank you, all of you. There's much too much happening of late to leave anyone comfortable."

Corin made a rude noise they all knew was his way of agreeing. The rest said their goodbyes.

"This place is horrid." Brolley Krous's voice was small. He stood only five feet away from Desh Krohan but from that distance he sounded almost like a child.

Desh turned back to look at the young man. "It is horrid. There were people here, Brolley. There was a town. And now?" He reached down and grabbed a handful of ruined earth. The black dust and ash mingled with the soil and he let it drift from his fingers. "Perhaps we will be fortunate and plants will grow here again someday."

There were ruins all around them. It had been a very long time since Desh had been to Roathes, but he doubted much had changed until recently. The houses were built to withstand rough storms and harsh gale-force winds. They should have taken anything thrown their way, but the fires had burned them down to skeletal remains.

"How did this happen?" Brolley shook his head and then brushed his thick hair back with his fingers. A trail of soot ran along his brow as a reminder of his actions.

"The Guntha Islands are gone, Brolley. They've been destroyed by that volcano. But that's not what did this." He pointed to the ground and the deep tracks that still showed in a few spots where the wind had not scoured them away. There were footprints, to be sure, human enough in size. There were also massive paw prints as well, treads with heavy claws that made deep impressions.

"The winds brought a lot of this ash, but they didn't bring these marks. Others have been here. Most likely the Sa'ba Taalor."

Brolley shook his head, and for a moment he seemed younger still, and then his face hardened back into a man's angered expression. "Haven't they done enough?"

"We've been preparing for war, Brolley. You know that. This is the first of many steps, I suspect. But we need proof."

"What more do we need?" The horror in the boy's voice pleased Desh, but he kept that fact to himself. Not that long ago, Brolley had been willing to get himself killed over a comment about the Sa'Ba Taalor. His actions had nearly led to a war by themselves. That had been the first step in the boy becoming a man. Apparently that particular transformation was continuing apace.

"A paw print that might be from a trained bear is not enough."

"Never seen a bear that size. Have you?"

"Oh, yes. They can be very large. Most of what you've seen have been cubs." He scowled. "Beastly habit, training bears to be pets. Never goes well." The fact that Brolley had once ranted and screamed for weeks about wanting a pet bear was not lost on Desh. Now and then he felt a need to remind the Imperial Family of their occasional lapses in judgment.

"Where are all the people, Desh?"

"Gone. I suspect a lot of them fled when the clouds came. We certainly saw enough on our way down here." Which was the truth. Nearly every town they'd passed had been inundated with families that had fled the ash and deadly winds from the ocean. A good number of the people travelling had suffered from deep, wet coughs and ragged breathing, a sign that they were suffered from inhaling too much of the poisonous fumes.

"Aye, we did. But not enough." Brolley shook his head. "Roathes was a large kingdom with a lot of people. Where would the rest have gone?"

"That's what we're examining here." Desh sighed. "If we are lucky we will discover that a lot of people fled to the south and east."

"And if we are not?"

"Then the Roathians have gone the way of the Guntha, and the lovely Lanaie is the Queen of a dead people." Brolley's brow grew stony indeed at that notion. He was as infatuated with Lanaie as Pathra had been, but not old enough to know it was merely infatuation. That was why he'd asked to come along on this journey, and why Desh had agreed. The others, the dozen soldiers standing in the distance, were there solely to appease Nachia's need to protect her loved ones.

"Barbarians." Brolley's lip curled in disgust.

"Barbarians? Hardly. They've lived in an area where few could hope to survive. The Sa'ba Taalor are violent, yes, but not barbarians. Warriors. Survivors. And currently they are our enemies, if I am right."

Brolley said nothing to that. Instead he stared out at the black waters and the black sky.

Desh shook his head. The air smelled of sulfur and worse, and the breeze from the waters was hotter than it should have been. That damned mountain growing in the distance was the culprit, of course.

"We have to move on."

"No. I think we have our evidence." Brolley sounded very sure of himself, sure enough that Desh turned to see what he was speaking about.

The woman stood exactly two arm lengths away from the Empress's brother, her arms at her sides, within easy reach of her weapons.

Desh Krohan had not heard her approaching, had not seen her, and for him that was a very rare thing indeed.

That she was Sa'ba Taalor was a given. Her skin would have given her away, the light gray color of it, so close to the ash that painted the ground. Her attire would have given her away as easily: the leather pants, the vest, the insane number of knives. The veil over her face. The eyes that glowed even in the light of the sun.

"You are the wizard, Desh Krohan." It wasn't a question.

Desh nodded his head and wondered if his cloak would stop whatever the woman intended to throw his way.

"This is for you." She tossed a metal tube at his feet. The dust kicked up when it landed. He watched the object as it rolled to a stop at the edge of his robe and when he looked back up the woman stood directly behind Brolley. "Read it. I will be here waiting for your response."

He nodded his head silently and lifted the container. He wasn't at all worried about poison or being attacked. If they'd wanted him dead he would have already achieved that state. The fact that the woman – by her stature he guessed "child" more accurate; she was likely no older that Brolley – had virtually manifested from nowhere made it clear that she could have killed him at any point. Even now the soldiers in the distance were just realizing that there was a problem. He could hear their cries of shock.

Desh held up a hand to warn them against any foolish actions. Despite their surprise, they listened. He could see the man in charge – damned if he could remember a name – pacing like a caged animal. No one liked to be caught completely unaware.

Desh read the scroll inside quickly. The note was five simple words: Do You Wish To Parley?

"Yes. Yes we do."

The girl nodded. He'd seen her before, he was sure of it. "When?"

"Choose a time and a place. We will meet for the parley." He kept his voice as calm as he could manage. "What happened to the people in this town?"

"King Tuskandru was attacked by your soldiers." Her voice was calm. "The Council of Kings felt a message needed to be delivered."

"I would imagine I'd have been just as happy with a note on the subject." He tossed the tube back to the ground to make his point.

The girl nodded. "Some messages need to be made more clearly."

"When and where do your kings wish to arrange a parley?"

"What your people call the Temmis Pass will do. Ten days from now, when the sun rises."

"How many people from each side?"

The girl tilted her head, considering. "As many as you like. This will be a discussion of peace."

Desh's eyes looked around a second time, trying to understand how the girl had seemingly manifested from nowhere. It took a moment, but finally he saw the marks in the ash-painted sand. "What if we had attacked you instead of agreeing to parley? What then?"

"I would have lived or I would have died and the Daxar Taalor would have had their answer either way." She slid back from Brolley, who, to his credit, did not try to reach for his sword. Desh had half expected the boy to try to defend his honor.

"Ten days from now. Until then we are at a peace?"

"Until then." She spread her hands out from her sides and bowed in formal accord.

Desh returned the bow.

A moment later she turned and walked away, heading toward the Blasted Lands. It would take her longer than ten days to get home and that in and of itself told him more than he had known before.

One of the soldiers looked as if he might go after her, but the commander said something from too far away for Desh to hear and the fool stopped. Good. That was good. He had no particular desire to kill a soldier who was only trying to do his duty.

Brolley took a step toward him and then shivered as quietly as he could. "By the gods where did she come from?"

Desh pointed to the marks in the soil. "She was waiting here."

"What?"

"She was waiting here. Waiting for us or for someone else, I'm not completely certain. But she was waiting. She rested under the sand."

Brolley walked over to the indent and shook his head, his face showing clearly his surprise at the notion. "For how long?"

"Who can say? Long enough to surprise us and we've been here for a few hours."

Brolley looked after the retreating figure. "Jost. I think her name is Jost."

"You're right. I couldn't think of her name to save my life."

"So they want peace?"

Desh looked at the Empress's brother and shook his head. "It's hard to say what they want. Peace? Possibly. Or they might be hoping to find us in a vulnerable position and attack then."

"Who will handle the parley?"

"That is for your sister to decide. And Merros Dulver as well."

Neither of the men said much more as they headed for their horses. They had the answer to what had happened in Roathes. They had all the answer they needed for the moment.

And they had new questions.

"What will happen in the meantime, Desh?"

Desh Krohan looked out at the bleak sea of ash and dead fish and shook his head. "I have hopes to accomplish several impossible tasks."

Danaher spread out before the Pilgrim, a collection of towns that had grown into one city over the course of centuries. The last time he had been in the area, the towns that had become a city had been little more than villages. Times had changed and for the better it seemed.

Still, looks could be deceiving.

He walked into Danaher without event, and only a few people noticed him at all. He had changed his clothes since awakening and his flesh had taken on a more healthy color.

Little remained of the towns he knew from long ago. Certain buildings, the way roads cut between two hills here or there. Mostly nothing was the same, but there were always exceptions. Near the lake's edge a rough wall – Danaher's Wall, actually, where the great man had first settled the area and decided to raise his family – ran for a quarter of a mile, holding back the earth that had, in distant times, been soft and prone to collapse. The roots of trees had long since hardened the earth's grip and the tendency to slough away was a thing of the past, but the wall remained, mostly intact. The Pilgrim walked the length of the wall and occasionally let his fingertips trace the rough stone. He followed the length of Danaher's wall to the temple of Plith. The path was clear of weeds and the stones placed for walking the length were worn from generations of feet.

Plith was the God of the Harvest, who aided the farmers in their efforts and, in her wilder days, had also been known to drive men wild with lust. In those times, she'd been portrayed as a beautiful woman with harsh features and vast antlers. The statue he saw of her now was a different thing entirely. There was a statue of a woman covered in vines instead of the lusty figure he recalled so well. He suspected there were changes in more than the way she was portrayed.

He would find out soon enough.

There were many people who spent lifetimes seeking to better understand the gods and those who wished answers often went to the priests and priestesses to get them. That was exactly what the Pilgrim did.

The temple itself was in fair shape. The original building had been expanded several times to make room for more worshippers, as was to be expected when a small personal temple became the center for something larger and far more formal.

Danaher had been a good man. He had also been an excellent leader of men. The temple was only one of his legacies.

The interior of the temple was clean and warm, inviting, as it should have been. Plith was not an angry god, but a generous one. Did she not offer of herself to strangers? Did she not help make the most meager of crops enough to allow a family to thrive? Had she not offered herself to the people of this region?

His presence did not go unnoticed. The man who approached him was smiling as he stepped toward the Pilgrim. "Welcome. Well met." The man held his hands together, cupped as if to accept water from a fountain. Puzzled by the gesture, the Pilgrim nonetheless returned it.

"How can we help you, my son?" The priest's voice was warm and soft. His eyes shone wetly in the well-lit temple.

"I would speak with Plith." The Pilgrim bowed his head in the old ways, showing his respect.

The priest's face worked in a strange way. "She is not here, of course."

"Where else would she be?"

"Well, Plith is among the stars with the other gods, looking down upon us all."

The Pilgrim's mouth cut into a harsh line. "Where in all the teachings does it say that Plith resides among the stars?"

Again the man seemed puzzled by his words, as if the Pilgrim was speaking in a language that seemed almost like one that made sense, but only sounded close to right.

"It is common knowledge."

The Pilgrim closed his eyes for a moment and then opened them after waiting for patience in the darkness of his head. "No. It is not. 'Plith may be found in her temples and in the great woods and in the fields when the harvest time has come.' This is her temple and I would speak with Plith."

"Plith resides among the stars, with the other gods. There is nothing that I can do to make her show herself in this place if she is not already here."

The Pilgrim took a deep breath and exhaled slowly. "Then you are not a priest of Plith and you should not be here."

"I am a priest of Plith, my son. I am the First Priest of Plith. The teachings of Fornuto and Polemea reside within this temple." The priest's voice had taken on an edge and his eyes looked past the Pilgrim, seeking, perhaps someone to assist him.

"Fornuto was second to Treidin and Polemea was a follower of Tyrea, not of Plith."

"You are mistaken, my son." The priest now spoke with a definite edge to his tone.

"No. I am not." The Pilgrim's hand lashed out, striking the priest in the throat. The priest staggered back and hit the wall, coughing, trying to understand exactly what had happened, his hands probing the damage.

The Pilgrim walked forward and held the priest's shoulders, looking into the man's panicked eyes.

"I would speak with Plith. Now."

From so very far away, he heard the voice of Plith. It was a faint sound, barely above a whisper as it came from the mouth of the priest.

The Pilgrim listened as best he could to the voice that should have been so very much clearer.

This was the first of his gods whom he sought to speak with. Plith would not be the last.

ELEVEN

After weeks of living on little more than scraps and dried goods, the feast was amazing. The meals he'd enjoyed in the palace in Tyrne had been extravagant, but they had also been terrifying things, with endless runs of cutlery and odd bowls and goblets for almost everything. True, most of the Sa'ba Taalor had ignored those sundry items, but Andover hadn't felt quite like he could, and so he spent most of each meal with others trying to imitate what item should be used with which bite of his meals.

This was different. There was a great deal of fresh food – roasted meats, vegetables, raw and cooked alike, and several different breads – and the only rule seemed to be to eat until you could barely move.

Andover had no problem with that notion. He ate a great deal and enjoyed every mouthful.

And when it was done there was only one speech. King Tuskandru stood where he had been sitting and raised one hand for silence. When most of the people were paying attention, he simply said, "The gods are generous today. Eat and celebrate that generosity." Had he not known better, Andover would have thought that the most rousing speech he'd ever heard by the way the people around him reacted. They roared approval and stomped their feet and drank their wine. And through it all Andover enjoyed his food with the gusto of a condemned man. He drank three glasses of the sweet wine he was offered and leaned back against a stone that had obviously been set where it was for the purpose of leaning against. There was no furniture, as such, but there were many spots like the one where he found himself, where one could settle against the stone and enjoy the view.

The air had cooled substantially, but he wrapped himself in his cloak. He looked at the stars above through their thin veil of clouds and down into the valley below. A good ways off, he could once again see the lights that burned near the lake. There were more than there had been before. A lot more. Enough to make him wonder if there was a city down there that he had somehow missed before.

Delil sat down beside him, sort of falling into a cross-legged puddle of mellow intoxication. "You should be celebrating more, Andover Lashk." She considered him for a moment and then took a drink from her flask, moving her veil out of the way and once again revealing a hint of a strong chin and jaw line.

"I've eaten nearly my own weight in food, and I'm drunk." He waved a hand in her direction and smiled. She was a welcome sight after being surrounded by strangers for the last few hours. Drask had already left, waving one time before he climbed on his mount and the beast charged down the steep slope to the pass. Bromt – never the most talkative of souls – had found a group of friends and gotten first drunk, and then rowdy. He wasn't quite sure how it had turned out but the last he'd seen of the man there had been a fight and at least one of the participants had been bleeding rather badly. Tusk was... well, Tusk was Tusk. That was all there was to it. And most of the others looked at Andover as a curiosity. A few spoke to him and a few did not.

He pointed to a man with only one arm and leaned toward Delil. "Why does he not have a metal hand like mine?"

Delil looked back at him and then touched his hand, her thumb caressing in circles over the palm, while her fingers wrapped into his. "The Daxar Taalor do not merely give away replacements. If they, did most of the people in this valley would be covered with metal. Metal skin, metal eyes, metal ears and noses." Her voice was low and soft and calm and soothed him. "Your hands are a blessing from Truska-Pren, who decided for whatever reason that you should be blessed. You are an exception. You were given your hands and then told to earn them. Most times, if someone wishes a replacement for what they have lost, they must prove their worth. If they are worthy they will receive the blessings of the gods."

For a moment he considered his hands and then thought how odd a man would surely look with an iron ear. "They can replace ears?"

Delil laughed. "I suppose they could though I have never seen a metal ear on the side of a head. Mostly if a replacement is made it is for a hand or a leg. On a few occasions I have heard of faces being replaced."

"Faces?" He looked at her and his vision swam for a moment. He would not have any more wine. He had learned a long time ago that too much would leave him hating his existence the next morning. There was also the chance that he would say something foolish and get himself killed, so best to stop before his tongue talked without his consent.

"One of the Kings in Lead once had most of her face destroyed in a battle. She won the fight, but it cost her dearly. Wheklam granted her a new face. She was fearsome in combat."

"No doubt." He nodded his head and then closed his eyes for a moment. The world finally stopped wobbling. "I'm to meet a god tomorrow, Delil." His voice was tiny when he spoke.

"That is why you should be celebrating, Andover Lashk. It is a great honor to meet one of the Daxar Taalor."

"What does one say to a god? How does one behave?"

"You answer the questions of the god. You behave with respect." She paused a moment. "Treat the gods as you would treat your parents. With respect and the knowledge that they can punish you and there is nothing you can do to stop that punishment."

"So it's all right that I'm scared?"

Her laugh came again and she nodded. He watched the way her hair curled and bounced along with her nodding face. "It is probably best to be scared. But I would also try not to let it show too much."

"All I know is that I'm supposed to climb up there," he waved in the direction of the top of the mountain, which seemed roughly half the distance to the Great Star from where they were. "And then I am supposed to present myself to Durhallem and offer my thanks."

She nodded. "Every person you see here has done the same. All but the children. They have not yet earned the right to see the faces of the gods."

"Have I earned the right?" He wasn't sure, and that was a large portion of his doubt.

"No. And yes." She shrugged. "You have not done all that most have to do to be presented to the gods. But you are also not from here and born of the Sa'ba Taalor. You are an exception that was made by the gods for the reasons they deem necessary. If you were not worthy, you would not be given the chance."

"What did you do to earn the right?"

Delil rolled her head to the side and considered him for a moment. Her eyes looked at his face and then at his body, her thumb continued to massage the palm of his hand. "I have lived and learned as the Daxar Taalor have asked, Andover. They told me to learn their ways and I did."

"What happens to those who fail, Delil?"

"Are you afraid of failing, Andover?" She had not answered his question. He only realized that much later. As with the lessons she had taught him, when she defended against his mad swings with his hammer or with his fists, she managed to evade and avoid rather than risk being hit.

"I am very afraid, yes."

She moved, and a moment later Delil was on top of him, her weight settled in his lap, her eyes looking into his, her hands holding both of his, fingers intertwined and palms pressed together.

Her lips pressed to his ear, the thin fabric of the veil tickling as she spoke softly. "So I will give you other things to think about for this night." He had no doubt at all what she was speaking of. He had never been with a woman, had never so much as kissed a girl, though he had often dreamed of the notion.

Somehow they rose from the ground. Somehow they found a private area, in the shadows, away from the celebrating crowds.

After that there was pleasure, and a little pain. There were awkward gropings and eventually there were matched motions and the most amazing, wondrous heat to counter the night's chill.

He did not think of Tega. He thought only of the woman he was with as his lips and fingers traced the scars on her flesh. He studied her as much as she would allow, knowing he could have spent an eternity learning the secrets of her form.

Andover was glad he had only had three cups of wine. More and he would not have remembered as much as he did of that night, and he never wanted to forget a moment of it as long as he lived.

Tega stood in the relative calm and looked at the area around them in wonder.

They'd made the Mounds with almost no additional troubles, but had decided to wait until after the latest storm before trying to find access to the frozen towers. It was a wise choice as just after the sun set and brought an even greater darkness, the weather soured and grew violent again.

The ground was locked under a sheath of ice. Opening the doors of the wagon had been a challenge and had involved the men using a wood axe to shatter the ice layers around the entrance before she could finally be freed.

The spokes of the wagon wheels were under so much ice that there were no longer any spaces between them. The entire wheel was coated in ice an inch thick.

Only a few feet away, the tent that the men had slept in was surrounded by a much thinner crust of frozen precipitation, but long sheets and shattered trails of the stuff lay all around it: signs that they'd been busy clearing the ice through the night.

For the moment, the storms were done, but they lost time getting free from the worst remains of their last encounter.

All of which paled when she considered the structures before them.

The Mounds.

They were not mountains, to be sure, but the spires and odd growths that thrust from the ground were monstrous in scale and even hidden they were unsettling.

They were layered by ice as well, but the thickness was far more than an inch. The Mounds were buried within ice and dirt and ash that had accumulated to a depth Tega doubted could be cleared by a single axe. More likely the blade would break before the frozen caul yielded.

Darus Leeds looked at her and kicked at the ice. "How are we supposed to get past this?"

Tega looked back at him and shook her head. "I'll see what I can do."

"What you can do?" He was frowning as he said it.

"I'm the apprentice to Desh Krohan. I have been taught a few things."

The man's eyes grew wide as she spoke. He'd forgotten why she was there, apparently.

Tega climbed back into her trailer with a sigh and closed the door. Beyond it, she heard Darus talking to the other men. "Where is she going? We have to figure this out."

One of them responded, "She has her ways. We have ours. Grab your axes, or a pick if you brought one. Does that sound right to you, Vonders?"

Vonders replied, "The gods of fortune are with you, my fellows. I happen to have several fine tools for just such purposes."

His words were met with grumbles. Tega allowed herself a smile and went in to get her supplies.

She could not leave. That would be foolish this far into the search, but she could consult with Desh or one of the Sisters. She sorted through her supplies for the right ingredients and then set about making her preparations.

Ten minutes later Tega fell back on her cot and closed her eyes. Moments after that, she was where she needed to be.

Desh!

The man looked at her and smiled, held out an arm for her to land on his wrist. He was not in the castle, but riding slowly along a well paved road, Brolley Krous next to him. Brolley seemed rather surprised to see her. He should have been. Not every day that a storm crow settled on the wrist of a wizard.

"What are you doing here?" Desh's voice was warm and he had a smile on his face.

She told him quickly of the Mounds, her eye locked on his to let him understand her words. She could not speak, of course, as she was not truly there. She was back in the camp and resting on her cot.

"Well, I certainly can't come to you right now, Tega. I'm afraid it'll have to be you. But if you think you're up to the task I have little doubt you can manage it. Just be careful. And prepare yourself. You'll be very tired when it's done."

She bobbed her head up and down a few times. The feeling was perfectly natural, as natural as the feathers on her wings and the claws at the ends of her talons.

I'll do my best, Desh.

"Do better than that. You have the knowledge and the skills. You just have to be patient. Don't rush." He paused a moment and then, "Have they been behaving themselves?"

Perfect gentlemen the lot of them.

"You are a bad liar. If they misbehave too much, call on me and I will resolve the matter."

She bobbed her head one more time and then launched herself into the air, her wings flapping madly to get the altitude she needed.

The bird went left, her mind went right. A few moments later she was opening her eyes and back in the cot, the cold seeping through to her bones.

She climbed from the wagon and looked to where the men had been hacking at the ice. They had cleared a surprising amount, but the ice must have been nearly as hard as steel, by the way they were attacking it.

Tega took a few deep breaths. "You should rest yourselves for a few minutes."

Nolan March looked at her for a moment, his dark eyes regarding her. He was a fine looking man, but the way he looked at her was not what she expected. Most men tended to examine her physique and went out of their way to smile for her. He did not seem to care.

Finally he nodded and stepped back, gesturing for the others to do the same. They did not take much convincing.

Tega walked over to the spot where they had been digging. The ground here was not jagged and rough but unsettlingly smooth. The ice layer had been hacked and brutalized and shattered by their work, but the surface below that murky layer had a look that was both organic and almost deliberate. Once, long and ago, the ground here had been boiling with heat and the spot where they chose to dig looked as if it might have hidden depths. She could see a darkness that ran low and deep into the earth there.

A tunnel, perhaps, or merely a pocket where air escaped as the ground here re-solidified millennia ago. Whatever the case, it seemed a good spot to try digging. If it was an entrance into the area forbidden by the Daxar Taalor all the better, but at the very least it might be a shelter for them should another storm come.

"You chose an excellent spot."

Vonders Orly nodded his thanks. "The only spot that looked like a possibility. Most of the other areas are too... jagged."

She nodded. There was little doubt in her mind that the man had looked around. His eyes were constantly scanning the ground and seeking, always seeking. His family was familiar with the Blasted Lands, had scavenged there before. She had already seen him seeking whatever might be close to the surface for him to claim, though so far with no appreciable luck.

"I would ask you to all stand back; I'm going to try to clear a bit of this away."

They did not hesitate to listen.

Tega eyed the area carefully and assessed the weakest spots and the areas most likely to collapse. Not the earth itself, hopefully, but the ice that surrounded the different structures. None of them were clear enough to make out. They were shadows within the ice, and even looking closely offered little but hints and vague possibilities. The ice was the issue in any event. Ice as thick as what she was dealing with might not respond to her attempts, or it might fall away in fragments large enough to break bones if it fell in the wrong area.

In the distance the horses let out several noises and Tega hesitated as the men looked first at the tent where the animals were sheltered and then to each other.

Maun spoke to the others in his soft voice and Nolan, Darus and Tolpen went to examine the situation. A moment later Tolpen called out and the rest ran to join them.

Tega let her curiosity win over for the moment and turned toward the sounds of the horses and the men alike. There was another noise, but not one that she immediately recognized.

It was inevitable that their luck, such as it had been, could not hold. They had managed a great distance without any encounters with the denizens of the Blasted Lands, but now she could see the Pra-Moresh as it came closer and the horses were not at all pleased with the creature's approach. It was only one, but it came in a stampeding rage, and even as she watched, the creature swept a paw in an arc and tore away half a mare's ribcage. The animal shrieked as it died and the Pra-Moresh greedily tore at into the flesh, unconcerned about whatever or whomever might approach.

The other horses reared and bucked and pulled at their restraints. Three of the leads holding them to the wagon's side snapped and the horses bolted, sliding on the ice, falling over themselves in an effort to escape the beast.

Tolpen Hart cursed and ran for the tent, ignoring the horses as they escaped. Darus and Nolan tried to recapture the animals, knowing that without them they might well be doomed in the wilds.

By the time the two of them had reached the wagon, the rest of the horses had broken free and the Pra-Moresh was looking up from its feast, blood painting the heavy muzzle a startling shade of red against the grey and black fur.

It screamed and laughed and whined as it looked toward them and reared up on its hind legs. By the gods, it was a massive thing, easily twice the height of a man.

Tolpen came from the tent with his bow at the ready and an arrow drawn back. He took careful aim and fired and the missile skidded across the monster's face, not even breaking the hide.

But it got the beast's attention. It looked toward the archer and roared. Tolpen was a hunter. He knew how to handle his weapon and he took the time to draw another arrow and aim as the beast charged. Nolan managed to get out of the way even as he pulled his axe. Darus was not as fast and was slapped aside as easily as a leaf. The poor man bounced across the ground. Even from her distance she could hear his grunts of pain.

Maun approached along with the other escort who'd been with her since the beginning of her quest. Both of them carried short spears and looked at the creature intently, even as it bore down on Tolpen.

Tolpen stood his ground and fired. He this time did better. The arrow drove into the open mouth of the Pra-

Moresh and then through the soft side of the creature's cheek. It reared up and roared-screamed-wept again, shaking its face as if to make the pain sail away as easily as Darus had.

While it was busy, Nolan came up from behind and brought his axe around in a hard swing at the beast's legs. Tega took a deep breath and let it out as the thing yelped and turned and swept both of its paws at Nolan. The man managed to duck away, but fell on the ice as he did so. He was surely as good as dead, might have died right then, but Maun and Stradly threw their spears and hit the thing. One shaft sank into the creature's bare abdomen and the other caught it in the shoulder. It turned to them and limped forward as it fell to all fours. The spear wobbled in its shoulder and it moved that limb with less strength, but still it charged. Blood fell from its hind side, but still it came at a frightening speed.

They were not prepared; it was as simple as that. The men had been trained to fight men, not monsters and the Pra-Moresh did not stop. It came for Maun and Stradly and they drew weapons and held their ground though she could see how desperately they wanted to flee.

Maun and Stradly were in front of Tega when it came for them. The thing looked so big already but grew at a horrible, sickening pace as it lumbered closer.

Tega concentrated and made herself remain as calm as she could. It was not easy. Calm went against her nature at that moment. What she wanted was to run from the unholy thing coming at her.

She said no words. They were not necessary. Instead she summoned the energies she had been studying for several years and forced her will upon the world.

And the world responded with a roar.

The Pra-Moresh exploded. Flesh and bone and fur and gristle went in every direction. The ground beneath the thing bulged and rippled and snapped in a violent wave, and Maun and Stradly, who were standing closest to the Pra-Moresh, were hurled aside and bounced and skittered as they tried to recover from the unexpected force.

The sound of the magic was as terrifying as the sight. The air roared with a force like thunder, loud enough to nearly deafen Tega. The air whipped from the center of the explosion and a few seconds later the remains of the thing rained down across the terrain.

She stared in horror, knowing full well that she had done that.

Past the ringing in her ears she heard the others calling out, looking around and trying to take in all that had happened. Maun lay on the ground, holding his stomach and grimacing. Stradly crawled over to him, looking at the spreading red stain on Maun's belly. Nolan March walked toward them, barely even aware of the axe he dragged behind him, and Darus tried to sit up. Tried and failed. She could just make out the sound of his moan.

Nolan turned to the other soldier and started looking· him over. Tolpen came closer, moving with extreme care, his eyes wide and worried. He did not understand what had happened, but only that the Pra-Moresh was gone in a wave of gore and violence.

Vonders understood well enough. He came up behind her and looked at her with horror in his eyes. "What did you do, girl?"

"I stopped it. It was going to kill them."

Before she could say more the ground beneath them roared. The air above them followed suit a moment later and the sound was so loud that thinking became impossible. It was all she could do not to simply fall down and scream. Heavy vibrations rattled her eyes in their sockets, her teeth in her gums and the flesh on her bones. Beside her, Vonders did fall down, howling into a noise that made his anguish silent.

They had heard the roar of the Mounds before, but always from a distance, from as much as a day's travel away. Now the sound came around them and shook the world. The ice that they had spent time trying to hack through shattered, in some cases falling away and in others sticking doggedly to the surfaces where it had adhered for who knew how long.

Tega turned in every direction trying to understand the nature of the noise, the source of the cacophony that dominated her senses and her ability to think. There was no one thing that she could see; there was only the sound.

And then the noise ended and she could breathe again and the pain faded to a tolerable level.

Vonders looked up from where he was laying on the ground, his eyes wider than before and a pained expression on his face. He was not injured, that she could see, but likely just overwhelmed. Aside from storms there had been nothing in their time traveling across the Blasted Lands and now all of this in only moments.

Within a few minutes they were assessing their situation. Darus had broken his left arm, and had several substantial bruises from being knocked out of the Pra-Moresh's way. Additionally, his left leg was either sprained or broken. He could stand but he could barely walk at all.

Nolan was unharmed. Vonders was unscathed. Tolpen remained uninjured as well, though he was still extremely shaken. She did not think he'd been as prepared as he'd thought he would be for the actual sight of a Pra-Moresh. Certainly she had not been ready for it. Stradly Limm was bruised across one half of his body. His right side had been facing the monster when the explosion occurred and his skin on that side was mottled and looked as if he'd been struck with a hammer across every inch of flesh. He was able to walk. He was able to stand. He did not look as if he was able to think clearly and his speech was slurred.

Maun was the worst of them. She did not think he would live through his injuries. One of the Pra-Moresh's teeth, a massive thing as big as her hand, had been blown into his stomach by the explosion. And while she watched, Nolan and Volpers did their best to pull the bloodied thing from his insides without tearing him up any further.

For almost an hour they worked at sewing his insides back in place, neither of them speaking more than in single words, mostly communicating in gestures for one item or another from a small surgical kit.

Maun was a quiet man, but he screamed a great deal as they worked on mending him. Eventually he fainted from the work and the silence was almost worse.

The horses were gone.

Darus doubted they would return. There was nothing for them in the Blasted Lands and they likely had only stayed because they were well trained, but now that they had broken free there was little to make him believe they would come back to the area.

By the time they were done with the surgery and had recovered from the madness of the moment the sun had slithered its way down toward the west again. The darkness would come back soon and none of them were in a state to attempt the Mounds.

Ultimately Tega decided they needed warmth and safety more than anything else. Though it was cramped in the extreme, all of them slept in the wagon that night.

Maun was still alive in the morning. The work that Nolan and Volpers had done was clean and efficient. Tega checked the wounds herself and used what ingredients she had to make a poultice to keep the wound clean from infection and to aid in healing.

None of them said anything. None of them blamed her, but she blamed herself. She had lacked the proper control. She had failed to restrain the power she wielded and when she could stand it no more she apologized.

"I'm so sorry you were injured, Maun and you, Stradly. I did not mean to do that."

Stradly had recovered a great deal from his earlier shock. He shook his head and winced. "Sorry for saving us, then?"

"What?"

"We were there, Mistress Tega. We saw the thing coming. We was as good as dead. Nothing to be done for it but to watch that evil thing eat our guts out. You saved us."

Maun nodded and spoke more softly than usual. "Aye. Might have been a trifle rough in the saving, but that you did. Only a fool would think otherwise."

Nolan nodded his head. "You were a ways off. I know how large the thing looked to you, but from where we were it was a lot bigger."

Vonders nodded. "Seen the head of one of those in the Duke's palace once. And saw the corpse of one that died of old age I guess. We'd have taken it back for the possible prize, but it was too rotted and too heavy and we had enough salvage. The one we saw yesterday was bigger than either. I pray they don't make them any bigger."

Tega had no true response to their words but thanked them with a smile and a nod of her head.

"So." Nolan looked around at the group and then looked rather pointedly at the door to the wagon. "When do we go exploring. Or do we, with what's happened?"

Maun was the one who answered. "We go. We have to. We've given our word to the wizard and we are on a mission to help the Empire."

Tega looked at the man and studied him. "Yes. That's the truth of it. But we go tomorrow and not today. Today we recover and we prepare." She was exhausted. She had never used so much energy at once before and, though she was young in years, she felt nearly ancient after the effort involved.

Maun nodded his head. "Tomorrow then. That should be soon enough."

There was nothing more to say after that.

TWELVE

There was no time in the morning to consider the magnitude of his night with Delil. The sound of great horns blaring out in the open echoed into his sleeping chamber and Andover awoke with a groan, sitting up in the cot and wondering for just a moment where he was. He reached up to rub the sleep from his eyes and barely caught himself before disaster. His hands felt, yes, and they moved, yes, but they were still forged from iron and he had already learned the hard way that rubbing at his eyes could leave him in agony and half-blinded. That was the last thing he needed when he was on his way to meet a god.

Meet a god.

"Oh." It was the only sound he could make.

Andover rose from his bed and quickly dressed himself. The room was empty. Delil sat up and dressed just as quickly, not speaking at all. She made sure her veil was in place before she stood and then headed for the threshold of the entrance.

"I... Good luck." She left before he could respond. That was just as well, he could think of nothing to say that would not come out the wrong way. Women always confused his tongue and after this? Well, "thank you" hardly seemed the right words.

He ran his fingers through his hair – taking a few strands along with his gesture – and then slipped on his boots. A moment later he walked out into the bright morning sunlight and found Tusk and several others waiting for him. They were a terrifying lot and for one brief moment he feared that he'd offended them. Was Delil someone's daughter? Betrothed?

Tusk dismissed any possible worries and added new ones, instead. "Andover Lashk of the Iron Hands, it is time to meet Durhallem."

Andover nodded his head nervously and stepped closer.

"No one faces the Daxar Taalor except on their own." Tusk's voice was not unkind. "You must walk." He pointed toward the top of the mountain so very far above them.

Without another word, Andover walked, heading toward his first meeting with one of the gods of the Seven Forges.

The palace was an endless hive of activity most days. There were people moving about almost constantly. Between advisors, guards, soldiers who were being trained as guards, chancellors, representatives from different kingdoms that sought to see the head of the Empire and all of the souls who took care to make every detail of the work seem effortless, it would have appeared to many that the people living and working in the palace never slept.

That was not true in most cases, but just at the present it was accurate.

Desh Krohan came back to the palace and moved directly to the throne room, not bothering to head for his usual stop at his quarters or anywhere else. When he got there Nachia Krous was already waiting and in discussion with Merros Dulver. The general was going over the maps with the Empress, showing her in careful detail the layout of the land as best they knew it and the places where he thought it likely they could manage to find access to the Blasted Lands and thus the Seven Forges.

Desh took one look at the maps and sighed. "We should prepare for war, yes – we have been preparing for war – but I believe we have a few other matters to attend to first."

"Desh, how very nice to see you." Nachia's voice was deliberately too bright and cheerful.

The wizard shook his head. "The Sa'ba Taalor are offering us a chance to parley."

Merros seemed genuinely surprised. "Really?"

"One of them was waiting for us. Had likely been waiting for a few days by the time I arrived." He looked at both of them for a moment to see if they understood. They did not. "She was literally waiting in the ashes, buried in the ground a few inches down. I would have never seen her had she not made her presence known."

"Oh."

"Exactly. It was an offer of peace and a reminder that for them the notion of sneaking in and causing mayhem is a minor thing."

"She could have killed you then?" Nachia's voice was small.

Desh shook his head. "Not likely. I am better defended than most. But she certainly could have killed your brother."

Nachia did not respond except to shift on the throne.

"The point is this. We have a chance to argue for peace before this gets worse, yes, but we also have a chance to move forward with whatever you decide to do, Nachia. We also have a chance to leave this city before it is too late."

Merros shook his head. His lips pressed together. "A nightmare of efforts, Desh, especially if your predictions are wrong."

He turned on the general and pinned him hard with his gaze. "How many people live in this city, General Dulver?"

"I'm not really sure…"

"I am. I have studied the surveys and the figures provided by the revenuers. We have almost thirty thousand people in the city of Tyrne and the surrounding areas. This is an old city and it has had a long time to grow in size. The occupation of the Summer Palace year round has already bloated the city over the last fifteen years." He waved a hand to stop the protest of Nachia. "I'm not saying there was ever anything wrong with Pathra choosing to be here instead of in Canhoon. I'm saying that the city has grown well beyond where it should have."

"I can see that. I've already discussed the need to fortify the walls, possibly to build another wall around the outer areas." Merros's voice was as calm as ever. He did a remarkable job of hiding his agitation. He was a proper soldier.

"That's only one of my points of debate here. Building a new wall would take a great deal of time and money.

We have the finances, of course, but the time is a different story. The Sa'ba Taalor would parley with us in seven days."

"Seven days?" Nachia sat forward in the throne.

"Seven days," Desh nodded. And if we fail in the parley or if they decide to break their word and attack, that is only seven days' time in which to try to build a wall. We would fail."

Merros shook his head. "And even if we should fail, we don't plan on letting them come to Tyrne without preparations, without moving the armies into position."

"And what then, Merros?" Desh tried to keep his voice from rising in volume with limited success. "You said yourself our armies are not at their peak. What happens if they send four hundred of their best against the city? We have battalions ready and waiting, but they move between the proper ranks of footmen and horsemen and charge on past on those demons they ride and they attack anyone they see, armed or not. You said yourself that ten of them eliminated over a thousand people."

"Then what do you propose we do, Desh?" That was Nachia, who rose from the throne and began pacing. The seat was uncomfortable at the best of times. Her response was simply to stand and move about.

"The Sooth did not say that the Sa'ba Taalor would attack Tyrne. They said that Tyrne is a doomed place. We cannot stay here. We should evacuate the city and immediately at that. There's no proof of what will happen, but I have been in places where disaster fell. Look at the Guntha! Look at what remains of them. Look at what that very disaster did to Roathes. The entire area is abandoned. The country is gone, lost in ashes and smoke. Gods, it's as bad as the Blasted Lands…" His voice faded away on that last part.

"Desh, what it is?" Nachia's voice took on that maternal edge he sometimes heard in Pella's tones. No matter who it was, the tone annoyed him.

He bit back his distaste for her concern. "I have not been to the Blasted Lands in a very long time, but I might be on to something there. The Sa'ba Taalor would not have a problem living in Roathes. Not like most would. They are better suited for it."

"No one would willingly live in the Blasted Lands." Merros shook his head. "And as someone who has been there, I can say that with ease and know I am right."

"That's not what I'm saying, Merros. I'm saying that they could *live* there. There was no one else there. No one at all. Not that I saw at any rate. And I'm still trying to understand that, because Brolley and I agree that there weren't enough of the Roathians on the return trip. Unless they all went to the south and east, there should have been more.

"They wouldn't go to the south and east. They wouldn't be welcomed by the Louron and I can't see them even trying to survive in the swamps. The land there is too dangerous."

"What land?"

"Precisely my point. You either know the swamps in Louron or you sink. There aren't enough people there to work as guides and even if there were, there's no love lost between the two peoples."

"Then where did they go?" Nachia's voice was taking on a frustrated edge.

Merros shrugged. "The last we heard there were black ships coming in. After that, nothing. It's possible they're all dead or captured."

Nachia frowned and looked at Merros for clarification. "Captured?"

"The Empire has a few countries that deal with slaves. Who's to say the Sa'ba Taalor do not also deal with them?"

"Did you see any sign of slavery when you were in the Taalor Valley?"

"No. But I hardly saw all of the valley. I saw a small fraction and we were moving at a hard ride for most of that time. They are a secretive people. Just think about the veils and you can see that."

Desh shook his head. "The veils hide a deformity."

"What deformity?" Merros looked at him with a doubtful expression. In that moment Desh understood that somewhere along the way the general had been intimate with one of the people of the Seven Forges. He had no notion as to which of them and did not care, but he saw the near-dread in the man's expression.

"Nothing like what the plague winds do. More like some sort of scarring. Like what the Brellar do to themselves."

Merros's body relaxed a bit. He could understand that idea well enough.

"That's not the point here in any event. The concern is what happened to the Roathians."

"Well. Perhaps that's something that should be addressed at the parley, then." Nachia spoke up, looking from one man to the other. "We have a week to consider what to do about that. We also have less time to consider moving everyone from this town if Desh is right, and much as I hate the notion of leaving, I believe we should consider the source here and prepare to move locations."

Merros looked long and hard at the Empress and nodded his head. He had likely come to the same conclusion on his own. Desh wished he could have said something to remove the sting from the matter, but there was nothing he could say. The Sooth had never lied about anything, not on a deliberate level. They were sometimes confusing in what they said, but there was no doubt at all what they were about in this case.

They had to abandon Tyrne and soon.

Merros sighed. "And why will we tell people that we must abandon Tyrne?"

Nachia asked, "Did the Sooth say when this great event would take place?"

"No. Only that it would be soon."

"So why don't we start by ordering the palace prepared for winter? Let it be known that I have decided to move back to Canhoon. That should start a lot of things happening by itself."

"Do you think so?" Merros wasn't completely convinced.

"Not everyone will choose to leave, but a good number will. Tyrne is a city surrounded by farmlands and one river. The industry here is mostly centred upon the palace and the seat of the Empire being here. Much of it will leave when we leave and take the soldiers with us."

Desh stared at the table for a moment, not sure how to approach the subject. "It might not be enough. I was thinking we might use the situation in Roathes to our advantage. We might tell people that the desolation there is growing." He held up a hand to stop either from speaking and both looked ready to. "Not that it's an immediate threat but something that could become dangerous later. It might make those who are only considering the notion of leaving lean toward moving faster."

Nachia shook her head. "Might well start a stampede, too. Best to avoid those, I would think."

True enough.

Merros spoke up. "I think we should pull the army from the area. Move them toward Trecharch and the Wellish Steppes. Send them back toward Old Canhoon. Announce the move to the proper palace and watch what happens. I think you're right. A lot of people will move on as well. And then when we've started that action, then maybe we talk of growing desolation to move the rest of them."

"I thought we were already there." Darus's voice had taken on a plaintive tone. No one really blamed him. The way into the Mounds was hiding itself – if, in fact there actually was a way in.

The ice had thinned, though it was not gone. The last roaring vibration had shaken a great deal loose, and even after spending most of two days in the wagon or the tent, nothing had come along to make the ice grow back. Nor had anything come along to remove it, come to think of it.

Nolan had doubts about that opening and about the ability of the people with him to do anything with it. Tega seemed nice enough but she was not designed for rugged climbing. Darus was not likely to climb with a broken arm, Maun was doing poorly at best and the big

man had made a good start at a recovery, but his body
was still swollen and he moved like an old goat that had
once lived on the farm. That is to say: he moved, but not
well and not without a good deal of bleating. Stradly was
a good man. He had a fine sense of humor and he was
strong as a horse, but whatever Tega had done to destroy
that Pra-Moresh, it had left him wounded deep inside.

No, none of them would be climbing, and that was
a problem since as near as Nolan could tell, whatever
entrances there were to the actual Mounds were high
up in the ruins.

Every entrance they'd tried along the lower levels
of the odd place was more like an ice pit than a
possible entrance. They went nowhere. They promised
possibilities of caves and tunnels, but ultimately even the
deepest of them only allowed entrance to another wall
of impassable stone.

The only person having any luck that wasn't bad was
Vonders, who had already gathered many small trinkets
to sell when he returned home. He showed them to his
companions and marveled at each of them, regardless of
how insignificant.

That was hardly fair. There were likely many who
found the items amazing, but to Nolan they had no
special qualities. They were shiny rocks and nothing
more. Neither his mother nor his father had ever been
much for trinkets. He shared that sentiment.

"Up there. Look." Vonders pointed toward one of the
towering masses around them. Nolan squinted along the
length of the thing and studied the surface. It was, as
with everything else, coated in ice and dirt, but he could
see what the ruin hunter was looking at. There was a

large hole in the side, almost a hundred feet above them. That hole looked deep, and he doubted it was merely a pit started by the wind. If one listened carefully, a note came from it when the air shifted the right way.

The Mounds were bizarre. They did not stand like buildings or like trees. There was nothing right or normal about them. They jutted from the ground at odd angles and some of the shapes looked like rocks and others like half-melted beehives. Some were long and thin and others twisted into shapes that made his eyes ache. All of them had the following consistencies, however: they were immense, and what could be seen of their surfaces looked burned and melted.

They had spent a night talking of the creation of the Blasted Lands. There was little else to do while they tried to lick their wounds and waited for the sun to rise. Surely no one felt like getting drunk, even if there had been a good tavern about, and even the most amorous of the lot had trouble considering Tega as a lover after what she had done to that monster. She was a lovely girl to be sure, but anyone that could simply destroy a Pra-Moresh was to be considered very carefully and for a long time before being approached along those lines.

There were a dozen stories or more. Old empires fighting and soldiers dying by the thousands, and then the Great Cataclysm. That was it. No one knew much more. Until Merros Dulver, no one had managed to get far enough into the Blasted Lands to find out about the Mounds or to even see the Seven Forges from up close.

Nolan looked toward the distant mountain range. The sun was up, the sky was calmer than it often was, and though he could not actually see the mountains, he could just catch a glimmer of the red light that stained the distant clouds where they stood.

How far away were they? He could not guess. Sometimes they seemed closer than others, and according to Vonders that was common in the Blasted Lands. The distant wall of the Edge was the only landmark his family had ever really used in the Blasted Lands, and that seemed to change all the time as well.

"We could climb it." Tega's voice shook him from his reverie.

"What?" He looked at her face for a moment and then back at the tower she was studying. The hole that gaped down at them from up high. "I'm not so sure."

"The surface looks tricky, yes, there's the ice to contend with, but we could climb it. Vonders says his family climbed down the side of the Edge on many occasions using ropes and spikes driven into the stone."

"The stone of the Edge is hard. It's granite, and even the stonecutters have trouble with it. We can't tell how solid that stuff is. It might have no more strength than unbaked clay."

"Nolan, have you seen anything else that looks like an entrance?"

A lot of them, but they were all lies. That was the only reason they were even considering this madness.

"And what if the winds come back while we are up there and holding on only by ropes? What if the ice storms start again?"

Tega looked at him and shook her head. "What other options?"

"There are still many structures we have not examined. Perhaps we should investigate the rest before we make a decision to climb that high with no guarantees." Her lips pressed together and she stared harder at him as if willing him to simply – *explode* – agree with her. "We are here to serve you, Tega. This is your expedition and your decision to make." He raised his hands in surrender.

She looked away from him and stared at the opening. Sixty feet was a long way to fall and the opening was at an angle that would make gaining entrance risky at best. And he still thought it looked closer to a hundred feet than sixty, but he was trying to be optimistic.

"We shall look a little further then, but let's mark this possibility."

He nodded his head. That was exactly what he'd hoped she would say. One thing to consider risking yourself and another when you risked the lives of the people with you. Had it been him alone, climbing the side would have been a more realistic option. With others? There were too many chances for people to die or get even more injured.

Vonders took in a deep breath. "What in the name of the gods?"

Nolan looked toward the man and then followed his eyes.

Just barely visible from where they stood, they could see a lone rider coming toward the Mounds. The figure came from the direction of the Seven Forges.

"I thought the Sa'ba Taalor were forbidden to be here?" Darus's voice was petulant, as if someone had taken away his time to play and given him more chores. Nolan liked his friend a good deal more when he wasn't injured and whining.

"We've no proof that whoever is coming this way is Sa'ba Taalor." Nolan shrugged, but he also reached for his axe's handle.

"This is not a good thing. I can feel it." Darus shook his head and frowned. His good hand felt along his broken arm for a moment and then he, like Nolan, sought the comfort of his weapon.

Nolan opened his mouth and then closed it. Finally he looked to Tega. "What would you have us do here, Mistress?"

Tega looked back to him, her eyes wide. "I... We should prepare ourselves."

"Prepare for what?" Darus said the words that Nolan was considering.

Tega looked toward the horizon and frowned. "Where did he go?"

"The rider?" Nolan looked away from her and back toward the spot where the rider had been. There was nothing. No one.

A chill that had nothing to do with the cold crept through him.

"Damn."

Darus nodded his agreement. "Whoever that is, I won't call it a good sign that we've been spotted."

"What makes you certain we were seen?" Tega's question was directed toward Darus. Nolan answered anyway. "We can't be certain, but we have to guess that the rider has seen us and does not wish to be seen by us. We must expect unpleasant intent."

Tega nodded. "Let's get back to the wagon then. We have to take care of the others."

Nolan bit back a response. They were soldiers. They were here to watch over and protect her, not each other.

Darus kicked at a loose stone with his good foot. "Where did Vonders go?"

Sure enough, the scavenger had vanished again. Likely off looking for something shiny.

Tega shook her head. "We don't know how far away the rider is. We have to get back to the camp."

Nolan nodded. "Vonders can find his own way. He's been leading us through half the pits in this area already."

Without another word they headed back for the wagon and the others. Nolan found himself wondering how good Tolpen was with his bow. He also found himself wishing he'd brought his crossbow with him.

Still, the weapon was waiting at the campsite and they'd be there soon enough.

Drask stared up at the Mounds and studied them. Brackka let out a low rumble and Drask patted the thick hide of his mount. "I know. I saw them."

He sighed and let his legs grip harder to the thick body beneath him. Brackka took his cue and moved quickly, bounding across the landscape in leaps that would have terrified anyone unfamiliar with how well the beast could move. It was only a matter of minutes before they were in the rough ground leading to the Mounds proper.

There was a flutter of unease in his stomach. It could not be called fear, exactly, but it was a close relative. For his entire life the rules had been simple enough to follow: first obey the Daxar Taalor. Second, stay away from the Mounds. Currently these two rules conflicted. Ydramil had spoken directly into Drask and told him to go to the Mounds. He had obeyed, readying himself for whatever might come his way in the process, but the notion of going to the area the gods forbade went against his upbringing. Still, the very first rule was to obey the Daxar Taalor, even if that meant going against every other rule in his existence.

The Mounds made no sense. They were vast and desolate. They were dark and jagged. The wind cut around them and brought with it an odd scent unlike anything he had encountered before, and he had seen more than most of his people had.

Standing in the shadow of the Mounds, Drask closed his eyes and offered a silent prayer to Ydramil. He had made his progress as the god demanded. Now that he was here, he hoped for more information. He did not expect it. He did not demand it. But he hoped for it just the same.

His only answer was silence.

When the gods do not give an answer there is as much of a reason as when they do. The process of becoming what the Daxar Taalor demanded was a lifetime in the happening.

"We go on then, my brother." He ran one hand over Brackka's neck and the mount let out a grunt. A moment later they moved forward and Drask let one hand rest on his throwing axes. There were likely threats, here. If those threats could be cut than he would bleed them. If they could not, then he would handle the matter differently.

There could only be one answer to the people he had spotted. They were seen at a great distance, but he suspected they were from Fellein, even without seeing them clearly. Many things lived within the Mounds, that was accepted, but Drask doubted that any of them were human.

The winds ripped across the ground and cast dust and ice into the air. The veil he wore for traveling caught the worst of the grit, but he narrowed his eyes against unwanted irritants.

Brackka moved up into the Mounds proper, breaking a sacred law as the gods demanded. The tension rose in both of them. One does not easily defy the gods' laws if one is wise. Even when the gods themselves demand it. Perhaps especially then.

From somewhere above him came a roar from the ground, enough to shake his body and Brackka's alike. They held their place and waited. The sound wrapped around them, crushed them in its grip, and finally released them when it had finished its course. Pra-Wren, the wailing winds. They had been a part of existence in the Blasted Lands for as long as anyone could remember. The Mounds did not rest easily. They never had.

He looked up at a towering arm of stone that reached for the heavens and pointed in the direction of the Seven Forges as if demanding that he retreat.

Drask sighed and once again they moved, climbing into the warped wasteland.

Somewhere ahead of them, the people of Fellein sought something. Perhaps he was here to stop them. Perhaps the gods had other plans. He would find out when the time was right. For now he looked around and expected the same of Brackka as they moved carefully into the forbidden.

Four days and nights of celebration were finally coming to an end, and Tataya could not have been happier about it. The Brellar had welcomed her and that was a good

thing. She had been treated with near reverence and
one of their chieftains – she could not quite decide how
many they had – had allowed her to learn their language
by touching his mind.

At first she'd thought perhaps she was expected.
The way the people reacted would have made it easy
to believe, certainly, but after they'd learned to share
languages, Tataya was informed that she was welcomed
because of her hair. Apparently women with red hair
were highly prized and even rarer than blond-haired
women among the locals. Near as she could tell no
one from the Brellar had any hair color but black.
They made up for the lack of variety in a number of
ways that seemed like lunacy to her. Still, Desh had
explained more than once that cultures found their
own ways to speak and words were only one example
of communication.

She'd known about the ritual scarring, but knowing
and seeing are different matters. The symbols they used
to write their stories on their skin were complex, and in
many cases the scars covered their entire bodies. Most
of the marks were tiny, smaller than her shortest finger
nail, but others were deep and thick on the skin, as
if to indicate they had a far greater significance. She
doubted there was any part of her history she wanted
carved into her flesh and left to bleed for days on end,
especially in the heat of the area, where infection was
likely a serious threat.

But the Brellar managed and she saw very few of
them who suffered drastically as a result of the markings,
even though several of the people she saw were covered
with fresh cuts.

The celebrations came to an end when she explained that she was not looking for a mate, but rather sought sailors for a possible war.

After that, the men she dealt with were strictly business.

Tomms and Laruth were the two men she was negotiating with, and both of them seemed amiable enough, though Tomms was still not pleased with her refusal to marry him. She lied and claimed that she was already married, but that didn't seem to matter in the least to him. He had three wives, and collectively those three wives had five husbands. While the notion was fascinating, she opted to hold off on studying the nature of their culture in quite such detail until after negotiations were settled.

Laruth was younger and possibly more ambitious. He was certainly more willing to negotiate. The men and two others of the same rank had gathered with Tataya and Callan to discuss prices. Captain Callan spoke their language with a bit of difficulty, but he did speak it and Tataya used that to her advantage, letting him handle many of the discussions while hiding exactly how well she spoke it herself. Not because she was hiding anything from Laruth, who'd allowed her to learn his language, but because she wanted to know if she could trust Callan.

Surprisingly, he seemed to be telling the truth and negotiating fairly. She was pleasantly surprised.

"So, then." Callan looked to her. "We have a deal? It's a fortune we're talking about here."

"A fortune, yes, but not paid in full until the deed is done." She leaned back and studied the four chiefs. They studied her right back, with varying degrees of interest.

She had dressed herself to add to their distraction and it was working just fine.

"How do you wish to handle this?"

She smiled at the captain. "I have a chest of gold with me, do I not? For just such contingencies."

Callan looked heartbroken by that idea. He had grown fond of that chest of gold. She'd caught him looking longingly at her cabin door on several occasions during the trip, and oftentimes she was surprised that he didn't merely break the door down. It wouldn't have done him the least good, of course, but that was something that he did not have to know.

"I suppose you do."

"Oh, calm yourself, Captain. You'll be paid first."

He looked at her with a wounded expression that held remarkably little conviction. "You cut me."

"So you've done all of this for love of Empire and will require no compensation?" She deliberately used an expression of hopeful ignorance that she knew would make the man crazy. He seemed to prefer his women on the naïve side. A little pout and widened eyes and the man was nearly ready to kill anyone who so much as looked at her the wrong way.

"Hardly." His response was dry and let her know he was on to her simple tricks. That was good. It was hardly fun playing with a new toy if it did not play back.

In perfect Brellar she replied to the waiting chieftains, "The terms are acceptable and I thank you for your honest and fair negotiations."

Tomms looked at her longingly. "You are certain your husband would not accept an offer of shared marriage?"

"He is not as generous with his wives, I fear."

The man sighed and waved a dismissive hand. "That is a pity."

She repressed a shudder and rose from her seat. It wasn't that Tomms was unattractive, exactly, merely that he seemed so desperate to add a red haired woman to his stable of wives. She was flattered and repulsed in equal measure.

Captain Callan stared at her with a dropped jaw and narrowed eyes, fully aware for the first time that she had understood every word he said, including quite a few that would have been deemed inappropriate. If Desh Krohan truly were her husband a few of the discussions would have ended with Callan dead instead of merely worried about his possible demise.

Desh did not defend the honor of the Sisters. They were expected to handle their own conflicts and call on him only as a last resort.

So far none of them had ever had to call on him for that purpose.

After formal goodbyes were said and arrangements made for Laruth's people to collect their advance, Tataya headed for the ship with Callan on her heels.

"You spoke the language the entire time?"

"No. Only for part of it."

"Which part?"

"You may rest comfortably with the knowledge that I heard your comments about what should be done with a woman who has a body like mine."

"Oh."

"I also heard your statements regarding the purchasing of slave-girls for the taverns in your home town."

"Yes, well…"

"Slavery has been outlawed in most parts of the Empire."

"But not all."

"True. Even so, speaking of women in that way will not endear you to most of them."

Callan smiled. "There are exceptions, you know."

"No doubt. I have known a few men who would be exceptions as well, but I have never respected any of them enough to want to be with them."

"You speak of relationships. I speak of rutting."

"We speak of the same thing, Captain Callan. I merely have higher standards."

He opened his mouth to retort and then apparently thought better of it. "So you're not upset then?"

"Not at all. I believe that everyone should speak their minds and have their beliefs. Especially when doing so reveals more about them than I would otherwise know."

"Is that why you left most of the negotiations to me?"

"No. Not entirely. At least two of the chieftains would have considered anything I said beneath serious consideration." She allowed a small smile. "Not all men are as enlightened as you, Captain."

They reached the ship in short order – most of the discussions had happened onboard one of the larger vessels and it was merely a matter of walking from one pier to another to get back to where they needed to be. By the time they'd arrived, the men Laruth had charged with taking payment were already waiting.

Tataya went to see about their payment and Captain Callan called out to his crew to ready for departure. None of the crew seemed the least bit upset by the notion. The ships around theirs were large, and even when they were silent, the knowledge that substantial crews of men who might or might not see them as enemies were stationed around them on all sides was not conducive to easy rest.

The men collecting the gold were familiar enough faces by now. They had been with the chieftain through most of his negotiations.

Within twenty minutes the payments had been made and the chest of gold first offered to Pathra Krous by the Sa'ba Taalor had been nearly emptied of coins. She rather liked the notion of paying for defense against the Sa'ba Taalor with their own offerings.

Another hour and they were ready to set sail. There were no challenges despite the worry that Callan held onto. The Brellar were indeed a strange people, but they wanted what everyone wanted. They wanted more than they already had.

They were well out to sea before the sun set. Captain Callan kept members of his crew on the lookout through the night, likely waiting to see if they would be followed.

After a while, day and night became irrelevant. The distance to the top of Durhallem was deceptive, and though he'd thought to reach the entrance to the mountain within hours, it seemed much longer.

Andover walked in heat that was blistering, and carried on through cold that left his teeth chattering and his toes numb, and still he walked. He did not stop to rest, because he had been told that his time for resting was done.

And so he walked. He moved up the side of the mountain, always angling higher, occasionally crawling on his hands and knees when the incline was too steep, and sometimes scaling sheer walls of stone. More than once he was grateful for fingers made of iron that were capable of gripping so much harder than mere flesh.

He walked until the snow started – a layer of white that hid the dark rock of the mountain. He continued higher still, feeling the ice beneath him and the biting cold of the air he breathed.

And in time, he could never say exactly how long with any accuracy, Andover Lashk reached the entrance to his destination. And seeing the entrance to Durhallem's Heart, Andover Lashk forced down his dread and walked into the simple cave. The floor was level enough, a rough black cut into the mountain's surface. The walls around him were obsidian – rich, black glass – and seemed to reflect his face back at him from a million or more uneven facets. He walked forward cautiously, barely able to see into the darkness, and he walked for a long time indeed.

There was no doubt in his mind as to where he was. How could any mere mortal doubt the presence of a god? He stepped into the cave and felt the heat of Durhallem's heart and the calculating rage that rested there.

Why are you here? He did not hear the words. He *felt* their meaning within his body.

"I am here to thank you." No. That wasn't right. Durhallem had done nothing for him. It was Truska-Pren who had given him his hands. "I am here to be judged by you." Yes. That was it. He was supposed to find out if he was worthy.

Did he see the force that came for him?

No. He saw nothing but darkness. But he felt it. He felt a powerful presence, a vast thing of impossible scope that *noticed* him for a moment, truly noticed him and examined him.

And judged him.

A moment later the pain came, a great searing agony across the left side of his face. Muscles spasmed, flesh twitched, bone moved within his face, and when he thought for sure that he must scream or go mad he remembered the words of Drask Silver Hand so very long ago now, as he prepared to be given his new hands.

Place your hands within the blessing box. Do not move them, no matter how great the pain, no matter how tempting. Life is pain, and if you would have hands that live, you must accept that pain. Do you understand?

He thought of those words and obeyed them as best he could. He did not move his face, despite the desire to do so. He tried not to scream and could never be certain if he succeeded there. The pain was unbearable, as great as any he could remember, but he did not move, he dared not move. The presence might notice him again if he did and he felt that would be a very bad thing indeed.

The pain disappeared as quickly as it had come to him. There was no lingering reminder of the agony. It was simply gone.

Andover closed his eyes and fell to his knees, able to breathe again for the first time since feeling the presence.

His hands clutched tightly to something he could not see. When he was strong enough to rise he kept his grip on that something and made his way to the entrance of the cave.

The stars were out and the night was cold and Andover Lashk walked carefully down the side of the mountain along a trail that had not been there before. He worked his jaw and felt the changes along the left side of his face and wondered what they might look like. His hands kept their tight grip on whatever had been given him by Durhallem, but he did not look at it. His eyes stayed on the path ahead of him instead. He understood in his soul that to look away would be to lose the path, and he was not sure he was strong enough to make it back down the mountain without it.

The sun rose, and still he walked, still he kept plodding along. In time he stopped, but only long enough to drink from a trickling stream of cold melt water. The ground was once more stone and the air was warm on his skin.

The sun was fading by the time he reached the village, and once again great fires raged within the pits before the cliff face dwellings.

Tusk came toward him and stopped a few feet away. His hand reached out and grabbed at Andover's face looking carefully first at his right cheek and then at his left.

And then the man roared, "He is scarred! Andover Lashk is scarred by Durhallem!"

Around him the people cheered and Andover blinked, shocked by the sudden noise.

The feeling that he was in a dream did not quite leave him, but it faded as the people came forward, many clapping him on one arm or the other, others, like Delil, embracing him briefly as if greeting a member of the family they had not seen in a while. It seemed that every person in the village came his way and offered their congratulations.

And maybe they did. He could not tell.

There was the talk of his being scarred and Andover let his hand drift up to touch his face. The right side was the same as ever but the left was changed.

His voice sounded strange when he spoke for the first time in over a day. "How?"

"No one can meet the gods and be unchanged, Andover Lashk. You have received the blessings of Durhallem. He has given you obsidian and your first Great Scar."

He nodded as if he understood, but the words only grazed the surface of his mind. He was tired and doubted he would ever feel as if he had slept enough again in his lifetime.

"You have wondered why we wear veils before your people, and now you know. Your people would not understand. They have not been blessed."

Tuskandru reached to the veil covering his face and pulled it back. A moment later the cloth was tossed aside amidst a faint tinkling noise from the thin links that adorned it.

Andover barely heard the noise. He was far too busy studying the markings on Tusk's face. They had no symmetry and each was as different as any of the marks on the man's flesh, save in that they were prominent and impossible to ignore. Along the left side of his face a thick scar ran from the cheek down to the jaw. Not but a few inches distant, another scar, heavy enough to stand out among the many scars on the man, ran above his mouth and almost to his nose. A third jagged across his right side, but that one seemed an open wound that would not bleed.

At least that was the impression until the wound moved. All three of the scars opened and flexed along with the broad lips of Tusk's mouth. And from the mouth and the scars alike Andover could see flashes of teeth, hints of gums. When Tusk spoke again all of the scars and his mouth moved, each adding a note of sound, and the apprentice blacksmith finally understood the source of the odd distortion in the voices of the Sa'ba Taalor.

"When we meet with the gods, we are gifted with the voices of the gods, you see? We understand them and we can speak with them. Once we are worthy, once we have proven ourselves, the gods bless us with their marks and their voices alike."

Delil peeled the veil from her face and he saw that she had two such scars, one on the right that ran along her jaw line, and one on the left that bisected her full lips. When the mouths were silent they did indeed look like scars. When she spoke they moved, they formed words and sounds.

"You are blessed today, Andover. Durhallem has accepted you."

Through the exhaustion that seemed to weigh him down, Andover felt a blooming understanding and a rising dread.

He spoke with both of his mouths. The one he had been born with and the one Durhallem had cut across the left side of his face. The mouth he had been born with let out a slight whimper and said, "Blessed?" And the other mouth, the scar that spoke in a slightly different tone said, "Blessed. Durhallem has blessed me."

He should have been horrified, but the exhaustion was still there, like the weight of too much wine upon him, and it crushed his panic.

But there was more. He could not fully understand it, did not want to make sense of it, but part of him was thrilled with the change.

He looked around him and saw the faces looking back, Delil, Tusk, Bromt and others whose names he barely knew and could hardly remember, and understood that they accepted him and reveled in the change.

They accepted him as one of them.

As an equal.

And it was good.

He fought back tears, not of grief but of joy. For the first time in so very long, Andover felt that he belonged.

THIRTEEN

When he stopped at Dretta March's home on his way to the palace and his offices there, Merros did so with mixed feelings. Since actually meeting her, the morning encounters had become a part of his life and he had come to truly enjoy them. On some occasions they merely ate in comfortable silence and on other occasions the two of them exchanged tales of Wollis and reminisced over the man they had both loved in their own ways.

It had become a part of his routine, and that was something that Merros was not used to having. His life had been broken into simple rituals since he'd joined the military, and while the locations changed the practices he kept seldom did. He woke, he cleaned himself, shaved and prepared for the day. He dressed, saw to his weapons and then went to the daily tasks, usually breaking his fast on the way out the door or occasionally when he reached his command.

Now the ritual had changed. Now he broke fast with Dretta, often eating nothing more than fruit, but sometimes having meals that required time and energy to prepare. A lot of time and a good deal of energy.

Roasted meats, pastries and breads served with preserves and honey, and the breads often fresh from the oven and still warm to the touch.

If this kept up he'd be having his uniforms altered to give his belly more space.

That thought brought a bittersweet smile. Because the chances were good that the ritual would be going away.

While they sat at the table outside of Dretta's home – to date he had never actually been inside the structure, merely beneath the cover of the patio – Merros chewed thoughtfully at his food and Dretta watched him with a wary expression.

As he was chewing on the loaf of crusty bread into which fruits and nuts had been baked – something he had never seen done anywhere but in the northern climes – Dretta finally had enough.

"What is on your mind, General Dulver?"

"Am I General Dulver, today?"

"When you are acting so formally and refuse to look me in the eyes I must assume you are here on official business." Her words were light enough, but her expression spoke of a deep and abiding dread. "Do you plan to tell me bad news of my son's fate? Is Nolan injured?"

He was horrified. "What? Gods, no, Dretta. Your son is fine. Nolan is on an assignment for the Empress, and I have received several reports on his condition. He is well." He could see her relax. She let out a deep breath and the tension fled from her face, removing years from her age. In truth she was younger than he was and younger by almost a decade than Wollis had been. She had married young and her husband had not.

"Then why are you acting like an ass?"

"What?"

"You've barely looked at me. You've not said four words. If I've offended you, then say how, and if I have not, then explain your silence before *I* take offense." Her dark eyes glared.

"I didn't mean–"

"You are a man. Men seldom mean to do anything. Wollis did not mean to leave me for months at a time. He did not mean to run off to all the cities of the Empire. He did not mean to die." She choked a bit on the last, but closed her eyes and continued. "Men never mean to. And yet they do. So I ask you again, what is it that bothers you?"

There it was, that knife of guilt. He made himself accept the wound without flinching.

"I have been trying to find a way to tell you that the city is going to be abandoned."

"Say again? I did not hear you well."

"I'm afraid you did. The Empress and the royal court are moving to Old Canhoon, to the original palace. The army will be leaving here. The people who tend to the army will be leaving and so will all those who serve the royal court. Everyone will be leaving."

"Why?" Dretta's had reached for a knife so she could cut herself a slab of the hearty bread. She dipped the edge of the bread into thick honey and began chewing slowly as she stared at him.

For just an instant he wondered why that should be so appealing a sight and then he pushed the thought aside. Dretta March was Wollis's wife. That was as far as he had to consider before moving on.

"Well, there seems to be some worry about the city meeting with disaster."

"That would be a thing to let people know, yes?"

"Well, yes, but there's the panic to consider."

"What panic?"

"If we tell the people that the city is in danger, they will most definitely want to leave. And they'll want to do so in a very big hurry. And if they all leave at once, there's going to be every imaginable sort of problem."

Dretta raised one eyebrow archly and studied him. Merros squirmed, feeling a bit like a bug under close scrutiny. Wollis had gone on at length on more than one occasion with stories of his wife's ability to make him feel like a complete buffoon with an expression. Merros was beginning to think his friend had been understating the matter rather than blowing it out of proportion.

"You understand the logistical dilemma, don't you?"

"How many soldiers do you have in this city of yours, Merros Dulver?"

He almost pointed out that the city wasn't his, exactly, but decided against levity. She might well take the knife to him, and he was still resisting a powerful need to squirm in his seat.

"Well, a good number…"

"And could they not be used to maintain order? Could they not be used to make certain that each avenue and street was emptied in a proper fashion before the people on the next street were allowed to leave?"

"Well, yes, but if someone decides to panic, or to protest, or to use a sword to explain why they should be allowed to leave sooner, there will no doubt be conflicts."

"Which soldiers are trained to resolve, yes?"

"Dretta–"

"You have only so many streets in this town, Merros. I know there are more soldiers than there are streets. There are more soldiers than there are roads away from the city. And so you have control. And if you are doing your job properly, as a general in charge of the army, then you should be able to schedule the evacuation of Tyrne."

"There are other considerations."

"Such as?"

"Mobilizing the army against the Sa'ba Taalor."

"Did you not tell me only yesterday that these Sa'ba Taalor wanted to sue for peace?"

"No. Not quite. They wish to discuss whether or not we will actually go to war or if we will discuss our way out of it."

"Well, then." She shrugged as if to say that settled the matter.

"No. No it's not quite that simple. In the event that they do not wish to end this, I have to have the military ready to strike."

"And do what? March all the way to the Seven Forges? Didn't it take you almost two months to reach them? How will an army get there any faster?"

He felt a headache growing behind his eyes. The problem was that her words made sense, but they did not take in to consideration all of the variables and he could not possibly educate her to understand them all.

"Dretta, I told you of this so that you could prepare. So that, if you want, you can move to Canhoon or back to Stonehaven."

"Why would I move to Canhoon?"

"Well, you wanted… I mean…" She was studying him again. He hated that. He had no idea what to do with himself when she studied him that closely.

"I came here to be with Wollis. Wollis will not be in Canhoon."

"He won't be in Stonehaven, either." The words jumped from his mouth before he could stop them. He was used to curbing that impulse, but here he was, making an ass of himself without really any defense against it.

"Yes." One word and it came out as cold as a blade soaked in ice-laden waters. "I am aware of where my husband will not be."

"Damn it, Dretta, I don't know what to say!" His voice was plaintive, bordering on whiny.

"Do you want me in Canhoon, Merros Dulver? Or do you prefer me in Stonehaven?"

And there it was. The very thing he'd been trying to figure out for himself. Did he want her in his life? Did he want her around him even as he prepared to move on to a different place?

"I want you in Old Canhoon, Dretta March. I want you near the palace there. Close enough that I can see you every day on my way to the offices of the Commander General."

She gave him nothing. Her expression could have been carved in stone for all the change. Still, her eyes regarded him and she said, "Then I shall move on to Old Canhoon, before the rest of this city moves on."

And he was relieved, because he had a parley to handle and possibly a war to fight and he wanted her safe.

The rest of their conversation was easier, but still she gave him nothing to hold in his mind save the memory of her eyes.

Nachia Krous did not walk the throne room. She stalked it, looking at every shadow, every window, every curtain, seeking answers to the questions in her mind.

Brolley, never accused of being the wisest soul, was smart enough to simply sit at the table there and watch her. He was wise in the ways of his sister if in nothing else.

Merros sat across from him, looking at a detailed map of the Tyrne, on which he had made several markings. The notion of changing the face of a map was one he had never felt comfortable with. They were damned hard to come by, unless one wished to hire a cartographer. The fact that he now had dozens of cartographers working for him did not change his basic philosophy on these things. He could have ordered a hundred maps and still he would have hesitated.

And yet, he grabbed the pen and carefully made a mark at the intersection of Winder's Way and the Harrow's Bridge. "Here. I think we can clear the city to this point before the first major panic starts."

Brolley looked, his face frowning in concentration. He had not said anything at all about evacuating the city, but he seemed intent on studying everything just the same. That was fine with Merros. If the boy wanted to learn, he would teach him. The fact was simple enough: he was a member of the Imperial Family, and as such he could eventually be called on to take up a weapon and lead. Better that he learn now than end up in another situation where he was an embarrassment to his bloodline.

Nachia stopped moving long enough to look at the map. "I don't like it. I think it's a mistake."

"Majesty, if we do not prepare the people and we have to evacuate, it's going to go from bad to worse. Riots have been known to break out over far less than asking people to move all of their belongings from one place to another."

"I thought we agreed to tell people we were moving the palace back to Canhoon and let them follow us."

"That is still the plan. What we are doing here is working on possibilities. Should we be forced to move people along at a faster pace, I thought it best that we have plans in place and routes by which the City Guard and soldiers can ensure the least amount of conflict."

She scowled at him. It was not an expression of anger so much as it was the face she made when trying to work things through in her mind. Had he not already gotten used to the expression he might well have worried whether or not she was going to have him executed.

"What of the City Guard. Have the issues you were having with them been handled?"

"Libari Welliso has taken command of the City Guard. From what I can see, he is the closest thing to an honest guardsman, and competent besides." Which was true enough. The man had been responsible for arresting and holding the members of the City Guard who'd beaten Andover Lashk and ruined his hands. He'd done so despite numerous members of the Guard making comments and a few of his superiors protesting the action.

"Majesty, have we had any contact with Andover Lashk since he left for the Seven Forges?" said Merros.

"Every attempt that Desh has made to reach the boy has failed. We either assume he is dead or we wait to find out his fate when we meet with the Sa'ba Taalor to negotiate a peace."

Merros nodded and pushed back a hard edge of guilt. Once upon a time he'd left one of his men behind in the Taalor Valley, Kallir Lundt, who had been ruined in a fight with the Pra-Moresh. He still had no idea if the man was alive, and if he was, what shape he might be in. He pushed the thought aside. Kallir Lundt had been promised safety by the Sa'ba Taalor. He had to hope they'd kept their word and if not, he would likely have a chance to seek revenge on the mercenary's behalf. Not that he expected that particular notion to go well.

"I shall make a note of it." And he did. There was a growing list of items to be discussed with whomever the Sa'ba Taalor chose as a representative. He wrote down Andover's name and as an afterthought scribbled Kallir Lundt's name beside it.

"How many days until this damned meeting?"

"We have to leave the morning after next if we intend to reach the meeting place on time." He almost mumbled the words. Much to his annoyance, the Empress intended to be there for the parley. Neither he nor Desh Krohan had been able to dissuade her.

Desh Krohan claimed he had a plan for that, but would not say what it was as yet. Merros didn't like plans that involved not being informed. They tended to make him nervous.

Nachia looked at him. Her expression made clear exactly where he could take his mumbling and his opinion of her choice to go along for the negotiations.

Brolley looked at his sister and shook his head. "You're being an ass."

"What?" Her voice took on a note that Merros had never heard. He'd never had a sibling, or he would have known that particular sound for the indication that long standing arguments had not been finished.

"You're in charge of everything. Nachia. *Everything*. What if this is a ploy to get you where they can kill you?"

"What if it's a genuine attempt at working out a peaceful ending? What then? What if it's a test to see if I'm brave enough to face off against one of their kings? How can I be a leader of an Empire if I'm too scared to look their leaders in the eyes?"

Brolley reeled back with each question she asked. Merros could see him trying to come up with good counterarguments and failing.

"What if they decided the only way to end this is to have a proper duel, Nachia? You and that Tuskandru fellow, one-on-one to the death for the right to rule over your Empire?" Brolley's words were just as harsh as his sister's. "Do you suppose that will go as well as my encounter with Drask Silver Hand?"

Nachia looked at her brother sharply.

Brolley continued. "I know exactly how fortunate I was. They were trying for peace. Wollis March screamed that into my ear for hours on end while he prepared me for my last fight and my certain death." Brolley stood up and pointed a thick finger at his sister. "I got a talking to from you on that too, as I recall. Several of them. So now it's my turn. Listen to Merros. Listen to Desh. They are here to advise you. If they say you should not go, then stay here, where you will be safe. You. The leader of the entire Empire."

Nachia's voice was calm and cool and slapped at the air like a lash. "Pathra was not on a battlefield when he was murdered. We have already seen that I am not safe anywhere. We saw that when Pathra died with a slit throat and got thrown from the window of this very room." She stabbed a finger in Merros's direction. "Want to know why I agreed to move to Canhoon? Because I can't stand knowing the room where I deal with the business of running this Empire is the same room where my cousin died."

The silence in the room was complete, save for a few small breaths from Nachia. "I will attend to the parley. That is my decision. If you have doubts, then bring enough guards to make our position on my living through this event clear. And bring your best, Merros. I might have to choose a champion."

Merros could think of no retort at that moment. Instead he gave a formal bow and left the room, leaving brother and sister to continue their debates in peace. It was best to know when to call a battle done. This one was finished.

Libari Welliso was a solid man, no two ways about that. He was older than Merros, but carried himself with the air of a man on a mission from the gods themselves. His uniform was in meticulous order and his sword's pommel was as well worn as the hilt. He was a man used to combat, in other words, and that won him a great deal of respect from Merros.

The fact that he was handling the clean-up of the City Guard as well as he was also went a great distance in the general's eyes.

Libari looked at the offices he was taking over with a clinical eye and nodded.

Merros could barely repress a grin. "Are they satisfactory then?" He already knew the answer.

"They're as pompous as I expected." He gestured at the walls. There were numerous portraits of the men who'd held the office of City Guard General before him on the walls and the desk was slightly larger than a wagon designed to be drawn by horses. The room itself was only slightly larger than the average home, which meant it was impressive, but not quite as large as the rooms where the Imperial Family went to piss in private.

"You can do whatever you please to make it yours."

"Seems a bit pointless to change things, doesn't it?" Libari eyed him critically. He had blue eyes that seemed almost out of place in his deeply tanned flesh. Unlike so many of the officers Merros had known, this one was used to being out on the streets and walking among his charges.

"How do you mean?"

"If the city is to be abandoned."

Merros nodded. "Heard about that?"

"It's hard not to. One has to know where to listen, but yes, I heard about it."

"It might be a temporary thing. It might be more permanent. No one knows yet, do they? We only know that Desh Krohan believes it must be done."

Libari nodded. "That was all the reason I needed to send my family to Canhoon. We have relatives there to take care of them."

"And yet you're still here?"

"I'm a soldier first. I don't abandon my duties."

Oh yes, Merros liked the man. They were going to get along well. "How goes the cleaning of the ranks?"

The smile Libari offered would have dropped a Pra-Moresh to its knees in fear. "I had a very long list of offenses I wished to see handled. The list is much shorter now."

Merros nodded and his smile came back. "I know exactly how you feel, Welliso."

"I know you do. I watched your disciplinary actions."

Merros felt himself nod again, his lips pressed into a hard line. "They were necessary."

"Has it ever occurred to you how annoying we must be to the younger men?"

"How do you mean?"

"Well, I can't speak for you, of course, but I have noticed a dreadful tendency to sound exactly like my father when I was younger. I've even caught myself saying, "When I was a cadet your age…'"

Merros slapped the man's shoulder and laughed. "I knew there was a reason I liked you."

"Why me, General Merros? It's not that I don't appreciate the opportunity, of course, but why me? There are other officers, many with higher ranks."

"There *were* other officers with higher ranks. They no longer have that advantage. And actually? You were chosen after a long discussion with Desh Krohan. You impressed his apprentice to the point that she spoke

288 THE BLASTED LANDS

often of your proper behavior when you took care of the matters with Andover Lashk."

That was obviously still a sore spot. "If he'd killed those boys it would have been easier. I keep having to lock them back up for begging."

"There are laws against begging?"

Libari nodded. "We only enforce them in certain areas. The areas where a beggar can actually make enough coins to offend someone."

"Perhaps we can find something to do with that problem after everything else has been cleared up."

Libari nodded again, his hands locked together behind his broad back. "So, when does this evacuation take place properly?"

"Soon. And when it does I'll need you and your guard handling a lot of the troubles."

"Just so. And how long will we be expected to watch over the city after the evacuation?"

Merros nodded his head again. The man was not a dullard.

"Likely for at least a month. Assuming whatever this threat is doesn't get resolved before then."

"I expect a few men to quit their contracts."

"I can bolster your ranks with soldiers."

Libari smiled again, a tight and cold smile. "Are you quite certain they'll stand for the demotion?"

There was a little flush of guilt at that. Merros was one of the many soldiers who tended to look down on the City Guard as secondary to real soldiers.

"They might not like it, but they'll follow your orders."

"Fair enough. If they fail to, I will treat them the same way I treat my men."

"Which is?"

"Precisely the same way I've seen you discipline your own men." He looked hard at Merros. "I don't like using a lash either, but it has to be done to make certain the men understand the proper chain of command."

"It's your command, General Welliso. You'll run it as you see fit."

"That's going to take some getting accustomed to."

"The title?"

"Indeed."

"You'll manage. I've started adjusting already and it's not even a year."

Desh Krohan looked at the bodies and felt his skin shudder with disgust.

Necromancy. That was one form of sorcery he'd never wanted anything to do with. He'd studied it, to be sure, knew about the ways of the dark art and the advantages to be found from employing it, but that did not mean he had a fondness for the subject. It wasn't the soul or the fact that dead flesh was used, really, so much as it was simple messiness of the subject.

Bodies rot. Flesh falls apart. Bodies decay. And in the process there were a great number of sounds and odors he could deal without in his life.

When he was a young man, one of the sorcerers who'd instructed him, Theurasa Sallis, had shown him how to revive dead flesh into a mimicry of living substance. It was a lesson he had never forgotten. The nightmares he suffered afterwards had lingered for a very long time indeed. The long-remembered incident – and the need to put down what he had created – were among the reasons that necromancy was now a forbidden art in the Fellein Empire.

And yet he was looking at the results of what had to be necromancy, though it was not anything he was familiar with.

Merros Dulver stood next to him. There were a dozen others there as well, all of them looking on as Desh studied the creatures brought back from the trail to Old Canhoon by the soldiers who had defeated them.

Besides the unclean things there was the body of an older member of the Sa'ba Taalor. Older than any Desh had seen, and withered. His mount was much the same, but beyond that it was almost impossible to say much about them. They'd both been trampled by the things that had followed them, and their remains were little more than broken, torn piles of bone.

Several different people had examined the remains, which had then been sealed away. Why? Because no one knew exactly how to handle them. The idea had been to hand them over to Desh Krohan to study and he'd certainly meant to, but there had been no chance.

And now there was no choice. They had to understand what the things were, not merely what they had been.

Desh reached out and touched one of the shields that had been warped and crushed into a new shape along with the bodies of soldiers. The Imperial Crest was clear on the malformed metal.

"So, what happened to them?" Welliso was the man's name. He seemed a decent enough sort. Certainly Tega thought well enough of him, and that was enough to garner him a bit of respect from Desh. His apprentice had a perceptive mind. If not, she'd have never become his apprentice.

"Well, they died, obviously." Desh looked at a corpse with a major's rank still evidence on the breastplate of his armor. "This one. I saw him when the fighting started with Tuskandru." His lip curled downward. "Wallford. Hradi's dog."

Merros started. He was not fond of the tone in Desh's voice. Still he was wise enough to keep his tongue.

"This is necromancy. Sorcery as dark as any that exists. But it is not a form of necromancy I am familiar with." Desh touched Wallford's dead face – which had been stretched and crumpled along with his helmet. The end result was not pleasant to view – and several of the people in the room gasped as the corpse's distended face twitched and the mouth opened and closed spasmodically.

"By all the gods…" He didn't look up to find the voice.

"Durst," Merros's voice warned the man speaking.

Desh looked up to see one of the soldiers, Taurn Durst, with his sword half drawn. He looked at the man for a long second and the man looked back, deeply afraid.

"The sword will do you no good. They're already dead. They've been dead. The only reason they stopped moving before is because whatever is controlling them told them to stop."

Durst looked at him and shook his head. "The soldiers hacked them to bits."

"The soldiers cut them, but they've been in here for a month or more and they're still moving. If they were alive and locked in a cellar for thirty odd days they'd be dead and rotting. These are rotting and they are dead but they are also moving. And they aren't rotting fast enough by half."

Desh plucked a deeply wounded, severed hand from the table in front of him and showed it to the solider. The fingers clutched at the air.

Durst grew several shades paler and staggered back, his hand reaching for a token of one of the churches.

And in that moment Desh smiled.

"Thank you, Durst. You're absolutely right."

"I... What?" The man looked to Merros for help and the general looked to Desh and then back to him and shrugged. "What did I do?"

Desh put the hand on the table and walked over to the stocky man. With the same hand that had held the dead, squirming flesh he clapped the general's aide on the shoulder.

"You're absolutely right! We need priests!"

Merros looked at him as if he'd grown a tree out of his eyebrow. "We what?"

"The Sa'ba Taalor have a close relationship with their gods. We need people who can speak on behalf of our gods. Durst here is going to go out running and bring back a priest from each of our churches." He looked to Durst. "Aren't you?"

Durst looked to Desh and then to Merros, his eyes growing wider.

Merros sighed. "Go find priests, Durst. Make sure they're ready to travel."

"Where are they going, General?"

Merros shook his head and scowled at Desh. Desh offered his best smile in return. "I believe the First Advisor wants them to come with us to meet with the enemy."

Desh straightened up and smiled. "There we have it. They'll travel with us and we'll ask them questions and get some answers. It'll be a wonderful and enlightening experience, to be sure."

He turned to leave the room. "Oh. And burn these things. Burn them down to ash. When you're done, take the ashes to the river and scatter them in the water past the city. Whatever metal is left should be brought back down here for me to study."

Merros looked to his men and nodded.

A moment later he walked into the narrow corridor leading from the long-disused holding cells where one of the previous Emperors had kept his favorite playthings and caught up with Desh.

"What are you thinking?"

"You said it yourself, Merros. We need to understand the Sa'ba Taalor better. We also need to understand the part their gods play in all of this."

"So how will priests from around here help with that?"

"They won't. But maybe having priests along with us will make them think our gods are ready to fight against their gods."

Merros nodded his head. He could see the logic well enough.

"They're not going to be happy about going along, I'd wager."

"That would be a problem the priests can take up with their gods."

FOURTEEN

How does one recover from being physically changed? Andover looked at his face, at the strange slash across his cheek, and then flexed his jaw. His mouths opened. Both of them. Rather than panicking, he considered the matter clinically. How does one recover? One does not. One adapts.

He looked down at his hands and at the scars where his old hands had once been attached to his body.

One adapts.

He sighed and heard the sound come mostly from his throat, but also from the smaller mouth, the "Great Scar" that moved and existed where before there had only been skin.

Andover did not understand all of the workings of the human body and he was exactly wise enough to know that he faced a mystery along those lines. His second mouth was a good deal smaller, and it could be hidden, he supposed, if he simply did not open his mouth. Mouths. That was going to take getting used to.

The polished metal he used to look at his face was not perfect, but there was only a small amount of distortion.

He knew that when he looked at the open scar and saw gums and teeth, they were real. He could even accept the change because he could see it. The parts he had trouble with were deeper than that. Below the surface as it were. He could feel the tongue in his new mouth. He could hear it speak from time to time.

More interestingly, he could understand the words it said, though before the changes Durhallem had made to him, he would not have heard anything but gibberish.

"Are you going to stay in there all day? Or will you come out and look at the farms as we discussed?" Delil's voice was without guile.

He thought about the feel of her body against his, the way her hands felt when they ran across his body, the touch of her lips on his neck, and his heartbeat increased.

"I'm coming." He set down the silver disk Tusk had found for him and stretched, feeling the play of muscles under his skin. The air was cool and clear and he felt surprisingly good. Part of him wondered how that was possible with the changes he was going through, but he suspected it was because of those changes, really. He had hands. The Sa'ba Taalor who had seen him as a stranger were now seeing him as an equal and that was an amazing thing.

The Great Scar left on him by Durhallem was a sign that he was an adult in the eyes of the valley people. He didn't understand all of their reasons, but he appreciated them.

The bag he grabbed held his belongings. It was time to leave Durhallem and move across the valley. There were other kings he had to meet. There were other gods he had to meet.

Gods.

His ears rang at the notion.

Delil stood in the daylight, her supplies already strapped across her back. She was alone. She tilted her head as she looked at him, squinting against the early morning glare. "You move like a glacier."

"A what?"

She shook her head. "A glacier. A frozen river. Never mind. You have to see one to understand."

"Are there glaciers in the valley?"

"No. There are three to the north of the Hearts of the Gods. Perhaps you will see them someday." She waved the notion away. "Come now. We have far to go."

He slung his pack over his shoulders and shrugged the weight into the now familiar place he had held it during his walk to the Seven Forges. "No one else is coming with us?" His obsidian, he held in a bundle of leather that he carried wrapped around one wrist. His hammer was slung over his other shoulder, ready should need it.

Delil looked over her shoulder and shook her head. "I will have to be enough for you." Her voice held a teasing edge and, despite how much he had changed, he still blushed at her comment.

Andover was not aware on a conscious level of how much weight he carried with ease, but had he tried carrying as much only a year before he would have fallen on his back like an upended turtle. He did not consider that the clothes he'd brought with him were for a smaller man, or how snugly they would have fit him now, because he wore the clothes of the locals instead. A vest and breeches and boots. More than that would have to be unbundled from his supplies.

Delil walked, heading quickly to the pens where Andover could see Tusk dealing with the massive mount he rode, Brodem. Even the animal eyed him differently as he approached.

"It is time for you to leave?" The words were stated like a question, but the tone was conversational. Tusk knew the answer even before he spoke.

Andover nodded his head. "Thank you. For all that you have done on my behalf."

"I have fed you and not killed you. Return the courtesy some day and we are even."

Andover grinned at that and the man smiled back, his broad face with its odd mouth-scars already becoming something Andover could easily accept. How quickly the mind adapts. "I think you are safe on both accounts, Tusk."

The King slapped his arm again and Andover braced himself for it, kept his balance.

"Show me the obsidian, yes?" Tusk pointed to the rolled leather. It seemed the man knew exactly where the two pieces were kept.

Andover crouched and unrolled the packing. The King squatted next to him and nodded. "What do you see Andover Iron Hands?"

The heavy axe blade was clear enough to understand. The other piece, the gift that Durhallem had offered up, was a curved, twisted line of obsidian that looked like nothing so much as a simple club. "I think you're right about the axe, of course."

Tusk laughed and slapped his arm again, his smile a broad, fearsome thing when all of his mouths opened and added their noise. And then the Great Scar on the left side of his face spoke clearly. "Durhallem has given you the handle for the axe. The Daxar Taalor agree."

The King gestured, silently asking permission to touch the pieces and Andover nodded his agreement.

He raised the clublike section and placed it in Andover's hand, moving Andover's fingers until he understood what the King was doing. The obsidian was uneven, yes, but there was indeed a purpose. Each of the odd indentations matched up with one of Andover's fingers. When he gripped the piece in his iron fingers the obsidian perfectly married itself to his grip. The heavier end of the club rested below his grip. The other end was not more delicate, thinner and pointed upward.

Tusk raised the axe head of obsidian and slipped it onto the thinner end of the volcanic glass in Andover's hand.

"You will need to work a way to connect them together, but they fit. How do they feel in your grip?"

Andover grinned as he looked at the weapon. There was no denying what Tusk had seen clearly. They were meant to be fused as one. The lines of the two pieces of darkness even matched up in the way their facets linked.

"They are connected already, aren't they?"

Delil chuckled and Tusk smiled indulgently. "Try to attack anyone and the head of your new axe would fall right off. Durhallem has given you a gift, but as I have said to others of your kind, you must make your own weapons. That is what the Daxar Taalor demand. You must find the proper way to bind them into one."

Andover nodded and watched as Tusk carefully took the two pieces apart and then wrapped them back together.

"What would you use to bond them Tusk?"

"Me? I would use a good length of leather." He stood up. "The gods say you have to make it work. They don't say it has to be hard work." He headed back to Brodem and turned his back on both Andover and Delil. "Go in health and walk with the gods."

A moment later they were on their way, heading down the side of the mountain. The journey was faster than the way up, but just as riddled with its own risks. Still, they made excellent time and before the sun was setting they had reached the edge of the valley proper and the farmlands that Delil had spoken of.

The ground was harder than he'd expected. Seeing the lush greens of the valley, he'd thought to see heavy vegetation and the sort of plant life he'd experienced on his way from Tyrne to the Temmis Pass, but instead there was little to see save hard soil and a short green moss that seemed to cover everything foolish enough to stand still for more than ten minutes.

"This is the farmland?"

Delil shook her head. "No. This is the ground when we do not till and work to make fields."

"How do you farm for anything in ground like this?"

"You say you have never farmed before?"

"No." He watched her as she stepped. Delil was careful about where she placed her feet, careful about how she settled her weight. A few missteps over the rocks told him why. The moss was solid enough, but the rocks it covered were often lose and he nearly twisted his ankle twice before he started paying better attention.

"The ground is hard. You have to break the ground, and you have to turn the soil and remove the rocks. Then you have to add ash to the dirt, because the ash from the mountains makes plants grow better. Then you have to plant the seeds and keep them watered. Then you have to wait and you have to protect the plants."

"Protect them from what?"

Delil stopped and looked back at him. "We are not alone here. There are other things that live in the valley and they are smaller than us and they fear us, but they are fast and they will eat the plants if we do not guard against them."

"What sort of things?"

"I thought you wanted to know about farming."

"I do. I just want to know the other things, too."

She shook her head. "When I have told you about farming you may ask more questions. Hold them until then."

They traveled a long way the first day, and never lacked for things to discuss. Mostly, Delil told Andover about the Taalor Valley and the local plants and animals. It seemed nothing went to waste in the valley. As proof of that, Delil hunted down and killed two small creatures the size of large feral cats, with thick hides and teeth that looked like they were designed to chew out a person's spine.

Delil held the jaw open on one of the creatures, and let him look carefully at the front teeth. "They are long and thin to allow for digging in the ground and for breaking the skin of the logga nuts."

"What is a logga nut?"

"It's what is farmed in this part of the valley." She dropped the corpse and reached into a pouch on her belt. There were four hard stones in her palm. No. He looked closer and saw the thin seam that ran along each of them. "Logga nuts." Using the hilt of one of her knives she hit the nut hard enough to crack the surface. The meat inside the nut was sweet and heavy. "They are good for traveling. They also make the bread you had at your feast."

"They grow on trees?"

"Vines. The only trees in the valley are much further down. You will see them."

As she was skinning the first kill – and showing Andover how he would skin the second – she explained that the very same creatures were the sort that stole from the farms.

He contemplated the teeth on the corpse, and the wide-set claws capable of tearing through the heavy moss or a person with equal ease, and asked, "Are these particularly large ones? I was thinking something more along the size of a rat."

"No. They are barely even adults."

"Oh."

While he skinned his meal, Delil started a small fire. It was blazing properly by the time Andover had finished his task. They ate the food together as the sun set behind Wrommish. A few small lights glittered on the side of mountain. More lights came from the valley, enough to hide much of the light from the stars.

Andover chewed at the meat. It wasn't as tasty as Pra-Moresh, but it would keep a belly full. "What's going on in the valley? I don't think there were fires so close to us yesterday."

Delil tore one of the legs from her roast and looked toward the fires. "They are moving closer. Yesterday they were still closer to the foot of Truska-Pren."

"Who is moving closer?"

"You were still visiting with Durhallem when we heard the horns." She looked at his scar for a moment and smiled. "That is the army of Tarag Paedori, the King in Iron."

The timing was good. As soon as she finished speaking the first horn blew a long note into the air. The call came from much closer than Andover would have expected.

A moment later four more calls echoed and joined the first. And a moment after that the entire valley seemed filled with the sound. From behind them on Durhallem and from Ganem and from Wrommish, they heard more horns calling to each other, the sound a powerful note that made Andover's blood race.

"What are they doing?"

"Tarag Paedori calls to the other kings. It is almost time."

"Almost time for what?"

Delil looked toward him in the growing night and her eyes once again glowed with a silver light all their own.

"Your people attacked Tuskandru. The kings spoke together on this matter. Tarag Paedori will now go to meet with your Emperor and discuss the attack and what will be done about it."

"And all of the horns? What do they mean?"

"Andover, the Daxar Taalor assign each king with certain tasks. They are prepared for those tasks by the gods themselves. Like Durhallem has given Tusk the order that he must always protect Durhallem's Pass. That is his sworn responsibility."

Andover knew she was preparing to say something but had no idea what it was. He wiped the grease from his fingers and focused his attention on Delil.

"Tarag Paedori is the King in Iron. He is the Chosen of Truska-Pren. Truska-Pren is the god of formal combat. He charges Tarag Paedori with ruling the armies of the Sa'ba Taalor."

"The armies?" He frowned at the notion. "I didn't think you had armies."

She rose from her spot and looked around for a moment, scanning the horizon. "Come." Delil moved quickly and he followed as she moved into a rocky area and climbed to a greater height.

Within ten minutes they'd reached a level where she could show him what she wanted him to see. The lights they had seen were closer than he'd guessed and far more numerous. There were hundreds of fires, most of them large enough to cook food as well as provide warmth. Large enough, surely, that more than one person sat at each.

Andover's throat was dry and he wished he'd brought water with him. Instead, he worked his tongue around until he could speak again. "How many people are there?"

"I do not know. But we will find out together."

"What?"

Delil clambered down the rocks as quickly as she'd climbed them and Andover did his best to keep up. Her eyes seemed better equipped for moving through the darkness of the valley. The fires were near, yes, but there was enough vegetation and enough changes in the landscape to hide most of the illumination.

"Where are we going, Delil?"

"You are to meet the kings, yes?"

"Well, yes, of course."

"If Tarag Paedori is to leaving the Taalor Valley, now is your best chance to meet him before he goes to face your Emperor."

He shook his head, not at all sure that her plan was a good one. She either did not see or did not care. Whichever was the case, she headed for the encampment. And after only a moment's hesitation Andover followed.

He'd planned to meet with Tarag Paedori, yes, but after a few more days at the very least and certainly not while the King was gathering an army to go attack or consider attacking the Empire he came from.

Following Delil was easy. She made it easy for him, turning around from time to time and gesturing him forward.

And then it was even easier, as they came upon the first of the fires. There were soldiers up ahead and no two ways about that. The figures he saw were dressed in armor as varied as he'd have expected. It seemed that none of the Sa'ba Taalor shared the same designs for their armor. Like with their weapons, the individuals who wore them created each piece of protective gear.

Delil looked at several of the shapes – each seemed more terrifying and less human than the last to Andover's eyes – and finally ran up to one, a bulky shape in the firelight that Andover could scarcely tell apart from any of the others.

Whoever he was, he lifted her into the air as if she weighed nothing and tossed her up and caught her twice before setting her back on her feet.

Each and every one of the faces he could see wore a veil, with the exception of himself and Delil.

Several members of the group saw her, saw him, and stared.

He stared back, his pulse hammering in his chest and his hand resting near the release on his hammer's strap.

Delil pointed toward him and spoke quickly to the man she was with. He in turn looked toward Andover and nodded his head. A moment later he called out in a loud voice and several others joined in. Andover did not recognize a single word they said.

Delil gestured him closer. Despite a growing unease, he listened and stepped up to her side.

Up close, the man she was with was no less a sight. He wore heavy plates of armor strapped over a dense chainmail. The helmet on his head was not as ornamental as many he'd seen – certainly nowhere as elaborate as Tusk's skull-like affair – but it covered his entire head, leaving only his eyes and his mouth clearly visible. His mouth was hidden under a veil. His eyes burned with that unsettling gray light.

Delil said, "Andover Lashk of the Iron Hands, this is Ventdril the Unbroken. He is my brother." The joy in her voice when she introduced them allowed Andover to relax a little.

The voice was milder than he'd expected from the monstrous shape. "Delil says you come from Fellein."

He nodded his head. "I was brought here to meet the Seven Kings and to speak with the Daxar Taalor." Both of his mouths spoke, the sound echoing oddly inside his head. He would likely never adjust to the change.

Ventdril spread his arms and then crossed them. "I have called for Tarag Paedori to meet you. He will be here soon." Andover studied the four knives strapped to the man's thick forearm and nodded.

"I am here now." The voice came from a giant. He was bigger than Tusk, bigger than Drask, bigger than most of the shapes standing around, and, as he approached, the warriors immediately dropped to one knee, many of them drawing swords or other bladed weapons, turning the hilts toward the giant striding toward Andover and offering the weapons to him. The move was so fluid that it had to be something done regularly.

Delil lowered to one knee and offered one of her swords. Andover looked to her, looked at the others around him and immediately dropped to one knee. The hammer was a heavy weapon but he offered it just the same, his arms straining from the awkward position he held it in.

Tarag Paedori towered above him and grabbed the weapon by the offered handle. He looked it over for a moment, his eyes quickly studying the shape, and then placed it gently back into Andover's grip.

"You are Andover Lashk. You are now called Iron Hands. Truska-Pren offered you a great gift."

Andover looked up at the man and nodded. "I have come to speak to you and to Truska-Pren, to offer my thanks for his gift."

Tarag Paedori made a gesture with one hand and the people around him rose from the kneeling positions, putting away their weapons. Andover followed their lead, and forced himself to breathe.

The King in Iron lived up to his name. His body was covered in iron, from the plates of the stuff that covered his boot tops to the shell of the stuff wrapped around his body. His hands were bare and his face, but almost every other inch of his massive shape was covered. Over that armor the man wore a dark red tunic and a black cloak. On his face he wore a veil that matched his tunic, and on his head he wore a simple crown of black iron.

His eyes regarded Andover for several seconds and Andover had to resist the burning desire to fidget. He had a powerful suspicion that moving around would be seen as a sign of weakness.

Finally the man gestured with one scarred hand. "You will come with me. We go to meet Truska-Pren."

Without another word the man turned and strode toward the side of the mountain. The Sa'ba Taalor parted for him, leaving a wide path that Andover followed as quickly as he dared.

Delil did not go with him.

The caravan was a compromise. The initial idea was for only a dozen or so people to head for the parley, but Nachia's insistence in being along changed everything. Desh Krohan could not stop the Empress from coming, but he could decidedly make sure it was more challenging for her.

Fifty of the Imperial Guards rode along with the caravan, dressed in full armor and prepared for any eventuality. At least Merros expected them to be prepared. They were among the best-trained soldiers Fellein had to offer.

Seven wagons of supplies rode along, including cooks, serving staff and a few surprises that Merros did not feel the need to share with anyone else. Desh Krohan had one of the wagons as his own, and Nachia Krous rode with him. It was a wagon that Merros himself had once been a guest in and though he could not prove it he suspected there might be something of a magical nature involved. The wagon looked as pristine as it had since heading into the Blasted Lands, while everything else that had gone along had been scoured by the winds and debris until paint and finish were ruined.

They reached the designated site well before they had to be there, and Merros was surprised to find Goriah and Tataya waiting for them. The Sisters were dressed for the weather, they had heavy cloaks and the rain washed off the well-oiled materials.

The Temmis Pass was nothing remarkable to see. Unless one knew what one was looking for, the spot differed little from the rest of the vast edge to the Blasted Lands. In this area there was a good deal of grassland and in the distance the town of Hallis crouched. Hallis could only properly be called a town if one was feeling generous. There were seven buildings all told, and half of them were abandoned and falling in on themselves, but it was the closest sign of human life.

The people of Hallis – all eleven – stared with wide eyes when the caravan rode past. One old man – Merros could not remember his name – nodded and waved when he recognized Merros. The general nodded back but did not wave. Though he could hardly blame the man for charging insane prices for his supplies, he still wasn't fond of anyone who charged that much for barrels of water.

This time they had plenty of water along with them.

Merros waved the caravan to a halt, and the Sisters looked in his direction and approached. He'd expected them to head for the wagon, but instead they came to him. Goriah smiled softly in his direction. "You are earlier than expected."

"I prefer being ready for when the Sa'ba Taalor arrive."

"They are still well away. You have time yet."

He did not bother asking how they knew.

"Excellent. We'll have a chance to make a proper presentation for them."

The Empress came out of Desh Krohan's wagon and headed immediately for the edge of the land where it fell away into the Blasted Lands. The perpetual storm below them was lower than Merros had seen it in some time, and through the clouds holding below that edge the distant spires of the Seven Forges were visible, though heavily sheathed in clouds of their own making.

"It doesn't seem that far to travel, does it?" Nachia's voice was low and her eyes studied the distant forges.

"It's deceptive. The storms within the area are constant and keeping any sense of direction is nearly impossible." He looked to the Sisters. "I have no proof but I suspect the journey might well have been aided by these ladies."

They offered no confirmation, nor any denial for that matter. Merros merely smiled. He was beginning to believe they'd be more likely to deny being able to do things rather than to confess what they might be capable of achieving. Like Desh Krohan, they preferred that an air of mystery surround them. Rumors had their own sort of power.

Both of the Sisters bowed formally to Nachia Krous and she nodded her acceptance of the gesture.

From the third wagon in the caravan a head appeared briefly and then vanished. After several seconds it showed again, just peeping past the door of the wagon, and then finally a man slipped free of the thing. He was not a very tall man, as it went. In fact he could be called short without stretching the truth in any significant measure.

If he was the scout for the party inside he barely showed it. A tiny gesture from Merros's hand and he was heading for Merros and the rest, ducking his head again and again, as if he were practicing how to bow while only involving his neck in the effort.

He came closer and kept his eyes on Merros. In the man's defense the general was the only one of the four carrying a weapon, but in truth all three of the women he was with were far deadlier.

Nachia turned her head and regarded the man for a long moment and as she did, Merros watched the subtle transformation in her demeanor. Her shoulders shifted a bit, straightening, and she lifted her chin. The lines of her face seemed to harden and the warm expression he was used to seeing grew as cold as the Blasted Lands.

The man came closer still, looking toward Nachia as if he were seeing her for the first time, and then remembered that he should bow to the Empress. Had a man ever looked more wretched? Not that Merros could remember.

"Your Manjesty…"

"Elder." Oh, how cold the woman's voice.

Teagus was an Elder for the Church of Etrilla. Near as Merros could figure it, Etrilla was the God of Cities. Wherever people gathered to live, the god was supposed to hold sway.

Merros gestured to the Sisters. "Teagus, this is Goriah and Tataya, two of the Sisters to Desh Krohan."

Teagus managed what should have been impossible. He simultaneously cringed and sneered at the two women. From what Merros had seen, that was his expression with all females.

"I am pleased to meet the both of you. May the gods always be kind to you."

Tataya, who normally managed to be pleasant and formal with everyone, made the barest nod in the man's direction.

Goriah smiled frostily and offered a formal bow.

Teagus then promptly ignored both of them and looked to Merros. "Is this the place where you are to meet with the Sa'ba Taalor?"

"It is. We appreciate your agreeing to join us on such short notice."

The cringe-sneer came back. "We were not exactly given a choice."

"Of course you were. You were given the choice to attend to her Majesty or to be brought along in irons. I feel you made the wiser of the two choices. I'm sure by now that two of your number would agree."

The cringing aspect of his demeanor grew more pronounced and the Elder wrang his hands. "Yes, well, that is why I am bothering you. They were wondering if they are to be kept in irons throughout the entirety of the trip."

Merros kept his stern expression despite the powerful temptation to laugh. There were eighteen members of the eighteen different churches present now and with the exceptions of the Deiber, the head of the Church of Lalos the Wanderer and Ellish, the head of the Church of Vendahl, the leaders of the churches had all come willingly enough when the Empress invited them along. Merros had taken the liberty of extending his own invitation to the reluctant duo.

"You may tell Ellish and Deiber that they will be allowed to move about after I have had a personal discussion with each of them regarding the proper response to invitations from the Imperial Throne." Merros shrugged. "I should be there within the next hour or so to have that discussion. Any who wishes to participate in the conversation is welcome to state their opinions at that time."

The Elder cringed and bowed and backed away as carefully as if Merros were aiming a crossbow at his testicles the entire time.

When the man had disappeared back into his wagon Nachia relaxed back into herself.

Merros resisted laughing and kept his stern demeanour. "Honestly, Nachia. You're a cold one. I thought he would wet himself."

"I wonder how he feels about the city being evacuated." Tataya's voice was low and conversational.

"I should imagine it's an affront to his position within the city. I can't imagine wherever he eventually relocates that the Elder in that city will appreciate the competition," said Merros.

Nachia responded, her voice carrying an edge, "As I understand it, the Elders of the Church of Etrilla must stay in the town where they are in charge. His being here is pushing the limits of what his faith permits. He must stay in Tyrne, even if the city is evacuated completely."

"Even if the Empress demands he leave?" Tataya asked the question in an offhand way, but her voice also carried an edge.

"The dictates of the church. He will leave when the time comes. I won't be giving him an option."

Merros looked from Empress to Sister. "Why do I get the impression there's more about this man that neither of you are telling me?"

Nachia let a smirk play across her face and then grew sober. She said, "Teagus has a long reputation for attempting to influence the youths of his faith." Nachia shook her head. "Do you know when I was younger I went to his church for one ceremony or another and he did his very best to bed me."

Merros felt his blood surge at the thought. "I do have extra leg irons in my supplies."

She chuckled and waved the thought away. "Mostly I just wanted to see if he'd remember me. His attempt to seduce me did not go well for him or for his church. Pathra nearly demanded his head."

Merros eyed the wagon and contemplated the leg irons. He was not fond of people who abused their position and that especially stood for anyone who would attempt to use that position to get between a child's legs. Nachia was the Empress, true enough, but a few years back she would have barely qualified as an adult.

Merros ground his teeth. "But nothing has been done about it?"

Goriah answered for the others. "There is a long standing tradition of allowing the churches a certain amount of leeway in their actions. It leads to less trouble between the Empire and the faithful."

Merros looked Goriah and shook his head. "Is that only within Tyrne?"

"No. The churches work throughout the Empire. They are a power to be considered, Merros Dulver. You would do well to remember that when dealing with them in the future."

He was not even aware of his hand resting on the pommel of his sword.

"The churches have their place. I'm not quite sure where that is, but I intend to find out."

Goriah brushed some of the blonde hair from her eyes. "Have you been studying the faiths your entire life, Merros?"

"No. I've been studying the military laws of Fellein. I have acquainted myself with the churches on the last few days. I'm still trying to understand the full hierarchy of the faiths."

She smiled at him, her eyes holding his attention as she stepped closer. "The hierarchy is uncertain at the best of times. The churches have come to a respectful accord. The differing faiths started throughout the Empire. Plith and Tyrea to the east. Kanheer to the south and east, where the Brellar often came in and took what they wanted. Kanheer is a war god. He is used to demanding sacrifices." She gestured toward the City of Wonders. "Vendahl and Luhnsh from around Canhoon."

The gods of wealth and beggars respectively. It made sense that they would be best known in Old Canhoon, where the two resided within the same walls as often as not.

"There are eighteen known gods and they come from all over the Empire, Merros. There is no hierarchy. The churches agree only to tolerate each other. And sometimes they do not do so very well."

Merros sighed. "Well, we have their gods outnumbered. I suppose that should be good for something."

Tataya looked toward the Blasted Lands. "Let us hope they feel the same way."

Nachia shook her head. "I will talk with the priests tomorrow, after the sun rises. Until then I prefer not to think about them more than I have to."

Merros nodded his head. "As you wish, Majesty." He did not feel completely the same way about the situation. At the very least he would be having a conversation with the reluctant duo and with Teagus. Of the three he suspected Teagus would like the conversation the least.

Nachia looked to the distant Seven Forges, their lights clearly visible through the heavy clouds that hid most of the Blasted Lands from this vantage point. She looked older than her years as she studied the reputed homes of the Sa'ba Taalor gods.

Merros turned away from the Empress and called to his soldiers. It was time to start preparing for the coming meeting.

Andover stared at the Iron King's city. Prydiria was a massive gray city built into the side of a gray mountain. Where the dwellings in Tusk's city were relatively new, these were ancient. Tarag Paedori continued his long strides and Andover did his best to keep up, taking deep breaths and fast steps to make up for the man's pace.

"I was to be the ambassador between our peoples, your Majesty."

The King in Iron looked his way and regarded him with eyes that offered no hint of kindness.

"I have spoken with your people before. I have talked with Merros Dulver and Kallir Lundt. You are not the first of your kind here, nor the first favored by Truska-Pren."

Favored? He looked down at his hands.

"Yes. Kallir Lundt was here before you and healed by Truska-Pren."

He had never heard the man's name mentioned before.

"He was given iron hands as well?"

The King turned to face him and slowly shook his head. "Kallir Lundt did not need new hands. It was his face that was ruined."

"His face?" There was a note of horror that Andover couldn't quite keep from his voice. He remembered the pain of his hands being ruined, and the even greater pain of having them replaced by the living iron hands he had now and shook his head.

"Like you, Kallir Lundt decided he would rather be complete than dead."

"Of course. I did not mean offense."

"There is no offense in simple truths, Andover Lashk." The man stopped and faced him. "You will meet Kallir Lundt. He has been waiting to meet with you for a long time. And then you will meet Truska-Pren. Be prepared for these things."

"Yes, of course." He said the words easily enough. But as his father had said more than once: words were easier to say than actions were to fulfil.

Had there ever been a place with so damned many stairs? Climbing the side of Durhallem had been a harsh challenge, to be sure, but Prydiria seemed harder still, with endless runs of staircases and level after level of hard angles and carefully carved stone. They climbed for a long while and Andover did his best not to show how tired he felt while the King continued to walk at a pace that would have shamed a few horses Andover had seen in the past.

Finally they moved into an area that forced Andover to stop. The opening they moved through was as tall as any of the others – tall enough to easily accommodate even the King in Iron – but, when they passed through, it opened into a cavernous area. The space was enormous indeed but, like everything else, was carved meticulously and filled with sharp angles. They were inside the mountain. They had to be. It was the only possible explanation that made sense to Andover. Light filled the area from dozens of stanchions lit with burning torches. He could not count the sheer number of lights that filled the area but it seemed nearly as many as there were stars in the heavens.

"This is Prydiria. This is my kingdom, Andover Lashk of the Iron Hands. And as long as you make yourself known to Truska-Pren, you are welcome here."

Andover nodded his head and swallowed. "You are most gracious, Majesty."

Tarag Paedori let out a sound that could have been a snort of laughter and nodded. "Come. It is time for you to meet Kallir Lundt."

Andover followed him, his heart beating too hard in his chest. The sense of wonder he felt as he stared into the amazing structure was offset by a growing sense of dread. He was to meet another god and once again he wondered if he would be found wanting.

Down another hallway that could have led almost anywhere, and then the King opened a door, speaking softly before entering. A moment after that, he gestured for Andover to follow.

The room had little by way of decoration, save for a bed and a long table. At the table a man sat drawing meticulous maps, carefully filling in as many details as the paper would allow. Andover knew what maps were, of course, but couldn't have guessed if this one were accurate.

The man rose and looked toward Andover.

Andover looked back, and forgot to breathe.

Kallir Lundt was a tall man, and thin in an athletic way. His muscles were solid and his limbs were long. He wore loose-fitting pants and a vest, and military boots that would have looked at home on any soldier from the Empire.

His face was hewn from black iron. That was the only way to put it. There was a line of scar tissue around that mask, but that it was fused with his flesh was obvious. The metal was angular, but it made human enough features, a broad mouth that pulled down in a slight scowl, an equally broad nose, and two eyes that lay sunken beneath a heavy metallic brow. If it had been a mask it would have been unsettling enough, but, as with Andover's hands, the metal moved. The mouth shifted and worked, and somewhere within that living mask, parts worked to make the mouth form words. Andover felt as fascinated as a child watching a street magician and a puppet show combined.

The iron face said, "You are Andover Lashk. We've been expecting you." The voice rang as if the man were speaking through a small metal tube. Perhaps he was, to some degree.

"Kallir Lundt?"

"I am." He could not really see the eyes within that mask, not with the lighting the way it was, but he could feel the gaze that studied him.

"How long have you been here?"

"Long enough to know that I am among friends." Lundt stepped closer. "In a few hours I will ride with Tarag. We will head for the Temmis Pass and discuss the possibilities of war with the Emperor and his people. I go along to do my part to keep things civil."

Andover nodded his head. "I am here to meet–"

"I know." The man nodded his metal covered face. "I wish you well with that." He regarded Andover for a long moment while Andover watched the way his features moved, amazed as he ever had been by the miracle of his own hands. It did not seem possible that metal could be so supple, could move so well. "Truska-Pren is a war god, Andover Lashk. His followers are soldiers first. Remember that when you meet. Discipline must overcome fear."

Andover nodded, trying to find the right words to convey his doubts. He was scared. He had been frightened when he met with Durhallem, but this was different. Durhallem seemed less imposing, his king seemed almost kinder than Tarag Paedori, and to say that about Tuskandru was something Andover had never expected.

"It is time, Andover Lashk." The King in Iron moved forward and looked to Kallir Lundt. "It is time, Kallir. Gather your armor and your weapons."

"It has been a pleasure meeting another blessed by the Daxar Taalor, Andover of the Iron Hands." Kallir's voice still echoed, but there was a warmth to his tone.

Andover smiled and held out one hand. "I wish we had longer."

"Soon enough, if the gods permit. First we both have tasks to attend to." He paused only for a moment before turning toward a chest that rested half beneath the table where he worked on his maps. "May the gods keep you safe and welcome you, Andover."

"And you, Kallir Lundt."

Tarag Paedori moved on and Andover followed, swallowing his fear as best he could.

"Where will I meet Truska-Pren?"

Tarag looked over his shoulder as he walked down the same hallway, heading at a rapid pace. "You will meet him in his heart. We are not far now."

That was not hard to believe. The vast majority of what he had already seen seemed to have been carved within the mountain itself, so how far could away the heart of the mountain be?

They walked until Andover felt winded, and he had not felt truly out of breath since he had entered the Taalor Valley. Part of it was the heat and the odd scent in the air. He knew both well enough. The heat was certainly similar to that of Burk's furnaces when the time came to smelt metal. The scent was most assuredly one he knew: iron and steel gave off a sharp, bitter scent when they were melting.

An immense door blocked the end of the hallway. Tarag Paedori opened that door with one sweep of his arm and the heat from the other side washed outward like a physical blow. How hot did metal have to be to melt? Hot enough to suck the moisture from the air and to crisp hairs on the scalp. The stench of molten iron was potent, but the heat was worse. Beyond that door was a furnace, a raging cauldron of white hot metal and burning stone.

Andover hesitated only for a moment and then stepped forward.

He had been an apprentice smith. The colors and scents were familiar enough, and in his heart he felt like he was coming home.

FIFTEEN

Tyrne was no longer a calm place. It had been called calm on many occasions, and a few visitors had referred to it as a "lazy town" when the summer heat came along. The main industry in the city had been the care and maintenance of the palace for over a decade. There had always been a certain amount of that, of course. The Summer Palace was occupied year round, even when the Imperial Family was not in attendance, but after Pathra Krous had decided to stay in the palace fulltime, the city grew more focused on tending to his needs.

Truly, the change in the activity was as sure a sign to the people of Tyrne as any other that the Emperor was dead. The decree had gone out that Nachia Krous would be moving everything to the traditional Grand Palace in Old Canhoon, and while the start of the exodus had been slow, it was now a driving force in its own right.

The armies of Fellein had been on the move, many of the regiments had been called to head for Tyrne, and thousands upon thousands of soldiers had come to the city. And now those very same soldiers were leaving, heading back the way they had come, toward Canhoon and other cities. And as they left they seemed to suck the very life from Tyrne in the process.

But if that were the case, the process was as slow and ponderous as the army itself. The soldiers gathered their belongings and formed up, and the supply lines that fed and cared for the soldiers moved too.

At first there was endless activity, and then the frenetic motion stopped, and the people of Tyrne looked around in wonder, surprised by the sudden silence where before there had been ceaseless commotion.

And then, in fits and starts, the people of Tyrne started moving. There was no choice for most of them. In one way or another they were dependent on the army or on the Imperial Family. Where those forces went they were sure to follow.

Not everyone, of course. Nowhere near everyone left.

In the palace itself, four members of the Krous family continued to occupy rooms. Brolley was packed, but he chose to wait for his sister's return before leaving. He had not gone with her to the parley, much as he'd wanted to, but he would be here for her when she returned. Whether or not he was accurate in his assessment, he had come to the conclusion that his sister needed him nearby, if only to make certain someone told her when she was being an idiot. Oh, to be sure Desh Krohan was doing that already, much as he had for Pathra, but he was still treading carefully, because even the First Advisor had to be careful when dealing with a new Empress. Brolley had the advantage of not worrying about a new Empress so much as dealing with an older sister. Blood had certain advantages.

Danieca Krous likely did not agree. She was still in a rage with how the accession had been handled. She was smart enough not to say anything in front of Nachia, but not quite wise enough to remember that Brolley was close to his sister. She had already said half a dozen things in his presence that could have been called treasonous.

Brolley was a Krous. He kept his mouth shut and listened. One thing to offend an occasional foreign dignitary – though to be fair he had learned his lesson along those lines – and another to ignore the ammunition one was given when it came to blood.

Towdra Krous remained in the city, but stayed at his own estate. The man had certain excesses he was fond of that were not the sort of thing even royalty should mention in public without fear of retribution. He knew that Nachia and the wizard wanted the city emptied and he would eventually listen, but first there were appetites to sate.

Hiding bodies had always been easier in Tyrne than it had been in Canhoon.

Laister Krous had no intention of going anywhere. He sat in his personal office within the palace and balanced the numbers on his estates as if there were nothing in the world to worry himself about.

Losla Foster was there to do his worrying for him.

"I'm thinking about marrying that little girl from Roathes, Losla."

"The Queen Lanaie?"

"That's the one."

"She's a queen, true enough, but she is currently a queen with no country."

Laister smiled. "I know this. I also know that she is alone in the world and in need of comfort. And that her title brings with it a certain level of legitimacy."

Losla looked at his employer for a moment and then poured a very small amount of the potent pabba fruit elixir that came from the far east. At one point it had apparently been a wine, but now it was thick and sweet and strong enough that a full glass of the stuff would have knocked a horse into a drunken stupor. He'd grown very fond of the elixir.

"You already have legitimacy. You're in line for the throne, should something horrible happen to the Empress."

Laister snorted. "Yes, I know that. But I would like to have a proper woman lined up to bear my children."

"Well, she certainly looks ripe enough to bear children." He sipped at the sweet drink and smacked his lips. "Still, you should move quickly. I understand she and Brolley have been making eyes at each other."

"Brolley," Laister snorted. "May the gods spare me from his imbecilic behavior."

"Apparently young Lanaie finds him quite handsome."

"Looks fade." True enough. In his time Laister had been the desire of most the women he knew. "Power and money stay. I have more of both and the girl knows it. If I approach her, she'll very likely say yes."

"What did you wish me to do about it, Laister?"

"I want you to look into who, exactly, controls Louron. I think it might be time to see about changing the map a bit."

Losla set down his glass. "Are you quite certain?"

Laister looked at him without speaking. It was best to remind the man who he worked for from time to time.

Losla cleared his throat. "I only ask because we are already close to a war with the Sa'ba Taalor."

"I don't care in the least about that. What better time to start making the proper adjustments?"

"Well, we could hardly use the regular soldiers in this case."

In the past there had been a few border skirmishes that had worked to Laister's benefit. Chief among them had been the situations with the Guntha. As the people in question no longer existed, that left a need for different catalysts to start his controlled fires.

"Yes, well, I have a few connections in Morwhen."

Losla nodded. "I'll make inquiries. Shall I be particularly discrete?"

"Oh, yes. I should rather not ruffle any feathers just yet."

Neither of them spoke of the assassins. They did not need to. If all went according to their plans, the parley would end with the Empress suffering from a wasting illness. And if things went astray, they would have their contingencies to consider.

In any event, Laister remained certain that he would be ascending to the throne within a reasonable amount of time.

One merely had to be patient, and that had always been one of his strong points.

Pella moved along roads she had not crossed since she was a child, and shook her head at how much had changed, but also how little. Far, far to the east of Tyrne the Empire was not the same. Here the royal family held sway in name, but not as an actual presence. Pathra

Krous had never once visited the eastern half of his Empire. He had left that task to his emissaries, and while they surely had their purposes, she was not here to deal with them at the moment.

The Imperial Army was a presence, to be sure, but nowhere near as noticeable as it was in the west. The closest thing to a truly vital Imperial city was Elda, and she walked through the streets of that city with impunity, knowing she would not be noticed unless she decided she wanted to be.

Elda was large, and the people were clean and did not starve. That made it an exception to many other areas in the east. Elda thrived on the backs of neighbors, as had almost always been the case. The military might in the city was enough to cause any force considering an invasion to hesitate. The soldiers from Elda were among the finest fighters that the Empire had, but the cost of keeping them was visited on the farming communities and smaller cities.

It seemed a full legion of smiths worked the forges in Elda, hammering out shields and armor, carefully honing the edges of swords, as surely as the young men brought to the city were shaped into soldiers.

She watched the practice sessions of the trainees, observed the use of crossbows and swords, and the marching formations of the troops. Merros Dulver might have approved of the practice, but he would likely have cut the throats of several instructors. They were brutal in the extreme, which he'd have accepted in preparation for war, but only a few days in the area had shown that they could be bought and paid for. Several men wore rank who had not earned it through time served but rather with gold coin. Fellein had thrived because that sort of practice was not permitted – excepting certain royals, of course. One could not demand that a prince be trained with the rest of the troops when the family could afford private tutelage.

Of course Pella was a casual observer in these things. She had never used a sword in her life and saw no reason to start. She knew which end was employed in the art of cutting, but that hardly made her an expert. Like her Sisters she was trained to know the nature of people. She observed and she reported. Her report to Desh Krohan would be a mix of good news and bad.

Morwhen was a different situation. The kingdom of Morwhen was run by members of the Krous family. That was surely the truth. That those members had almost nothing but blood in common with the rulers of the Empire was also truth. Theorio Krous had nothing but a name in common with the likes of Danieca and Towdra. He and his kin held to the beliefs of Morwhen, and she doubted that any loyalty the man had would go so far as to send his soldiers into the rest of Fellein. They were fearsome. They had earned a reputation as violent and cruel savages. Somewhere in the past they'd sued for peace with the Empire and won it by marrying into the bloodline.

Theorio did not recognize Pella. She had no desire to be recognized. He had aged very poorly and she doubted that he would last another year on the throne under ideal circumstances. He had two sons and three daughters. Pella had no notion as to who would rule after the old man died. If she had to guess, no one within the family knew either, and that made the situation volatile.

To the south of Morwhen, things got more interesting. The city states in the area were familiar enough and had changed almost not at all, but there was talk of a resurgence in the old faiths.

Pella listened intently to those claims, not because she thought the situation was of great importance, but because she knew that Desh would want to know. The most interesting aspect she noticed was how many of the older temples – many of which had nearly been abandoned – were now active again. People gathered in the halls dedicated to the gods and prayed. She had seen very little of that to the west.

Several weeks after starting her observations Pella found a properly secluded area and fell into a potent sleep.

As she had done many times before, she dreamed of herself as a storm crow and made that dream come true.

In that way she made her way back to Desh Krohan and her Sisters.

They were not surprised to see her.

"Pella!" Desh Krohan held his arms out at his sides and Pella moved to him, hugging his ribs warmly. Several of the soldiers watching the embrace likely envied the man just then.

"I've missed you, Desh."

"And I you. I like having my Sisters together again." He smiled and she returned the smile, her eyes locked on his.

Without any more theatrics, he headed for his wagon and Pella followed. Not far away Merros Dulver was speaking with the men he'd brought along, enough trained soldiers to terrify most towns along the way. He saw Pella and nodded his acknowledgement, but he did not stop dealing with his charges. There were issues he wished to see handled, chief among them the protection of a headstrong woman who refused to understand her importance in the grander scheme of things.

Nachia Krous stubbornly refused to stay in Tyrne. Desh was actually quite pleased with that part, though he'd have preferred she be in Canhoon and safely hidden away in the palace. Naturally she disagreed. Had he told her the skies were clear when there were no clouds to be seen, she would have found a way to argue the point with him.

It was what she did.

Pella poked his ribs. "You are being harsh."

"It's my duty to be harsh. And I'm not wrong." He paused for a moment. "Also, if I were Merros, I'd be ready to chastise you for reading my thoughts."

"If you were Merros your thoughts would be decidedly more lusty."

He smiled at that. "Fair enough."

They entered the wagon together. Tataya and Goriah were already there and after a quick embrace they got to business.

Anyone entering the wagon would have heard only their pleasant conversation, which was exactly as they preferred it. The reality was hidden from prying ears.

There was a reason that the Sisters could read thoughts. Desh Krohan liked to share secrets only when he wanted them shared.

Pella asked, *How goes the clearing of Tyrne?*

Desh responded, *Not as quickly as we would like. There are troubles with the people not wanting to leave.*

Pella frowned and went to the small fire where water was already boiling. Goriah had beat her to it, and tea leaves were already steeping within the waters. *The Sooth say disaster is inevitable?*

Desh sighed and leaned back into one of the cushions spread around the interior. *The Sooth nearly screamed it. There is danger, but they cannot or will not say what that danger is.*

Pella scowled at that. The Sooth were not her favorite entities. She preferred to observe for herself. *I do not trust the Sooth.*

That makes you wise, Pella. They are not trustworthy, but they do not lie in this. I am convinced.

She was not foolish enough to doubt him. If there was anyone more adept at dealing with the Sooth she had never encountered the individual. *When?*

No one can say, not even the Sooth. Soon, but how soon I do not know.

How long until the Sa'ba Taalor arrive?

They should be here within a day.

Pella poured herself tea and then explained what she had encountered on her journey to the east. There were stories to share, and decisions to be made.

Merros looked out at the Blasted Lands again, watching the agitated clouds seething and drifting in the distance. They reminded him of the ocean on a turbulent day, but the smell was wrong and there were no sounds of crashing waves. The air here was acrid, and if one caught enough of a breeze from the area where no sane person went without good reason, a taste like ash and dust crept into the mouth and lingered.

Nachia Krous came up next to him, and he looked her way and bowed immediately.

"I told you that you don't have to do that."

"I know, but the troops are present and I'll not have them getting the idea that they are free to ignore protocol." He looked at her from the corner of his eye, still mostly facing the ruined land that had changed their lives recently. "I'm wondering if we would have been better staying away from here."

A smile played on her lips, but it was the dry humor of a cynic that made that expression show itself. "Desh would likely point out that you are now in charge of the Imperial Army and that I am now the Empress and say that there are worse fates."

His smile mirrored hers. "Mmm. There is that. But we've both lost people and I wonder how much more we're going to have to go through before this is resolved."

"Pathra used to sit in his throne room and sip at his wine and stare out his window for hours, Merros. He wanted to see the world so very badly, but he was a prisoner in his castle. Do you know why he preferred the Summer Palace?"

"No. I hadn't given it much thought."

"Because the view is better. Look west and you see the Wellish Steppes. Look north and if the day is clear enough you could almost see Trecharch through the hills. South and there are towns and the river that runs all the way to the ocean. East and there are farmlands and, beyond those, more hills.

"Look out the windows in the palace in Canhoon and all you see is Canhoon. He did not like the city. He wanted to see the world."

The Empress put a familiar hand on his shoulder. He was tempted to brush it away. Not because he did not enjoy the familiarity, but because he didn't want anyone starting foolish rumors. Ultimately, however, he did nothing. She was the Empress, and if Pathra Krous had made the exact same gesture he'd have felt no reason to act as if anything were amiss. If rumors started they would die just as quickly. That was mostly the way with fancies and little lies.

"Why didn't he move about a bit more then?"

Nachia took her hand from his shoulder and shook her head. Her hair was carefully brushed and styled, and he knew she probably hated the effort but, like him, knew appearances had to be kept. "He felt he couldn't. Too much to do and not enough time in the day. I think Desh probably encouraged that. Better to keep the Emperor safe and all."

"Yes. Well." He didn't have to say that Desh's efforts had failed. They both knew it.

Nachia said it though. "My cousin was murdered in his home. He stayed there most of his adult life, and he never indulged his desires to go anywhere. And in the end he died just the same."

Merros nodded but said nothing. She had more to say and he could tell it.

"He would have given away the throne just to make this trip. I know that. I will not be in the same situation. I will go where I feel I must." She smiled at him. "Oh, I know you hate that, but you're good not to say it."

"You are the Empress. It's your decision to make." What else could he say?

"Here's the thing of it. I think that Pathra staying locked away made him want more of the journeys into the Blasted

Lands. Whenever the expeditions actually made it back, he got a trinket of some kind. Maybe a piece of ancient pottery, possibly a melted piece of gold. Whatever the item, it let him look away from the windows and imagine a bit more of what the world was like outside his palace walls. He used to practically interrogate me whenever I came to visit. He wanted to know about the places I traveled to, and believe me, Merros, I traveled a great deal. I have spent a good portion of my life already on the road to one place or another and usually with a retinue to keep me safe."

Nachia turned and looked at the caravan, at the tents aligned along the road and the soldiers who were stationed around the area, wisely at attention and careful to stay alert.

"None of this is especially unusual to me. Better organized than I've seen often, but not unusual. I saw more of this Empire as a little girl than my cousin saw in his entire life. And I think if he had seen more of it we would have never continued the quests into the Blasted Lands."

"Weren't those Desh's doing?"

Nachia nodded and looked out at the cloud cover in the distance. The sky above the Blasted Lands was gray, and more clouds were moving in, mirroring the ones below in the valley. There would very likely be rain coming. Whatever fell into the Blasted Lands, Merros knew, would fall as freezing sleet and howling winds. The clouds hid so much of the raging fury just below them.

Nachia said, "Absolutely. He paid for the expeditions himself. But he would not have done so without the permission of the Emperor and in the past there were less of them. Pathra encouraged the explorations. Pathra wanted to see more."

Merros sighed and looked again at the wasteland just a stone's throw from them, contained by a sheer cliff and little else. He could not for the life of him remember if he could see the Seven Forges in the distance the first time he'd been in the area. Mostly he'd been drawn to the turbulent motion of the storm clouds.

"So whatever the case, I think we would have met with the Sa'ba Taalor sooner or later. Hopefully we can make peace with them before it is too late."

Merros nodded his head. "Hopefully, indeed, Majesty." He feared it was already too late. But hope was a lovely thing to cling to when the winds were raging.

Andover Lashk met his second god. This time he was not alone. Tarag Paedori stood at his side, unflinching in the face of the raging heat and the boiling magma. Hot as it was, Andover could still breathe and his flesh did not burn. That seemed a miracle by itself.

The walls in the room ran with liquid fire. It drooled down along the sides, its heat mingling with that rising from the floor. The ground where he stood, the same as the gray stone that the castle was cut from, was not burning hot and the molten stuff never touched it. Instead it fell into deep cuts along the floor and slipped harmlessly into whatever lay beneath.

A wide metallic face stared at him from the wall. It was untouched, the sweating fiery metal and molten stone never quite reached this centerpiece of the room.

He had seen the face before. The exact same one had adorned the blessing box before he was gifted his new hands and learned that pain could be a healing thing as well as a hurtful one. The light of the raging volcano below and the smoke rising upward highlighted rather than obscured the edifice.

The face glared down from that wall, the mouth open in a cruel sneer. Truska-Pren seemed an angry god.

Just the same, Andover Lashk lowered himself to one knee before the face, and offered his hammer handle first, exactly as he had done with the King in Iron. "I am Andover Lashk, of Fellein, and I am here to thank you for the gift of my hands and all the blessings you have afforded me."

He half expected the face before him to grow animate, to work as easily as the iron features of Kallir Lundt, but nothing happened.

Nothing physical, at least. Instead he felt the presence come into the area, a powerful thing, vast and potent, that if it had mass it surely would have crushed him beneath it without even noticing his insignificance.

It was not fear he felt when Truska-Pren came before him. It was awe.

His hands tingled. They did not burn, but when he looked at them the metal glowed, growing first red and then yellow and finally white with heat. By all rights his arms should have burned away but there was nothing – no pain, no bubbling meat and burning blood. Instead that presence grew even greater and he understood that Truska-Pren was studying his hands, a god examining the work it had offered to a mere mortal.

It was Tarag Paedori who spoke, though his voice was not his own. His voice echoed with the presence of the Daxar Taalor. "You have proven worthy of this gift, Andover Lashk. You have shown yourself capable of defending yourself. You have faced the trials I demanded and you have triumphed."

The King in Iron stepped forward and placed one finger against Andover's lips as if to shush him. Instead of demanding silence he pressed his finger down harder, and Andover froze, feeling the pain come on him as it had when Durhallem had touched him.

He did not scream, but only because he could not. The heat that he should have felt in his hands directed itself across his mouth, his face. He did not smell burning meat, but it seemed to him he should have. The King in Iron's other hand grabbed the back of Andover's head and held him in place. "Do not move, Andover Lashk. Do not flinch. The Iron God offers you a gift this day."

The blessings of gods, it seemed, never came without agonies of their own.

What was it that Drask Silver Hand had said to him? Life is pain.

Oh, how he lived just then.

SIXTEEN

Captain Callan unloaded his cargo along with his men. He commanded the ship, he made a good wage, but he did not shirk his portion of the workload. That was why the men liked him well enough to let him call himself "captain". By the time they were done he was pleasantly tired and his crew was happy for the break. Dealing with the Brellar was always a risk, but this time it had paid off handsomely.

Freeholdt was busier than usual and he rather liked it. The port town was always busy, yes, but this time around, the activity was not as simple as he'd have expected. There were ships unloading cargo, but there were just as many hauling new cargo onboard.

What he found interesting, though he was barely aware of it, was how few of the Guntha or the Roathians he saw in port. He'd expected to see a good deal more of both, seeing as their lands were gone. Instead there was just business and, more business, with none of the begging masses he'd half dreaded encountering. Business was excellent in Freeholdt.

That meant a good chance at another commission. Commission meant a good chance at enough money to celebrate properly. After spending time with the witch Tataya he had a powerful desire to find a dozen wenches and rut himself senseless. Paying for it hardly bothered him. He wasn't likely to be around any port town long enough to make a relationship, but he could surely spend enough time to handle the finer physical aspects of one.

Vondum climbed the gangplank back onboard with a grin on his face. "It seems everyone wants to leave the area, Callan. But wave a flag to let them know you're ready to negotiate and you'll have a dozen passengers and their goods to carry out of this town."

"What? Why?" He smiled as he asked. The reasons hardly mattered as long as the money was good, and by the smile on his first mate's face the passengers seemed willing to pay good coin for their travels.

"The Empress heads back for Canhoon. People either take their wagons along the Imperial Highway or they take the Freeholdt River to the Jeurgis and ride into Canhoon in safety and comfort."

"So people are heading south to get to Freeholdt so they won't have to take a wagon north?" Callan chuckled.

Vondum laughed out loud. "Isn't it lovely?"

"By the gods, man, anyone willing to take a long way to a short cut must be willing to pay good coin indeed." Callan's grin refused to go away.

"I say we spend a night celebrating, restock in the morning and then head out tomorrow night, Captain."

Callan nodded. "Whores, supplies and feasts, in that order."

"Feasts, indeed. We have some of the finest of Tyrne's merchants looking to take their supplies and stock to Canhoon."

"Well, if we could find the finest brothel willing to transport their whores by river, we could sail out tonight." Callan wiped at his brow and looked out at the town.

"I don't think we'll be quite that lucky, Callan, but it would be a lovely thing."

Callan shrugged. "Tell the lads to enjoy their night. We're going to see about earning some extra gold and heading into Canhoon." They didn't often take the river routes, but they could. That was one of the things about a smaller ship that Callan liked. The Brellar's vessels would have managed nothing but getting themselves mired in sand bars if they tried a river run. Callan's little ship was a deal smaller, but also faster and mobile. Still, he'd actually have to work this time around. Piloting through the rougher areas of the rivers would take concentration.

Vondum said he'd pass the order around and Callan took him at his word. His second had long since earned his trust.

The night was spent exactly the way he'd wanted, with three lovelies who did their best to take away the hurt of never bedding the redhead who'd paid him handsomely to get her to her destinations safely.

And in the morning the lads looked as ill as he felt, but most of them managed a smile just the same as they started restocking the holds. The trip would take a few weeks, but not much more so they went light on supplies. Better to hold a little storage space for the customers who wanted to move with their possessions.

Sadly there were no brothels willing to transport their wenches as cargo. One could only get so lucky.

By the time the sun had reached its zenith and started a leisurely crawl to the west, Callan, his crew were helping a few very wealthy folks get their cargo stowed and were nearly salivating over how much they were earning.

The captain was considering the merits of leaving in the morning versus leaving earlier for a bit of extra coin when Vondum reported the news that set them for immediate evacuation.

Three words made all the difference. "Black ships, Captain." Vondum pointed to the horizon, in the direction of where the Guntha Islands had been.

There were indeed black ships. Callan couldn't see exactly how many, but it was enough to make his blood sing and his testicles try to hide themselves away. He found himself thinking of the redhead again and wishing he had a way to warn her that she was right. It seemed the black ships were looking to Fellein, and at the moment that meant they were looking at Freeholdt.

He wondered how long it would be before news of the port town being attacked made it to his ears.

He hoped it would be a long time, and possibly never. He feared it would be much sooner.

Either way, he'd be heavier with coin before this trip was done. One merely had to polish the silver to make it reflect properly.

Drask eyed the sloping mountain of ice before him and nodded. Brackka was nearby, but currently had no interest in climbing.

Drask did not have that option. Ydramil demanded and he obeyed, and so he set his hands carefully into the places where the ice had broken away and started climbing.

The surface was pitted with hundreds of spots where a hand or foot could find purchase, but most were filled with ice. It took time and patience to start scaling the structure. And it took a good axe to make fresh handholds. The silver hand held him with ease, the fingertips crushing the ice into a new shape when he gripped. He used his other hand to cut away the ice and allow him a fresh grip before moving upward again. It was an arduous task, but one he managed well enough.

By the time he'd reached an area where he could stand and walk, the sun was almost up and he had a perfect view of the wagon and tent where the others slept.

They'd danced around each other for over a day now and he was tired of it. Rather than worrying about them he chose to observe what they did for the day without conflict.

Drask crouched and dug into one of his pouches until he found a few nuts and dried meat. Better to have a bit of food in his stomach while he waited for the foreigners to start their explorations again.

The winds were starting up again with proper fury and he pulled his furs closer around his body, taking the time to tie them to his wrists and ankles. The hood was drawn over his head and he crouched lower. The winds could be damned for all he was concerned. He had a task to do and he would do it.

Soon enough he was rewarded.

Nolan climbed from the tent and shook his head.

The air outside was bad. The stench inside the tent was worse. Maun was dying, but taking his time about it. His breath stank of infection and his skin was pasty white and sweaty.

Stradly was no better. The man's body had taken on a yellowish tint. His eyes were also yellowing. Nolan was not a healer, but he knew that the colors were bad. The large, jovial solder was not dead but he was definitely dying.

Vonders and Tolpen were as fit as Nolan himself, uninjured by the Pra-Moresh or whatever sorcery Tega had done. But Darus was not well. His arm had swelled, the fingers barely recognizable, and he was in agony. The best plans for seeking a way into the Mounds had fallen quickly into ruin and there was nothing to be done for it.

Vonders climbed from the tent next and the worried expression on his face made clear he knew exactly what Nolan did, that their three companions would not survive this trip. With Vonders along they might survive themselves, despite the lack of horses, but he was having doubts.

Tolpen was a hunter. He'd spent the last day looking for anything he could hunt, but so far had failed. If there were creatures out there, like the rider they thought they'd seen, then the wind was scouring away any tracks that might have been left in the drifts of dirtied snow or on the rare patches of bare ground.

And off to the left was the wagon Tega slept in. The damned thing seemed nearly unaltered by the ice and sand and wind. The ground under Nolan's boots crunched with every step he took, but the wagon remained untouched by it. He resented the damned thing, irrationally, he knew. It had certainly proven a worthy shelter when they had stayed in it.

One of the men in the tent let out a moan and Nolan closed his eyes. At least one of them would die today, he could feel it.

The sun was up, which meant that the darkness was kissed with lighter shades of gray and brown.

The structures around them, the towers and lumps that made up the Mounds, took on detail again. The closest of the things had a beauty to it he'd deliberately refused to acknowledge before but after days on end of nothing, he allowed himself the pleasure of staring at the texture of the thing. There were striations of what looked like ice or glass, fused with flecks of metal and layers of different stones. The feeble sunlight washed the surface and let him see all of that under the thin layer of ice that had grown over the last two days. No noise from the Mounds, which meant nothing to break the ice away and so it was thickening again, like a scab over the open sore of the slanted tower itself.

"Maun won't make it." Vonders's voice was soft, just loud enough to make the distance between them past the wind

Nolan nodded. "I don't think any of them will. We've no way to take care of them properly.

Vonders glared at the wagon and Nolan knew he was thinking that Tega was to blame. She had saved them. She had damned half of them. That was still something to consider. She was powerful, but she had flaws. Didn't they all, really?

Tolpen came out of the tent, his face pale and grim. "Stradly is dead."

Vonders spit. Nolan nodded his head. "Best tell Tega."

Without waiting for one of the others to do it, he headed for her wagon.

So he saw the thing first.

It was moving not far from the wagon, not really looking at anything but the ground as it shuffled forward. He doubted it could have moved faster if it had to.

There was no sense to it. The skin of the thing was mottled gray, and covered in several places with bubbled clusters of watery blisters. At the very best it made him think of the monstrous lumps they'd fought on the road to Tyrne, but the comparison was merely because, like those beasts, it hurt his eyes and head to look at the thing. It was bloated and its body was squat. The torso was as wide as three men and the limbs on it made no sense.

It moved forward on one foreleg and two rear legs, none of which matched in thickness or length, which lent it a very uneven shuffling gait. A second forelimb was there, but like the rest did not seem to fit. It was much shorter than the – it hardly seemed right to call it a mate – other foreleg, and ended in a mass of stubby clawed fingers, and a thumb. The body was heavy, yes, but muscular. The four legs differed so much that none even matched in width. Judging by the mass dangling from its hindquarters he suspected the beast was male, but, frankly, he didn't want to consider that appendage, as it was as malformed as the rest of the thing.

None of which prepared him for the face. There were two eyes, but neither of them matched. One was as large as his balled fist and the other, higher up on the left side of the face, no bigger than a grape. Both gave off a pale gray light that Tega said the Sa'ba Taalor also cast from their eyes. The nose was a gash in the front of the face. The mouth was a great, drooling, uneven thing, an angry slash that had somehow sprouted teeth and a tongue.

Nolan noticed all of that at the same time that the thing saw him and looked him over from his head to his boots.

For exactly four heartbeats he thought the thing might simply keep going. His hands shook a bit and he almost reached for his axe before he remembered that it was back in the tent. He'd only come out to relieve his bladder and had certainly not planned to meet a fiend or learn that one of his companions was dead.

And then that great mouth opened and the thing grunted.

And then it charged him, screaming out a shrill battle cry. It did not roar. He knew a battle cry when he heard one. Hell, half the soldiers he'd trained with tended to let them out when they attacked.

Nolan threw himself sideways and dodged as the malformed brute came for him. His elbow slammed into the thing's face, hitting and mashing the oversized eye on its right side.

It yelped and the foreleg it ran with slapped him across his chest and staggered him backward. Had he not already been in motion it would likely have caved his ribcage in.

"Attacked! Arms!" It was all he could think to say.

The thing looked like it could barely stand, but it charged him again, as fast as the attack dogs his uncle had trained. Nolan let out a scream of pure panic and cuffed the thing in the face a second time, feeling its wet breath blast across him. Gods, it gave off a frightful heat.

His knee came up into the side of the thing's face as it lost balance and tried to recover. The blow was good and it fell back, grunting again. Nolan danced back, repulsed, his heart hammering and his eyes wide.

Vonders called out, but Nolan didn't have time to focus on him because the thing was coming again, loping forward, and as he watched, the thing planted both rear legs, squatted and then jumped at him, clearing the distance with ease.

Nolan did exactly as his father had trained him to do and caught the immense weight, pivoted his body at the hips and helped the thing on its way, adding his strength to its momentum.

It crashed into the side of Tega's wagon, hitting one of the wheels and disproving his thought that magic protected the wagon. The wheel broke, several spokes snapping, and the wagon rocked on its axles.

The thing was back up before he could even congratulate himself on the maneuver. That mouth, that ugly slit in its face, bloomed open until it was large enough to give a Pra-Moresh feelings of inadequacy. Those mismatched eyes glared at him as the thing jumped again and Nolan met it head on, slamming his body against the thing's bulk, hoping to kick it aside.

He failed. He staggered backward, tried to find his footing and instead slid and skidded like a skipped stone, bouncing along until he ran into the side of the tent. His ears rang and he tasted blood in his mouth.

Tolpen put an arrow through the hellish thing's fat, bruised right eye. It let out half a squeal and fell on its backside. It was possibly dying, but it was not dead. It kicked and shrieked and rolled itself to hands and knees and then flopped down on its face. Still, it managed to get back up, its one remaining eye glaring undying hatred in Tolpen's direction.

The hunter let out a curse under his breath and reached for another arrow from the quiver at his feet. His hand was shaking and the first arrow slipped from his fingers. His calm demeanor broke as the thing came for him, once again leaping instead of running.

Vonders tried to step in with a spear to stop the thing's charge, but instead was knocked aside.

Tolpen gave up on the arrows and swung his bow like a great sword, clubbing the misshapen face with all the strength he could muster. The thing fell to the ground again and let out a squealing noise.

The wagon door opened and Tega stepped halfway out. Without even considering, Nolan moved to stand between her and the monster. His duty was to protect her. His father had always taught that duty was all a soldier had to concern himself with. The rest was dressing.

Tolpen whapped the monster's head four more times with his bow, screeching with each blow delivered. As his arms rose up for a fifth, Vonders caught his elbow and shook his head. "Might need that bow yet."

Tolpen glared for only a moment and then calmed down.

The thing let out one long sigh and seemed to deflate a bit. The body relaxed to the point where Nolan knew it must surely be dead. He stayed exactly where he was, however. Some dead things didn't stay as still as they should. That was a lesson he would not easily forget.

Tega stepped from the wagon with surprising calm and looked down at the dead thing.

Nolan turned to her and relaxed a little. "Stradly is dead." He had no desire to protect her from the truth and no reason to. She had seen as much as they had and still she held herself together.

Tega's face lost composure for only an instant and then she nodded. "I had thought it would surely be Maun first."

She pointed to the dead thing on the ground. "Roll that over, please. I want to see it better."

Nolan almost told her where she could take her desire to examine it, but remembered that, while here, he worked for her. Instead he nodded and, with Vonders's help, maneuvered the thing onto its back.

The monster obliged him and remained dead.

He silently thanked all of the gods for that small blessing.

And then he watched in mute surprise while Tega studied the body and cut samples of the hair and the skin from it.

Drask watched the fight in absolute silence. He did not move. He did not consider helping either side. Instead he studied every move the Fellein made and filed the information away. Better to know an enemy than to guess what might be in their hearts.

The Broken they fought was not very skilled. They killed it with ease and all of them lived through it. Still, he stayed where he was as the girl – he thought it might be the sorcerer's apprentice, Tega, but could not be certain from this distance – first looked the corpse over and then began cutting.

If she planned to eat the flesh it would go poorly for her. The Broken had poisoned flesh. That was part of the punishment the Daxar Taalor rewarded them with for their failures.

They could no longer offer anything to anyone. They were useless. They were broken.

They were godless.

The men with the blonde girl stepped away as she started her examination, and shortly entered the tent and came out with the body of a man who was older than the rest of them and flabby besides. Drask shook his head. He had seen several people in Tyrne who were overweight and the notion horrified him. That anyone could consider themselves capable of fighting when they weighed so much... Still, there were a few among the Sa'ba Taalor who were as large and carried extra flesh and they were only alive because they were skilled combatants. Physical prowess alone did not make a warrior.

After a bit of discussion, the group decided the man needed to be burned. They managed to start a small fire and lit the man's clothes, which smoldered and sputtered and finally burned. When his remains were burning well enough, they dragged the Broken over and cast it into the flames.

Through it all, Drask stayed on his perch, moving his legs from time to time and carefully stretching to avoid letting his muscles cramp or his joints lock.

And that was how they spent the day, killing a Broken and burning corpses.

It was a wonder to him that the Fellein ever managed to accomplish anything.

From his perspective Drask saw the troops moving from the Seven Forges toward the place the Fellein called the Temmis Pass. He nodded his satisfaction at the careful movement of the soldiers. He did not know exactly what Tarag Paedori was planning, but he also understood that there were no better tacticians for a land battle among his people.

They moved at night, and from this distance they were little more than a smudge on the horizon. He doubted that any of the people below him would have spotted the army moving.

He could not guess how many of the Sa'ba Taalor were moving in that column, but part of him longed to walk with them.

• • •

Andover Lashk stepped from the castle at Prydiria and moved into the daylight. The skies above were mostly clear, and the temperature was pleasant. His skin felt dry after what seemed like days in the intense heat of the god's heart. Seemed like days. In truth he could not begin to guess how long he had been in the presence of the Iron God.

All he truly knew was that he was changed. Again.

Some truths seemed to remain constant no matter what. One did not face a god and come away unchanged.

The second Great Scar on his face was larger, and bisected his mouth. He could feel the changes in his flesh far more easily this time. Below his nose to just above his chin there was a line of flesh that split his mouth in half. That line could move and could open, and when it did he suspected he looked like a monster. He understood now why the veils were important. Anyone not prepared for the ways of the Sa'ba Taalor would have been terrified by what they saw when they looked upon the warriors.

Andover knew that he *should* have been horrified, but he was not. The culture he was with admired scars as signs of achievement. Great Scars even more so. A person with no Great Scars was either young or, in the eyes of the people of the valley, godless. What could be worse for them?

He had never cared much for the gods when he was growing up. The gods, it seemed, had never much cared for him, either. But here, in the Taalor Valley, the people and the gods had a relationship that was extremely different. He was only beginning to understand it, but it seemed to him that it might be something wondrous.

He looked at his hands and the iron rings that he held in his grip. The rings, like the scar, were a gift from the god of the mountain. He suspected he knew what they were for.

Delil waited nearby, sitting on a flat stone that had been carved, smoothed, sanded and polished until it was as flawless as still water and almost as reflective. The woman was sharpening one of her swords and had several other weapons nearby. There were daggers and throwing knives and several long, thin darts that looked like they should have been harmless. He'd seen her use them and knew better.

She smiled at him as he approached and he smiled back. Her face was revealed to him. Andover felt like she and the rest of her people had given him a great honor by taking their veils away around him.

She looked at his face and saw the new scar and as he came closer she stood up and ran one callused fingertip across it gently.

"You are blessed indeed, Andover. Two gods have favored you in less than a week. That is very rare."

He looked into her eyes and smiled. "Where did everyone go?" The last time he'd been outside there had been crowds of armored Sa'ba Taalor around, most of them with weapons and supplies aplenty.

"They have gone to meet with your rulers to discuss whether or not a war will happen."

He felt oddly relieved. He'd felt a certain dread that the King would make him go along. He was supposed to be an ambassador, according to Drask. "Is there anyone left here?"

"Oh, yes, there are many people left here. But they are training."

"Training for what?"

"If there is to be a war, everyone must be prepared." Her voice carried an odd tone to it. He couldn't decide if she was disappointed that she was still with him instead of with the rest of her people. He also wasn't quite brave enough to ask her. Andover had dreamed of being with a woman and Delil had made that dream come true, but he didn't know the intricacies of what happened next. He had never been close to a woman before this journey.

Delil stood up and started putting away her weapons. He was amazed even after months of being with her by how quickly she could slip the various blades into their sheaths. "We should go now. There are places we have to take you yet and time is short."

"It is?"

Delil looked at him and nodded, her expression solemn. Behind the scars and the gray skin and the odd silvery light of her eyes she was rather average in looks, but that did not matter. He'd grown very fond of her and knew he could trust her and the lingering memories of what they had done together made her lovely.

He pushed away thoughts of what they had done, how her flesh had felt in his hands, and touched by his lips, and made himself focus as she started to speak. "Time here is short. There are places you must see within this valley and there are other places you must go as well, Andover Lashk."

"How do you know that, Delil? How do you know what I must do?"

She tilted her head in that odd way of hers. He understood what it meant now. The way she looked at him sometimes was both an expression of surprise at how naïve he was and exasperation that he could ask so foolish a question. "I know because Wrommish tells me. You have been marked by the Daxar Taalor, Andover Lashk. You should start listening when they speak to you."

Shame washed through him quickly but was shoved aside by irritation. "This is new to me, Delil. You have had a lifetime to learn how to listen to your gods. I have not."

"And that is why I am here. I am here to help you listen." Her voice was surprisingly light. She finished strapping her weapons in place and grabbed the bundle of clothing she'd been carrying. Somewhere along the way he had left his behind. He was about to start cursing when she reached to the side of her perch and lifted his supplies. "Come."

"Not yet." He shook his head.

"What?"

"The Daxar Taalor have spoken to you and they have spoken to me, too. I was told to finish this before I go further." He unrolled the bundled goods and took out the separate sections of obsidian. Putting them back together was easy. They fit as if they had always belonged together.

Andover stared at the assembled axe with a critical eye and considered how best to make sure the pieces would stay together. Delil looked with him and finally nodded her head.

"You need hide."

"Hide?"

"You killed Pra-Moresh. You took their fur for your own. The skin of the beasts is good, tough leather. A little and you can tie it. Or better still, you could use metal wire." Her fingers touched the edges where the two pieces joined and she ran a line of imaginary wire, showing him how she would secure the two segments.

Andover nodded again and then rolled the iron rings between his thumb and forefinger. They were just the right size to wedge into the obsidian and lock the parts together. "I think maybe the gods have plans for me and though they may not speak as clearly to me as they do to you, the Daxar Taalor are still telling me things."

The rings locked into the socket of the obsidian blade, above and below. Once in place the blade that had wobbled was properly secured.

Delil squatted and watched as he worked the metal and the volcanic substances together. She spoke very softly. "Never have I seen the like."

"What? An axe?"

"No," she responded. "Two gods working together on one weapon."

That was all she said on the matter. When she stood again she started walking, moving down the path away from where they had already been and moving deeper into the valley.

Without another word Andover followed her. There were places to go and according to her they were running out of time.

"What did Wrommish tell you, Delil?"

"That we must visit each of the mountains before the time comes to leave the valley."

"What? I thought I was supposed to stay here with the Sa'ba Taalor."

"No, you are supposed to stay with my people, but you are not supposed to stay in this valley. We are not staying in the valley forever. It has almost served its purpose."

"What do you mean?"

"I mean what I say, Andover." She was growing tired of his questions and so he shut his mouth. He would wait a while for more answers. Still, he looked around as they continued walking and wondered why the people would leave.

And, of course, he wondered where they would go. There seemed only one possible answer and he found that answer lay uneasy within him.

The streets in Tyrne were crowded with people and supplies. Many of the people looked shocked to find themselves on the streets and moving away from their homes, but more were angered by the idea.

At first, when the announcement came that the Empress would be leaving Tyrne and heading for Old Canhoon, there was shock and disappointment. Several times gatherings of citizens attempted to reach the palace and ask their new ruler to change her mind, but they were turned back. Surprise was the usual response to that. Pathra Krous had almost always managed to find time for concerned citizens of the city. Pathra Krous was well thought of, and had been a boon to Tyrne.

And now his replacement came along and changed everything without warning. At first it was just the increased military strength in the city, which, after the murder of the Emperor most people could understand. Then came the decision to leave Tyrne. And then, oh, the madness, the latest insanity.

Town criers had been about, announcing the Imperial order to leave the city within days. There were a few people who scoffed. No one wanted to believe the decrees. That was when the madness began.

Libari Welliso had been warned to expect trouble, but this? He shook his head at the reports coming into his command center.

In the Gardens district, where many of the fine old homes had walls and gates and guards to keep the families safe from intruders, a few families were refusing to vacate. That was to be expected, really, as many had been situated in the same place for generations and had more invested in the property than merely possessions.

Libari sent guards to explain the position of the City Guard: if the people in those palatial homes wished to stay, there would be no one to assist them. Their guards were being told to leave as well, and the families of their guards. That seemed to make it through a few people's heads and several families prepared to move their possessions to other places or at least to lock up their homes. Some of the newer inhabitants had already left, which was a pleasant surprise.

To the south, where the largest collection of immigrants congregated, he had less trouble and more chaos. The Roathians who'd made it to the area were already homeless and few of them had possessions. The families he saw looked wounded at the idea of moving on, but few of them protested.

The biggest problem in that part of town was caused by his own guards, some of whom felt that they should be allowed to take out their frustrations on the poor wretches who were already lost and abandoned. He was doing what he could. Currently seventeen of his City Guard were awaiting his punishment for complaints ranging from abuse of authority to rape and murder. Welliso ground his teeth at the thought of administering justice, but he would do it, if only to guarantee that others were not foolish enough to think they could get away with breaking the rules.

Still, he'd never gelded a man before. It was not a task he looked forward to performing.

Around the palace, where the majority of houses and apartments were used by the people who served at the palace, the city was calmer. When the Empress and her entourage had moved on to handle the parley, those who served at the palace began the massive task of moving the offices of the Empire to Canhoon. Many of those very same people were moving too, preferring to keep their jobs and relocate to the old capital.

There were entire streets that were abandoned. Walking the same places he had walked for most of his life, Welliso felt his skin crawl and his hackles rise at the unsettling silences.

But mostly, in the other parts of the town, there was chaos. It took time to pack belongings and most did not want to leave behind anything that might be important. Wagons that were overloaded with worldly goods lumbered onto streets never meant to accommodate the sheer volume of traffic trying to leave Tyrne, and in short order tempers flared and the fighting began.

The City Guard and the Imperial Guard worked together to clear the streets. The situation was growing worse, despite their efforts.

In the westernmost part of the city someone had either been careless or had deliberately set a fire. The blaze was growing and there seemed little that could be done to quell it. Soldiers were attempting to put the fire out with buckets of water run up from the Freeholdt

River, but with little success. The river was too far away and the way to the wells in the area were blocked by the growing blaze.

The people there were going out of the city by heading either south or directly across the city to the Eastern Gate, the main access to the river. The only obstacle in their way was, of course, the palace, which lead to a lot of name calling, stone throwing, and worse forms of civil disobedience. The congestion had reached a level where no one was moving anymore and the City Guard were doing what they could to break up skirmishes and calm down the already angry and distressed citizens.

And the Imperial Army was doing what it could to back up the City Guard.

And ultimately, nothing was getting accomplished.

Libari Welliso had no choice, not in his own opinion. He brought the combined forces down to hammer out the problems quickly and efficiently.

The clusters of traffic that blocked the roads were broken apart. The soldiers under Welliso's command pushed carts from the road and ushered people and their draft horses out of the city, often insisting that the ruined wagons be left behind. A few fools tried to grab at the remaining supplies and the soldiers put an end to that action as soon as it started. The damaged wagons were confiscated, either dragged away completely or rolled far enough off the road to allow more evacuees through.

A few of the first people who encountered troubles tried to protest the rough treatment, but Welliso had his orders and he intended to keep them. The first time he whipped a man in public was enough to stop most of the protests. He took no satisfaction from his task, but he did it.

He would do all that he could to see Tyrne cleared of people as effectively and quickly as possible, regardless of how that made him look in the eyes of the people. The City Guard had been feared and loathed by a good number of people over the years and some things simply did not change.

Of course some reputations are earned, even if they are earned for all the right reasons.

Several skirmishes broke out along the road to the Summer Palace.

Had Merros Dulver been there to discuss the matter with Welliso Libari he'd have likely told the older man to let them stay if their lives meant less than their possessions. But Merros was not there; he had his own troubles to deal with at the edge of the Empire.

Instead, Welliso did what he thought best. His people followed orders and the Imperial Guard followed his orders as well. It was only a matter of hours before the city's cells were filled with angry citizens who'd attempted to fight. There had been no fatalities because Welliso refused his forces the right to attack with swords, but there were broken bones and busted skulls aplenty, and that was on both sides of the law. More than one of the aggressors were either soldiers themselves or had trained to defend their homes. Tempers flared and fights broke out, and in the end peace was restored again and again, only to face another disruption.

And that was only on the first day of the forced evacuation of Tyrne. There were plans in place to start sweeps of all the streets after the majority left the city. City Guard walked the areas where people had already moved on, making sure that homes were left abandoned and did not become victims of looting.

Libari Welliso came home from his first day of the evacuation in a state of exhaustion unlike any he had dealt with in his career. Tyrne had always been a peaceful town, regardless of its size, and he had never run across the sheer volume of people in motion, the large number of angry citizens or the massive swell of traffic at any point in his life. Dealing with all of that together was enough to make him consider moving on and forgoing the rest of his career with the Guard.

Of course his wife, Annushi, would have put an end to that notion. He smiled when he thought of her. Annushi was more than he had ever hoped for when he'd agreed to the arranged marriage. She was smart, funny, lovely and strong of will. All things that he admired.

They were fighting just now, because, after sending the children on to Canhoon, she had insisted on staying in the town with him until he was ready to leave with her. She was a stubborn woman and he loved her for it, even when the risk to her life made him nervous.

He opened the door to his apartment and started to call for her when he saw her corpse on the ground.

Annushi. Dead. He walked into the room and looked down, his eyes staring at the ruin of his beloved, uncomprehending.

There was no moment when he thought it was a joke. There was no time when he expected his wife to get up. She was dead and there was no denying it. Her throat was cut. He could see that as soon as he entered the room. She had been bathing, perhaps, or she had planned to bathe, because her body was naked and Annushi was nothing if not modest. She seldom let him see her without clothes unless they were making love.

"Annu?" She did not respond. She could not. She was dead. He knew that. But even though he could see she was dead – murdered, surely – he could not make his mind accept it. "Annu, what are you doing down there?"

All thoughts of the City Guard he had to punish, the people he had to let free from their cells when they had calmed down and the evacuation of the city were gone. What little they planned to take with them from the city was already packed into several bundles; Annushi had been busy preparing for their journey. She'd been optimistic about his promotion and looked forward to seeing new places. Like Welliso she had spent most of her life in Tyrne and had considered Canhoon only as a place where powerful people lived. The thought that they would move there had excited her and her enthusiasm had been infectious enough to make him look forward to the idea.

Annushi did not answer him.

Could not.

He stepped into the room properly and walked toward her body. Annushi stared past him at the wall near the door. There was nothing particularly exciting about that spot. He had looked at it many times. It hardly seemed like a thing she should have been stuck with as her last sight in her life. He would have hoped she could see a thing of beauty as she died.

Libari did not believe in the gods or in any sort of afterlife. He had always believed solely in what he could see with his own eyes.

There was a dryness in his mouth. His eyes felt wrong. His heart had gone still, near as he could tell, and his ears rang with a light note that took away all other sounds.

Annushi still stared at the wall, dead, as he moved closer to her and crouched beside her, reached to touch her face. Maybe she was injured, but alive. Perhaps there was a chance that she could still be mended, saved from death. He did not truly believe that, but he had to try because the thought that she was gone from his life was simply too large for him to consider.

His hand touched her lips, felt for a hint of breath. Her skin was cold. She was not freshly dead, but had been killed at least a few hours earlier. He had seen enough dead bodies to know that much.

Libari tried to stand but his legs did not work.

"Annu?" How had his voice gotten so small? He wasn't quite sure.

"She will not answer you. She is dead."

Libari turned his head and looked to the voice that spoke. A woman looked back at him, her eyes studying his face.

"Did you do this?" Blood surged in him as he stared. She had dark hair and dark eyes and was dressed for the road. He had seen a hundred or more just like her through the course of the day and wondered if the woman he looked at was one he had offended somehow through his actions.

She did not seem offended. She looked at him without much expression on her face at all.

"She had to die. Just as you have to die."

When Libari tried to move again it was easy. He thought of Annushi and the woman who had killed her and he thought of how much she would suffer at his hands. He was not angry, not really. He merely knew that she would be dead soon and then he would allow anger and grief to take better rein of his heart.

He had ordered his men not to draw their swords against the citizens of Tyrne. Libari Welliso did not follow that rule himself. His blade slid from the scabbard with a whisper and then sang as it cut the air and sliced toward the bitch who'd murdered his wife.

She was not there.

The blade clattered and rang out against the wall where she had been leaning, but struck nothing aside from the plaster over the stone of the wall itself.

He looked around, eyes rolling with a sort of madness all their own, and heard himself growl as he sought the woman out.

She crouched on the other side of Annushi's body, her left foot resting in the blood that was congealing into the floor.

Her face was still calm and she continued to look at him.

"Kill you. I. Will. Kill. You." He spoke the vow softly and adjusted his grip on the blade.

"No. You will not. You are already dead."

Libari moved one step forward and his leg collapsed under him. He fell to his knee and grunted, puzzled by the lack of strength.

It was only then that he felt the pain of the cut. As he had tried to strike, she had done the same, but she had been successful. The blood flowed down his side, from a deep incision in his stomach.

A cut, yes, but not enough to stop him from his revenge.

Libari tried to rise a second time and moaned instead. His legs would not hold him, would not move. His arms felt too heavy to lift. The sword dropped down, cutting a bloodless wound into Annushi's calf.

He looked down at his wife's new wound and felt his eyes water. Never in his life had he ever meant to cause her harm.

Libari toppled, then, falling across his dead wife's body.

The poison in his system was quick but not quite fast enough to prevent his suffering. The last thing he ever saw was the floor beside Annushi's cold hip. He had hoped his last sight would be something more beautiful.

Swech searched the man's corpse and found the key she was looking for around his neck. There were things she needed from the palace and without a key it would have taken too long to get to them.

Time was becoming a rare commodity and she had spent too much of it already in the city of Tyrne. She had places she needed to be that had nothing to do with the place.

The blade went back into the sheath along her left hip. Moments later she was gone from the building and heading for the offices of the General of the City Guard.

The gods made demands and Swech obeyed, grateful for the chance to please the Daxar Taalor.

SEVENTEEN

Tuskandru looked down from the top of Durhallem and studied the Blasted Lands. The air was thin here and the cloud that usually hid away the devastation beyond the Seven Forges was sparser than he had ever seen it. He could see the Mounds from where he stood and he could see the distant wall of the barrier that separated the Blasted Lands from the Fellein Empire. Somewhere in that vast distance an army moved and prepared themselves for parley.

A thin smile crossed his lips as he considered that notion.

Beyond him, the rest of the mountains stood silent guard over the valley. The gods were generous with their protection. How then could the Sa'ba Taalor be any less than obedient to the wishes of their benefactors?

Durhallem touched him, allowed him to see further than should have been possible. It was almost time. Before the sun set, the world would be changed by the Daxar Taalor and he would be prepared for his part in that change. He had to be. It was what he was meant to do and what his god demanded of him.

He reached down and grabbed the helmet resting by his foot. The great skull-shaped helm slipped over his head and fit as perfectly as it ever had. The teeth of his foes moved around his neck and along the edges of his vision. The teeth were reminders to him, yes, but mostly they were simple adornment. The enemies of his people were odd indeed and many of them looked upon death as something to fear. He did not share in that sentiment. Death merely was. It held no power over the gods and therefore held no power over the faithful.

Stastha came up from behind him, the horns of her helmet pointing toward the ground as she stepped closer.

"We are ready when you call us, Tusk."

He nodded his head without answering. Tusk did not like to speak at times like this. He preferred the silence. Stastha knew that and slapped his shoulder with her hand as she turned to walk away.

"Sound the horns, Stastha. Call them all home. It is time." He did not have to turn his head to know that she was smiling. Stastha was a warrior, one of the best he knew, and, like him, she thrived on the smell of blood and the sound of battle.

Stastha raised her horn to her lips and blew a long harsh note that echoed down the side of Durhallem and carried across the valley before coming back as a whisper. Long before that soft sound returned, the other horns called, demanding that the followers of Durhallem join together in the time of war. The Wounder called to his children and they obeyed.

It did Tuskandru proud. "Brodem! Come to me!" Tusk's voice called out and was answered a moment later by the content rumble of his mount. The great beast rose from the rocks where he had been staring into Durhallem's blazing heart and leapt down to where Tusk waited. Tusk climbed aboard Brodem's broad back and checked that his weapons were in place. The beast roared and he roared as well, his blood rising in preparation.

The sun would soon set and, before that happened, the world would change. He intended to make the Wounder proud.

Along the Mounds the air was surprisingly calm. The clouds were a thin scrim above, and the sun almost managed to show through. Tega looked at her target and sighed. There would be no better time.

Not far away the fires still burned. She tried not to think about them or about the smell of roasting meat. Her stomach rumbled in appreciation of the odor but the notion of eating that particular flesh repulsed her. Maun had not been a friend, but he had been a companion, and both he, and his partner in the flames, Darus Leeds, deserved better than a funeral pyre in the Blasted Lands.

Still, they were dead and she had been given a mission by Desh Krohan. It was time to fulfill her orders.

Nolan March let out a small cheer and Vonders Orly joined him. The fourth arrow that Tolpen Hart fired into the wall of the Mound stuck true and the rope dangling from it swayed enticingly in the breeze.

Now, finally, was the time for her to prove her worth.

Tega concentrated on the arrow and the rope and focused her will. This was a subtle thing, not a harsh assault, and her faith in her abilities was high. Still, it would not do to allow herself to lose control, and so she settled herself on the ground and cleared her mind of distractions.

Her hand touched the rope, felt its coarse texture and the thickness of it. Then she let her senses follow the rope to the anchoring arrow and to the surface where it had stuck precariously.

A gentle touch, a strong will, and she forced the change to occur.

The rope sang beneath her touch and the arrow's head pulsed where it broke the surface of the stone. All three men with her let out small noises as the fibers surged and changed and the arrow changed with it.

"Done. It is done." She looked at the finished result of her spell and smiled.

Nolan was the first to touch the silk. It was thick and would hold them with ease.

"Where is the arrow?"

"It's still there. It has just become something stronger than it was. It will hold us. Have no doubt of that." She tried not to sound smug. It wasn't easy.

Tolpen grabbed the silk chord and pulled, throwing his weight into the maneuver, as well he should. After too much time spent searching and hoping for a better entrance into the Mounds, they had finally accepted that the hole high in the side of one malformed column was their best bet.

They had to climb to use it. The first two arrows Vonders had managed to use had broken against the stone. The third had held but only until he pulled with his body weight. After that Tega said she would try to help with the anchoring of their only hope of reaching the proper entrance and now, finally she had succeeded.

Vonders pulled several times, making certain for himself, and then he started climbing the side of the column. His grip on the heavy silk was solid, but he moved it around his waist for extra support as he climbed, careful to place his feet firmly with each step he took on the slippery surface.

The rest of them waited below until he reached the hole in the side of their target. It had seemed a small area when viewed without perspective, but the higher Vonders scaled, the more Tega realized the opening was anything but. She wouldn't quite manage to park the wagon inside of that opening, but it was a close thing.

"This is madness." Tolpen spat and watched the other man climbing. "What if he falls?"

"Then we know this was a bad idea." Nolan shrugged and stepped closer to the silk cord. "We have been told to handle this. We must." Vonders slipped his leg over the lip of the breach in the side of their target and settled his weight, panting as he recovered from the climb.

"It's a tricky climb!" Vonders'svoice called down to them, and he settled himself as best he could within the spot.

"Can you see anything in there?" Tega wanted to know what they were in for if it was possible.

He nodded. "It's hollow. Hard to say how far it goes down. I can't very well climb it until the rest of you are up here."

"Or you could take another rope, tie it in place, and then climb down." Nolan spoke as he started up the cord himself. He had a bundle of rope around his waist. Vonders did not.

Nolan made the climb look easy until a little over half the distance to the top. That was when he slipped and nearly fell to his death. He caught himself and bounced along the side of the tower a couple of times, cursing and spinning before he managed to regain control and his composure.

When he finally settled himself, one leg on either side of the entrance into whatever lay inside, he carefully unwound the rope from around his waist and looked for something to anchor it with. Finally he tied it to the rope they'd scaled to reach the spot.

Tolpen looked at Tega for a moment and cleared his throat. "Do you know how to climb, milady?"

Truthfully, she did not. Because she had been trained to know that pride is often a waste of breath, she confessed her ignorance.

"Would it be best if you waited here?" The man meant no insult. He was simply trying to figure out what to do about the matter.

"Can you teach me to climb?"

"No more than I can teach you to properly hunt. That is to say it would take more time than we have. Perhaps after I've scaled the side we can pull you up with the rope." He sounded doubtful. It wasn't her weight and she knew that. It was that there was little enough for them to hold on to as it was and carrying a person's weight would make their perch even more dangerous.

Vonders said something from above and Nolan cursed softly.

"What is it?" They had a much higher vantage point. Whatever it was they saw, Tega saw nothing when she looked in the same direction.

"Don't know, but it looks like foot soldiers. A very large number of them. Hundreds at the least."

Tega felt her heart drop. Secrecy was the key to what they were doing. As far as they knew, the Sa'ba Taalor could not come to the Mounds, were forbidden from entering the area, but that was only what they had been told, and the truth of the matter simply had not been tested.

"Where are they? Are they coming closer?"

"No." Nolan looked down at her. His face from this range was unreadable, not that he was normally very expressive.

"Well? Where are they going?" Tolpen's voice was edged with frustration.

"They head for the Temmis Pass, near as I can figure."

"So they are Sa'ba Taalor." Tega shook her head. Even if they got the information they needed, getting it back to Desh Krohan was looking to be more and more of a problem. She knew that people could walk the Blasted Lands. At least she thought they could. She knew that Andover Lashk had left into the area with a few of the Sa'ba Taalor, but they had been prepared with mounts and supplies.

"I can't say how many. I think it could be hundreds, as I said, but it's impossible to tell. There's too much of this damned filth between us." He gestured to indicate the air. Though the day was calmer and they could almost see the sun in the sky, it was still overcast and the air still tasted foul.

"We can't concern ourselves with them."

Tolpen looked at her as if she'd suddenly sprouted wings on the sides of her head. "What?"

"They are there. We are here. This is where we have to be. We must do as Desh Krohan has commanded. We have to know what is here." As she spoke she glared at the hunter. He was as polite as he felt he had to be, but she also knew that of the three men still with her he was the one who thought the least of her. His expression said he felt she was pampered. His eyes tended to look anywhere but into her eyes when he spoke.

Tolpen's eyes looked at hers now, as if to prove her wrong. "Then we best get to it."

Without another word he grabbed the silken cord and started hauling his body upward, his arms bulging with corded muscle and his legs kicking furiously against the side of the Mound. He scaled at almost twice the speed of the other two, the better to get away from her, it seemed.

She watched his movements and nodded to herself.

He did not understand how sorcery worked or what was required. He did not begin to know how much time was afforded to studying the ways of the world before one considered trying to change it. First came examination, then comprehension, and then experimentation; then and only then did a person hope to begin the proper focus required.

Tega had never climbed a rope in her life. She grabbed the cord and slipped it loosely around her waist as she had seen Vonders do. Her arms moved through the cord and she pulled herself up and off the ground. A moment later, her legs found the side of the Mound's wall and she balanced herself. One arm pulled, and then the other. She slid upward. Her left leg pushed and she stepped up the side of the Mound. Her right foot followed. Her arms shifted and pulled and her body already ached, but she climbed, one step at a time, and forced herself upward, looking at the men above her and determined not to let them think her foolish or weak.

Her arms shook. Her legs shook. The effort was immense. She made herself breathe, and pulled and stepped and pulled and stepped, and when her right foot slipped she shifted her weight quickly to compensate and caught herself before she could spin as Nolan had before.

Above her Nolan's eyes studied her and he nodded silent encouragement. Vonders did not look at her. His teeth worried at his lower lip as he carefully set about tying the other rope in place. Tolpen watched her, but his expression was impossible to read.

He did not matter. There was only the climbing. Until she reached the lip of the opening and Nolan's hand was gripping her wrist and her elbow as he steadied her and she swung one leg over the side of the entrance and straddled the cold stone.

The wall they rested on was thick, at least as thick as her waist, and unyielding.

She looked out toward the horizon as her pulse calmed down and her breathing returned to normal. Her body shook not only with exertion but also with a hint of fear. She had never climbed so high in her life and the notion of falling had never quite seemed so real.

Out in the distance there were shapes moving, and yes, they looked like troops on the march. She had certainly seen enough soldiers marching in her time at the palace.

It was more than a few hundred if she had to guess, but from this range it was hard to say. They were just small shapes. For all she could truly see there might well have been a dust storm running along the side of the distant cliffs.

No. Dust storms seldom stayed consistent in their height.

"Do you see them?" Vonders looked up from his business and yanked hard on the rope he'd been tying in place. The rope stayed where it was and so did he. That was as good a sign as she could expect.

"Oh, yes. I see them. Now we have even more reason to go about this. If those are the soldiers of the Sa'ba Taalor it is possible that war comes even sooner than we feared."

"Are we not already at war?" Nolan frowned and continued to look at the distant column.

His father, of course, had already died. She'd let herself forget that fact.

"We are engaged. I do not know if they call this a skirmish or a war yet, but I think wars are bigger."

She nodded to Vonders. "Are you ready?"

"No. But I'm going anyway." Without another word he started down the inside of the cavernous darkness. They had no light, no torches, nothing of the sort.

"Wait. We need light."

"No, I don't think so." Tolpen spoke softly and pointed down into the depths of the Mound. Tega looked and frowned.

It was faint, but there was something down there. She could see Vonders, though he was now well below the light from the entrance. And below him, below the level of the ground even, she could see luminescence. It was a cold light, and it set off a winter storm within her heart and her stomach alike.

Vonders kept sliding down the rope, carefully descending. Below the ground, now, and deeper still. From time to time he looked up, but mostly he panted and made his slow drop into the place where the gray-skinned Sa'ba Taalor were forbidden to journey.

Drask watched them scale the side of the tower and then slip inside. It took them a very long time to manage it.

When they were gone he finally let himself move, sliding one leg and then the other from where they had been resting and stretching the muscles that had spent far too long in the same position. His practice of moving and keeping his circulation steady had been halted when there was a chance that they would notice him. Patience was one of the hardest things to learn, for him. It had always gone against his nature. He was born and raised to fight and to kill and those were situations that required speed and skill and strength of body and mind.

Patience required only patience.

It was not his strongest characteristic.

When they had finally dropped completely from sight Drask climbed down from where he had been waiting and stretched, rewarding his body's patience with relief from threatened cramps.

And then he squatted low to the ground, stared toward the Seven Forges and prayed silently to Ydramil. He had been told to come here. He had not yet been told why.

The world around him was nearly silent. There was the wind, and the sound of grit and dust skittering along the ground, and there was the slow and steady sound of his breathing.

And then there was the voice of Great Ydramil speaking to him, into his very heart.

Drask looked around at the Mounds, the forbidden territory that always waited. His feet touched the forbidden. He breathed in the air of the same.

And now he would once more break the rules he had been taught for as long as he had been alive.

He nodded and waved one hand and Brackka came closer. The mount had never been far away. His place was where Drask could call on him and he knew that well enough.

"I go after them." Brackka panted and pushed his face closer to Drask's. His hands moved behind Brackka's ears and scratched and the great face pushed against him. "Wait here. I will be back as soon as I can. Or I will not, as Ydramil decides." When he let go of his mount his hands reached out and took a small selection of weapons. His long bow stayed where it was. The shorter one he took with him, along with a quiver. One sword. Four axes and an assortment of knives. Anything else would have to wait with Brackka for when he came back.

The mount let out a grunt and moved away, circling the area slowly. He would wait and he would hunt when he needed food. That was the price he paid for his past sins. He would be faithful, because that was all that was left to him.

Drask would be faithful, too. He moved to where the people from Fellein had left a gift for him, a rope that dangled down and made his climb easier than he'd expected.

From the top of the climb he could see the columns moving toward the Temmis Pass.

There were so many more than he had expected to see.

Drask waited only a moment before he started down the rope that was, once again, foolishly left to allow him an easy descent.

In his heart there was no fear. He went where his god commanded. There was nothing for him to be afraid of.

The sun set.

King Tuskandru, Chosen of the Forge of Durhallem and King in Obsidian, called to his people and began their sacred journey.

• • •

The sun rose in the east and as the first light of the day made itself known, Merros Dulver stepped from the tent where he'd slept, dressed in his uniform and ready to deal with whatever came his way.

Well, as ready as he could manage when he felt like he was going to his death.

A quick gesture and the troops were called to order. He would inspect them soon, but first he wanted to see if there were any signs that the Sa'ba Taalor were ready to discuss grave matters.

The Sa'ba Taalor wanted to parley, and he hoped and prayed that was a good thing, but he was not one hundred percent sure. He wanted all to go well. He wanted peace between their people.

He wanted to cut the throat of whichever bastard king had ordered Swech to kill the Emperor. He wanted to see justice for Wollis March.

He wanted not to feel shame because he enjoyed his talks with Dretta March.

He wanted a thousand different things that he suspected would not be a part of the day's work.

Desh Krohan was already waiting near the Temmis Pass. It looked much like all of the other spots until you looked past the edge and saw the wide span of rock that gradually wound down to the floor of the Edge.

Desh stared out, his cloak drawn around him and his hood up. He looked scarcely human. He was an intimidating figure.

"Well. Here we are." Merros looked at the start of the pass himself. There was no sign of anyone.

With the cowl over his face the man sounded different. Merros had to remind himself that the same man he'd had a few pleasant meals with was under that thing. "There's something odd going on."

"What do you mean?" said Merros.

"The cloud cover. Look at it."

Merros looked out toward the Blasted Lands and frowned. The mists seemed lower.

"Is it calm in there? That seems unlikely."

"It's calmer. The storm seems to have weakened and, while it has been a few decades since I was here, I've never heard of such a thing."

"Neither have I."

It was at that moment that the first shape started rising from the mists where the pass lay. It only took one look for Merros to recognize the man. He struck a powerful figure, dressed as he was in his red tunic and dark armor. His thick hair ran in the same curls as before, but this time the body was hidden behind a full suit of plate mail armor. The cloak he wore was the same as before: black with scrollwork of silver and gold, and a heavy cord of gold that held it in place. A sword that should have looked preposterous rested at one hip. On any other man it would have seemed a man's sword worn by a child. Paedori was large enough to carry it with ease.

The iron crown sat on Tarag Paedori's brow. His eyes looked coldly at each of the people before him, his face once again hidden by the veil that obscured most of his features. Still, there was no mistaking the man.

"We meet again, Merros Dulver." He nodded. If he was at all put out by Merros not bowing to him he hid it well.

"I wish we were meeting under different circumstances, Majesty."

The Iron King nodded his head slightly and gestured. "I bring with me your charge, Kallir Lundt."

Merros blinked and felt a heat of shame bloom in his chest. He'd forgotten the man again. A charge that he should have never forgotten, now returned to him by the King who had promised to do what he could to mend the injured wretch.

Kallir Lundt stepped from up from the edge of the Temmis Pass when his name was called. He was a tall man, but small in comparison to the king. To be fair, most men were dwarfed by him and that included all but a handful of the Sa'ba Taalor Merros had met.

Kallir Lundt wore an iron mask over the ruin of his face. There was a twinge of guilt there again. The Pra-Moresh had attacked and torn the bastard's face away. That he had lived at all was an accomplishment.

And then Kallir spoke, his mouth moving, his iron face changing as he spoke and Merros felt his knees go weak.

"It is my pleasure to see you again, Merros." He smiled and showed teeth – some of white enamel and some that seemed cast in iron – and gums of red flesh beneath the moving iron.

"How?" It was the only word Merros could manage. Desh Krohan said nothing, but merely stood where he was and watched in silence.

"The Sa'ba Taalor are generous and their gods can be merciful. I am here as proof of that, Merros."

He felt himself staring, but could not stop. The face *moved*. It was impossible, of course, but so were the hands of Drask and Andover Lashk. Still, this was different, or it *should* have been. By the gods, how had the man endured having the metal cast upon his flesh?

"I am still Kallir Lundt, Captain Dulver."

"I know." He managed to look at the darkness where the eyes should have been visible. There had to be eyes, of course. It was merely hard to see them through the rest of the black iron face. Merros shook his head. "I know and I am truly grateful to see you again, my friend."

He reached out and took Kallir's hand in both of his, shaking it warmly. The tint of his skin was wrong. He had a sickly cast to his flesh. Still, he was alive, and he moved and saw and spoke. That seemed nearly impossible.

"Are you here for the parley, Captain?"

Merros nodded. "General. I'm General Dulver these days."

Kallir looked at him and slowly nodded.

The King in Iron stepped forward. "Is it you I am here to speak with, Merros Dulver? Or does your Emperor's replacement come to speak as well?" He looked at Desh Krohan as he spoke.

Desh replied in the language that Merros had learned through sorcery. He spoke softly, but carefully. "Nachia Krous, Rightful Empress of Fellein and Ruler of the Twelve Kingdoms, is here to negotiate with you. She will join us soon, Majesty."

Tarag Paedori nodded again and crossed his arms.

Desh stayed nearly motionless, but Merros doubted that anything remotely like calm was going on under that cowl.

The Sisters came out from the main tent and with them came Nachia Krous, dressed not in finery, but in armor of her own. Merros tried to hide his surprise. He had no idea she owned armor, let alone knew how to wear it. The armor was functional and fit her like a second skin. That was for the best when wearing the stuff. It stopped a body from getting battered and reduced the encumbrance caused.

She wore a crown, but not the one she given to her at her coronation. The simple band was as unadorned as the Iron King's though made of finer metals.

Merros Dulver called his men to attention and they listened, moving quickly to form a rank along the passage the Empress would walk. The men were in armor as well, each of them bearing a heavy sword and a light spear. They stood at attention and faced the Iron King and Kallir Lundt. The two men scarcely seemed to notice.

As Empress Nachia Krous stopped before him – looking really quite tiny in comparison, but holding her head and posture as she had been trained to for her entire life – the King in Iron offered a formal bow. His eyes did not leave her face.

After just exactly enough time to avoid insult, Nachia Krous returned the bow.

Desh Krohan spoke. "Empress Nachia Krous of Fellein, ruler of the Twelve Kingdoms, this is Tarag Paedori, Chosen of the Forge Truska-Pren and King in Iron." He stepped forward and moved next to the Empress. "We meet here on this morning to discuss the difficulties between the Sa'ba Taalor and the Empire."

Nachia Krous spoke clearly. "You have called for parley, is that what you and the other kings seek?"

Tarag Paedori spoke just as clearly, his voice holding that odd echoing quality that all of the Sa'ba Taalor shared. "Empress Nachia Krous of the Fellein Empire, your representatives sought to capture and hold a King of the Seven Forges against his will. He was within his rights to defend his honor and struck down the agents sent against him."

He looked to Merros. "We had your men delivered back to you. Should we see more of them we will do the same."

Nachia's face remained calm, but Merros could see the tension under the surface as it rose. "Your people came to us as guests. One of them, a woman called Swech, murdered the Emperor, my cousin, and killed several others before fleeing the palace and the city. At the very least we demand her return to us, so that she may be punished in accordance with our laws."

The man loomed over her and let his arms rest at his sides, far too close to that insane sword of his for Merros's comfort. "Swech Tothis Durwrae followed the orders given to her by the Daxar Taalor. If she killed your cousin it was because the gods decreed it was his time to die. In addition she has not been within the Taalor Valley or within the Seven Kingdoms of the Seven Forges in well over a month."

"Then where is she?"

He could not see the King smile, but Merros could hear it in the man's voice. "She remains among your people."

Nachia lost a bit of her composure. "Should we find her, we will kill her. She will suffer for what she did."

"You will not find her unless she wishes to be found." A gesture with one hand, a dismissal of the conversation and just exactly casual enough to be insulting. No one missed it, least of all Nachia.

"If you do not seek parley, why do you come here, Tarag Paedori?"

"I offer you the mercy of a surrender. Should you offer yourself to me as a bride, your Empire will be spared the pain of being destroyed by the Sa'ba Taalor."

Desh Krohan made a noise. Merros made a noise of his own. Neither was precisely polite.

Nachia Krous shook her head. "Go back to your Seven Forges and your kingdom in the dust." She turned her back on him, the insult very clear in her dismissal. "You and your filth are no longer welcome here."

The behemoth laughed at her, and Merros felt winter bloom in his guts.

"Tuskandru said you were a fool, Nachia Krous. He was right. I have offered you the only mercy possible and you have denied it."

"You have offered *nothing*!" She jammed one finger toward the King in Iron. "You have offered me a chance to grovel at your feet! I should have my men kill you where you stand as a lesson to your people. We are an Empire! Run back to your foolish gods and hide in the cold and dust, you swine!"

Merros stepped closer to his Empress and let his hand rest on his sword's pommel. If there were bloodshed, he would die defending her.

Behind her, the priests and the soldiers and the entourage that had come along stood and watched. The soldiers at least were prepared to stand with him and kill, or die as their Empress demanded.

"Here is my offer to you, Tarag Paedori." She stepped closer to him and Merros moved with her. Desh Krohan watched on, but there was a presence about him that rivaled that of the Iron King and even the monarch noticed it. For the Empress herself, she held her temper at bay and stared coldly at the man who stood before her without an army, without support of any kind. "Lay down your sword and surrender. Offer me your fealty and I will spare your life and that of your people when the rest of your kingdoms are foolish enough to attack my Empire. That is the one mercy I will offer you."

When Tarag Paedori spoke again his voice was calm, but low with menace. "Mock me if you will. Mock my fellow kings and our people, but mock the Daxar Taalor and you risk their wrath."

The King in Iron drew his sword and raised it high above his head with both hands. Merros stepped toward him, pulling his weapon, looking for any weakness in the heavy armor the man wore. He prepared to strike and stepped between Empress and King.

And Tarag Paedori drove his sword into the ground before him, breaking the hard soil with ease.

The King in Iron spoke in his own language, but the words were understood by Merros and Desh Krohan. "The Daxar Taalor are not kind to their enemies."

The ground shook.

Not close by, but far away.

Tarag Paedori pulled his blade from the ground. If he so much as noticed Merros standing before him and ready to fight, he hid it well. He stepped back four paces and Kallir Lundt moved with him.

Kallir Lundt said, "I am sorry for this, Merros Dulver, but they gave me back my life." His voice was heavy with regret.

And the ground shook on, a growing vibration that reminded Merros of the Mounds deep within the Blasted Lands, though the vibration came from the wrong direction.

"By the gods, no!"

He turned his back on Tarag Paedori and stared at the column of clouds rising into the sky in the distance.

He did not need a map to know, of course. He knew even before he looked, knew it in his heart and felt a sorrow that could not be turned back.

Great gouts of flame and smoke ripped into the sky, but from several days' march away.

From the direction of Tyrne.

The ground shook only once and then exploded.

The black rock punched through the ground as easily as a dagger through a heart. Tyrne screamed as it died and burned.

The Summer Palace shuddered and the stone and mortar that had formed the walls broke, falling and crumbling even as the first tide of magma boiled from below. The heat was enough to melt steel, to incinerate paper and to boil flesh from bones. There were many people left in Tyrne when the eruption started, but for most of them death was quick.

It was the people beyond the outer wall of Tyrne who suffered. The great clouds of burning ash and fiery gasses scorched flesh and lungs, seared eyes in their sockets and burned hair to scalps. Those who thought to breathe in, the better to scream, filled their lungs with smoldering soot and died quickly before the ash buried them.

Still the ground shook and the skies screamed and the black rocks rammed their way from the ground, rising higher and higher, pushing aside the accomplishments of men and nature alike, even as those monuments were incinerated or crushed.

Fire. Ash. Fury. The lands around Tyrne had not been marked by anything so violent since the Great Cataclysm.

The mountain rose slowly, pushing itself from the ground, forcing itself upon the Fellein Empire with no regard for the history, for the city or the people who had once lived there.

Tyrne died, and the skies above wept lightning and thunder on the growing mountain to mourn the city's passing.

On the Imperial Highway many people screamed when the eruption took place, and just as many found themselves praying to the gods.

Swech rode among them and prayed, but not to the same deities.

On the Jeurgis River the boats that carried passengers from Tyrne rode on, and Captain Callan thought about how very fortunate he was to be on the water when the fires started. The heat was fearsome but not enough to stop them.

Later he would hear tales of the birds that fell from the sky, poisoned by the very air they breathed, and he would feel a deep and abiding fear creep through him. The closest bird fell dead only half a day from where he was traveling when the city died.

Far to the east of Tyrne the Pilgrim stopped in his tracks when the ground split and the fires tore the skies asunder. He was too far away to hear the sounds or to feel the ground shudder, but still he knew.

It was his place to know these things.

It was his place to try to stop these things.

He hoped, briefly, that he was not too late and then lowered his head and moved on.

There was no time left. No time at all and he had so very far to travel.

Desh Krohan shuddered within his cloak. The winds picked up and whipped furiously at every single one of them as he watched the Sooth's warning come true.

He stepped closer to Nachia Krous even as the Sisters moved closer to him. The same instinct drove them all: there were loved ones who needed protecting.

Merros Dulver looked back toward the King in Iron with a horrified expression. He did not speak. There were no words left in him at that moment.

The winds lashed harder still and several people staggered as the heated air came in a rush.

Nachia Krous was not staggered. She looked at the sky and looked at the place where Tyrne had been and felt her heart clutched in a gigantic fist of sorrow, but she did not flinch.

When she turned back to look at the Tarag Paedori she did not make threats. She marked him in her mind and studied him carefully.

And she vowed to herself that she would see him dead at her feet before she died, no matter how long that might take.

The winds pushed harder still and caught the veil of clouds over the Blasted Lands pushing them aside, scattering them and revealing the land below for the first time since the Cataclysm.

And revealing the vast forces waiting on the fields below.

Tarag Paedori swept one hand back to gesture toward his armies.

Merros Dulver looked down and saw the people that he would be asked to defend his nation from.

There were so many more than he had expected.

They were small from here. They were far enough below that they looked like ants, really. Ants with banners and sigils and weapons and armor. Ants regimented into companies, and battalions and legions.

He could not count them all. There were simply too many.

Even as he stared, the clouds took back what was theirs, fighting against the winds and winning. The veil of mists that hid away the Blasted Lands thickened quickly, boiling his view of the enemy into obscurity.

When Tarag Paedori spoke again his voice was bereft of all humor. His tone was a lash across the back, a vicious cutting hiss. He had to bellow to be heard over the roaring winds and the death of Tyrne. "For one thousand years we have trained ourselves. We have dedicated our lives to our gods in preparation for this day." His eyes sought out Nachia Krous and narrowed with barely restrained hatred. "Your Empire rose on the ashes of our people, on the blood and bones of Korwa and the First Empire. You killed us a thousand years ago, but you did not kill us all."

He sheathed his sword.

"Gather your armies. Prepare your weapons. If you can even remember your gods, find them and pray to them. You will find the Sa'ba Taalor are ready for you and you will find the Daxar Taalor are unforgiving."

He stepped toward the Temmis Pass and looked at Merros Dulver. "Like your people before, we came to you and offered gifts. Like your people before, we offered friendship and a promise of peace. And like your people before, we have drawn first blood. As our ancestors were betrayed by the Fellein, so we have betrayed."

Finally he looked back to Nachia Krous. "Prepare yourselves. We will destroy your nation, your twelve kingdoms and you."

WAR IS COMING

SEVEN FORGES

JAMES A MOORE

A swashbuckling tale of assassination, inventions and families at war, from a secret corner of history that is more familiar than you know.

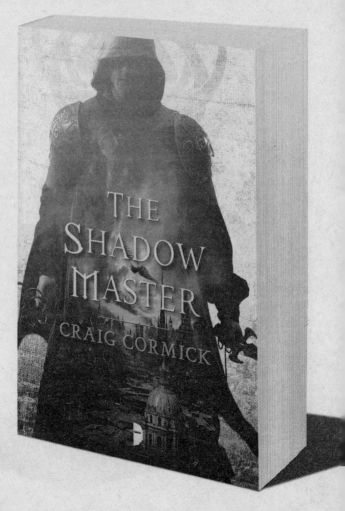

It's *Supernatural* meets *Men in Black*
in a darkly humorous urban fantasy
from the author of *Nekropolis*.

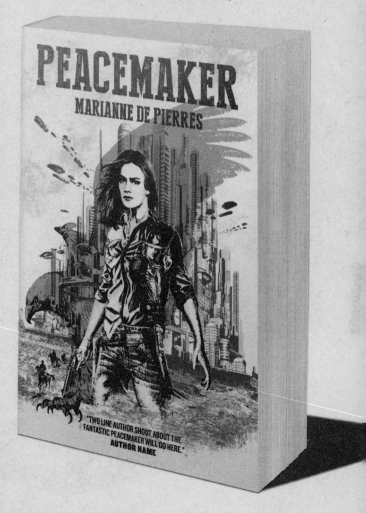

PEACEMAKER

MARIANNE DE PIERRES

"TWO LINE AUTHOR SHOUT ABOUT THE FANTASTIC PEACEMAKER WILL GO HERE."
AUTHOR NAME

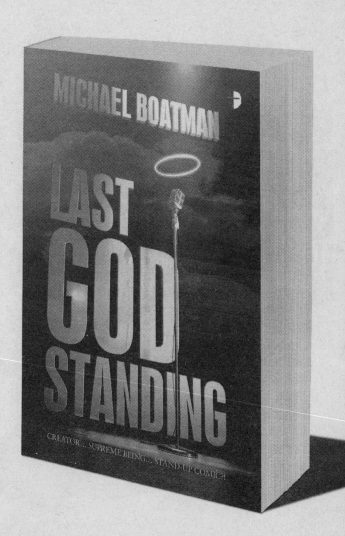

The quest for the Arbor has begun...